Spinning Thorns

Spinning Thorns

Anna Sheehan

Copyright © Anna Sheehan 2015
All rights reserved

The right of Anna Sheehan to be identified as the
author of this work has been asserted by her in accordance
with the Copyright, Designs and Patents Act 1988.

First published in Great Britain in 2015 by Gollancz
An imprint of the Orion Publishing Group
Carmelite House, 50 Victoria Embankment, London EC4Y 0DZ
An Hachette UK Company

A CIP catalogue record for this book is available
from the British Library

ISBN 978 0 575 10481 5

1 3 5 7 9 10 8 6 4 2

Typeset by Born Group within Book Cloud

Printed in Great Britain by Clays Ltd, St Ives plc

The Orion Publishing Group's policy is to use papers
that are natural, renewable and recyclable products and
made from wood grown in sustainable forests. The logging
and manufacturing processes are expected to conform to
the environmental regulations of the country of origin.

www.orionbooks.co.uk
www.gollancz.co.uk

For Jennifer,
my perfect, beautiful, wonderful sister
who has never burnt any of my books

Chapter 1

* * *

Once Upon A Time is how they begin the story. Once upon a time there was a beautiful princess, cursed by a wicked faerie, to prick her finger on a spindle and die on her sixteenth birthday. Another faerie softened the curse and the princess and her entire court fell instead into a hundred-year slumber, while vicious, man-eating thorns grew up around the palace. After a hundred years, a handsome prince made his way through the briars, and kissed the princess awake. They married, had two beautiful daughters, and lived happily ever after.

Everyone forgets about the wicked faerie, whose curse was spoiled, and whose name was disgraced. But I couldn't. I was reminded of it daily.

'Faerie! Demon!' Someone shouted that day's reminder at my kit sister. 'Nameless! Oh, gods, protect your children! Get her!'

I looked up. I was too far away to be of much help immediately. My sister and I hadn't exactly been together. It was sheer folly to be seen beside each other in a public place, but we weren't very far from each other, either. We would work together to get food to eat. The kit had a gift of illusion, so it was easy for her to conjure up a bird or a dog that would distract stall owners so that I could steal a loaf of bread or a withering winter apple. Unfortunately, the kit's magic doesn't work very well when she's scared, and

1

the moment someone recognized her as what she was, she panicked. Her only choice then was to run, and of course I had to stay with her.

It was usually the kit who gave us away. As a man I could wear a hood, and so blended more easily into human society. The kit was still a child, and female at that, so she couldn't conceal herself as deeply as I could, hoods being distractingly unfashionable for girls. She was also so stunning her features were too recognizable. Faeries don't look like ordinary humans. We're usually considered unnaturally beautiful, just a little too graceful. Our limbs are longer, our heads are proportionately small, our eyes proportionately large. We're naturally taller. And of course we have pointed ears. Some faeries have wings, which makes them even more obviously inhuman. But there was one literally glaring difference between my family and ordinary faeries.

Most faeries glow with magic. It's a slight glow, one that makes them look as if they're perpetually standing in the sunshine, even in darkness. My mother, my kit sister and myself were constantly in shadow, even on the brightest day of summer. If we can hide that we're faeries at all, we can blend in with human society, if we're careful. If we stay indoors or stick to shadows no one really notices that we aren't glowing. Unless someone notices that we're faeries, in which case, we end up running for our lives from angry mobs.

A whole pack of human boys was after the kit this time, all between the ages of sixteen to twenty, each of them eager to prove himself to his mates. I bolted through them. At first they thought I was one of their own, and they let me through. But then I caught up to the kit and helped her turn the corner, and one of them shouted, 'It's another one! Get him!'

The kit was too terrified to do any magic, and my best spells took more time to spin than I had. We ran down the frozen market streets while the boys shouted behind us, 'Thief! Nameless! Demon! Get them!'

A horse shrieked as a cart piled high with hay pulled into the cobblestone street before us. The kit shrieked back, launching herself up over the back of the cart and over the driver, who fell from his perch like a sack of potatoes. I wasn't so lucky. The cart came up too quickly, and I skidded on ice. A collision seemed inevitable, and I distinctly heard one of the boys behind me shouting, 'We've got him now!'

He didn't know much about faeries. The cart had fairly high wheels. I bent backward under it as I skidded, nearly touching the back of my knees with the top of my head. But as I came out from under the cart my loose shirt caught on the splintered wood and pulled up over my head. I heard a clatter, and my heart stopped beating. No! I let myself fall onto my back, and the air was forced from my lungs. I looked up, and saw two things at once.

The first was the kit. She had vaulted from the hay wain and set off down washer's alley, where half a dozen laundresses plied their trade. The shouts of 'Nameless' and 'Demon' had preceded us, as had the curses of the fallen driver. I watched as one of the washer women, her face like a gargoyle and arms like iron tree trunks, lifted up her washtub to throw the ten gallons of water and lye onto my kit sister. The second was my wooden drop spindle, fallen from my shirt onto the icy cobblestones, with the last of my wool still clinging to it.

My choice was terrible, and I hesitated a second too long in making it. Before I could sit up to protect my sister or fetch my spindle, a two pronged pitchfork pinned my hood to the cobblestones. 'Got you!' the owner of the pitchfork gloated. It was the fallen driver, dirty snow and ice ground into his hood from his fall. My mind refused to work fast enough, and in the corner of my eye I saw the kit plastered against the wall of the alleyway, the steaming wash water impacting her with the force of a body blow.

The rest of the mob would be on me any moment. My magic was stronger than the kit's, but took more time to implement. I'd lost my spindle. It all seemed finished for me, but I was lucky. The kit saved me.

It was her best spell, the first spell she'd ever learned to cast. The kit yelped and suddenly half the street was engulfed in blue and white foxfire. People screamed. Horses whinnied. Shouts of 'Fire!' echoed over the houses. My captor hesitated then dropped to his knees, trying to shield his face.

Yes! I twisted the pitchfork away and threw it as far as I could into the blinding fire. Pausing to snatch up my spindle, I ran to catch my sister and pull her away from the coming mob, which would soon realize the foxfire held no heat.

'You all right?' I asked as I pulled her along behind me.

'My eyes hurt,' the kit said.

'If you were human, you'd be blinded for life,' I pointed out. 'Come on, we have to hide.'

She blinked at me, and despite the dire circumstances, she giggled.

'What?'

'You'll have a hard time. You're glowing.'

I looked down at myself. The kit's foxfire surrounded my hands, and my clothes bled white tongues of flame. It tended to stick to magic, and I was always doing magic. I shook the flames off so that I wouldn't be a glowing beacon to anyone persuing us. 'This way,' I said, and I ducked away from the marketplace.

The marketplace sprawled just outside the main gates of the palace, with a wide margin separating the town from the hedge of thorns that protected the royal house. To the west were the residences of the more affluent townsfolk, who looked upon

4

the somewhat tamed hedges as an advantage, particularly in the summer when the roses bloomed. To the east were the slums, which had been forced in that direction by the more aggressive thorns. I pulled the kit towards the deserted eastern wall of the palace. There was quite a gap between the houses and the thorns here, and the people tended to look on the hedge as nothing more than a hazard. 'This way.'

The kit baulked as I tried to lead her towards the eastern wall of thorns. 'That way?'

I glared at her. 'You have a better idea?'

The shouts of the mob behind us grew louder. The kit's fire would be dying now, leaving, unfortunately, no damage. If I had my way, every last one of the bloodthirsty black-guards would be burned to a cinder, but that wasn't the kit's magic. The kit swallowed. 'No?' Her fear made it come out as a question.

I pulled her towards the palace and the hedge of briar roses. 'I'm sorry,' the kit said as she followed me. 'I'm so sorry. The breeze came up, and my scarf blew, and . . .'

'I know,' I said. 'It's not your fault you were recognized.'

The poor kit was beyond beautiful, and that was most of her problem. I was the plain one in the family, and thanked the stars for my features. I took after our da, a fox faerie my mother had taken up with against, apparently, the advice of general faerie society. Before we'd lost our Light, my ma's family had been considered rather high rank amidst the faerie clans of the area. Fox faeries were more earthy, more mischievous, more bestial, and usually dismissed by the greater clans. Most of them were loners who made no claim to the great clans of most of faerie society. My mother was the worst off in our family, as she was still tall and noble and beautiful, and moreover, bore wings she could not hide. The kit and I took after earthy Da, and were, fortunately, wingless. I hid

5

my more overt features beneath a hood, summer and winter. It was aggravating that my sister couldn't wear such a thing without drawing too much attention.

With the kit's white hair and her white skin and a pair of huge amber eyes which glinted with mischief, she was far too noticeable. She tried to hide her ears beneath her hair, and in winter she could don a scarf, but she was so stunning, and so out of proportion for a seemingly eleven-year-old child she had a much more difficult time than I did. And she was so white that her shadow was obvious.

We were shadowed because we were disgraced. There's a name for us. The only name left to us. We were of the Nameless.

Humans don't fully understand what a terrible thing it is for a faerie to be without a name. To a human being, a name usually means only what someone is called. It is a label, an appellation. As one would title a book or a play, to change the title is not to change the play itself.

But to one of my kind, a name *is* self. To change or remove our name is to burn the parchment the play was written on. The play no longer exists. Oh, the players may remember the parts. They may act out a scene or two. Members of the audience who saw it may remember the play in passing. But the play itself is lost.

I wasn't born lost. My mother remembers when I had a name. She doesn't remember my name, of course, or her own. I was an infant when we lost ourselves. My kit sister had a name, when she was born. If I tried very hard I could almost remember noticing it, the blood connection she had with her brother granting me that taste of her instant of self. It lasted about a second before the curse took effect, and her baby glow was cast into shadow. Now she was just another fox kit fae, like me. Nameless. Stationless. Considered a criminal, almost a demon. Laws forbade harbouring us, dealing with us, feeding us. We were lower than vermin. We were considered plague carriers, fit only to be exterminated. Hence the angry mob. Hence why we were risking our lives sneaking into the thorn hedge surrounding the palace at Lyndaron.

The leafless briar roses shivered as we stepped into their winter shadow. They pulled aside as if to welcome us. I knew better than that. I pulled out my spindle. 'No, don't!' the kit cried, looking behind us.

'You want to die?' I asked.

The kit frowned. Using the spindle was illegal, but we were already being hunted for our lives. She gestured that I should go ahead.

This wasn't the first time I'd spun my way around the palace thorns. They were a useful place to hide, if you had no other options. No one would possibly follow you in there, not the most bloodthirsty murderer. To enter the briar patch was death.

I pulled a few fibres from the wool in my pouch and fed them onto the thread I already had on my spindle. I closed my eyes for a moment to find the feel of the thread, and then spun the spindle, letting it swing like a pendulum beneath me. The wool became thread, and I poured my magic in with it, forcing my will upon the thorns. They began to twist and sway, spinning quietly aside. I nudged the kit forward with my foot and followed in after her. Once inside, the magic followed me, closing us into a tiny bubble of clear space into which the thorns could not follow. When we were deep enough inside the hedge I grabbed the spindle and the thread, holding the spell taut around us.

Within a few more minutes several of the mob appeared beside the hedge. They'd brought dogs. I heard one of them yelp as he got too near the hedge. 'Hey, Ralph, get back from there!'

I wanted to scoff. The damned dog had a name. The kit and I were below even that.

It wasn't through any fault of ours. The Nameless are made Nameless through a consensus of the faerie clans, usually because of some heinous act. Ordinarily, the Name is stripped only of the malefactor, but in this case the malefactor was the head mistress of our clan. The only way to make her of the Nameless was to strip her of her clan name as well as her own. Which meant the entire clan suffered, including my cousins, my mother and myself.

My mother's aunt was to blame. As for what she did, the stories were garbled. It was clear she cast some kind of curse on Princess Amaranth, but precisely what it was and what her motives had been had been lost. I was too young to follow the faerie gossip before we were made Nameless, and my ma wouldn't discuss it, but from what I had been told as a child, she had tried to kill Princess Amaranth, and had cursed the royal palace with the thorn hedge. The very thorn hedge the kit and I were hiding in, as the mob bayed for our blood.

The thorns still surrounded the palace, attacking the unwary. The writhing, twisting briar roses seized innocent victims whenever they could and drained them of their very blood. It was quite a spell. Even twenty years after Queen Amaranth's resurrection, the thorns still grew over and around the palace. They tried to cut them down, but the only thing that had worked so far was to drive them out with strong ivy, which sapped the ground of the nutrients the thorns needed to survive. Some areas of the thorns, like the western wall, had been tamed by interbreeding them with ordinary roses, but these were expensive, didn't always take, and needed to be imported from distant countries. The truly deadly thorns were now fewer in number, mostly surrounding the eastern wing of the palace. Unfortunately, the thorns that were left now seemed more aggressive, more hungry for the blood of passersby. Eventually, so the royal family swore, they would have eradicated the thorns for good. I wished the thorns would last forever, and eat the royal family into the bargain.

Unfortunately, they seemed about to eat my sister. 'Ow!' she hissed. 'It has my leg!'

'Be still!' I crouched down and twisted my spindle another time. The thorn complained, creaking its hunger, but slowly released its hold on the kit. She heaved a sigh of relief, but only whispered her thanks to me, keeping hidden from the mob and their dogs. Not that they could get at us in here.

Many in Lyndaria don't know how spindles work, even in the ordinary way. They've been banned since before the interregnum. I've had to make my own. Even if I was human, if anyone saw what I hid beneath my tunic I'd be arrested. Once they found out that the malefactor was also one of the Nameless, I'd probably be executed. The Nameless are not allowed second chances. My drop spindle looks a bit like a wooden top, with an extremely long handle. When I attach a bit of hand-twisted thread to the lower end, I can start the spindle spinning, and use the weight of the round 'top' section to pull the thread from the wool. Which is what I was doing now to still the thorns, pulling from the little bag of wool I always kept on a belt beneath my tunic. I have the Spinner's Gift. It is usually considered a women's gift. It isn't a very common gift in men. I inherited it from my mother, along with my Namelessness.

In Lyndaria, which looks down on magic to begin with, this is a thrice-cursed gift. I am a faerie, I am Nameless, and I am a spinner. If the queen knew of me, I'd be above mass murderers on My Lord Provost's list of Evildoers To Be Disposed Of. Spinning magic caused the interregnum, and caused beautiful Queen Amaranth to spend a hundred years asleep in her briar-guarded palace.

I sometimes wondered why the thorns were so difficult for me to subdue. If it was indeed my aunt who had summoned them, they should respond to the traces of her blood I carried in my veins, and bend to me like a lover. But they didn't, and I was forced to maintain a constant spell with my spindle.

'Let 'em go, Reg!' shouted one of the mob. 'They're long gone or eaten by the hedge. Let's get out of here. These plants scare me.'

'Too right,' another replied. 'Do you know how many hundreds have died in their clutches?'

'I heard a story about a pair of lovers,' began another voice, and as he told his tale they all began to fade away down the paths. A dog barked one more time in our direction, but was quickly called back.

We weren't out of the woods yet. I still had to bring us back out of the briar patch without getting caught and bled. 'You go on ahead of me,' I told the kit. The sweat was beginning to stand on my brow. The thorns were battling me with a hundred years of strength.

'R-right,' the kit said, and took a hesitant step away from the palace wall. I kept up a constant spin as I walked behind her out of the hedge. Finally we were far enough away to be safe. I heaved a sigh of relief and let go of my thread.

I had been a bit cocky. With a crack, a branch of thorns lashed for my ankles, trying to drag me back into their clutches. I was out of range, but only by an inch. The kit yelped, and I jumped out of the way. 'Whoops!' The kit grabbed me and pulled me away from the hedge. 'I'm all right!' I snapped. I was ashamed of myself. I should have kept the spell going until we were well out of range. You'd have thought that a hundred and twenty years of Nameless wandering would have weaned me away from such folly. I pushed the kit away.

It was only then that I noticed how cold she was. The water was dripping from her rags, and her eyes were red. 'Let me see to you,' I told her.

'I'll b-be all r-right,' she said. 'I'm just c-cold.'

'How are your eyes?'

'Fine. A b-bit blurry.'

'Here.' I was tired from spinning the thorns into submission, but I could do this. I reached for the kit's white hair and twisted two hanks of it into an elf knot. She sighed with relief as the pain faded from her eyes.

'Thanks,' she said.

'Can you get home alone?'

'You're not coming with me?'

I shook my head. 'Not unless you think you can't make it. We shouldn't try going back through town together.'

She shuddered. 'I c-can't. N-not all wet like this,' she said.

I nodded. 'Don't move.' I pulled out my spindle one more time and tried to shake the weariness from my eyes. With a deep breath I set the spindle going again. 'Spin!' I told her. She spun quickly, turning sunwise like my spindle, and the water around her flew out in a sudden circle, dropping in a ring around her, and splashing my trousers.

She looked at me. 'Sorry,' she said.

I sighed. 'It's all right,' I said. 'It was my spell. Can you make it now?'

'Still cold, but I think I'm all right.'

'Good. You go the outskirts. I'll go through the town. I'll meet you at the burrow.'

She nodded and slipped through the poorer houses back towards the distant forest, and our burrow.

I looked down at my sodden trousers. They were freezing in the snow. I didn't want to waste the wool to shed the water from them. And I'd sent the kit the safer route – I

11

would now have to make my way back through the hostile town in order to walk back to our tiny, filthy burrow. I was a bug. A Nameless, filthy, sodden bug. And inside that huge, beautiful palace behind me sat Fair Queen Amaranth, her prince charming, and her two devoted children. And what did I have? A price on my head and an empty belly.

It wasn't fair. So Queen Amaranth had to spend a hundred years asleep because my aunt was a drag at parties. All was well now, wasn't it? Why did they have to continue to hold her curse against my family? After all, what had we ever done? My ma, the kit, myself, my cousins, what exactly had we done to warrant the theft of our identities? Queen Amaranth the Asleep knew who she was. Everyone knew who she was. Even I wasn't allowed to know who *I* was. My cousins had all disappeared years ago. They had probably been killed, the same way the kit and I were always in such danger. We were alive only because of the strength I had in my hands, the skill I had with my spinning, the knowledge I constantly sought as I strove to improve my magic. Only these had been our protection, since Da left.

That thought did cheer me up a little. Not as much as seeing Queen Amaranth and her daughters carted off to be eaten by trolls would have done, but the thought of my magic always warmed me. And there was one good thing about having to go through the town. I could stop off at Madam Paline's bookshop.

There was a book at Madam Paline's I was slowly getting through. It was a trick reading at Madam Paline's. She didn't approve of people without money going through her stacks. However, she was trying to slim her waistline (a venture which struck me as pointless. If you have enough for food, you should have the courage to accept the consequences. It's far better than starving). So she would frequently skip lunch.

If I arrived shortly after midday, I could tie a knot in my spool and tease her hunger, which would make her head off to the nearest tavern.

I could have stolen the book. I frequently considered it. I stole food, clothes, wool and flax. Somehow, whenever I left Madam Paline's, it was without a book in my hands. Part of it may have been because I knew I couldn't keep it safe — my family and I frequently had to run from our makeshift lodgings, and were almost never able to take anything with us. But there was more to it than that. I may not have been honest, I may break the law every day of my life spinning my magic, but I wasn't about to steal from a bookseller. If the booksellers went out of business, where would I find books? And particularly from Madam Paline's, the only place I'd ever found any books on magic.

Besides, Madame Paline's was considerably warmer and more comfortable than our tiny, filthy, freezing burrow. So I'd tease her to luncheon and spend an hour reading blissfully amongst the stacks. The book I'd just found was called *The Ages of Arcana*, an old book on magic theory, which had miraculously escaped the purge. Most books on magic were burned with the spinning wheels when the then-Princess Amaranth was cursed at her christening. While the laws against spinning had never been revoked, the laws against magic were eventually lessened, until magic as a whole was only frowned upon, but not forbidden. Still, most of the old grimoires and spell books were lost in the purge, so a book on magic theory was a rare find indeed. I was very much looking forward to reading through another chapter. Particularly as there was a chapter there about the theories of healing magic. I wanted to be sure I could protect the kit's eyes.

With one last impotent curse toward the palace, I set off for Madam Paline's.

Chapter 2

Will

There was a trick to sneaking out of Rose Palace without being horribly killed. It took a pinch of magic, a great deal of courage, and some plain old-fashioned quickness. Willow had mastered the trick some three years since, but even she felt nervous when she passed the hedge. She was always afraid that the leaves of the ivy used to combat the thorns would turn out to be the briars, and they'd find her bled white in the morning, hung upside-down with her skirts around her ears.

They said that the palace wasn't always so dangerous, but no one Will knew really believed it. For more than a hundred years the palace had been immersed in deadly briar roses, and Will was sure that a hundred years on they'd still be finding the unaware hung up in their twisting coils.

The thorns were a curious curse. No one was really sure why they were included in the curse that had troubled Will's mother. Everyone knew the story of beautiful Princess Amaranth, and how the thirteenth fairy arrived at her christening and cursed her to fall down dead when she pricked her finger on a spindle on her sixteenth birthday. The curse was softened by the youngest fairy who had not yet given her gift and, instead of dying, Amaranth fell into an ensorcelled sleep for a hundred years.

Many people were of the opinion that simply letting her die would have been kinder for the kingdom. The interregnum caused chaos and confusion and wars without cause and seemingly without end. The kingdom would have utterly dissolved but, as luck would have it, politics intervened. Seven years after the princess's curse befell, the king of a neighbouring country, Hiedelen, pledged to annex Lyndaria, and sacrificed his firstborn son to the thorns. Prince Alexi had tried and failed to pierce the hedge at the palace at Lyndaron. His death was witnessed by hundreds, and as much of his body as could be retrieved from the thorns was carried in a state procession through Lyndaron to be buried back in Hiedelen.

From that first princely sacrifice, the Hiedel line had sacrificed one son a generation to the thorns. Their perpetual sacrifice rallied the people, and Lyndaria was ruled through those hundred years by the Hiedelen kings. Will had to honour those four dead princes. Everyone did. The princes' memorial was a national holiday.

Will's father's name was Ragi, and he was the Hiedel prince who finally made it through the hedge and woke the sleeping beauty with a kiss. (Ragi always said it was a little more complicated than that, but that was the official story, and no one had ever written down anything different.) Twenty years before, Will's mother had been awakened and become queen. Everyone thought that the thorns would disappear then. But they didn't. Instead they renamed the palace at Lyndaron 'Rose Palace.' The kingdom was too poor to build another royal seat, and the city of Lyndaron couldn't be moved from the banks of the River Frien. It was cheaper to battle the thorns from the palace than to build a new one.

They told the story far and wide. It had almost become a legend already. The beautiful princess, deep in an ensorcelled slumber, in a palace guarded by briars, is one day awakened by a prince, and they live happily ever after. The thing about 'ever afters' is that 'ever' is a very long time, and 'after' involves more than people expect. Including, it would seem, Will and her sister Lavender.

Will's mother was the sleeping beauty herself. Will's sister Lavender, the eldest, had also always been considered the beautiful princess. And Will? Well, she was glad she didn't make people scream when they looked at her. No one fell at her feet with protestations of adoration, either.

Not that she needed suitors. She'd been betrothed from the age of nine, when the Hiedelen king's youngest grandson was born. Will had grown quite used to Narvi, who was also some distant cousin of hers – very distant, she thought, if her suspicions were correct. They sent him to Rose Palace regularly to learn Lyndarian law and for official functions. He spent three months out of the year at Rose Palace. He was a nice enough boy. Of course, she didn't love him.

It wasn't expected that either of them would amount to much. Narvi was little more than a lesser duke, and while Will had the title of princess, it was not a title of inheritance. Lyndaria would go to Lavender. Will's fate was most likely to be shunted to some cornerstone duchy and invited to Midwinter's and royal christenings. Narvi and Will would marry dutifully when he turned sixteen. Their children would be marriageable pawns to strengthen Lyndaria's alliances. That was always to be the case, and Will had been content with that. Until she had the misfortune to fall in love.

She knew how banal it was. It was not something she was proud of, and not something she indulged. But she couldn't help it. Anyone could understand why she should love Prince Ferdinand. One had only had to look at him. Prince Ferdinand was tall and courageous, with white-blond hair, a hawkish profile, ice-blue eyes that could pierce to the core of your soul, and a dignified and genteel manner. He was also betrothed to Will's sister.

To understand this, one had to understand Lavender. There could be no mistake about it – Will's older sister Lavender was beautiful. Small and willowy and graceful as a swan, a fine embroideress, an excellent dancer. Hair like autumn leaves. Eyes like the summer sky. Skin soft and pure as spring rose petals. Voice clear and crisp as a sunny day in winter. She looked just like her mother, and was as beloved as Queen Amaranth had always been.

Will loved her, she supposed, but in truth she also loathed her. It turned out that, contrary to popular opinion, those two emotions were not exclusive. And when looked at together, it wasn't hard to figure out what Will's resentment stemmed from. Her name of Willow was a cruel joke fate played on her parents and herself. Willow was not willowy. She was not graceful. She was not delicate. She was tall and stocky, a combination which made seamstresses throw up their hands when they tried to fit dresses to her. By the age of sixteen she could wear her father's clothes, and frequently did when she snuck out of the castle. By eighteen, even her father's clothes were tight in some awkward places. She was not shaped like a man, but she took after her father. She felt, with some resentment, that she should have at least had the regal bearing of the Hiedelen line, but she didn't.

Her father didn't, either. He'd been considered the black sheep of the family, and wasn't even the son of King Lesli himself. He was the son of King Lesli's brother, the Prince of Ethelbark (a small province of Hiedelen). Ragi wasn't even a prince. Technically he was the Duke of Rendaren (an even smaller province of Hiedelen) and when he was selected as the representative of Hiedelen to try and wake Princess Amaranth, he was convinced that King Lesli was mostly trying to get rid of him.

There was some question as to Ragi's legitimacy. Apparently he'd been born more than nine months after the Prince of Ethelbark died in a 'hunting accident'. Princess Meggi (who was herself of the Hiedelen line, though rather distant) insisted that she'd been pregnant when he died, and it was a story she stuck to. Despite this, all his life everyone had looked at Ragi askance. The fact that he had made it through the thorns was taken as proof that he was in fact a legitimate prince.

Will was inclined to believe otherwise. Though she never told anyone her findings, her study of the hedge had led her to believe that the briars had a taste for royal blood. One was considerably more likely to get through if one was an honest woodcutter's son than a royal prince. But all of the honest woodcutter's sons that had made it through the hedge (and there had been a few) had all succumbed to the sleeping beauty's contagious sleep once they set foot in the palace. There was a small pile of honest miller's apprentices and virtuous woodcutter's sons discovered in the receiving hall upon Amaranth's awakening. They were all so handsome and bold and kindly and clever they promptly ended up married to Amaranth's ladies-in-waiting, most of whom had lost their betrotheds during the interregnum.

Which was why the hedge was so confusing. One could only battle the sleep if one was of royal blood, but that was less than helpful in getting through the hedge. And it wasn't that the hedge invited virtue, either. There were several thieves discovered upon Amaranth's awakening, too, who had planned to rob the sleeping palace. Many of them were wretched and sinful in the extreme.

In the end, it was the thinness of Ragi's royal blood which enabled him both to bypass the hedge *and* battle the sleep. Unfortunately, that same thinness of blood left Will looking, she felt, like a soldier off the battle field, or the daughter of an ogre. Her face was too strong to be considered handsome as a woman, and her body so large that she towered over visiting princes. She towered over Ferdinand, too, which only served to remind her how futile her love was.

Prince Ferdinand was fiercely in love with Lavender. He had saved her life. She was abducted by a dragon while out picnicking on Midsummer's Day. (Will had told her it was a stupid thing for a princess to go and do.) She was missing for six months, and all were sure she'd been killed. Will had had the horrifying prospect of being groomed as the heir. They'd already fitted a new wardrobe for her, and had doubled her diplomacy lessons, which left her even less time to pursue her magic. Then Prince Ferdinand arrived on a white horse with a white hound at its heels, holding a white hawk on his arm, with Lavender riding pillion behind.

The adventure surrounding Prince Ferdinand's rescue of Lavender was daring and clever. He was the youngest son of the king of the distant country of Illaria. His father had set him out to make his way in the world. Very traditional story – Ferdinand gave his last piece of bread to a beggar woman, who turned out to be a faerie and gifted him with the three animals who led him over hill and dale, through a dozen different adventures, until he finally slew the dragon through courage and cunning and freed the kidnapped princess. And almost from the moment he arrived with Will's sister, Willow had been desperately in love with him.

It was torment. It was also flat stupid, she knew, far more foolish than going picnicking on Midsummer's Day while being a princess. Ferdinand was handsome and clever and bold. He had wit, a sense of honour, a charming and noble grace. Who wouldn't have fallen in love with him?

Anyone with a modicum of self-control, Will supposed. But, she reasoned, not everyone knows themselves well enough to control themselves. And those who do, don't always have the power. Like the roses, she thought. They could train them and guide them, but if they left them alone for long they'd take over the entire castle.

The evening she realized she was in love with Ferdinand was agonizing.

It was less than three days after Lavender's return. They were holding a ball in honour of her survival, and her betrothal to Ferdinand. Will hadn't wanted to go. For one thing, though she was glad Lavender had returned and Will was no longer going to be saddled with the running of the kingdom, she was envious of all the extra attention Lavender was receiving. Moreover, Will couldn't dance. She may have been fast for a noble, and she may have been strong for a woman, but she felt clumsy when it came to dancing or embroidery or curtseys. Her deportment tutor had given up on her years before, focusing her attention on Beautiful Princess Lavender. (Sometimes, Will suspected that this might have been one of the reasons why she was so dismal at it, as she was mostly forced to struggle though on her own.)

At this celebratory ball Will mostly loitered around the buffet table, tripping on her skirts (which were not accurately tailored to her frame) feeling as useless as a fifth leg on a horse. Amaranth and Ragi and Lavender and Ferdinand danced like butterflies around each other, while Will sat stuffing her face with pheasant, trying to figure out how soon she could make her excuses and escape.

'What are you doing here all alone?'

Will turned and gaped at Ferdinand, whom she'd barely spoken to in the three days since his arrival. They hadn't had much time for ordinary pleasantries. What with hearing his story, confirming the destruction of the dragon, contacting Ferdinand's kingdom, announcing Lavender's return to the populace, and arranging the betrothal, there hadn't been a moment of his day that wasn't scheduled. He and Will had been formally introduced, but that was about it. Will found him a little intimidating. As far as the men in Lyndaria went, he was quite tall, and fair. His skin was tanned golden from his adventures, and it made his fair hair look almost as white as his beasts'. He tended to dress in black, which made his fairness shine out all the more, though for this ball he had brightened his sober colours with a lavender cravat that matched his beloved's dress, and of course the medals of bravery that Queen Amaranth had bestowed upon him at Lavender's return.

'Ahm . . . just . . . here,' Will said. She was famed for her wit. She had no idea where it had gone in that moment.

'We haven't had much chance to get to know each other,' Ferdinand said. 'I hope we can come to be friends, Willow.'

'Will,' she said. 'Call me Will.'

He smiled, easily. He had a nice smile. 'Will.' He took her hand and kissed it gently. 'I had a sister,' he said. 'We spent many hours together before Father shut the door on me.'

'Why did he do that?' Will had heard the official story about his dragon slaying, but hadn't heard much about him otherwise. He still held her hand. Will found it distracting.

'A prophecy that I'd come to more if I was banished from the kingdom. Scant evidence for disowning your youngest son, but inheritance was difficult. I had two brothers, and Victoria needed a portion of land and a title as her dowry.' He made a small, sad sound in his throat. 'I miss having a sister.'

'I didn't,' Will muttered.

Ferdinand laughed. 'I suppose you don't get to be queen, now,' he said. 'That must be frustrating.'

'What?' Why was he laughing, Will wondered, if he thought she was ambitious and jealous? 'Oh, no, keep the kingdom, I honestly don't want it. Please. Take it off my hands.'

He cocked his head, like a bird. There was something Will found quite birdlike about Ferdinand, something hawkish, like his white falcon, which was currently perched atop the back of the Queen's throne. He rarely went anywhere without the thing. He said it was known to talk, and gave him advice as he battled the dragon. His horse, hound and hawk were magical of origin, that much was obvious, but Will suspected whatever magic they had possessed was spent in the course of winning Lavender. 'You don't want to be a queen?'

'I never wanted to be queen,' Will said. 'I barely like being a princess. But look at her!' She gestured to her sister, who was dancing prettily with their nine-year-old cousin Narvi. Will frowned at her supposed betrothed. She wished their engagement could be thrown by the wayside. He was too young for her. 'The whole country went into mourning when she disappeared. Have you been hearing what they're saying? They all thank the gods they won't have this hulking beast of a princess as the heir. Lavender's *perfect*.' Will sighed. 'I wish she'd just develop a flaw or two. Or that I wasn't . . .' She gestured down at herself, protruding awkwardly from her ill-fitting dress. 'Me.'

Ferdinand placed his warm hand on her shoulder, sympathetic. 'I felt the same way about my brothers,' he said. 'They were both taller and stronger than I, better at the sword, better with the lance. And yet, they never had a chance to use their skills. You don't have to be better than everyone else. You only have to be good enough.'

Will eyed him. 'Who are you quoting?'

He grinned. 'Prince Ferdinand of Illaria. He's a very wise philosopher.'

She laughed.

'You have a nice laugh, Will.'

Will's laugh caught, and she blushed.

'I hear you're interested in magic.'

Will looked about, to see if anyone was listening. 'That is something of a family secret, you know.'

'Yes, so Lavi tells me. She warned me not to bandy that knowledge about. Why?'

Will shook her head. 'Magic is somewhat frowned upon in Lyndaria. It's caused so much mischief. Until recently there's been an out and out ban on witches. The laws have gotten more lenient, but it's still not considered, as it were, couth.'

'I'm not sure I approve of that,' Ferdinand said. 'There were all kinds of magicians in Illaria. And I owe my happiness to faerie gifts. Without magic, I would never have rescued my Lavender.'

'I agree,' Will said. 'But that didn't stop a century of Hiedelen law which made it illegal. It's hard on magic users. Particularly the faeries. So many of the clans have emigrated out of Lyndaria, and I think that weakens us. When my mother was born there were thirteen faerie clans, most with at least a half dozen members. A representative of each of them were present for her christening. It's why she's such a fine queen.'

'What happened to them all?'

'Well, during the interregnum one of the clans was condemned, made Nameless and disbanded. Eight clans left Lyndaria for more magic-welcoming kingdoms, two clans died out, and one, the Winnowinn clan, retreated to a fastness in the highest northern mountains. I've met a few of them. They're pale and icy. Their glacier is what feeds the Frien, you know, so we're very respectful of them. They don't like to talk much. The last one, the Caital clan, was reduced to only a single member, Mistress Cait herself. It's rumoured she lives deep in the enchanted forest. Since she's supposedly the one who enchanted it, that kind of isn't surprising.'

'Have you ever met her?'

'Not so as I would remember. Technically, Mistress Cait is my godmother. Both mine and Lavender's. I'm told she was at my christening, but I haven't seen her since. She was the one who saved Mother's life when the thirteenth faerie gifted her with the virtue of Death. Cait gifted her with Life, and the two virtues clashed and created the hundred year Death in Life of the interregnum.' Will frowned. 'It all comes back to the interregnum. Hiedelen's hold on us, the kingdom's poverty, why everyone distrusts magic.'

'So, then, why do you . . . indulge?'

'It's a bit hard to explain,' Will said. 'You see Lavi, right?'

He turned his gaze back to her. She was dancing gracefully with King Ragi, who was at least keeping up. She was dressed in swan white with lavender trim, and her autumn coloured hair caught the torchlight. Will was annoyed to see that it glowed as brightly as the flames. Ferdinand's face softened a bit as he looked at her. 'Yes.'

'Well, she got most of my mother's virtues. The useful ones, anyway.'

'Virtues?'

'Yes. When Mother was christened she received eleven virtues from the representatives of the faerie clans which had been invited.' She ticked them off on her fingers. It was a well known litany. 'Beauty, Wisdom, Kindness, Generosity, Patience, Wit, Bravery, Honesty, Mercy, Nobility and Grace.'

Ferdinand blinked. 'You have that memorized?'

Will frowned. 'Why wouldn't I?'

'Lavi couldn't get through more than five.'

Will laughed. 'I'm not surprised. Let me guess, Beauty, Kindness, Patience, Grace and Nobility.'

'How do you know that?'

'Because those are the ones we know she's got,' Will said. 'I'm left with Honesty and Wit, which tends to annoy people, Bravery, which is useless in a princess, and Mercy, which pretty much makes me feel guilty for being a princess in the first place, without the kindness which enables me to want to do anything about it.'

'Perhaps you were also gifted with the Wisdom to know you can't,' Ferdinand said. 'I can give my last crust of bread to a starving beggar woman, and have. That doesn't mean she won't be starving again tomorrow.' He frowned. 'Who got Generosity?'

'Probably her,' Will said ruefully. 'But Mother raised us both with a sense of altruism, so it's hard to tell.' She pointed at her costume again. 'You'll notice this dress isn't silk. Fine linen, but not silk. We don't waste taxes on frivolities. We feed our people, instead. We are not a wealthy kingdom. The interregnum raped our land, and most of our wealth ended up in Hiedelen. Half that dragon money you brought us is probably going to go to healers guilds and orphanages.'

Ferdinand laughed again. 'Why didn't you mention Wisdom?'

Will shrugged.

'Could you have grown your own virtue?' he asked.

'What?'

'Modesty.'

Will blushed again. 'What makes you think I'm wise?'

'Because I know Lavi. She's clever enough, but she's silly. She's delightful, but I wouldn't call her wise. Unlike you.'

Will had never really been given a compliment before. Not on anything that ever mattered. Whether someone told her that her dress looked nice or that she'd done a good job at her riding lesson had never mattered to her. But to have a handsome, charming prince approach her and call her both Wise and Modest did strange things to her insides. 'Thank you,' Will said, and her voice came out very soft.

'So how does that lead you to magic?'

Will shrugged, and tried to find her voice in amongst the billows of feathers which seemed to be choking her. 'Not much else to do. Besides, maybe—' She bit her tongue.

'Maybe what?'

'Maybe . . . once I've learned enough . . . I could change people's minds. Our ban on magic leaves us vulnerable to another kingdom with military mages.' She shivered. She was ashamed to realize it probably had more to do with Ferdinand's hand on her shoulder than it had to do with fear at a non-specific potential threat. 'Maybe I could make a difference there. Maybe there'll be something I can do to make things better here. Besides trip over my feet at dances like this and dutifully marry my young cousin.'

'You'll find something,' Ferdinand told her, with an air of certainty. 'You'll do something amazing with your life.'

'Why do you say that?' It actually came out as a whisper, and Will hated herself for it.

'Because I did,' he said. 'I think I was more like you. Youngest son, didn't really seem cut out for much. And look at me. Lyndaria's hero, wealthy on dragon's gold, betrothed to the most wonderful princess any man could ask for.' He flashed that beaming, charming smile at her again, and her heart throbbed, melting all over her stomach. 'You'll find what you're meant for, Will. I have faith. Each virtue went where it was needed the most.' He held his hand out to her. 'Would you care to dance?'

Will shook her head. 'I didn't get Grace.'

He laughed. Will found she wanted to make him laugh. She liked hearing him laugh. He sounded like a mother hawk chuckling to her chicks. 'I'll lead,' he said. 'Grace is supposed to be my job. All you have to do is let yourself follow me.'

Will found her hand reaching for his, and he led her out to the dance floor. And he was right. With his strong hand on her waist, his sure feet guiding her, the gentle pressure of his fingers warning her when the steps changed, she was as graceful as her mother, who was twirling like a snowflake across the ballroom with King Ragi. Will stared into Ferdinand's ice blue eyes, and saw herself reflected there. And for once she wasn't horrified by what she saw. Though she was an inch taller even than him, he carried himself with such nobility that they didn't look out of place together. Her hair like winter leaves and her eyes like a glowering sky didn't seem so plain when she stood with him. With Prince Ferdinand guiding her around the dance floor, Will felt as if she'd earned the virtues of Beauty and Grace and Nobility.

And when the dance was over he bowed regally, kissed Will's hand, and went back to her sister, taking Beauty, Grace, Nobility – and Will's heart – with him.

Will was shuddering as she made her way to her chambers. She shouted at her chambermaid (not granted the virtue of Kindness) ripped off her ill-fitting party dress and dropped it on the floor, (not gifted with the virtue of Patience) flung herself onto her bed and cried and cried and cried and cried and cried.

It was awful. It was stupid. It was dangerous. She was deeply, desperately in love. In love with her sister's betrothed. Her perfect, beautiful, flawless sister. It was hopeless. It was wrong. It was cruel, to Will, to Lavender, to Ferdinand. Will had only one choice, and that was to swallow the huge lump of unrequited love, force it deep down inside, and bury it there until it died, or it killed her.

So Will did the only thing she could do. She buried herself in her studies. She avoided Lavender and Ferdinand as much as possible. She avoided her mother and father. She avoided the courtiers. She avoided everyone. She reread every magic book she had, hoping she'd somehow missed a spell to make someone fall out of love. She was half afraid she'd actually find it. If she did, she wasn't sure who she would use it on – herself, or on Ferdinand. If she could make him fall out of love with Lavender, could Will make him fall in love with herself? Could she cast such a spell on Lavender, cause her to reject him? No. That would have been wrong. Whenever her thoughts reached that height she was hit by Mercy again (which was a virtue she frequently wished would simply go away) and she knew she could never do such a thing.

It didn't matter. She never did find such a spell.

Once Will had fallen in love with Ferdinand she tried to think of nothing but her magic. Which was why she had to escape the palace secretly. A princess of Lyndaria couldn't be permitted to go into the city alone, and certainly couldn't be seen buying books on magic. Which meant she had to wear father's clothes, hide her hair, and sneak through the secret passage and past the thorn hedge.

Trying to practise magic without a teacher was exhausting. It involved a lot of trial and error. Most of the time when Will recited a spell or brewed a potion nothing happened at all. Sometimes the wrong things happened. Sometimes *very* wrong things happened, such as the time Will had inadvertently summoned a demon. She had been lucky in that it had been a night demon, and she was able to keep it busy with riddles until dawn, but that had been a close one.

The spell Will used for subduing the thorns didn't always work. It was, if one could describe a spell as such, temperamental. Ideally it was supposed to bend the thorns from her, as if she was a hot fire they needed to pull away from. Usually the best she could do was keep them still, and keep them from actively seeking to pierce her flesh. Sometimes all it did was slow them down, and sometimes it did nothing at all. And sometimes, (rarely, but often enough to aggravate her,) it seemed to anger the briars, and make them come at her even more violently than usual.

So. Which would it be today? Will took a deep breath, closed her eyes, and recited the spell.

> *For everything that grows and every leaf*
> *That hangs upon the climbing vine or tree*
> *with sweet flower, wondrous belief,*
> *That my poor will can overpower thee*
> *For I am nature's strength, her arm and hand*
> *That can, for beauty's sake, for wonders great*
> *That binds the fruitful bounty of the land,*
> *And so becomes the instrument of fate.*

Ah, that was good. It was going to work today. The winter thorns parted, leaving her a small window from her palatial prison. Will carried her cloak rather than try to wear it through the briars. She tensed up her muscles, waited until the thorns looked peaceful, and started to run.

They closed behind her as they always did, but her spell made them slower than usual. She could almost hear them growling as they grew and grabbed, trying to catch her in their coils, hungry for her royal blood. She leapt the last few steps in one bound and landed rolling, holding her cloak against her face to protect it from the dirt.

She took a deep breath once she'd made it. Now that she was out of the briars' reach they seemed to mutter in disappointment and then settle back down into false dormancy. 'Until next time,' Will said with a slight bow to her adversary. The briars never bowed back, but sometimes, she felt as if they'd heard her.

Will knew she was mad, but she almost liked the violent briars. Not the sort of secret she could tell anyone, though. 'I don't know how anyone could stand to live here!' visiting nobles always said. At least until they saw the palace in summer.

Rose Palace was considered the most beautiful castle in the seven kingdoms. The tamer roses climbed the walls, framed the arches and lined the paths, only swaying prettily when people passed by, wafting their scent into the air. Even the predatory hedge, which had completely overrun the East Wing and which they could not seem to tame, was stunning for three seasons of the year. The roses grew in a subtle rainbow, no two colours clashing. Will always thought that evil faerie must have had a brilliant sense of colour, for all the artistic arrangement of her roses.

In the spring, summer and autumn Rose Palace was permeated with the scent of roses. People claimed that it was like an ocean of scent, and if the wind was right the fragrances of the many roses could be carried for miles into the country, causing farmers amidst their pigstys to suddenly lift their noses into the air and inhale deeply. As the spring roses faded and the summer roses took their place, showers of petals fell to earth. The palace employed special teams, with long poles to keep the thorns at bay, who collected those petals. They were used for perfumes and sachets which were sold all over the seven kingdoms. It was Lyndaria's most profitable export.

Those who lived in the palace did not need buy those perfumes; the scent permeated the very walls. Even in the dead of winter, to walk into Rose Palace was like walking into a garden. The courtiers' clothes always smelled as if they had been washed in rose water – which in truth, they might as well have been. The heavy tapestries exuded a constant scent. In the summer months, those who lived in Rose Palace could tell where people had been by the scent they carried with them. A subtle sweetness? They'd just been near the receiving hall. A spicy tang? They'd been ambling near the queen's chambers. A savour of fruity musk? Must have been consulting in the kitchens.

In the winter it was not so overpowering, but the scent of roses never really faded. Once people visited Rose Palace, they believed they understood why the royal family never left it, despite the deadly, predatory thorns. They forgot to take into account Lyndaria's inherent poverty. The interregnum was not kind to the kingdom. It was hoped that Lavender's marriage to the wealthy Ferdinand would help with that. Will hoped they wouldn't leave their seat at Rose Palace, regardless. Her albeit limited control over the briars gave her a sense of self. She didn't have much control over what else went on in her life.

Not that she could control the briars very well. Most spells she couldn't do, anyway. She had no formal magical training. There were no more official magicians living in Lyndaria, not openly. Will had never even met any magicians, unless you counted the faeries, and it wasn't really fair to count them. Faeries were in a class by themselves.

No one recognized Will as she walked through the town to the booksellers. No one ever did – her face was not as well known as her sister's, and no one expected to see a princess in that part of town. Madame Paline's book shop was the worst book shop in the city. It held penny dreadfuls and ancient warped door stopper books which would be better turned to papier mâché than read. Her tomes were worm-eaten and weather-beaten and dusty and musty and often profane. Which was why Will could occasionally find books on magic there. Any used magic books which found their way to the more reputable booksellers were usually burned unceremoniously.

Will was at Madam Paline's for over an hour and found nothing. She browsed and dipped, searched corners and peeped into unlabelled books. Her hands grew dirty and her father's doublet was smudged and she sneezed from the dust. Then, in the most unlikely of places, her search was rewarded. It was hidden behind a collection of out-of-date atlases, which showed the continent of the seven kingdoms with the borders from when they were still five kingdoms. It was called *The Ages of Arcana*, and it seemed to be a book on magic theory, and the history of spell making. Will's heart caught in her throat as she held it, a treasure beyond all sense. What she didn't understand was what it was doing hidden behind the atlases. It was so unlikely a spot that she was pretty sure it had been hidden there deliberately.

Still, it was hers, now. She carried the book with her to the front desk, where Madam Paline lounged reading a penny dreadful.

'I'll take this one,' Will told her.

Madame Paline held up a finger, as she was clearly at a good spot in her romance. 'One minute,' she said absently.

Will sighed. She did have to grant that Madam Paline, for all her unsavouriness, did adore books. Or rather, reading, as she didn't bother to take good care of the books themselves. Madam Paline charged her books by the pound, so Will set the book on the paper scale next to the desk and pulled her purse from her waist. It was likely to be rather expensive, by Madam Paline's standards, because it was old and thick with a heavy binding.

With a creak the scales shifted, and *The Ages of Arcana* was snatched from under Will's nose.

Will's head snapped up, annoyed. 'You're excused, *sir*,' she said, grabbing it back.

The little hooded figure whose sticky fingers had tried to purloin her book shocked her the moment he turned to look at her. The first thing she noticed was a pair of piercing red-brown amber eyes, which caught her with the same power and strength as a falcon. They were so stunning they made her feel ill.

'Am I?' he said with a smile which made his teeth glint. 'Ah. Good to know. I shan't ask for such pardon, then.' There was a cutting edge to his last words, and he snatched the book back from her again.

He was still dressed for the winter weather, bundled tightly against the cold. The thought which echoed back and forth in Will's head was, 'Fox.' His clothes were russet, rumpled and dirty, as if he slept in a burrow. The patch of forelock which peaked through his hood was ginger, as was the hint of beard which considered gracing his chin. His skin was darkish and dappled, as if a man naturally disposed toward pale, freckled skin had spent so long out of doors that his complexion finally relented, and stopped burning him. Moreover, he was a little man. He slunk, like the old faerie tales of the red fox Reynard. A fox at the hunt. And Will had the unnerving sensation of being a silly goose.

The only remedy was not to act like one. She glared. 'That's my book, sir.'

'Have you paid for it?' he asked.

'Not yet.'

'Then it does not, in point of fact, belong to you. Would you care for a copy of *Lyndarian Property Law*? I don't quite have it memorized, but I'm sure if we dig in the stacks we can find a copy here somewhere.'

Will wanted to laugh, but she kept her face stern as she looked down at him. She was used to her great height intimidating people, and she liked to use it when she could. 'No, thanks ever such.'

'In the meantime,' said the little red man, 'this book is not yours. And until such time as it is, it is well within my rights . . . to read it.' And he plunked himself down in the nearest chair and opened the book at the ribbon.

Ah! Will realized. This must be the perpetrator who had hidden the book. Which technically meant that he had found it first. But, just because he expected to be able to read it anytime he wanted to without buying it didn't mean that she had to defer to him.

'I happen to be in the process of paying for it,' Will pointed out.

'Not done yet!' the Reynard barked.

'Give it here, and it will be!' she demanded.

'And when I don't?' he said, not looking up.

Will noticed he'd said, *when* not *if*. 'I'll call the bookseller.'

'And where is she?'

She looked at the desk, half expecting Madam Paline to already have set down her book to prevent antagonism in her shop. But Madam Paline was nowhere to be found. The chair behind her desk was empty. 'She was just . . . here . . .' Will said. She didn't want to walk away, for fear Reynard here would walk off with her book.

'No more. She's off for her luncheon.'

Will frowned. 'Why would she go for her luncheon when I was just about to pay for a book?'

The Reynard glanced up over the top of the binding. 'Because I made her hungry,' he said. 'Which means she shan't be back for another hour, at the least. At that point, you may pay for this book and take it to whatever fine home you are most privileged to sleep in of an evening. In the meantime, you can leave me alone. I am busy.'

Will wasn't about to leave it at that. She wondered if she was in the presence of a real, live magician. 'You made her hungry? How?'

He rolled his piercing eyes. 'Are you really this stupid, or are you only pretending?'

'You're a magician,' she accused.

'And how did you come to that?'

'Oh, I don't know,' she said. 'Perhaps it's because you're reading a magic book and making cryptic little remarks and don't seem to feel any shame about stealing a book out from under my very nose.'

'Ah, yes,' he said. 'Your perception astounds me. And because I am such a fine magician, I should like to get back to my book.'

Will's hunger burbled. She had never met another magician before. 'Where did you learn magic?'

The Reynard closed his eyes for a moment and then glared at her, incredulous. '*What?*'

'Where did you learn magic? What made you interested in it? Can you do many spells?'

He snapped the book shut and leaned his arm carefully atop it. 'Listen here, young man. I realize that you're probably very used to servants and peasants and other pitiful peons of Lyndaria fawning over you and your fine garb as if you were King Ragi himself, yet you shall not get such attention from me. I realize you would like to take this rare and beautiful tome home with you because you think it would look very nice beside the basket of fruit your tutor is making you paint for a still life, or perhaps would grace your half-barren shelf and possibly make you appear learned. I, however, am attempting to broaden a portion of myself, a kind of abstract concept we call a *mind*, which I'm sure you've never encountered before. Because of that, the book actually has to be open and studied, and a lack of brainless prattling would be greatly appreciated, if not actively praised.' He reopened the book and leaned back as if he expected her to flee, crying.

'Indeed, my supercilious friend,' Will said, returning his arrogance head to head. 'You are correct, I do tend to get a great deal of "pitiful peons", as you call them, fawning at my feet, much to my chagrin. It is not something I particularly enjoy, which is one of the reasons why I avoid my duties and my family and indulge in such a questionable pastime as magic. But without any assistance in that area, I find it very hard to improve, which is why I spend a great deal of my time actively searching out books such as the one you are currently holding.'

'Would you shut up?' he asked casually.

'No. I've never met another magician.'

'You don't get out much,' he said absently. Then he looked up from the book, realizing what she'd said. He looked her up and down, incredulous. 'You're a magician?'

'No, when I said, "another magician" I was not referring to myself, but my invisible friend. Yes. I'm a magician.'

'You shouldn't admit it,' the Reynard said. 'An interesting hobby for you, young man. You don't look like you're starving.'

Will didn't quite know how to take that statement. 'I didn't know starvation was a prerequisite.'

'Foreigner, are you? From a kingdom more happily situated when it comes to the politics of magic? To whom are you apprenticed?'

Will was heartened. She'd always wanted to talk magic with someone, but it was so frowned upon that she didn't quite dare. 'No. I'm from here,' she said. 'No trainer. No master. I study, on my own. From books, like that one. I don't know any magicians, and I can't leave Lyndaria to get apprenticed.'

'What prevents you?' he said, and Will detected scorn. He looked her up and down again. 'Not money, obviously.'

'Not shame, if that's what you're thinking,' she said. 'I'm needed here. My family wouldn't allow it. If it became known why I left, it would besmirch the family name.'

Reynard's face darkened and he glared at her. 'Yes. I can see how that would be a problem for you. Good afternoon.' He turned back to the book.

'I didn't say it was a problem for me,' Will said. 'It is a

problem for them. As far as I'm concerned, the name means nothing to me. But as much as I wish it otherwise, very few of us actually have control over our own lives.'

Reynard twitched an eyebrow. 'This is true.' He hesitated, then looked up at her. 'You truly intend to buy this book?' His voice had changed. The growl was still there, but the bark had gone out of it.

'Of course,' Will said. 'There aren't that many tomes that survived the purge.'

Reynard cringed, then sighed and closed the book with a quiet finality. He laid it aside. 'Is there anything I could say that would dissuade you?'

'If you can make Madame Paline hungry, can't you just make me not want it?'

'I've tried,' he said with a little growl. 'You haven't left yet. It only works on very simple minds.'

Will was a little confused by this. 'Well, I suppose you could start with, "Please don't buy this book", but I'd kind of like to know why.'

'Because I can't afford it,' Reynard said with what was clearly painful honesty. 'And I don't want to steal it.'

'Would you steal it if you had to?' Will asked, more curious than disturbed.

'Very likely,' Reynard said. 'But I probably wouldn't be able to take care of it, and the trouble involved in the theft is a little more than I feel up to handling just now. I've already run enough today. What can I do to make you leave this book here?'

'Nothing,' Will said.

He sighed. 'Very well.' He stood up and made as if to slink out of the store, book in hand.

'But if you'd like to read it after I buy it, it wouldn't bother me.'

He turned his smouldering eyes back on her. 'You what?'

Will smiled. 'Very wise move,' she said. 'I was about to shout "thief". Listen, you have as much right to knowledge as I do. I'm hoping, if enough people of Lyndaria stand up and declare magic to be no more dangerous than any other tool, we could change the laws. But we have to have people in the kingdom who know magic to prove it. If you'll tell me who you are, I'll meet you at the Princes' Monument of an evening, and you can read it.'

'Tell you who I am?' Reynard laughed. 'And who are you, young man?'

Will opened her mouth, and remembered she was dressed like a boy. 'That's no concern,' she said.

'Then no thank you.' He pressed the book into her hand. 'I've just decided this is not worth the trouble.' He turned his back.

He was definitely going to leave now. The only other magician Will had ever met, and he was about to walk out that door and away forever, taking all his knowledge with him. 'I'm not trying to make trouble for you!' she cried. 'Please, don't run away. I only want to talk a bit, maybe work through a few spells I'm having trouble with.'

'You having trouble with spells doesn't surprise me in the least,' Reynard said. 'Good day.'

'It'll be an even trade,' she said. 'In exchange for telling me a little about what you know of magic, I'll share my books with you.'

He stopped as if his feet had sunk into mud. He turned his head to her slowly. 'Books?' he said.

'Yes,' she said. 'I collect books on magic. I have quite a collection by now. Nearly a hundred.'

He blinked. ' A *hundred* books on magic.'

'Well, closer to a hundred than it is to fifty. I haven't counted recently.'

'And you will allow me to read these.'

'Gladly,' Will said. 'If you'll just go over some of the spells with me. I have one I *need* to make more powerful, it isn't very reliable, and my life keeps depending on it.'

He tilted his head, considering. His smouldering eyes narrowed. 'One spell for each book you bring me.'

'One evening for each book, as many spells as we can cram into an evening,' she bargained.

'As many *attempts*. I can't make you gifted at magic if you simply don't have it.'

'I have it,' Will said. 'I've just never had much chance at practical applications.'

'Fortune has smiled on your life,' he said bitterly. 'We have a bargain?'

'Done,' she agreed. 'Now, tell me your name so I know who I'm bargaining with.'

He laughed. 'All we need to know is where to find each other. The Princes' Monument?'

'One hour after the curfew,' she said.

He took a step back. 'Why after curfew?'

'I told you I had an interesting family. They keep my day pretty full. But I should be able to get away after curfew sounds. Provided that spell that doesn't always work is working for me.'

'We'll work on that one first, then,' Reynard said. 'You'd best fetch out your money. Madame Paline is returning.'

Will turned to see Madame Paline through the window. She was relieved until she saw she was flanked by two palace guards in the royal livery of red and white. More than just palace guards. These were Jakin and Jared, two brothers who served only at the queen's whim. Will sighed. There was only one reason why the Terrible Twins would have been within a hundred yards of Madame Paline's. Amaranth had sent them after her wayward daughter.

Will tucked the book under her arm and stretched to her full height. 'Your Highness,' said Jakin as he passed under the lintel.

She tried to pretend he wasn't addressing her.

'My lady,' said Jared. 'We've been ordered to escort you back to the palace.'

'Very well.' She reached into her purse to get Madame Paline the coins for *The Ages of Arcana*, hoping that no one would notice the title. As she fumbled for the coins she saw Reynard staring at her in horror. Will froze in surprise. In his shock he'd stopped his slinking hunch and had stood to his full height. He was taller even than she was. The only man she'd ever known who was actually taller than her was her father. He noticed her looking at him and hunched back down, slinking a few steps away. Will dug out the coins and handed them to Madame Paline. When she looked back to confirm her meeting with Reynard, he was gone.

Chapter 3

* * *

I was talking with the princess! I had been laughing and ribbing with the princess of Lyndaria! The personification of the enemy! I shuddered as I fled from the bookseller's. I'd spun a web of invisibility around myself to escape without anyone seeing me, breaking the law right in front of *a Princess of Lyndaria*!

I couldn't believe I hadn't recognized her. That damned Lyndal face of the wretched Lyndal Queen was on all the money. Not that I had much chance to look at money, now that I thought of it. And she had been dressed like a boy. Tall as a boy, too. Hadn't really looked Lyndal. It had to be the younger daughter, Ash or Willow something, not the Lovely Lavender, whose image was touted by all as the personification of Beauty and Loveliness, and whose disappearance, reappearance and now betrothal had her face splashed all over the broadsheets.

What had the younger Lyndal daughter been doing, dressed as a boy, buying a magic book at one of the seediest booksellers in Lyndaron? It was as shocking as the idea of Queen Amaranth making a quick copper or two down at the local brothel.

And I had been talking with her. By my lost name, she'd touched my shoulder! She'd arranged a blasted magical tryst! I felt ill. I'd had a Lyndal princess right before my eyes, and I hadn't spat in her face. I'd joked with her. I'd laughed with her. I was horrified by all the things I did and didn't do during that encounter.

I didn't know where I was going until I made it to our burrow, a hole made quite literally below the roots of a choke cherry tree, at the edge of the enchanted forest. We'd settled in there that autumn, as it became too cold to sleep out of doors. The burrow was big enough for all three of us to stretch out flat in it, and tall enough for us to sit upright, but that was it. It was a temporary shelter, at best. It was only barely warm enough, and that was only because, unbeknownst to my mother, I'd spun a web of insulation around the drafty corners of the hole. I wasn't supposed to use my spinning magic, but it was what I was best at. All other types of magic seemed watery and weak to me.

They were watery and weak to my mother, too, who still refused to touch a spindle. Which was why the fire by the door to our cave was thin and cold. We could only gather what wood we could find, and that was usually green and unseasoned. If our mother had wanted, she could have spun the heat out of that fire, wrapped us in a cloak of warmth, and kept us toasty as that blasted princess in her fine palace. But our mother would never touch a spindle, even to save her life.

The kit was huddling right beside the fire, still shuddering from her dunking. 'Aren't you warmed through yet?' I asked when I saw her.

'N-no,' she stammered.

'Where's our ma?'

'Sh-she went out to try and find a chi-chicken.'

'Good,' I said. I pulled my drop spindle out of my shirt.

'No, don't!'

'You want to freeze to death?' I asked.

The kit looked down at the ground. I'd sounded more harsh than I'd intended. I was still put out by my encounter with the princess. 'Hold still.' I spun out another strand of thread, spinning the fire into a tight whirl of heat. The fire looked much smaller, but the heat which came from the green logs was three times hotter. The kit groaned with joy as the heat reached through to her bones, and she leaned into the warmth. 'Not too close, it'll burn you,' I said. I snuck in under the blanket with her and settled her on my lap. Between my fire and my arms she soon stopped her shuddering.

'What's wrong, my brother?' she asked me once her voice was under control.

'Nothing,' I said.

'You can make light of something, but it is eating at you. I can feel it. Not our close call this morning?'

'No,' I said. That was just a matter of course.

'Then what is it?'

'I said it was nothing. I only betrayed myself and the family, nothing of any concern.'

Since I was clearly not grabbing all our meagre possessions and running for a new shelter, as I would have done had our burrow been revealed, the kit only snuggled closer to me, leaning her head on my shoulder. 'And how did you do that?'

'I met the youngest daughter of Queen Amaranth today,' I said. 'And I didn't kill her on sight.'

'You saw Princess Willow?'

'I met her,' I said. 'I spoke with her. She offered to loan me her library. And I didn't spit in her face. I did not snap her fingers one by one as she begged for mercy. I did not spin her into a noose and watch her dance, turning blue in my gallows. I did not cut out her heart and send it to her mother in a box with a ribbon.'

The kit laughed. 'You wouldn't have done those things, anyway.'

'Don't be so sure,' I whispered, and I kissed the kit on the temple. If the kit had died this afternoon, I might just have tried to do those things, to anyone and everyone. I knew how strongly my anger raged when someone I loved died.

'What was she like?'

I couldn't believe what I was hearing. 'What?'

'Princess Willow. What was she like?'

'Since when do you follow royal gossip?'

'I'm just curious. Was she as haughty and greedy as you said?'

My face twitched as I tried to figure it out. 'No,' I said. 'She was haughty, all right. I suppose she might be greedy, too. But not in the ways I would have thought.'

'What else of her?'

'She smells of roses,' I said, and blinked. I hadn't noticed that I'd noticed. One of the annoying things about being Nameless was that I didn't see myself very clearly, so I sometimes ended up doing or saying things I hadn't planned or expected to do. The memory of the princess's scent batted at me with soft paws. 'And she's very tall,' I added. 'To begin with, I had no idea it was her. She's stocky, and was dressed as a boy.' I spun the story as I would my thread, until the kit was laughing in my arms. At least I could get some good out of my humiliation.

The kit was impressed by the story. 'So are you going to meet her at the monument?' she asked.

'You're joking,' I said. 'I only agreed to that when I thought she was some rich merchant's son, not the thrice blasted Princess of Lyndaria.'

'So?' the kit said. '*She* knew who she was all the time.'

'She doesn't know who *I* am,' I growled.

The kit nuzzled her nose deeper into the blankets. 'Neither do I. But I think you ought to meet her.'

'Why?'

The kit shrugged. 'I just think you should. Think about it. What have we got to lose?'

'Our lives, I suppose,' I said, but she was right. There wasn't much else they could take from us. And there was *much* I could take from her. 'You really think I should go to the monument?'

'At least see if she really shows up,' the kit said. 'Maybe she won't now she knows you know.'

'And what would I do there? Tie her up and hold her for ransom?' That was an idea, come to think of it.

'No,' the kit said. 'I think you should tell her what's happened to us.'

'I'm not going to do that!' I snapped. 'She wouldn't care, anyway. Stuck up, spoiled princess.'

'But she's studying magic,' the kit said. 'Surely she can't be entirely unsympathetic.'

'Yes she can,' I said. 'You think they don't know what they've done to faeries and magicians around here? She's probably just trying to annoy her mother. She looked like the type that likes to annoy.'

The kit squirmed and glared at me. 'So are you!' she said pointedly. 'You have two choices. Either sit here in this hole and simmer in anger, or go talk to the princess and maybe do something about it.'

'What do you think she could do?' I asked. 'She's not going to change public opinion on magic, she won't set about lifting the ban on spindles, and she certainly can't give us back our name.'

'Before she does any or all of those things she'd have to be convinced,' the kit said. 'And if anyone could do it, I know you could.'

I frowned. 'I couldn't convince her of anything.'

'You? The biggest rake in Lyndaron, couldn't convince a lonely princess?'

My brow furrowed. 'What makes you say she's lonely?'

'Everyone knows she's lonely. She's been of age for more than three years. Most say she's too tall, but some say she's too clever. Whatever the reason, she hasn't had a single suitor, not even those love games with poetry and dances they play up at the palace. Who better to sweep her off her feet than my handsome brother?'

I looked away, unconvinced. She wasn't wrong about my being a rake. It wasn't anything I tried. Faeries are naturally beautiful, and that included myself and the kit. And since, being Nameless, we didn't have the natural glow of other faeries, people didn't always recognize where the allure was coming from. It never got me very far. A few kisses. Some hurried, illicit fumbling in dark corners. But the moment someone spotted my ears or noticed my proportions, I'd be shunned instantly. I was once snatched nearly bald by a girl who had sworn she loved me, until she realized I was a Nameless faerie. Not to mention that terrible affair in the meadow, seven years ago . . . I turned my head from the memory.

'I've seen you do it before,' the kit continued. 'You have something she wants. You are who you are. Something can come of that.'

'She can't change our lot,' I said. 'All I could take from her is my revenge.'

The kit frowned and held her hands to the fire. 'Maybe,' she said. 'But at least it isn't sitting in this hole.' She looked back at me. 'I'd go to her.'

She was right. I was sick of skulking and hiding and living underground in every possible way. At least plotting my revenge against Queen Amaranth through Princess Willow was something more constructive.

Chapter 4

Will

When Will got back to the palace she was told that her mother wanted to speak to her, in the formal audience chamber. She swallowed. Will found Amaranth rather intimidating. She tended to bring out the worst in her. She and Lavender both did. Will had barely spoken to either of them since she had fallen in love with Prince Ferdinand. The wretched thought of *him* made her heart beat a little faster, and she was suddenly terrified lest he be in the audience chamber as well. 'Might I go and change my clothes first?' she asked the guards.

'Our orders were to take you directly to the queen,' said Jared. 'As soon as possible.'

Will sighed. She wouldn't be able to stash the book, either. She tucked it under her arm backwards, hoping it would look like any book of stories. She gathered her dignity, lifted her head to its full height, and told the footman to announce her.

'Her Highness the Princess Willow Lyndal,' said the footman, and stepped out of the way, holding the door.

Will strode in, holding her eyes directly on the queen. There was a small collection of people there already. Will didn't know why they had to have this encounter in the public audience chambers.

She looked about a bit and she glimpsed a golden crown which was not her mother's. Will's memory came flooding back. By all seven hells, this was the formal reception of King Lesli of Hiedelen! Will had forgotten it. He and some of his court had come to Lyndaria as honoured guests for the Midwinter Ball. It was also to be King Lesli's formal introduction to Ferdinand. The alliance between Hiedelen and Lyndaria was so strong that his approval, though not exactly required, was to be expected.

Many of the older citizens still thought of King Lesli as the true king. Until Amaranth's awakening he had been king, for nearly a quarter of a century. It had been conjectured that Lyndaria should never have severed rule with Hiedelen at all, despite Amaranth's resurrection. King Lesli was experienced, was of the line which had sacrificed their sons for the good of the people, and had ruled well enough.

Ruled well enough, indeed, Will thought. *Oh, aye, he had only tapped the people of Lyndaria for soldiers for his wars five or six times. He only took a modest tribute, over and above the regular taxes. He'd only raped the land to line his own coffers.* But, particularly to the older generation, Lesli seemed considerably more experienced and regal than the true Lyndal line, Amaranth only sixteen and Ragi barely into his twenties. It had only been Amaranth's prompt marriage to Ragi, and a series of tributary treaties which had prevented civil war.

Now King Lesli was in his sixties, hoary but hale. Lyndaria still sent Hiedelen a yearly tribute, but Amaranth and Ragi had been slowly lessening the amount for the last ten years. Will still remembered the unrest when they'd first reduced the tribute. She'd only been eight at the time, but she still remembered the mustering for war. A marriage between Lavender and Lesli's younger son Dani had been arranged, which prevented this war.

Now, unfortunately, the situation was shaky. Dani had been killed by the very dragon which had abducted Lavender, on the very eve of the announcement of their official betrothal, no less. Since all of Lesli's other sons and grandsons were already married, save for young Narvi, who had already been promised to Willow, the announcement of the betrothal to Prince Ferdinand had not been taken as an immediate declaration of war. All the same, there was a certain amount of tension between the kingdoms, and the state visit over Midwinter was intended to smooth this rift.

And I've been so selfishly, hopelessly in love that I managed to forget all about it, Will thought.

She could feel her cheeks go hot as she walked across the carpet to the dais at the end of the audience chamber. She was dressed in her father's clothes. Her cloak was still snowy from the outside. She was holding a book of magic. And she was late. Princess Willow Lyndal, the last chance at a tacit alliance between Hiedelen and Lyndaria, was disrespectfully late.

And Prince Ferdinand *was* there, of course. He flashed Will a sympathetic smile as she crossed the floor. Her heart twisted in her chest, and she felt about nine years old.

'Well, dear daughter,' Amaranth said as Will came into conversation range. 'We had expected you here to meet with King Lesli.'

Curtsying without a dress looked a little silly, but Will took a fold of her cloak and bent into a respectful one all the same. 'Your Majesty,' she said to Lesli. 'My deepest apologies for my tardiness, and my appearance. I had mistaken the day of your arrival. I beg your forgiveness.'

King Lesli regarded her, his stern face entirely unchanged. 'Hard to imagine that you had forgotten the day a once beloved ruler of Lyndaria would return.'

Every word in a state audience was recorded meticulously. The court recorder duly jotted down his statement. For Lesli to bring up his previous status as Lyndaria's tacit king in such a setting was audacious. 'I could never forget such a day, Your Majesty,' she said, her teeth hurting at the blatant lie. She could use sarcasm without pain, and she was perfectly capable of keeping her mouth shut and omitting pertinent facts, but outright lies were difficult for her. Honesty was another virtue Will wished would disappear. 'Rather I am such a fool I had mistaken the very day it was. I believed it was the Sunday.'

'It is Moonsday, dear daughter,' Amaranth said. Will could read her eyes. *I'm not asking about your apparel in court, but you had best have a damned good explanation.* 'Before your arrival we were hearing a brief report on the state of the kingdom, for King Lesli's benefit. Perhaps you would join us?'

Will curtseyed again. 'Indeed, Mother.'

Amaranth gestured to her right, and Will cringed. The chair which was usually taken by herself was occupied by Ferdinand. He was sitting regally, affectionately holding Lavender's hand. As Lavender was the heiress, her consort merited a chair, of course. Will was merely the second child. But unfortunately, court protocol dictated that her place was directly behind them. Will took a deep breath and took her place, standing directly behind their chairs, trying not to look at the couple, at how happy they were together, at how, oh, by all the gods, his hand was running sensuously up and down her back. Lavender was naturally pale. At court she wore face paint, so the deep blush Will could see colouring her ears was probably invisible to the audience, but his actions were distracting her. They distracted the hell out of Will.

She didn't catch a word the herald was saying. She didn't follow the tension-filled 'friendly' discourse between King Ragi and his 'Uncle Les'. She did not hear how Queen Amaranth tried to defuse Lesli's complaint about yet another reduction in tribute. Instead she watched Ferdinand's fingers as they played with Lavender's laces, as he reached up and fingered tresses of her autumn-coloured hair, as he lightly traced her neck above the collar line, causing Lavender to repress a shiver of excitement.

Lavender was repressing those shivers. Will was less fortunate. Nobility and Grace were far beyond her, and she wasn't wearing face paint, and her men's clothes were still wet from walking through the snow. At one point a footman did manage to take her sodden cloak, but by that time the wet had already soaked through, leaving her shoulders stained dark, and her skin breaking out in goose pimples. Her cheeks continued to flush. She hoped it was only the cold. Every time Ferdinand moved his hand she was hit by another case of the shivers. Her feet were turning numb with the damp cold. The audience chamber was not adequately heated. The throngs that huddled together, witnessing the discourse, probably didn't notice, but up on the dais the draught whistled cruelly.

Will was shuddering, but felt hot and cold by turns, as if she were feverish. She couldn't stop herself from imagining *she* was the one sitting in that chair, that *she* was the one feeling Ferdinand's fingers trace patterns on her back, caressing the skin on the back of her neck, his hand travelling down and down her spine until . . . oh, by all the gods!

She realized she'd made a sound when King Ragi turned to face her. To his credit, Ferdinand did not give himself away by snatching his hand back. Rather he very quietly shifted in his seat, casually moving his hand as he did so. 'You disagree?' Ragi asked.

Oh, seven hells, what were they talking about? 'I think it would be best to know every particular before any decisions are reached,' Will said, pretty sure that would cover anything.

'You see?' King Ragi said. 'Our daughter agrees with us.'

God of Death, what had she just agreed to?

'Of course she does,' King Lesli said. 'But my great-niece is notoriously absentminded on many subjects.'

The laugh this brought from the audience at Will's expense was a sprinkling of sugar atop the day's humiliation.

'As I was saying,' King Lesli continued, 'if you cared to look at my dealings in timber you will see that the cost involved in replanting seriously depletes the profit of the project. If you did not waste your funds on such frivolous ventures, you might not have such a poor coffer, and I would not be forced to so often forgive a portion of your tribute.'

Queen Amaranth's voice was very serious when she said, 'The depletion of our tribute is less the monies spent in projects such as replanting than it is the necessity of maintaining a kingdom over more than one generation.'

King Lesli shook his head. 'Without the immediate revenue to maintain the kingdom, the chances of it lasting until the next generation is negligible. Replanting forestry is a waste of time and resources. If you would be willing to follow my example in this, you would increase your timber revenue by likely treble, and we wouldn't have to worry about not having such ready monies.'

'Of course!' Will said, unable to keep her tongue still. 'You are so brilliant at this, Your Majesty. Why waste the resources in revitalizing the forests? It would be much better to simply clear the land and let all the game and foresters die, or move elsewhere. If this should result in a lack of charcoal for your blacksmiths and a winter of bitter cold for your people, what should it matter? By all accounts, soon enough, *you* at least will have fluttered off the mortal coil, and it certainly shan't be a trouble for you. You can always bring in metalworks and fuel for your people with all the revenue the forests will have brought you. In the meantime, you can dress yourself and your household in velvet and silk, throw lavish parties and turn forests into frivolities. Of course, by the time the revenue is needed, you will already have spent it on your parties and silk, so perhaps it would be best simply to declare war on a neighbouring kingdom and take their revenue. They would still have forests of their own, of course, because they will have bothered to replant. So you'll have the revenue needed to maintain your palace, *and* your people, however many are left after the cold has killed off the weak and the wars have killed off the men. You can then level the forests of the country you have invaded, producing more needed revenue, more lavish parties, more shivering, starving people and more devastated landscapes. You have such brilliant economic solutions, King Lesli!'

By the time Will was finished with that little burst of Honesty and Wit, her father had buried his head in his hands, and Amaranth and Lavender had turned perfectly, nobly still. Prince Ferdinand looked as if he was trying not to laugh. Will took heart from that.

'You must forgive my daughter,' Queen Amaranth said into the stunned silence of the chamber. 'I fear the cold has befuddled her. She is not at all well.' She turned to King Ragi. 'My dear, if you would see to our guest. I must ensure that our dear Willow is properly tended to. Your Highness,' she added to Lavender. 'If you would be so good as to assist us?'

'But of course, Mother,' Lavender said, standing up so quickly Will suspected Ferdinand had been caressing her again.

Will was seized by two graceful, noble hands and marched quickly and quietly out of the room. Her only comfort was that Prince Ferdinand remained behind with King Ragi.

Amaranth led Will to her private antechamber, a room well appointed for use as a study, with couches and curtains for the use of waiting nobility. The antechamber was much warmer than the chill throne room, a blazing fire dancing in the hearth.

Amaranth gestured for Lavender to shut the door. She did so, and then whirled on Will. 'Willow!' Lavender screeched. 'What in the name of all the gods were you thinking!'

I was thinking about Prince Ferdinand nearly consummating his upcoming marriage at court, Will didn't say.

Amaranth's voice screeched less, but was no less angry. 'Have you any idea what you've just done?' she asked. 'You have publicly insulted your great-uncle, a king of a powerful nation towards which this kingdom owes all allegiance. On a delicate state occasion, you have shown the worst disrespect any noble can show another. You arrive late, in disarray, in your father's clothes, no less. As if you were the jester, making fun of the entire court! We are trying to prevent a war! I do not know how I shall gather the courage to face that man again. If your father is able to convince him not to run to his coach and return directly to Heidelen, I will be amazed. Where is your head, child?'

They wanted Will to apologize. She knew they did. Lavender was about to demand it outright. 'I'm not sorry,' Will said. 'To let him believe that we agreed with that damned fool wasteful timber plan—'

'He can believe whatever he wishes,' Amaranth said. 'And we can continue to do as we always do.'

'But don't you see that letting the populace think you agree with him makes us appear less?' Will said. 'If we appear weak in our stance and our dignity, that is more likely to cause unrest.'

'Insulting King Lesli is likely to start a full-out war!' Amaranth said. 'The Hiedelen kings have sacrificed for generations for our people.'

'The Hiedelen kings as a whole may have done,' Will said, 'but I see no sacrifice in Lesli's history, or in his robbing our country of our gold like a common highwayman! King

Lesli's sacrifice consisted of sending us his least respected, thinnest-blooded relation, hoping he'd be killed and taken off his hands.'

The queen went white at these words, and Will feared she'd have to face her cold wrath. But it was Lavender who turned on her. 'You impolitic wretch!' she screamed at her. Amaranth glanced toward the door, afraid the words would travel to the audience chamber. 'Insulting Father like that!'

'I have nothing but respect for Father,' Will said. 'His blood is mine, but I very much doubt King Lesli's is, and I owe no honour to him.'

Lavender lunged at Will and grabbed her by the front of their father's coat. 'I'm trying to get married!' she yelled. Tears were streaming down her flower petal skin, falling from her summer sky eyes. 'You wretched little worm! You're going to ruin this for me! I can't live without him!'

'I don't see what your betrothal has to do with this,' Will said.

Amaranth placed her hand on Lavender's shoulder, trying to calm her. 'Can't you see, Willow?' she said. 'If we don't make a good impression on this visit, allow Lesli to feel that his influence in our kingdom is not diminished, he will take it as both a state and personal affront. He will dissolve the alliance and use his considerable influence to cause severe unrest in Lyndaria. There might even be civil war. The only way to quell such unrest would be an indelible alliance with the Heidelen line, marrying the heir to Prince Narvi.'

'But Prince Narvi is already betrothed. To me,' Will added with disgust. Narvi was well enough, he was too young to have developed any truly hideous traits, but that didn't mean Will was thrilled about the idea of being his bride in another seven years.

'Betrothed,' Amaranth said. 'Not wed.'

The full implications of this slowly dawned on Will. She swallowed.

Lavender was still weeping. 'If Lesli isn't satisfied with this visit, he'll forbid my marriage to Ferdinand! Mother, I can't live without him, Mother! Don't let her ruin this! We must do something!'

Amaranth cuddled Lavender under her arm. 'Hush, dear, we'll do everything we can.'

Comforting Lavender. *Where's my comfort?* Will thought. 'But what would happen to Ferdinand?'

'Likely banished or executed,' Amaranth said, 'if King Lesli's wishes were to be followed. Which they would have to be.'

Lavender sobbed louder.

Will banished an uncharitable thought of Lavender and herself switching their betrothed, Lavender safely married to Narvi, leaving Ferdinand and Will free to find each other. 'That wasn't what I meant to do,' Will said honestly. 'But I'm still not sorry for what I said to Lesli.'

'Oh, you horrid little vixen!' Lavender said, somehow able to sob without her voice breaking, a trick Will would have killed for. She grabbed Will again. 'You've never been in love! You'll *never be* in love! All you love is your self and your magic and your wretched books!' She ripped Will's new book out from under her arm. 'Ach!' She pointed at the book as if it were an apparition. '*Mother!* Mother, see what she has!' She pushed *The Ages of Arcana* under Amaranth's nose.

Amaranth frowned at the title. 'Is that what you were doing this afternoon?' she asked. 'You snuck out to get a book on magic? On this, of all days?'

'I . . . I forgot,' Will said. 'I really didn't know what day it was.' She'd been trying to forget. She'd been trying to forget everything. She'd been trying to forget Ferdinand's ice-blue eyes and the chuckling hawk of his laugh and the warmth of his fingers and the sound of his voice. Will was near crying herself. She only wished what Lavender had said was true; Will wished she'd never fallen in love.

'You're *still* doing magic?' Amaranth looked astoundingly sad. 'I've told you and told you what that would do to the opinion of the populace. Willow, what is *wrong* with you? Why won't you listen?'

'I can't!' Will said.

'You won't try!' Lavender said. 'You never try at anything!'

'I *do* try!'

Amaranth shook her beautiful head. 'Willow, it was magic that caused the interregnum, magic which made the thorns that are *still* killing innocents every year, magic which made us beholden to Lesli in the first place. Why do you insist on dabbling in something this dangerous?'

'Yes, magic got us into this,' Will said. 'So doesn't it make sense that it might get us out of it?'

'It's been tried,' Amaranth said. 'All it does is make things worse. We haven't found a single spell that will eradicate the thorns. All that happens is they grow angrier, faster, killing more subjects. We abandoned all attempts as too dangerous before you were born. All we can do is slowly choke the briars out, tending the ivy, grafting the more violent bushes with more benign ones. You just have to trust that we know more about these things than you.'

'You insist you know everything,' Will said. 'And everything just stays the same! Maybe you could *stop* trusting that you know everything and try and learn something new.'

'Maintaining this country takes experience and wisdom, not unproven invention,' Amaranth said. 'We can't afford to fail. It's too important.'

Will tried to keep her anger only simmering, instead of boiling over. 'We're already failing if one little criticism over 'timber maintenance can cause a civil war,' she pointed out. 'Maybe keeping an open mind is just as important.'

'I know you don't care what's really important to this country,' Amaranth said, which was both insulting and untrue.

Will's fist clenched. She wanted to hit her own mother, but she wouldn't dare. 'You can believe that if you want. I know that *you* don't care what's actually important to me.' Will had meant to add that the country was just as important to her as her magic, but she didn't get a chance.

'You dare say that?' Lavender cried. 'You dare say we don't care? You don't care about *me*! You don't care if I lose my true love! You only care about your stupid magic books!' She grabbed the book from Amaranth's hands and flung it at the fire.

Even as it flew Will was sure it would fall to the ground, would bounce against the wall, couldn't possibly land in the fireplace. The gods couldn't be so cruel. But it did. Lavender's aim had been perfect. *The Ages of Arcana* flew like a bird, its pages spreading open, the ribbon streaming behind it like a tail, a phoenix, ready to rise again from the flames. But it wouldn't rise again. One of the few books on magic theory that had survived the purge, and it went up in flames.

Will screamed. It was as if Lavender had flung all that was left of her heart along with that book. 'No!' Will shouted. She dived for the fireplace, trying to grab the book from the flames before too much damage was done. It was hopeless. It was a cold day, and the flames had been burning hot, to fight the chill. Her hand closed on the fiery book and tried to pull it from the flames, but it crumbled to burning ash. The pain didn't register for a moment. Then Will screamed again. It hurt too much to be real. The sleeve of her shirt caught fire. Her very face was smarting, and strands of her hair singed in little comets past her eyes. Lavender started screaming. Amaranth lunged for Will and pulled her from the fire, smothering the flames in her fine burgundy skirts.

Will's hand was in agony, but it was better than the pain in her heart. She stared up at her sister, her perfect Beautiful, Kindly, Noble, Patient, Graceful, horrible sister. She had everything. She had all the best virtues. She had the kingdom's respect. She had Ferdinand. And she had to burn the only thing Will did have. 'You didn't!' Will yelled at Lavender. Her voice sounded deep and deadly, as if it came from someone else's chest, or through a long tunnel. 'Why did you do that! Why did you have to do that? I'll kill you, you hear me? I'll kill you! *Why did you do that?*'

Lavender had stopped crying and was staring at Will, realizing, belatedly, exactly what she had done. She did have the virtue of Kindness, after all. But her lack of Mercy had burnt Will's own heart. Will curled in on her injured hand and sobbed and sobbed.

'I'm sorry,' Lavender whispered, but Will was past caring what she said. Her very world was reduced to flames. It was only one book, but it seemed to represent everything, her hopeless love for Ferdinand and her hideous, useless place in the family and her despicable penchant for magic and the general wretchedness of her life. All of it was fire, burning her, until she was nothing but the pitiful black ash of those pages, unreadable, lost forever.

Then Will felt her father's arms around her and he lifted her to her feet. Will was already at the seventh level of her own personal hell when she discovered there was a hitherto unknown eighth level waiting for her. Lavender's screams had made her swain come running, and not only was Ferdinand witnessing Will's pitiful sobbing, but half the populace of the audience chamber seemed squeezed around the open door of Amaranth's antechamber. Will couldn't be certain, but she thought the court recorder was still taking notes. She let her head drop onto her father's shoulder. King Lesli of Hiedelen was standing a little behind the crowd, only visible because he, like Will, was half a head taller than everyone else. Not as tall as King Ragi, but taller than the Lyndarons. He was watching Will with eyes like razors. There was really only one thing to do. Will grabbed her chest and cried, 'Oh! Oh, my heart!'

It wasn't really a lie. Her heart was indeed broken. Her next actions were the lie. Will rolled her eyes back in her head and pretended to fall into a dead faint.

There. Will wasn't at all well. Maybe now everything could be smoothed over.

Chapter 5

* * *

I debated with myself for hours before I decided to even leave the burrow. I finally left only because our ma had returned, and there really wasn't much space. Sometimes we could huddle together and tell stories, or use our smallest magics (never the spinning magic, but other kinds) to entertain each other in our tiny, chill space, but I wasn't up to it this evening. Our ma had risked her very life stealing a chicken to make a broth for the kit, and stealing always made her irritable. She wished she didn't have to, but even if we could have gotten our hands on some money, no one would sell anything to her. Making us Nameless had forced us into being criminals, in a self-fulfilling prophecy. Our ma with her wings was more obviously a faerie than me. More clearly a faerie, and more obviously Nameless. The kit and I were very pleased we'd inherited Da's more earthly magic, and weren't cursed with useless, Nameless wings.

I missed Da. He'd finally left after the kit was born Nameless, and he knew there'd never be any hope for us. We weren't sure where he'd gone. Back down into the earth, or left Lyndaria, lost in his fox form. It didn't matter. We'd never see him again. The kit didn't even remember him.

There was only one place to go unless I wanted to wander aimlessly in the cold, and I didn't. I kissed the kit goodbye and told her I was heading for the club.

The club was in fact an abandoned townhouse off the market. It was condemned, falling down in places, and extremely dangerous. It was also where every magician in Lyndaron gathered to meet.

There were never any formal meetings. For those who could read, a board was up in what had once been the parlour, asking questions and dropping hints about certain spells, or some Morality Coalition which was cracking down on magic in this or that neighbourhood. It was close enough to several taverns, so it was easily accessible. Magic was so looked down on that we kept the club a clandestine affair, only telling other magicians of its existence and its location. This was the third house the club had been housed in in two years. I rather liked this place, though the sagging floors worried most of the others. I'd surreptitiously spun some strength into the ageing foundation shortly after the club had taken residence there. I was far and away the strongest magician who ever frequented the club, but I kept that fact as closely guarded as the shape of my ears.

I ducked in through the kitchen window, the only entrance which hadn't been nailed over. Even inside I was careful to keep my hood up to hide my ears. It didn't look out of place. The temperature had dropped, and everyone was huddled against the cold, despite the feeble attempt at a smokeless witchfire someone had thoughtfully coaxed into the crumbling kitchen hearth.

The members of the club were of course all magic users. Magic being almost illegal, viewed in the same light as prostitution and gambling, they were also all thieves, cutpurses, whores, liars, sluts, and scoundrels. They were also the closest thing I'd ever had to friends.

I never really knew why, when I couldn't be completely honest even with them. They did not know I was a Nameless fae. But it was probably for the same reason the princess wanted to meet with me; magicians tend to stick together. We couldn't meet up outside the club – if one person was found out, all of his or her acquaintances would fall under the same suspicion.

When I ducked into the otherwise empty kitchen, I was greeted by Shadow. We called him Shadow because he was a pickpocket. Most of the members of the club knew only a handful of spells. Faeries are born with magic. Most humans have to learn it, acquire it, build it with rhymes or music or ritual. I could use these things too, but ultimately I didn't have to. In theory, as a faerie, any spell I knew I could *will* into being. In truth, we too were often specialized. I was a spinner. I could do other magic, and spinning magic was a skill I could strengthen, but it wasn't something I could ultimately teach. I could teach how to spin a fine even thread, but to use that spinning for magical purposes wasn't a gift that was easily passed on.

Shadow knew a shadow spell which made him semi-invisible of an evening. I knew he wasn't going to stay much longer. The sun was setting, and the night market taverns would be in force until first curfew. The curfew wasn't deeply enforced. No one breaking it would be arrested, but they would be told to run along home. Mostly the curfew kept people from loitering in the streets after fourth night bell. 'Aren't you running late?' I asked him.

'Well, if it isn't the old rumpled one. Haven't seen you about in a while.'

I grinned. 'Rumples' was the closest thing I had to a name. Old rumples or rumpled or rumple. It was because of the excessively baggy clothing I wore to hide my spindles. It wasn't a real name, because even that wouldn't stick to me. No one here really noticed that I'd never shared a name, and rarely noticed that even 'rumpled' was more a descriptor than a nickname. Most of us went by descriptors here, anyway – it wasn't always safe to have a name to share. 'I've been here,' I said. 'You're usually gone by the time I come. Why aren't you out at the taverns?'

'Oh, there's gossip from the big house,' Shadow said. 'Pretty sketchy yet, but the agony sheets'll be coming out just after first night bell. I'll be following the printers. They'll all be too hung up on the gossip in the broadsheets to notice a little Shadow, slinking amongst them.'

'What sort of gossip?'

He shrugged. 'Some blow up in court. Hiedelen king. We'll know more in a bit. Always easy pickings when the Hiedel king's over for a state visit.'

I shook the snow off my coat and hung it over my arm. 'Who else is about?'

'Oh, the witch and the whore are arguing over love spells somewhere,' Shadow told me. 'And I saw that holier-than-thou sparkly flitting about earlier.'

I nodded. The 'sparkly' would be Junco Winnowinn, a faerie of the Winnowinn clan, visiting from his northern fastness. Though low in his clan order, he was still a faerie. He very rarely came down from the mountain. 'What's he doing here?'

'Damned if I know. I'm vanishing. See you around.'

'See you, Shadow.'

'No you won't.' Shadow muttered his spell, stepped sideways, and vanished into the gloom. It was a good spell. I could just make him out with my faerie eyes, but only if I already knew he was there. I could barely detect him slipping out the door.

I left the kitchen and heard shrill voices arguing in what had once been the drawing room. But I was accosted by a bright glow in the hall.

Junco lurked by the rickety stairs. Faeries lurk badly, unless they're Nameless like me. Junco didn't quite cast a cheerful glow through the hallway, but he shone quite clearly out of the darkness. The Winnowinn clan were white and blue in colouring, with white wings like snow angels. I always felt like I was speaking to ice when I spoke to Junco. 'Well, well,' he said, smirking. 'If it isn't the Nameless one.'

'I'd thank you to keep your voice down!' I hissed. No one else here knew I was a faerie, and I wanted to keep it that way. The club might be full of thieves and cutpurses and disreputable whores, but they were all human. Magic might be accepted here. The Nameless were not.

'Oh, they can't hear me,' Junco said, jerking his head toward the argument in the drawing room. 'Aren't you dead yet?'

'I'm sure that would give you great satisfaction,' I snapped, 'but no, I'm not.'

'I wouldn't feel anything, satisfaction or otherwise,' Junco said.

'Then why do you even talk to me?'

'Perhaps I enjoy watching your envy,' Junco said icily.

I suppressed a growl. I did envy Junco. I hated every faerie who wasn't disgraced like myself. But hostile as I was toward him, Junco had never revealed who I was to the others, for which I was grudgingly grateful. I suppose he had that, *There, but for faerie grace, go I,* feeling about me. I doubted he liked me at all, though it was hard to tell. The Winnowinn clan was known for their icy countenance, and Junco had a sense of humour that was difficult to detect. 'What are you here for, anyway? I was under the vain hope that you and your clan were iced into that glacier permanently.'

'Clan Mistress Isolde thought someone should come down and see the young Prince Ferdinand. Rumour was he was a magician.'

'A magician?' This was the first I'd heard of that. 'The princess's husband is a magician?' That would change everything.

Or would it? Princess Willow apparently dabbled in magic, and no one knew about that, either.

'Not her husband yet,' Junco reminded me. 'And not a magician. He earned himself some faerie gifts is all, one of the clans in Illaria, where he comes from.'

'He has faerie gifts?'

'Just the typical questing beasts. The horse that can outrun the wind, the hound that can track through water, the hawk that can tell you the route to take. Their magic is all expired by now, of course. Fool still clings to them like a child's doll. Still, they won't throw bad offspring, he's not wrong to keep them.'

'You were at court?' I asked.

'No, strictly incommunicado, this visit. Only keeping the clan abreast of the changes in the wind.'

'You don't sense any change in the opinion on magic?'

'Not a whiff,' Junco said. 'This new prince's affection for faerie magic might even make things harder on those like us, since he seems to be causing some political troubles. Scratch that, things can't get much harder for *you.*'

'Thanks ever such,' I muttered.

'The death of Prince Dani and Princess Lavender's betrothal to Ferdinand has caused some tension between the Lyndar and the Hiedel. Apparently King Lesli has come up himself for Midwinters.'

'Hope he starts a war,' I muttered.

'He may,' Junco told me. 'At least that's what his guards are thinking. You might want to scout out a place to hole up if that happens.'

I glared at him. 'I suppose you expect me to thank you.'

'No,' Junco said. 'Not *you.*'

'God of Death!' shouted someone from the kitchen. A half-rate middle-aged necromancer we called Riverbottom, due to both his area of operations and his personality, came running through the hallway, nearly crashing into both of us. Without pausing to apologize he waved a broadsheet in the air and dived into the drawing room shouting, 'Witch! Get over here, you've got to hear this!'

Junco and I glanced at each other, and then followed after him. I let Junco go first, and when we entered the dilapidated drawing room I stayed as far from him as possible. I may not be obviously a faerie, but I wasn't so dull-witted as to stand beside one and let people notice the similarities.

The whore stood in the centre of the drawing room staring at the broadsheet, which she had clearly snatched from Riverbottom. The whore was less than twenty, and used glamour to entice her customers. She was actually quite hideously ugly, her face pockmarked, with a long, crooked nose, a cleft palate and several teeth knocked out by her drunken father. But when she put on her glamour, even I found my eyes drawn to her, and I could see through it if I squinted. Today she was wearing an image that was almost, but not quite, the mirror of the Princess Lavender, her autumn-colored hair twisted into a bun to show her graceful neck. 'Read this!' she was saying to the witch. The witch perused the broadsheet and rolled her eyes. 'It's nothing,' she said. 'Just gossip.'

'Oh, do it!' Riverbottom said. 'You read better than I do.'

'Come on!' the whore pleaded. 'Have a little pity. Read it aloud.' The whore, like most of the lower classes, couldn't read. I was fortunate in that my mother had taught me how. Nameless we may have been, but our clan had once held good standing in Lyndaria.

The witch sighed. 'I didn't learn to read so I could spill worthless gossip at street urchins,' she muttered, but she turned her eyes back to the broadsheet. 'Princess Willow Takes Ill at Court,' she read. She looked up. 'That enough for you?'

'You know it's not,' the whore squealed. 'Read the whole thing!'

'It's worth it,' Riverbottom said with a chuckle.

The witch sighed. She believed she was better than most of the rabble at the club, and she was probably right. She was a middle-aged herbwoman who was once an apothecary's apprentice, but was banished from the guild for poisoning someone. (I never knew if it was on accident or by design.) Now she eked out a meagre living by mixing small charms, most of which were pure fancy, but some of which smelled nice. The whore bounced up and down with excitement. She preferred news about the heiress, but Princess Willow was almost as exciting. I had to admit, I was a bit curious myself. *Had* the Princess been ill? Was that why she was looking at magic?

'Queen Amaranth's youngest daughter Willow was taken ill with brain fever today at the reception of Hiedelen's king, and Lyndaria's one-time regent, King Lesli.' The article continued on about the history of the two families, but I tuned most of that out trying to arrange myself across the room from Junco, somewhere in a shadow.

'Princess Willow was heard to question, "Why waste the revenue in revitalizing forests?" thereby proving her ignorance of the pertinent issues. Later on she was heard to sound her opinion for war, citing needed revenue as a legitimate reason. It is in the opinion of this chronicler that our "Princess Will" should be "Princess Won't".'

More than half the room groaned at the pun. The tale went on that Princess Willow began to feel flushed and faint, and the queen and Princess Lavender led her into the antechamber to try and refresh her. 'Whereupon the princess, shrieking at hallucinated demons, fell senseless to the floor. There was some speculation that the Great Sleep had again come to the palace, but it quickly became apparent that the only problem was with Witless Willow herself.'

I didn't listen to the rest of the agony sheet, which had clearly been written as salaciously as possible. The idea of the Princess Willow falling into a dead faint had caused the wheel to spin in my mind. 'Excuse me,' I muttered to no one in particular, and skirted back up the stairs to the collapsed room we called 'the observatory'.

The observatory was an upstairs chamber on which the roof and one wall had fallen in. It enabled one to look out over the city, but more importantly, to my mind, it enabled me to look out at Rose Palace, looming over the rest of the town like a great spiky dragon.

I pulled out my drop spindle and dug in my bag to measure my wool. I didn't have much. I usually tried to save it, portion it out sparingly. It was a consistent nudge in my mind – unspun wool made me uncomfortable. Even to think of it was to make my hands itch to spin it into thread. But to spin it up meant I could not spin it into spells, and that left me helpless. What I wouldn't have given for a immense flock of sheep, an entire barn full of wool or flax, enough to keep me spinning until my fingers bled and I itched all over with loose fibres.

I'd have given even more for a true spinning wheel. When I was a child, our ma still kept one, before hardship and fear had broken her. We'd had to leave it behind in one of our moves, and I remembered seeing it thrown on the fire. It had felt as if I'd lost a member of the family. I hadn't seen another spinning wheel from that day to this. I made do with the drop spindles I made myself. I still ached for the feel of a wheel at my fingertips, for a treadle to push, the gentle whirr-click of the footman turning the wheel.

No matter. There was only one spinning wheel left in the entire kingdom of Lyndaria, and it was under lock and key at the palace. And I had no flock of sheep, no acres of land on which to plant flax. I had only what wool I could rescue from thorn bushes. Once I'd stolen a whole bag of fleece from a shipment that was on its way to Hiedelen for processing. That had been a glorious year, with enough wool to keep me in spells to my heart's content, so long as I was careful. But the wool had been used up all too soon.

All the wool I had in my shirt was all the wool I had in the world. And all the wool I would have until spring, when, with luck, I could steal a fleece, or at least follow the flocks to pull wool from the brambles again. It wasn't much wool at all, and even carded as carefully as I could manage it, it was very poor quality. But maybe, if I used all of it, it would be enough.

I was going to take my revenge on the Lyndar line. I wasn't cruel. I wasn't going to kill them. But they deserved to be punished for my life, for the kit's life, for every terrible thing that they and their laws and their supposed morality had taken from me. They deserved to hurt. And I would make them hurt. I would remind them of our power, and I would make them hurt.

I pulled the thread that I had already spun off my spindle and folded it carefully into a skein. Sometimes I could do things with the thread itself, though it was easier to only spin the magic, rather than try to twist it out of already established thread. There was nothing wrong with the thread I'd already spun, except that it was spun sunwards, toward my right. I knew, for this kind of curse, I would need to spin widdershins.

Widdershins meant turning the spindle to the left, and was better for darker and more sinister magic. I didn't use it very often, usually only for defensive spells to protect myself or my family. Using a piece of thread from my old spinning I attached a leader thread to the spindle. I drew the fibres out from the wool and set the spindle off. The leader thread slowly unwound, then rewound widdershins, drawing the new wool with it. The spell drew itself from me as the thread drew itself from the wool.

The spell took me with it as the thread wound tight. I didn't simply spin a sleep. I spun my hatred. I spun in every stone that had ever been thrown at me, I spun every woman who had ever spurned me, I spun every cold, wet night without shelter. I spun in my fear for the kit and my anger at my father, who had abandoned me just when I needed him most. I spun in my resentment of my mother, who refused, blatantly refused to spin to make us safe. I spun in hunger. I spun in fear. I spun in despair. I even spun in that terrible day in the meadow, though it nearly made me sick to think of it. I spun all of this into the wool and wrapped it around and around the spindle.

By the time I was done I could barely look at the thing. It fairly reeked of my hatred. This wasn't simply spinning magic. This was a Nameless spell. I could see that Light would not shine upon this thread. I wanted to smile at my handiwork, but it made me feel ill. I was exhausted, and rightly so. I'd woven half my life to date into that thread of sleep. A thread of sleep with dreams. Those who fell victim to my sleep would not be granted peace. They would suffer the nightmare of my existence, the horror of Namelessness, the brunt of all the bigotry, the pain of every jibe and jab, every stick and stone. It was high time they knew how it felt. Them with their palace and their high name and their fancy victuals.

The only problem was how to set it? The spell was wound into the wool, but how to turn my sleep loose upon the palace? My aunt had used a spinning wheel with a sharp spindle, a pointed metal tip which would work the spell into the blood. I couldn't do that, not with a wooden drop spindle. But what could I do?

The answer came as I let the spindle go. The top of the thread came unwound, and some of the spell weakened with it. That was it! I took the remainder of my wool and spun in a catchment. When the thread was unwound the spell would take. Without being able to bring it into the bloodstream it would only work for a day and a night, but that was enough. A day and a night of contagious sleep, and all who woke would have suffered the same nightmare. Until the thread was destroyed, it would keep weaving its way into its occupants, knocking them to sleep again and again. Perhaps it would take some days to discover that my thread was the source of the spell. Perhaps people would keep falling into nightmares, on and off, for months. I liked that idea. I hoped it would take Queen Amaranth. And that foolish clod of a husband of hers, too. And that prissy little Lavender and her dashing swain. They deserved a taste of my fate.

I could trust that curious dabbler of a younger princess to wonder what the spindle was, and unwrap some of the thread. She wouldn't even know what a drop spindle looked like, most likely. She'd think it was an ordinary spool, such as was imported all the time. All I'd have to do was plant it on her, and hope she'd wait until she got to the palace before anyone discovered it.

I felt pretty good about myself as I left the club. Of course, it would all depend on whether or not the wretched little princess would show up at all.

Chapter 6

Will

Will was carried to her bedroom, changed into a fresh, warm dayrobe, tucked into bed, fussed and fretted over, poked at by a leech, and finally diagnosed 'overtired' and surrounded by warm blankets. She artfully opened her eyes when the healer came by, so that things wouldn't get too out of control. Then she pretended to get back to sleep until everyone left.

Almost everyone. Someone remained, waiting by the fire. Will opened her eyes, expecting to see her chambermaid, but it was her father. 'Don't they need you downstairs?' she asked quietly.

Ragi smiled. 'Despite having known the man since I was born, your mother is far more gifted at diplomacy with King Lesli. Possibly because of that, actually. He hasn't liked me since I spilled cider on his throne when I was four. He sat down before he'd noticed it.' Ragi pulled his chair over to Will's bed and lifted her non-injured hand. Her right hand still felt like it was on fire, but it hurt less than the pain of simply being Will. 'How are you?'

'My hand hurts.'

'Let's see what we can do about that.' He went to the window and swung it open on its hinges. 'Ah!' He took Will's face bowl and filled it with snow from the windowsill. 'Here,' he said, bringing it back. 'Put your hand in this.'

Will did. He was right. The pain diminished almost instantly. The cold hurt, but not nearly as badly. 'Thanks,' Will said. 'Does Mother know you're here?'

'Yes,' he said. He sat at the edge of her bed and pushed a tendril of hair off her brow. 'Now that no one's trying to make you apologize, you want to tell me what happened this afternoon?'

'You don't want me to apologize?'

He looked away for a moment. 'Politically speaking, it would probably be best,' he said. 'Though I'm not so sure. It might just bring everything back up again. Your mother has a much more generous opinion of Uncle Les.'

That made sense. 'Do you think this will start a war?'

'Not since your artful faint,' Ragi laughed. 'It might make things difficult with Lavender, though. If you aren't a fit consort for Narvi, that would count against her.'

Will groaned, her heart breaking in three separate pieces. She often hated her sister just for being as perfect as she was, but she was still her sister. Will loved her, too. Between her and Ferdinand and the good of the country, Will felt in the worst possible situation. 'What can I do?' Will asked.

Ragi shook his head. 'I honestly don't know.' He patted her hand. 'You don't really want to marry Narvi, do you.'

Will sighed. 'I don't hate him or anything.'

'But how can you love a young boy?' he asked. 'It must seem as if Lavender gets everything, doesn't it?'

Tears stabbed Will's eyes and rolled into her ears. 'Why'd she have to burn my book?' she whispered. 'Why?'

Ragi shook his head. 'She doesn't understand,' he said. 'She never felt the sacrifices her place has put upon her. She was willing to wed Dani because that was her place, just as she is willing to be queen because that is her destiny. She feels no sacrifice in spending her days studying history and diplomacy, does not feel it tedious to spend hours flattering visiting nobility, does not find any hardship in being the ideal figurehead for her people. Because she's never felt any of it a sacrifice, she doesn't realize that you do.'

Ragi shook his head. 'It wasn't until Ferdinand rescued her that she's ever wanted anything besides what has been placed before her. As if she sat at a banquet with all her favourite foods, and only now has she had her first taste of a wine which might be taken from the table.' He stroked Will's hair. 'All her life she's seen you at the same banquet. It's never occurred to her that you might have a taste for different fare. And therefore, have gone hungry. She sees only that your plate is full, and you're even allowed your magic, this illicit treat under the table. While we frown on it, no one is threatening to take it from you. Politics is against her and Ferdinand.'

He understood very clearly. Amaranth was the one with faerie-granted Kindness and Wisdom, Willow thought, so why wasn't she here making sense out of this? 'So she burned the book out of envy? Of me?'

'Yes. She sees that you still have everything, and all she wants might be taken from her. She doesn't see that you'd be starving to death but for your magic. That's why your mother and I haven't forbidden it,' he added. 'We know it would hurt you too much.'

'Mother knows?'

'Of course she knows. She doesn't understand it herself, either, but she knows.'

'You understand it?'

He sighed. 'A little. I never fitted in much, either. I don't know where you got the gift for magic, though. It did not come from either your mother or myself.'

'It's not a gift like blue eyes, or Mother's Honesty,' Will said. 'I just learned it. Like an instrument.'

'And there are those who can't carry a tune no matter how hard they try,' he said. He touched Will's nose. 'I've got something for you. I used the poker. I couldn't save much,' he added, pulling a handful of singed papers from under his coat. 'But some of it is still readable.'

The sight of the burned pages made Will tear up again. She'd only just remembered that she'd promised to lend the book to Reynard in exchange for his help with her spells. 'Take it away,' she sobbed.

Ragi nodded and slid the pages into the drawer of her bedside table. 'You can decide what you want to do with it later,' he said.

Will moved her aching hand in the snow. The parts of her skin which weren't blistered burned with the cold. 'Father?' she asked.

'Yes, Will?' He was the only one of her family who had agreed to call her Will.

'What am I?'

'What do you mean?'

'What's my purpose? Am I just a thread, useful only as a tie between us and Hiedelen?'

He pursed his lips. 'Am I just the questionable son of a Hiedelen prince, useful only as a sacrifice?' he asked. 'We are who we are. I know, whether you are the final link between us and Hiedelen, or not, that you can do something amazing with your life.'

That was what Ferdinand said. Maybe that was what she liked about him, she thought. He reminded her of her father.

The door burst open revealing Lavender, her face glowing with happiness. 'Willow!' Lavender screeched. 'Willow, Willow! Oh, are you all right?'

'Ye-es?' Will said carefully.

'Oh, Willow, I can't believe it! I'm so sorry for everything I said to you!' She rushed forward and kissed her, again and again. 'I love you, I love you! Anything you want, it's yours. Anything. You want my rosebud silk gown? It'll look beautiful on you!'

'It wouldn't fit me,' Will pointed out.

'Oh, right. Sorry. Well, anything. I'll sew you a gown! Myself. With my own hands. And I'll prepare your trousseau. I'll embroider willow branches over everything. Thank you so much!'

'Wait, wait,' Will said, glad Lavender wasn't still mad, but still feeling resentful over her book. 'What are you thanking me for?'

'For formalizing the engagement with Narvi!' she cried. 'Thank you *so much*. I know it'll be strange being married to a boy, but Mother says we'll send him to college, bring him back in half a dozen years. And you'll get to see Hiedelen – ask them to take you to the seaside. I hear they have an ocean. You've never seen the ocean. I'll be your maid of honour, I'll do everything for you, you won't have to lift a finger. You'll be the most beautiful bride!' She jumped forward and caught her in an extremely tight hug. 'I can't begin to thank you enough!'

'Lavi,' Ragi said, 'what are you talking about?'

She looked to him. 'Oh, Mother didn't tell you? Willow and Narvi are to be married at Midwinters! Isn't it wonderful! Narvi will be safely attached, our kingdoms will be allied, and I can have my Ferdinand!' She kissed Will again. 'Thank you, thank you, thank you! Can you ever forgive me for all the awful things I said to you this afternoon?'

Will's hand closed in the snow. Her eyes shut tight to block out the light. 'I forgive you,' she whispered.

'Oh,' came Queen Amaranth's voice from the door. 'If you two don't mind, I need to talk to Willow for a moment.'

'It's all right,' Will whispered. Her voice wouldn't come any louder than that. 'I know all about it.'

'Oh. Lavender, you didn't!'

Lavender sounded flustered. 'You mean she . . . this wasn't her idea?'

Great. So now not only was Will still thrown to the fire, now she wouldn't even get Lavender's gratitude for it. 'Please,' she said, as loudly as she could muster, which wasn't very. 'Please could you all leave me alone for a while?'

Amaranth frowned. 'I still think we need to talk.'

Ragi took that as his cue. He stood quickly, kissed Amaranth's cheek, and then led Lavender out of the room. Lavender cast one last confused look back, and followed him.

'Willow . . .'

'You really don't have to do this,' Will said. 'I won't argue. I know why it had to be done.'

Amaranth sat demurely in the chair Ragi had vacated. 'What you don't know is how proud I am of you for taking this so gracefully. I know that your will is such that you could make this extremely difficult for everyone, if you didn't understand.'

'I understand,' Will said. 'Three weeks. Seven years. It doesn't really make much difference. If it's best for the country, I'll do it now. I know we need the dragon gold Ferdinand brought as much as we need Hiedelen's favour. I know. Can we let it go at that?'

'We can,' Amaranth said gently. She gently touched Will's cheek. This surprised Will. Her mother was kind and loving, but she didn't touch people very often. She wasn't like Ragi, who used contact in ordinary conversation. Every time her mother touched her, it meant something. 'Something you don't know, though, is that I know how you feel.'

Will couldn't quite suppress a scoff. 'Thanks,' she said, without feeling.

'I know how hard this is for you. Do you think I really *wanted* to marry your father?'

Will blinked. 'But . . . he rescued you.'

Amaranth nodded. 'He did. And I spent a hundred years asleep, dreaming of my prince charming. And when I open my eyes, what do I find? A hulking, coarse-faced lesser noble, with a thick Hiedelen accent, looming over me, his clothes all rent and ragged from the thorns. I nearly screamed. I was only barely able to gather the dregs of my dignity and bring myself to request an introduction.' She shook her head. 'I ran downstairs as fast as I could. I found your grandparents in the throne room, and told them point blank that I refused to marry that man.' Will could imagine how well that went down. Her grandparents were old when Amaranth was born, and very, very old-fashioned indeed. They'd both died when Will was still a child. They would never have permitted defiance in anything. Amaranth shrugged, gracefully. 'You know how that worked out. We owed Hiedelen our kingdom. And that meant I was destined for Ragi.'

Will sat up, bringing her bowl of melting snow with her. 'Are you telling me you don't love Father?'

'No. I'm telling you I came to love him. Marriage isn't so much a meeting of hearts as a meeting of minds. Ragi wasn't sure he wanted me, either. He said he'd look a clod beside me on a dais.' Ragi had a point, Will thought. 'But in the end, he knew what was best for both our kingdoms, just as I did. And he is a kind man. It took less than a year before I came to love him.'

'But Narvi is *nine*.'

'And you are eighteen, and your blood runs as hot as mine did. You have the urge to explore, and the courage to try anything. But that was my undoing, in the end. If I hadn't been so keen to learn, I'd never have touched the spindle.'

Will swallowed. The fated spinning wheel was on display in the Great Hall, surrounded by glass and iron. The spindle had been removed, destroyed, but the wheel was viewed by visitors to the palace, and was kept under twenty-four-hour guard. It was the only spinning wheel left in Lyndaria. Will could easily envision herself being fascinated by the whirring wheel, the spinning thread. She'd have touched it, too, she realized. Particularly if, like her mother, she'd never seen such a thing before. Lavender would have sat demurely and let the spinner continue, not wanting to get in the way. But Amaranth and Will, they both liked *doing* things.

'You've already said you'll do the right thing. But I want you to know, you aren't abandoning your dreams. Narvi is a good boy, and will grow to be a good man. We'll send him to a college of *our* choosing, so that he will learn how we rule here in Lyndaria, and not the kinds of practices Lesli prefers. Part of the arrangement is that you spend some of your time in Hiedelen, but I'm negotiating your own estate, so you won't have to live at court with Lesli. All it takes is patience. And in the meantime, your life won't have to change very much unless you want it to. We're all very proud of you.'

'Mother?' Will asked. 'Could you . . . just leave me alone? I know you mean well, but . . . I just . . . .'

Amaranth nodded. 'I understand,' she said. 'You rest and get used to the idea. I do have to tell King Lesli that there will be no difficulties in this.'

Will nodded. Amaranth stood and kissed her forehead. 'I'm so proud of you, Willow. Everything will turn out right.' She slid like bright shadow out of the room.

Will lay there trying to grieve for her dream of lost freedom, but her snow melted, and her hand felt on fire. She tried to tough it out, but she couldn't bear it. She climbed out of bed to the windowsill and gathered more snow. She did this three times before all the snow on the windowsill was gone, and she was left clenching her teeth at her burns. She needed more snow. She could have just rung the bell and asked a serving maid, but the idea of getting it herself appealed to her. And since she was getting dressed and going downstairs anyway, why not keep her appointment with the Reynard? *The Ages of Arcana* was burnt, but she had other books.

She dressed in a winter dress, unwilling, while King Lesli was here, to again be caught in men's clothes in what was essentially a court function. So long as there were visiting dignitaries, she had to be ready to receive them at any moment.

Which of course meant that sneaking out after first curfew wasn't the most prudent of actions, but she was feeling rebellious.

Will kept her books behind a panel in her closet. This led to a secret tunnel, entirely disused, except by Will. The secret passages were only known about by the royal family. Keeping them clear was the one chore they had to do themselves. Ragi had performed the spring task of setting rat poison and clearing out the spiders, until Will had turned thirteen and offered to help. He'd left the tunnels to her care since then. They allowed hidden access to some few rooms of the palace, such as the royal bedrooms, the antechamber of the throne room, the library. Yet the routes were narrow, chilly, dark, and generally spooky. They had once had access to the outside, but in that aspect they were now entirely useless. Except to Will.

They were useless in the sense that they were now death traps, leading directly to the briars. Will couldn't bring *The Ages of Arcana*, but since Reynard had said the two of them should work on her thorn spell, she grabbed the book on green magic she'd found that particular spell in. Then she wrapped herself in a cloak and headed out into the night.

Chapter 7

* * *

When the bell sounded first curfew I made my way towards
the Monument for the Fallen Princes. The Monument had
been constructed by King Ragi just after the end of the
interregnum. It was a solemn testament of gratitude for the
generations of fallen Hiedelen princes who had sacrificed
themselves to the thorns. I found it rather amusing.

I hadn't been very aware when the first so called 'sacrifice'
had stupidly walked to the thorns, but Da had told me what
he remembered. Prince Alexi disobeyed his father and ran off
hot-blooded to earn his manhood. His father had intended
to annex the kingdom without sacrificing his son. Alexi must
have had some sense of honour, because he disliked the idea.
He had flung himself full onto the thorns expecting them
to simply part for his royal greatness. They hadn't. They'd
drained his blood very quickly.

The next, Prince Tenni, was a simpleton. Truly a simpleton,
he drooled and sucked his thumb, his mind barely more than
that of a toddler. He'd learned to ride but never to read. It was
likely someone who did not have his best interests at heart had
suggested he try for the Princess of Lyndaria. Either that or
they had exhausted every other hope of finding him a royal
bride, and he had braved the thorns in a kind of desperation.
He'd expected brute strength and an axe would be enough

to hack his way through the thorns. He was probably the only true innocent to ever die upon them.

The third 'sacrifice' had attempted to kill his older brother for the heirship. He had failed and was offered the choice of standard execution, or the chance at freedom and a kingdom as a sacrifice to the thorns. He'd chosen the latter, and died rather honestly.

Then it was King Lesli's generation. Lesli had clearly taken a lesson from the last sacrificed prince. Lesli was the second of three brothers, and had not been originally destined to be king. According to one story, Prince Lesli and his eldest brother had ridden to the thorn hedge at the palace at Lyndaron, with Lesli saying he intended to try his luck at it. He and his brother had gotten quite drunk, and Lesli managed to persuade the crown prince that he was no man if he did not brave the thorns at least once. The crown prince swallowed the bait and committed suicide by stupidity, leaving 'poor Prince Lesli!' to mourn his brother's corpse all the way to the kingship.

Then, at a time when Lesli needed soldiers for his armies and Lyndaria was again wondering why they kept honouring a monarchy who wasn't really even theirs, Lesli had known it was time for another sacrifice. He had sent his youngest brother's possibly-not-really son to get rid of the poor lad, and Ragi had made it through the thorns. Lesli was likely very peeved about that.

There were some interesting things about ageing five times slower than most everyone else in the country. You knew the truth behind all the old legends.

The Monument for the Fallen Princes was a dome held by four pillars. In the centre was a fountain of pure drinking water, which did at least lend the monument one useful aspect. Each of the four pillars represented one of the fallen princes. Only the last two held much resemblance to the princes' actual faces, and the simple Prince Tenni's face was a total fabrication. He looked strong and proud, and they'd omitted the drool.

In the winter the fountain froze, and the monument was fenced in by removable walls. I knew it was full possible to sneak around them, and clearly the princess did too, or she wouldn't have suggested we meet there.

I fingered my poisoned spool of thread. My aunt used a better spindle, with a real spinning wheel, rather than the rough wooden thing I was forced to spin with. I was sure she had had fine flax, or even an exotic silk to spin for her curse. I was left with the waste wool I could pluck from the hedges during the summer, following the sheep. Still, I was rather proud of my Sleep. I wasn't being cruel. My aunt had tried to spin a death. I was only spinning a reminder. If I still had to suffer for my aunt's transgression, the Lyndal line should as well.

I waited until rather later than an hour after curfew sounded. I was freezing. I had no wool left to spin up a warmth spell, and I was tired from spinning up the Sleep. Sleep. I yawned. My prison of a burrow seemed comforting at that moment. She wasn't coming. I should go home, keep the kit warm. So much for my revenge.

The smell of roses caught my nose. One of the false walls warped at the edge and a figure richly bundled up scrambled through the small opening. She hoisted herself upright and tripped over her own feet. Perfect opportunity to get my hands upon her. I darted forward and caught her by the shoulders. 'Well, well,' I purred into her face. 'The little hen has left the coop.' She shivered in my arms, and I flashed her a sly grin in response. That made her shiver again. I let her go. 'You're looking lovely this evening,' I added for good measure.

She started and looked at me. I realized that was probably the wrong thing to say. I hunched, hoping she wouldn't notice the extent of my height. I could do nothing about the length of my fingers except keep my hands closed. Hopefully she wouldn't notice the size of my eyes. The proportionate small-ness of my head and the length of my neck, not to mention my pointed ears, were all concealed beneath my russet hood. I did not like her looking at me. I felt on display. Finally she looked down at her own fine woollen dress and absently brushed her hand down it, as if embarrassed.

I realized she'd been looking at my clothes. Where they weren't actively ragged they were patched. I selected brown when I could, because it blended easily into the background, and they were dirty from crawling into the burrow. She turned her gaze back onto my face and frowned. She was thinking. That worried me. 'I'm surprised you actually came, Highness,' I said.

The princess's eyes flashed, not quite in the way I would have hoped. She seemed annoyed at me. 'Don't call me that,' she muttered.

Anger surged in me. I rarely called anyone by their name if I could help it. It felt like rubbing it in. 'Oh, did I get your title wrong, Splendour? So sorry Your Grace. You must forgive this poor peasant, Your Majesty.'

She gazed at me sardonically as I danced through various noble titles. 'Done?'

'Probably not,' I smirked. 'What should I call you, Excellency?'

'Will,' she said.

Short. Terse. Awfully informal. I hadn't expected that. Still. I couldn't resist. 'Won't.'

'Very droll. Quite original. I had no idea magicians were so amusing. Since pleasantries are obviously not to be expected, shall we come down to cases?' That brought me up short. Wasn't I supposed to be seducing her? It was as if my carefully constructed lines had fallen out of my head. Before I could come up with anything charming, she pulled a thin, tattered green book out of her muff. 'I need help with this spell.'

She was so brusque and businesslike I despaired of the kit's advice. Instead, I turned mercenary. 'Now wait a moment, Princess. Where is my payment?'

'Pardon?'

'Don't be coy. If this is a business arrangement, I expect to be satisfied. I want to see *The Ages of Arcana*.'

She pulled herself up to her full haughty height. 'It is my choice which of my magic books I allow you to read. Tonight, I choose this one.'

I stood taller myself. If this was to be a challenge, I was as game as she was. Simmering, I pulled myself a little too close to her and glared down into her eyes. It was surprising how tall she was, for a human girl. 'You are coming perilously close to making me lose my temper,' I told her with gentle menace. 'You're the one who came up with this ridiculous scheme, which let me tell you, is not a risk I take lightly. When you were merely an annoying but wealthy brat, the risk I took by agreeing to meet with you was slight. As it seems you are the princess, I am risking my very life, not to mention that of my family. Even by spending time with you I could be accused of kidnapping a princess, or robbing you of your virtue. I could be executed for treason if the right reason were invented. So unless you have something more reasonable than your royal whims as your excuse for negating our agreement, I'm going to back out of this mad situation before I see myself hung.'

'Hung? Aren't you overstating your peril?'

I nearly hit her. My hand clenched impulsively, but I managed to take a step back instead. 'Fare thee well, Princess,' I growled.

'Please, wait,' she said as I turned. Her voice was very quiet and calm. 'I didn't bring the book because I don't have it any more.'

I turned back to her, simmering, but steady. 'Why not?' I asked evenly.

'It was burned,' she said with grim finality. 'I couldn't stop it.'

It was like hearing of a murder. I think I went white. I know I went faerie still, which is something I try not to do. Perfect stillness is no more a human trait than overly quick movement. 'How?' I finally asked.

'I told you my family does not approve of magic.'

'You told me you could keep it safe!' I exploded.

'And you were going to steal it!' she snapped back. 'Is that keeping it safe?'

'Get away from me,' I snarled. 'I'm leaving. I should have known you weren't serious about magic. You're just dabbling. Tossed the book in front of My Lord Provost showing it off, did you? You didn't think, didn't care what might happen to it.'

'Didn't care?' she hissed. She pulled her hand out of her muff and held it out at me. 'Didn't care? Does this look like I didn't care?' She forced the hand into my face. It was covered in fierce burns. I blinked at them. I knew exactly how much those had to hurt. 'I couldn't stop it – Lavender threw the book in a huff, and I couldn't stop her. I singed half my hair and would have been willing to burn my hand off to save it!' She kept advancing on me, and I shrank down, abandoning my height. 'I'd rather have lost an eye.' She was nearly in tears. 'And it doesn't even matter, because now you're going to run off, and I'm going to end up married to Narvi and shuffled off to Hiedelen. You think you'll be in trouble if people think my virtue in question? I'd be cast down as a handmaiden to the Vestal Virgins. I shouldn't have even come here, alone, without guards. I care about my magic. That much should have been obvious, even to a scavenger like you.' She put her hand back into her muff, which I noticed, finally, was filled with snow. No doubt it was keeping the pain at bay. She closed her eyes and took a deep breath. 'I have the books. You have the experience. We both want to learn magic.' She glared at me. 'I'm sorry about *The Ages*. You have no idea how sorry. But I brought this book to lend you, and . . . I don't want you to leave.'

I blinked up at her. I was surprised by my own reaction. She'd nearly pushed me right across the room. Faerie Light, this woman was strong. Any magic aside, her personality was strong enough to cow a faerie, and a nameless one at that. I suddenly realized seducing her might not be possible. At the same time I was even more interested in the challenge involved. Rather than snapping back at her, I grinned. 'All right,' I said, trying not to laugh. I wasn't sure why I wanted to laugh. It was pure delight, but I didn't know where it came from. Quicksilver changes of mood were something I was used to, though – a trait of the nameless. 'Let me see it.' She passed the book to me. It was called *A Greenwitch's Almanac*, and seemed very well read. She was probably giving me her oldest and least interesting book. Unless this spell was so important to her that she was giving me her most cherished and studied. I longed to ask her, but I was afraid she'd catch on to my game. 'What spell did you need?'

She turned to a creased and dog-eared page marred by smudges of dirt. 'This is the Stillness Spell for greenery that I use on the hedge. It's not very reliable, and I'd like to know what I'm doing wrong. If anything.'

I flipped through the book, considering. It wasn't a proper spell book. The book had some ordinary weather predictions, details of which plants grew well together in the same plot of ground, and a great many tinctures and potions which one could use the plants for. The Spell for Stillness was one of the few actual chants in the book, and stood alongside a chant for dispelling unhelpful insects. I looked back at her, then back at the spell, blinking.

As it was, the spell was simply for helping the formation of aspiliated fruit trees and the growth of topiary, but that was only because it was at minimum strength. Greenwitches weren't considered proper magicians, for all they could work miracles in gardens. I was surprised that she managed to get it to work on the thorns at all, in the form the spell was in. She must have some real skill, despite being utterly untrained. I glanced back at the princess appraisingly. 'And you use this on the briars?'

'Yes.'

'And you can get through the thorns with it?'

'Sometimes.'

I frowned. Even the kit couldn't keep the thorns still enough to survive passage through them, and she was a faerie. Well, at least I wouldn't have to lie about the princess's abilities. 'Well, it's pretty mundane,' I said. 'The spell is at dabbler's strength. It lacks a word of power. You hear this section where the metre slips? That's where the word goes.'

'What word is it?'

'Usually it's hidden somewhere in the description. Let me see.' I muttered over the page. 'For the control and stability of growth of plants, vines and trees . . . etcetera, etcetera. To have integration of the seasons, etcetera . . . . There! *Blessed* with the gift of growing things. Do you see the extra spaces around the word? That's usually an indication.'

'I thought it was a mistake by the printer.'

'No. There was a time the printers wouldn't put the spells on their presses unless they were marred in some way. This was the only way around it. Blessed. A pretty common word of power, an easy handle for those who lack faith in their own ability. They can use the belief in a greater entity to power their own magic. "*Blessed* with sweet flower." Now, you're using this on the briars?'

'Yes.'

'Hm. They're wildly magical in their own right. First off, you should add back the word of power. If you're using it on the thorns the spell should have a rhyming couplet to punctuate the strength on the end of the spell. Let me see . . .' I muttered through the spell, and my mouth caught on the final verse. 'That's it. These two lines are only draining power. They're there for aesthetics, and you aren't trying to make the briars look pretty. If you cut the second and fourth lines out of this verse, it should have more strength to bind. You can recite it faster, too.' I showed her the book.

'Six lines instead of eight?'

'The world loves a hexagon. Look at beehives and snow-flakes. Six is stronger. And . . .' I ran through the spell in my head. 'Yes. If you have the first verse memorized, which, as you aren't a complete imbecile, you do, you might be able to get away with just the final couplet, in an emergency.'

She blinked. 'Really?'

'Only if you have faith in your own magic, of course.'

'That would have saved me a dozen times. I'd have paid my teeth to know that earlier.' She sounded a bit rueful. The princess frowned at me. 'How do you know all this?'

'What?'

'How do you know the spellmakers hide words of power?'

'I read, just like you.'

'I haven't seen that anywhere in my books.'

'Well, *The Ages of Arcana* had a chapter on it early on.' I looked up at her, and I'm afraid I probably glared.

The princess flashed an irritated wince. 'But what about the other part? How do you know how to shave a spell to make it more powerful? I would have thought more detail would strengthen it. I mean, all the spells I've seen for summoning demons are high power, and the incantations go on for pages.'

'Don't be a fool,' I said. 'You can summon a demon with a single word. The pages of incantations are to keep it from running amuck.'

'See? All I know is what I've managed to read, and that's cryptic enough. How do you know these things?'

I shrugged.

'Are you apprenticed to anyone? Who taught you all this?'

'No one. No apprenticeship.'

'So how do you know it? I only know as much as I do because I have enough money and leisure time to find the books and do the research. You don't give me the impression of being someone with that kind of luxury.'

I frowned. 'I thought we were supposed to be talking about the spell, not me.'

The princess sat back on her heels. 'Well, terribly sorry,' she said, sounding like she wasn't sorry at all. 'I thought it was only fair, seeing you know everything about me.'

I glared. 'I know *nothing* about you.'

She leaned back as if affronted. 'Good gods! I'm learning about magic from an illiterate! You can *read*, can't you? Do the daily agony sheets somehow not float up to your magical ivory tower?'

'No,' I laughed. 'They get weighted down by the snow halfway up.'

She cracked a smile too, though it seemed to cost her. She had lost a great deal of spirit since I'd seen her that afternoon. She was very pale, and her burns obviously hurt her. I peered at her intently, trying to figure out what else was different. What if she really was ill? 'Are you all right?' Now what prompted me to ask that? It wasn't as if I cared about her.

'I'm fine,' she said brusquely.

'It's only, I heard you were ill.'

She looked sad. 'Ill. Furious. Easier to pretend I was sick than try and explain my behaviour.'

'What behaviour?'

She blushed and looked down. 'I was rude at court. I don't lie easily, and I don't like King Lesli.'

'Who would?' I muttered.

She laughed ruefully. 'Half the kingdom.'

'Fools,' I spat.

She hesitated. 'Poorly educated,' she said finally. 'They grew up hearing Hiedelen's propaganda, and they still believe it. I wish we could afford to found a university. Teach our people what freedom really means.'

'A university?'

'Well, public schools first. For children. Do you know how many of our people cannot read? Even much of our nobility are functionally illiterate. If you don't know the history, how can you understand the difference between justice and injustice? Knowledge versus prejudice. That's all this onus on magic is, equating it with prostitution. It's all just prejudice.'

I gazed at her. There were depths to this princess that made me uneasy. 'And you want to change that.'

She frowned. 'I want to change anything that is a remnant of Hiedel law. Nearly a century of Hiedelen rule has not been good to this land. The people are uneducated, the economy is geared entirely for export and support rather than self-sufficiency. It worries me. We have almost no army, and we're landlocked, apart from the delta off the River Frien. So far the only reason some other country hasn't invaded is because we're still Hiedelen's protectorate. But their demands are draining us, and making us even weaker. Mother's been trying to change things. You know the laws on magic usage have changed in the last ten years. Now they have to prove that a witch or hedge wizard has been doing evil or committing crimes with their magic, not only that they were doing magic at all. But the onus is on the magician, and the bias is so strong . . ,.' She shook her head. 'Never mind. It's all politics, and that bores everyone, including me. In answer to your question, no, I'm not ill. I'm just frustrated. I can't seem to make myself into what the country seems to need. They need another Amaranth, or a wiser Lavender, and I'm neither.'

'Poor princess,' I whispered. I wasn't sure whether I meant it or not.

'Everyone's always glaring at me and whispering about me,' she muttered, almost as if she was talking to herself. I wondered if she had anyone to talk to at home. 'I'm being judged all the time, and I keep being found wanting. Everyone is just waiting to pounce on the least little mistake. And I'm always making mistakes. I can't seem to stop doing it. So I'm always looking behind my shoulder waiting for someone to pounce.' She glanced at me and shook her head. 'Sorry. No doubt it all seems pretty silly to you.'

Her little speech had touched me. Was it right for me to punish this princess? She hadn't done anything horrid to me. It was her mother I really wanted the revenge on. For a brief moment, my resolve wavered. 'Not silly,' I said. 'I think there are others who feel the same. Having to hide who you really are. Everyone always watching and judging.'

'Even you?' she asked.

I was about to confirm, adamantly, when I remembered I didn't want to give her any clues as to my identity. 'Well. What magician isn't frowned on in Lyndaria?'

She shrugged. 'Well, the faeries are accepted, in their way.'

I scoffed. 'They're frowned upon, too.'

'I know, but not at court.'

I scowled. 'Don't talk about things you don't know anything about, little girl.'

'You're not *that* much older than I am,' she pointed out, and I realized from her perspective that was true. I didn't look much older than twenty. 'And I happen to know some faeries personally.'

'*I* know faeries,' I told her, quite truthfully. 'And if they ever come to your court, it's because they're too scared not to.'

She blinked at me. 'Why do you say that?'

'Why do you think there aren't many faeries left in this kingdom? They use magic. We're all frowned upon, faerie or no. Why do you think Mistress Caital buried herself in her enchanted forest? Why do you think the Winnowinns barricade themselves into their mountain fastness? It isn't because faeries are loved and revered.'

'I know that. But everyone knows faeries have to do magic or they'd . . . I don't know. Melt or something.'

I laughed. She was such a child. 'Waste away,' I corrected her. 'Lose strength. Start to become mortal, turn old and die.'

She frowned at me. 'How do you know that?'

Oops. Said too much. 'Well . . . I-I'm a magician,' I said lamely. 'It's my business to know.'

'But you're wrong. Faeries don't get old, do they?'

'No books on faerielore in that palace, apparently.'

'No,' she said. 'My grandfather burned them all first thing. The only reason the faeries weren't banished completely is because of Mistress Caital. And she hasn't aged a day.'

I shook my head. It was a common misconception that I wished would go away. We weren't human, but were weren't gods, either. 'Faeries age four to six times slower than your average human, depending on their heritage, and what kind of magic they do,' I told her. 'They do age. But if they stop doing magic their age catches up to them, and then yes, they will die. It's an awful cycle, because the less magic a faerie does the less it *can* do, so once age starts to accelerate it's nearly impossible to stop the process.' I think I wasn't able to keep the worry out of my tone as I said this. My ma feared her spinner's gift and only used the smallest of magics, and I was beginning to see her age catch up to her. It might have just been hardship, but I couldn't tell.

'You know a lot about this.'

I cursed myself. I should learn to keep my mouth shut. 'I told you. It's my business to know.'

'Hm.' She seemed to be considering this. 'Still, people know faeries will do magic. It's expected of them. But that's not the case for you and me.'

For you and me. I stared at her, sitting on the edge of the frozen fountain in the lamplight. She was risking everything for the chance to improve her skill. 'Isn't it?' I asked her. 'Do you think you could just *stop* using magic, just because someone says you should?'

She smiled wistfully and pulled off her snow-filled muff. 'Does it look like I could?' she said, holding up her burned hand. She gazed balefully at the burns and moved to put the muff back on.

This was it. The perfect opportunity to earn her trust. 'Wait,' I said. I forced her back onto the edge of the fountain, pulled the wet muff off again, and examined the burns. 'I might be able to do something for that.'

'I tried already,' the princess said. 'But I don't have any spells for healing burns. A few for cuts, but nothing for burns. They wouldn't adapt.'

'I've got something.'

'What?' she asked, interested.

There was nothing for it. All my other magics were too small to heal burns this deep. I thought about this. 'Close your eyes,' I said.

'Why?'

'Because the spell will work better,' I lied. The lie parched my throat. Faeries have the natural virtue of Honesty. I swallowed the burn away and reached for my drop spindle. Damn. I'd forgotten I'd already woven the Sleep onto it. The last of my wool had been used for the final catchment, that would let the spell loose when the thread was unwound. Well . . . maybe that was for the best. I couldn't have her realizing my magic was anything spectacular. She might suspect me. Instead I used the opportunity to plant the spindle in the hood of her cloak. Hopefully it wouldn't start to snow and she wouldn't pull the hood up until she got back to her palace. By then, I'd be far away, and no one would be able to blame me for it.

Then, of course, I was forced to try and pull a healing spell out of sheer willpower. Actually, her having her eyes closed probably would help, here. I placed my hands on her shoulders, to distract from the pressure of what I'd just placed in her hood. 'Think about your other hand,' I said, keeping my voice low. 'Think about how it feels to not be in pain.' I took her injured right hand in mine. It was very cold, and very, very smooth. She hissed. 'It's all right,' I said. 'Think about not feeling pain.'

I placed my thumb atop one of the deepest blisters. She hissed again. 'Ow!'

'Shh!'

Without a single tool I twisted the state of her two hands together in my mind, twisting the healthy hand over the injured one. 'Thy pain be done, there will be none,' I muttered, twisting the spell into the words. As a human, words would work much better than pure mind magic. She needed the focus. I looked at her face. Her nose was less than an inch from mine. She had opened her eyes. I hadn't realized how little they looked like the queen's famous sky-blue ones. Hers were grey and ominous, like a winter's storm. She had very long lashes. The scent of roses was enough to make me dizzy. 'Can you remember that?' I whispered.

'I think so,' she answered, and I could feel her breath against my skin.

'Repeat that when it starts to hurt.'

She seemed to have trouble finding her voice, and her eyes were fixed on mine. 'Th-thanks,' she said.

I pulled away a little. Didn't want her to realize I was *trying* to seduce her. 'It's getting late.'

'It is.'

'And you have your spell.'

'I do.'

'You should be getting back to the palace.'

I could tell she didn't want to. She looked very reluctant as she said, 'You're right.'

I could barely wait for her to leave. The presence of my drop spindle in her hood made me uncomfortable. I thought at any moment that she'd discover it, and accuse me of something. Though I didn't think she would recognize the sleep woven into the spindle, not being exposed to spinning magic. 'Fare thee well, Highness.'

'Will,' she said firmly.

I did not want to give her her name. I flashed the book at her to remind her I was taking it. She'd probably never see it, or me, again. 'Goodnight.'

Chapter 8

Will

That roguish Reynard was up to something. Will didn't trust him an inch. As he slipped out the door she recited one of her favourite spells.

> *Evening shadows, autumn shadows,*
> *Come to find a certain space*
> *Dawning shadows, sunset shadows,*
> *Bathe me in thy dusky grace*
>
> *Brightness now will I abandon*
> *I must be as dark as thee*
> *I will shun the light of heaven,*
> *Evening shadows, come to me.*

The book she'd gotten it from called it a shadow spell. It was all but useless during the day, but at night it would almost turn her into a shadow. So long as she kept to darkish places she was nearly invisible. Moreover, it made her silent as a shadow. It wasn't really an invisibility, but it had served the purpose well enough in the past. Will loved it, as it was one of those spells that wrapped around her and made her feel powerful, but she didn't use it often; it made her tired, and as a spell it felt dark – sinister. It was a spell that gave one the power to do very unsavoury things. But if Will was going to know anything about Reynard, she knew she had to balance the risks with the rewards.

She became a shadow and followed him.

At first it was difficult. He moved much more quickly than she did, and he too had a tendency to stick to the shadows, so it was hard to keep an eye on him. While they were in the city Will was panting trying to keep up with him. But after some time he turned down a side street where the snow had not been churned to a muddy slush, frozen now in the night air. The barely disturbed snow showed only a few footprints, including a fresh set which belonged to her magician. Will followed, carefully setting her feet directly in his footsteps.

Once she had footprints to follow she let him go on ahead. She hardly had the energy to keep up with his long strides, anyway. By the gods, he was tall. It unnerved her. They followed the side road until suddenly Reynard's footprints turned and set off across country. They passed through a meadow, where the only footprints were Reynard's and a few rabbits'. Beyond the meadow was a copse of trees, followed by some fallow winter fields. The moon was obscured by clouds, but the sky glowed with its light. Everything was grey and blue, and seemed to be asleep. Despite Will's shadow spell, her footsteps still squeaked slightly in the snow.

At first Will thought that Reynard was heading toward some farm house, but as she passed through the little copse and looked out across the fields she knew that was not the case. Mistress Cait's enchanted forest loomed ahead of her, and Reynard's footprints headed directly toward it.

Will frowned. The enchanted forest wasn't exactly welcoming to casual visitors. Still, Reynard had gone there. She would go only to the border, and see where he had entered.

Will's shadow spell blinked out as she left the copse and let herself be exposed to the moonlight. She hesitated. If he was still within sight of her, he could hardly miss her coming, a dark, hulking form against the snow. Finally she shrugged. What had she to lose? She followed.

As she approached the enchanted forest she was struck by the sheer size of the trees there. Twice as wide as ordinary trees, they were as tall as some of the turrets of the palace. The only plant she'd seen nearly that size were some of the briars which had been left to overrun the disused East Wing of the palace. That section of the palace was now so overrun with thorns it was a deathtrap with walls. Apparently the chamber Queen Amaranth had slept in was up one of those towers. Will had never been in there, stilling spell or no.

Her shadow spell flickered back as she stepped into the shadows. She let loose a little breath of relief. She was pleased to see that Reynard's footsteps did not plunge into the forest but instead skirted alongside. She followed them, darting between the border trees, until she smelled smoke. Smoke? Did he have a cottage in there, then? It was risky business, living by the enchanted forest; the trees were known to grow up through your sitting room of an evening.

Will crept forward, listening. She thought she heard voices. She couldn't make out what they were saying, but one voice was clearly Reynard's. The others were higher, feminine. She poked her head from around a tree, but saw no house. Only Reynard's footprints, which vanished into a hole that glowed from beneath the roots of a tree. Did he have some kind of underground fastness, then? That made sense for a magician.

It didn't matter. If she ever needed him, she knew where to find him now.

She skulked her way out of the border forest and back into the fields. Across the fields she could see a few scattered lights from Lyndaron, lit by those who started their day before the cock's crow. The twisted towers of the palace grew above the town, like a little thornbush all its own. With its spires and towers it was as pretty as the briar roses, and seemed just as deadly.

Will had walked farther than she'd intended, and had a long walk back to the palace, but she took it with relish. She could spend the day 'convalescing' in her room after her 'attack' yesterday. It was the perfect excuse to avoid having to deal with King Lesli. If she was extremely tired and spent the day sleeping, so much the better.

She was weary but content as she neared the palace. She didn't feel quite up to experimenting with Reynard's altered spell, and besides, it was already full morning. Rather than brave the thorns and her secret passage, Will approached the palace from the front, heading toward the main entrance.

The main entrance was heavily protected by ivy and walls, a broad carriageway bordered by footmen and guards. It should have been perfectly safe. Indeed, as Will came through the front gates she spied a handful of palace children and young people engaged in a sprightly snowball fight in the gardens. She even caught sight of Lavender, laughing merrily as she pelted Prince Ferdinand again and again with snowballs, which he seemed to be going out of his way to be struck by. He had snow in his yellow hair, and his fine features were red with the cold. And there was Will's nine-year-old betrothed, the odd one out of the bunch, being systematically slaughtered by the Lyndar noblemen's children.

That didn't seem at all fair. Narvi was the only Hiedelen child there, and it wasn't his fault that his grandfather had designs on the kingdom. Narvi was shy and quiet naturally, and he kept trying to laugh off the attacks, but his coat was caked with snow, and as Will watched a snowball hit him in the face with enough force to bruise.

Will shook her head, almost amused. This was likely the most fun she was liable to have with her husband-to-be, for at least some years. She decided it would be prudent to join in the fray, give her young betrothed someone to watch his back. She shouted and waved, announcing herself to the snow party.

Lavender started and stared at her, as if ashamed that she'd been caught out at something so undignified as a snowball fight. She hadn't thought such things beneath her dignity even three years ago. Will had to hand it to Ferdinand – he had reminded Princess Lavender that there was fun to be had in the world.

But Lavender's gaze glanced from Will to Narvi, and Will saw her turning to Ferdinand. Will realized that she was probably a sore point with Lavender just then. Lavender was still a bit of a sore point with Will, but at least Will wasn't dwelling on it. She took a step back, debating the merits of joining in, or simply giving a distant curtsey and seeking out her bed.

Before she had made a decision, she felt something wrap around her ankle.

She knew it was the briars without even looking. She was standing rather close to the hedge, although the thorns in this part of the hedge didn't usually reach out for people. Will was royalty, though, and the hedge had a taste for royal blood. Fortunately her ankle was wrapped in a heavy winter boot, so it hadn't pierced her flesh yet. Will sighed. This wasn't the first time she'd had to sacrifice her fingertips to the thorns to rescue an ankle or the hem of her skirt. She tried to remember the alterations Reynard had suggested for the stilling spell.

But Lavender screamed as if Will was about to die. Will looked up, bemused, and saw Lavender rushing toward her, Ferdinand hot on her heels. The palace children mostly stared in numb stillness, but Will spied Narvi quickly running in the opposite direction. *Oh, my brave swain!* she thought, rolling her eyes. 'I'm fine!' she tried to call to Lavender, but Lavender was too busy screaming Will's name in panic.

'Willow! Willow!' Lavender fell prostate at her feet, her hands scrabbling for purchase on the thorns, which were slowly tightening around Will's leg.

'Really!' Will tried to explain. 'It's all right!' Then she realized that Lavender had no idea that Will dodged through the thorns on a regular basis. Lavender had no interest in all the studies Will had done on the hedge. Will knew how the thorns worked, how quickly they were apt to attack, how deeply embedded one had to be before it was impossible to extricate oneself. Lavender knew none of this. She only knew that once the thorns had hold of you, they slowly bled your life away.

Her panic was only making things worse. The thorns reacted to fast movements, and new tendrils reached out from the hedge, grasping at Lavender's skirts. 'Get back,' Will told her. 'There's nothing to worry about.' But Lavender was making a high-pitched cry of panic that drowned Will's words. Ferdinand arrived then, and of course he made to rescue Lavender. He pulled the reaching briars from her skirts with a ripping noise. Suddenly he hissed with pain as a long thorn pierced his hand.

That did it. Will opened her mouth to recite the stilling spell.

She knew she had no one to blame but herself. Will knew the old version of the spell very well, and when her mouth began reciting it should have gone with the old recitation rather than experiment with the new one without preparation.

For everything that grows and every leaf
That hangs upon the climbing vine or tree

with sweet flower, and belief,
Blessed with flower, and belief
That my poor will can overpower thee
For I am nature's strength, her arm and hand
That can, for beauty's sake, bind the fruitful bounty of the land.

It was abysmal. She forgot the word of power and tried to insert it afterwards, and then forgot how much of the verse to cut. Whatever Will had done to the spell, it wasn't going to do what she wanted. The thorns suddenly went wild, constricting around her legs and grasping at Ferdinand's hands. He pulled away with a sudden cry, and a huge gash opened on his palm. Will was too distracted to worry about Ferdinand at that moment, however, as the thorns thrashed, throwing herself and Lavender, still tangled hopelessly in the briars, high over his head.

'Oh, you wretched fool!' Lavender cried out, her voice sounding beautiful amidst its high panic. She hung upside down, and her autumn colored hair was pierced through with combs of briars. 'What did you have to do that for!'

'What did you have to go panicking for?' Will retorted, trying to wrestle her arm free. 'If you'd just stayed put I'd have been over to join you in two breaths!'

Lavender didn't respond, except for a scream as another bramble twisted around her skirts.

'Hang on to me!' Will shouted. She was going to get that stilling spell to work if it killed her! 'Do you hear me? Lavender, hold on to me, I'll get us out of this!'

Lavender looked both doubtful and desperate. She had no faith in magic, but she wasn't about to reject her current only hope of rescue. 'You'll just make things worse!' she cried, grabbing for Will's hood.

'How could things get worse?' Will asked, and Lavender didn't respond except by grabbing hold of her even tighter.

A thorn was digging into Will's thigh and her arms were twined round with them and her foot was starting to go numb, but all of those were pleasant compared to Lavender's graceful arms, which were, annoyingly, around Will's throat, preventing her from uttering another word, let alone a chant.

Will still thought she might get them out of there herself, but it would have been an iffy thing. Rescue was at hand, however, and a series of jarring thumps shook the briars. Gasping for breath around Lavender's stranglehold, Will glanced down to spy Ferdinand hacking at the base of the briar that held them with a broken battle axe. Standing behind him was Narvi, out of breath, holding the broken end of the axe. Will's opinion of her betrothed went up a good few notches. The boy had had the presence of mind to go and fetch the axe from one of the front doorkeepers at the palace.

Will did manage to get a muffled, 'Let go!' out of her strangled throat, and Lavender loosened her hold. Will took some much needed gasps of air and began the first line of the stilling spell. 'For everything that grows, and every leaf—'

She didn't get a chance to finish any more, as Ferdinand had finally hacked through the key stalk. The briar that held them stiffened, then loosed its hold. They fell eight feet to the ground, and Lavender's grip tightened around Will's shoulders again. Even Will shrieked as they fell. They landed with a bruising thump on the snow, and Will felt something snap under her back as they landed. She was afraid it was a bone, and wondered if it was her own or Lavender's but was too stunned to feel any specific pain. Lavender had landed first, and Will had landed on top of her, and some terrible bruising force had crunched under Will's substantial weight.

Ferdinand dragged them away from the hedge, and Will pulled herself off Lavender as quickly as she could. She was frightened.

Lavender wasn't screaming or sobbing or laughing hysterically. That wasn't like Lavender. Will turned and stared at her in horror. She was completely unconscious, and a smear of red blood shone stark on the white snow where they had landed. 'Lavender?'

But Will's cry was utterly overpowered by Ferdinand's, who rubbed Lavender's hands and touched her face and loosened her cloak. A piece of stick was embedded in Lavender's right shoulder – too high, Will thought, to be fatal, but it would have ruined any prospective career as a soldier. Her mind, still in a panic, was unable to separate important thoughts from trivial ones. She thought of all of Lavender's skills, and decided dancing and diplomacy would be unaffected, depending on the damage her table manners might need to be adapted, and it was possible, but not likely, that her embroidery would suffer. And off the shoulder evening gowns were going to be a thing of the past, unless she opted for a sash of some sort . . .

The little thing which had impaled her was inconsequential, however, because she was unconscious. A tangle of rough grey wool, like the kind Lavender purchased to knit stockings for the poor, was twisted into her hair, matted together with the blood. Will reached for it, and her hands closed on the blooded wool. It wasn't right, that grey wool, as if it was turning her sister into a lifeless rag doll. Ferdinand pushed her out of the way, and Will wasn't even sure he knew who she was. His eyes were only for Lavender. The fall. It had to be the fall. Will wanted to take Lavender's hands. She wanted to tell her she was sorry. But she couldn't move. She just stood there in the snow, gasping for air, as she watched the love of her life try, desperately, to bring life back into the love of his.

The printers had a wonderful day with the broadsheets, even before anyone really knew what had happened.

The king and queen and the royal healer had Lavender carried to her chambers, while Will was dragged by the healer's apprentice to her own. There she was passed off to the town healer while the apprentice went back to assist her master with the princess. The healers poked and prodded at Will, putting plasters on her scratches and checking her all over for damage. Her dress was the worst casualty of the ordeal. Officials asked her questions, and she answered them as well as she could, but she was exhausted and giddy. Narvi was the most reliable witness to the whole affair, and through most of it he had been running back and forth fetching the axe.

Will held the tangle of grey wool drenched with her sister's blood in her hands. It felt sticky, and it was filled with rubble from the thorns. This was so like her sister. She'd gone outside intending to sedately knit along the sidelines while everyone else played in the snow. And so like Ferdinand, to draw her out of herself and remind her how to play.

Eventually the healers pronounced Will sound and left her to her own devices. Will's chambermaid offered to help her change, but she dismissed her. What she really wanted to do was sleep. She sat down on the edge of her bed, then shifted as she realized she was sitting on something hard. Someone had lain her cloak over the bed and Will had inadvertently sat on it. What was hard in her cloak? She prodded at it until she found a round piece of wood with a broken stick through it folded into the hood. Now how had that gotten there? Moreover, what was it? It looked like a wheel from a toddler's pull toy, with the axle snapped. A piece of Lavender's wool had tangled – or somehow tied itself – to the wood.

She frowned at it. She debated throwing it into the fire, but it seemed like too much trouble to get up. Instead she reached over and tossed it into her bedside drawer, alongside the burned pages of *The Ages of Arcana*. Lavender. Will hoped she was going to be all right. The surgeon was tending her shoulder, and the healers had reassured Will that there was no reason to suspect that Lavender wasn't going to recover. Despite that, a feeling of deep foreboding troubled her. She ran her fingers over the bloodstained wool before stashing it in the drawer alongside the broken wheel. Then she pulled out what her father had salvaged of *The Ages of Arcana*.

There wasn't much. Most of it was unreadable, and much of it crumbled to ash in her hands. After sorting through the most useless pages, she found she had about ten pages from a chapter at the centre of the book, a chapter on sympathetic magic. If magic were performed on one part of a thing, the same spell could be performed on the whole of the thing, even over great distances. To her annoyance, the pages were utterly useless to her. They referred only to the power of great magics, the kind of magics she could never learn without more sacrifice than she would ever be willing to endure – taking out her heart, for example, or possibly someone else's – but it was interesting nevertheless. She fell asleep with the singed pages falling from her hand.

She awoke a short time later, feeling uneasy. She blinked at the light from the windows, the floating blue of twilight. She was surprised that no one had woken her before then. Wasn't she supposed to have some formal luncheon with Lesli and Narvi? Shouldn't someone have inquired after her continued health? But there was nothing. She could hear voices in the corridors, but they seemed subdued. She changed into an afternoon dress and left to inquire after Lavender.

It was pretty easy to guess that Lavender hadn't recovered. Half the corridor outside her chambers was packed with courtiers and recorders and priests. Will pushed her way through the worriedly whispering crowd and stepped into her sister's lavender and lace apartments.

The princess's favourite colours were lavender and dusty rose. Her room was warm, but pale. Will tiptoed across the pink carpets to the lavender bed, where her parents and Ferdinand sat an anxious vigil. 'She hasn't awoken?' Will asked.

Ragi was pacing worriedly, but he turned to look at Will and smiled with relief. 'No, she hasn't. Your mother wanted to send someone to check on you, but I thought you needed your rest.' He came up and gave her a formal embrace, as there were a dozen witnesses which had crammed their way into the little room. In *sotto voce* he added into her ear, 'Next time you sneak out all night have the wisdom to lock your bedchamber door, please? I had to pretend I'd seen you this morning before all this happened.'

Will looked up at him with chagrin. 'Sorry,' she whispered. 'I've come to see Lavender,' she added, loud enough for the courtiers to hear.

Amaranth shifted to allow her through. The princess lay on her lavender bed, her head resting prettily on her lace pillows. Her long autumn hair was braided neatly, and lay across her shoulder like a bandolier. She'd been bathed and changed, and she looked considerably more hale than Will felt. Will's face was marked with red lines and she stung from what felt like a hundred different scratches, but Lavender hadn't a scratch on her. Even out like a lantern, she was unfailingly beautiful.

Everyone's face was grave. Amaranth was unknowingly wringing her hands quietly. As soon as Will touched Lavender's hand Ragi resumed his pacing, as he always did when he was upset. Lavender's ladies were huddled quietly in a corner, all of them miserable, whispering sadly to one another. A few were in tears. But the thing that dropped stones into Will's chest was Prince Ferdinand.

He sat stricken at Lavender's bedside, gripping her pale, delicate hand. His eyes never left her face. His proud shoulders were hunched in worry, and his laughing mouth was turned down in quiet agony. Will wanted to run to him and pet his head and tell him everything would be all right. But he didn't want her words of comfort.

'Hey, Lavi. 'Tis Will.' She touched her rosy cheek. She looked up at Ferdinand. 'What do the healers say?'

'They say she should have come to by now,' Ferdinand said, his voice husky. 'They say . . .' He couldn't speak.

'They can't do any more,' Ragi said quietly.

'Have you considered . . .' Will began, but she bit her tongue at a look from her mother. Suggesting magic at this stage wasn't prudent, given the fireworks of the day before. Will wondered if Amaranth also knew she had been out all night. Instead of suggesting it, she reached for Lavender's hand again.

Lavender's hand rested beside her little dog Dash. Dash was a silly, silky, yappy thing that Will usually despised. It had a shrill, piercing little yip that always threatened to give her a headache. She frowned. Why hadn't he barked at her when she opened the door? He usually did every time anyone entered Lavender's rooms. With all these people around, Dash should have been racing around the room yelping bloody murder and threatening all the ladies with torn skirt hems. Right now he was curled up by Lavender's hip, his eyes closed. He was asleep. Will's eyebrows furrowed. Dash woke up at the sound of a dropped embroidery needle. Why wasn't he up and panting, yapping at all the strangers in his chambers? She reached out to touch him. She half expected him to leap up and growl at her as he always did. The other half already suspected what would happen.

The dog stayed perfectly still, breathing evenly. She poked him again. Nothing. Finally she picked him up. Dash remained limp and lifeless, like a rag dog. She'd have said he was newly dead, except he continued to breathe in and out peacefully. But his loud, obnoxious throat remained quiet. 'Mother. Father. I don't think she was injured by the fall.' Will looked up at them. 'Or rather, I don't think that's all of what's wrong with her.'

The queen frowned. 'What do you mean, Willow?'

Will held the sleeping dog out for her to see. 'Dash is asleep too. I think this sleep is contagious.'

One of the ladies behind Will gasped and fell senseless to the floor. Most of the others screamed as she fell. Some of the more sensible ones tried to wake her. 'She's caught it too!' screeched one of the ladies, Will thought her name was Ginith. 'We'll all fall asleep! The curse is upon us again!'

'Quiet!' Ragi snapped, his head up at his full height. 'She's only fainted! The Sleep doesn't come upon you like that.' He pointed at the two most sensible ladies. 'You, get her out of here. All of you, go. And don't go spreading gossip, we still don't know *what's* wrong.'

'Hettie, Mercy, help me,' said one of the girls, and they carried the weakly moving fainting victim from the princess's chamber. Ragi indicated that the rest follow them, and as soon as they left he closed the door on the curious onlookers in the passageway.

Once the ladies in waiting were out of the way Ragi turned toward Will. 'Now, show me this dog.'

She held Dash out for him to see. He picked the dog up in his hands and turned him over, lifting his eyelids, listening to his breathing. Will realized Ragi was the only one who had actually been awake to see the effects of the Sleep. His face was intent to begin with, but quickly turned grave. He looked up at Amaranth and nodded his head. To Will's surprise, Amaranth's face crumpled, and she began to weep. Will had never seen her mother cry before. She hadn't realized until that moment how much her mother grieved for her lost century.

There was a miserable silence for a moment in Lavender's room, the only audible sound her even, delicate breathing. Then Ferdinand's face lit up. 'Wait!' he said. 'If this is the Sleep, then I should be able to wake her!'

A dull hope shone in the king and queen's faces. Will's face darkened further. She hoped it would work, but watching Ferdinand kiss her sister, saving her again, wasn't something she wanted to see. But she would stay and watch it; she had to know that Lavi was all right. 'Try it!' the queen whispered.

Ferdinand looked up at Ragi. 'Any advice, sir?'

'Be gentle,' he said. 'She may be disoriented.'

There was a ruefulness in his tone that made Will curious. She wondered exactly how distraught her mother had been at finding Ragi bending over her. Had there been a physical confrontation?

Ferdinand bent over Lavender's sleeping face. 'Come back to me, my beloved,' he whispered, twisting Will's guts. Time held its breath as Ferdinand brushed his lips gently across the princess's full, red mouth.

Nothing.

'Try again,' said the king. He'd been so delicate, Will might have suggested that herself. Was that even a kiss?

Ferdinand tried once more, a real kiss this time, his lips closing over hers with tenderness.

No change.

He stared down at her sleeping form. His ice blue eyes were wild. 'No!' He kissed her again, passionately this time, forcing her lips to open, to accept him. Will was crying by that time, but only inside. She forced the tears back down her throat until she choked on them.

The princess lay as still as death. When he finally pulled away Lavender sighed in her sleep and shifted her head a little on the pillow. 'Oh, please!' Ferdinand whispered. But she did not move again. He gripped her dress and held her to him, kissing her face, stroking her hair. 'No!' he cried. 'No, I'm not letting you go!'

Ragi pulled him away from the girl's sleeping form. 'Stop. Stop! You'll hurt her!'

Amaranth went back to her daughter and smoothed her mussed braid. Lavender's face was smudged with red from Ferdinand's kisses. 'So much for that,' the queen said. 'I never could understand why that worked in the first place. Willow,' she said quietly. 'Have you any idea why this might have happened?'

Will was surprised that she asked her. She shook her head. 'I have no idea. Unless . . .' Then she stopped.

'Unless what?' Amaranth insisted.

'I really don't know.'

'What is your theory?' she asked patiently.

'Perhaps . . . perhaps the thorns?' Will asked. 'The Sleep came upon you because of the spindle, and the thorns came because of the Sleep. Maybe the thorns recognized Lavender as the heir and started the cycle over again.'

'Why do you say recognized her as the heir?' Ferdinand asked. 'Couldn't it have cast the Sleep onto anyone?'

'Possibly,' Will said. 'But I've been pricked a hundred times, and I've never fallen asleep.'

Both Ragi and Amaranth looked at her darkly. 'A hundred times,' Amaranth said, voicing their joint disapproval.

'Yes,' Will said, after a nervous swallow. 'They aren't that dangerous if you know how to handle them.'

'I'd ask you to be more cautious,' Ragi said. 'You know full well they nearly killed me.'

Will opened her mouth to tell them about the stilling spell, and then realized it would probably only make this conversation worse, especially considering it was the botched spell which had caused Lavender to be injured in the first place.

'So, we have a working theory, though in truth we can't know what caused this,' Amaranth said, returning to the matter at hand. 'We know that a kiss from a prince won't reverse this magic.'

'What can we do?' Ferdinand asked. 'Whatever it takes. I will undertake any hardship.'

The king looked blank. Amaranth looked up. 'We can try and contact Mistress Cait. If we can find her. No one has seen her since Willow's christening. I'll send a messenger to the Winnowinn clan as well. Ferdinand?'

'Yes?'

'Do you think you can find whoever gave you those beasts?'

He shook his head. 'I never even knew who she was. I gave her my last crumb of bread, and she told me that the beasts were waiting for me in the stables of a giant. Which I had to kill first. Nothing is given easily by a faerie. She told me nothing more.'

'Could you go back to where you found her? Try and see if she's still there?' the queen asked.

'No!' Ferdinand shouted. 'That was in Illaria, six months' journey away by horseback! If this is indeed the Sleep as you say, by the time I got back it would be too late!'

'But if you could try. Whoever gave you those gifts must have known a great deal, and showed you great favour—'

'Mother! Stop it!' Will cried. All eyes turned to her. 'Don't ask him to leave her for an uncertainty. He can't.'

Ferdinand's eyes closed in silent thanks. Will winced at the pain this caused her, but she swallowed it.

Amaranth stood up from Lavender's bed. 'Mistress Cait's our best chance,' she said. 'But I don't know how much good it will do. I've invited her to the palace half a dozen times in the last eighteen years, and none of my messages have been answered. Usually my messengers return home seven weeks late, confused and half enchanted.'

'Why?' Ferdinand asked.

'Mistress Cait lives in the enchanted forest,' Will said. 'One treads through there at one's own peril.'

'Let me go,' Ferdinand said. 'I will mount my white steed and use my hawk and hound and I will quest for this Mistress Cait. I will save my beloved!'

'Don't be mad!' Ragi said. 'That hawk hasn't said a word since you arrived. The dog's nothing miraculous, and the horse has already lost half a dozen races. You'll only disappear, and we may still need you to wake her. We may only be doing something wrong.'

'But that hawk led me to her before!'

'And if it suddenly tells you where to go and what to do, listen to it,' Ragi said. 'Until then, we must be rational about this.'

'But there has to be something we can do!' Ferdinand cried.

Suddenly a terrible scream issued from the bed, and Lavender thrashed. All four of them rushed back to her. 'Lavender!' Ferdinand sized her hand. 'Lavender, it's me, you're back!'

But she wasn't back. Her eyes were still closed, and her movements were the blind thrashings of a victim of a nightmare. 'What is it?' Ferdinand asked. 'What's wrong with her?'

'She's dreaming,' Ragi said solemnly. 'I saw this before, too. But only in some of the sleep victims. Those with seriously guilty consciences. The executioner, the lawmen, some of the ladies prone to intrigue.'

'But what nightmares could be plaguing my Lavender?' Ferdinand cried.

'I can't think of a thing,' Ragi said.

'I could . . . ' Will began, and all of them stared at her. 'I know how you feel about magic, but . . . if she's dreaming . . . '

'What?' Amaranth asked.

'I have a dream-sharing spell,' Will said. 'It might take me a bit to work it, but what if the key to her sleep is in her nightmares?'

There was a long silence. 'Do it,' Amaranth said quietly.

'I'll need to double check the spell.'

'Do so,' Amaranth said formally.

Will took a deep breath, curtseyed neatly, and fled back to her chambers through the crowd of anxious courtiers. The dream-sharing spell was one of the spells hidden in *The Zarmeroth Cycle*. Zarmeroth was a long ago king of Lyndaria and well known to be one of the more powerful human wizards ever. Will wasn't related to him, to her chagrin, his line having been conquered more than seven generations before by the Lyndar line (whose name apparently hadn't been Lyndar before they'd become kings, but something like Halflenger). Zarmeroth had lived more than five hundred years before, and some said he was actually a faerie, or half faerie, though there was no proof of that. Until the purge, his spell books were reprinted and annotated and considered the superior work on magic in Lyndaria. The three volume set was the most practical treatise on magic that Will owned. It was also the rarest, having been one of the first to burn. Will had gotten her copy from the personal library of a courtier so old he'd only lived a week after the Sleep was lifted. He had apparently been too old and befuddled to search through his library for magic books after young Princess Amaranth had been cursed, and *The Zarmeroth Cycle* was overlooked.

Will glanced at the dream-sharing spell, but it was rather ambiguous. It wasn't a chant or a potion. It was just concentration, and putting your mind 'in synch' with another's. That was going to be interesting – getting Will's mind in synch with Lavender's was going to be next to impossible. But it was worth trying.

She fled back to her sister's chambers and told her parents she needed to hold her hand to continue. She sat down beside her and closed her eyes, trying to find her sister in her mind. She held her warm hand. For some reason, she suddenly thought of Reynard, and his seemingly innate ability to understand how spells should be moulded to fit. She wished he was here now, to give her some pointers on moulding her own mind to make the spell fit. Still . . . nothing for it but to try.

And it was easy. Surprisingly easy. And Will immediately wished it wasn't.

Pain, fierce and deadly, pulsing the life's blood from my chest. There is anguish, too, and guilt, but the pain is what drags me, pulling me down and down. I can see my blood pulsing onto the ground, and I know that I am dying. I can't move. I'm frightened, so frightened, and so hurt . . .

There was more to the dream, but Will didn't dare reach for it. She opened her eyes, shivering. 'Pain,' she said. 'So much pain.' She wasn't sure whether she was shivering from a memory of the dream of pain or from fear. 'She's dreaming she's hurt,' Will told them when she could find her voice. 'Mortally wounded. She's in pain.'

'No!' Ferdinand flung himself back down at Lavender's bedside. 'Beloved, I will bring you back to me! You must come back to me! You are my heart, my joy, my sun, my spring! I cannot live without you! There must be a way. Please, all the gods above. Show me the way.'

Will hated seeing him like this. Every word was like a stab to her heart. She wished her love for him would simply go away. It was the most terrible thing that had ever happened to her. She wanted to make him happy, so she wanted to give him Lavender back. But his being happy with Lavi wouldn't make Will happy. Quite the contrary. Her heart was torn in two different directions, and she hated herself into the bargain. Never mind that she couldn't bring Lavender back.

Or could she?

Reynard knew faeries. He had told her so. And he lived at the edge of this enchanted forest. If anyone had the chance of finding Mistress Cait in time, it was probably him.

But did she dare ask him? No, she couldn't ask. But perhaps, just perhaps, she could purchase his services. There was only one thing she knew he wanted. She closed her eyes. She'd have to offer all three volumes of *The Zarmeroth Cycle*. She had notes on it, of course, it wouldn't be a total loss, though it would be a wrench. To get Lavender back, it would be worth it.

If Lavender didn't recover soon, Will knew what she had to do.

Chapter 9

* * *

I often thought of our burrows as prisons. Of course, my very Nameless existence was a prison of sorts, with everyone in the land as my gaoler. The afternoon that news of the new Sleep came to us the burrow was more a prison than ever.

'What have you done?' my mother shouted at me. She barely had to shout. We were curled up sitting on opposite sides of the burrow. My mother's wings were drooping from the cold. It was freezing because I no longer had a spindle, and I'd used up all my wool even if I had had. 'You've ruined us! We'll be cursed forever!'

'We were already cursed forever!' I snapped.

'But now they'll all say we *deserve* it! The other faeries will have nothing to do with us now.'

'They've never had anything to do with us before,' I said, 'I can't see how this could make it any worse.'

'Trust me, my son, this can make things *so* much worse.'

'I don't see how,' I said. 'It's only a temporary spell. She'll be awake within twenty-four hours. Thirty-six at the most. I only had a drop spindle, the spell hasn't poisoned her blood.'

'But it was a spinning spell!' my mother pointed out. 'They'll know it came from one of us!'

'They don't even know us,' I said.

'That princess you cursed does.'

'She doesn't know I did it,' I said.

'She will when she wakes up!'

'And *when* she wakes up, maybe she'll know why I did it!'

The kit had been sent outside after she'd returned with the news she'd overheard in market, about the princess being cursed with the contagious Sleep. My delighted grin when I heard this was all my mother needed to know it was my spell. Motherwise, she always knew when I misbehaved. Technically I was a full-grown man of my own, but faerie clans typically stay together, and in the absence of my aunt, my mother was clan leader by default. I should have obeyed her injunction against spinning magic. I should have asked her permission before I set the curse on Princess Willow. I did neither of these things, and she was furious. Nameless or not, my mother was still a faerie, and a faerie's anger can be caustic. The kit was better off outside.

Or so I'd thought. 'My brother, there's someone out here looking for you.'

My mother and I both stared at each other. 'This is it,' she said.

'Hide!' I cried to the kit. I got to my hands and knees to climb out and protect her.

'What for?' the kit asked. 'She's not dangerous.'

The kit had better instincts for that kind of thing than I did, but not strong enough to trust absolutely. 'She?' I asked.

'Aye,' the kit said. 'She was calling out, "Hello? Hello?" so finally I answered her. She asked if I'd seen a young man in a russet hood. That would be you.'

'And you led her here?' I snapped.

'No,' the kit said. 'I led her away from here. She was already coming straight towards us, I thought you'd be pleased.'

I climbed out into the snow. 'Where is she?'

'Down at the spider clearing,' the kit said. 'I'll show you.'

'No, kit, wait!' I called after her, but she was already running between the trees, her white hair disappearing into the snow. I chased after her, wondering who in all the seven hells could be looking for me? One of the witches from the club?

I should have guessed, but I'd been convinced she was asleep and dreaming of my Namelessness. Princess Will stood in the centre of the clearing which, due to the patterns of the wind, held vast numbers of spiderwebs in the autumn, so that it glittered all over with gossamer. Now the clearing was bare and cold and bright enough that I had to be sure I kept to the shadowed edges. Willow stood in the sun. She looked pale and tired, but very much awake. Her dark hair had tints of red in it in the sunlight.

She knows! I lunged to grab the kit and put her behind me. 'What do you think this is going to achieve?' I shouted at the princess. 'You think you'll get back at me, do you? You know full well I owe you nothing. Nothing!'

She didn't look frightened, or angry. 'You're still here!' she said, with what I read as relief. But that couldn't be right.

The kit pulled away from me and went up to her, careful to stay in a shadow from a tall tree. Despite the kit's care, I was terrified. 'No! Get away from her!' I yelled.

The kit looked at me, confused, and then shook her head. 'Are you the princess?' she asked.

Will sighed, looking tired. 'Sort of,' she said. 'And you are?'

'He's my brother,' the kit said, pointing at me. 'I like your scarf.' She fingered the edge of it. 'I've never seen anything more beautiful.'

The scarf Willow was wearing with her cloak was of a royal blue, and made of a thick, rich wool. The ends were fringed with amber beads that clicked as the kit fondled them. 'Here,' said Willow, and she took the scarf off and wrapped it around the kit's shoulders. 'The amber matches your eyes.'

I was afraid she'd look too closely at the kit's eyes. I jumped forward and snatched the scarf away. 'We don't want your charity,' I snapped, handing it back to her.

'Hey!' the kit said. 'She gave that to me!'

'Aye!' Will said, glaring at me. 'You think I'd curse it or something? You think it'll make you beholden to me? I've got dozens of the things.' She took the scarf out of my hands and placed it back in the kit's. 'Don't you let him take it from you,' she hissed.

The kit stuck her tongue out at me and ran into the woods, wrapping the scarf around her head.

'What are you trying to achieve, Princess?' I scowled at her.

She scowled right back. 'What? She looked cold.' She shivered. 'It's not as if I'll suffer from the loss of it.' She smiled after my sister. 'She's cute. Doesn't look much like you, though. A little bit about the eyes, maybe,' she added.

Hoping to distract her, I shifted to another part of the clearing. I took care to stay in the shadows so my darkness wouldn't be noticeable. 'How did you find me?'

'Oh, I followed you,' she said.

I blinked at her. 'You *what*?'

'I followed you,' she said. 'That night after the Monument, I followed you here. You live somewhere over there,' she said, pointing toward the burrow. 'Under some tree. Do you have a magical house under the earth?'

A burrow scratched out of the frozen ground. 'Something like that,' I said. 'What are you doing here?'

She didn't answer at first, and looked down at her hands. 'It's a little hard to explain.'

I couldn't fathom what might be in her mind. If she had been truly frightened by my little curse, she'd have brought her guards. Her face held no remorse, so my attempt at making her understand my suffering had either failed or caused a backlash. So she could only be annoyed at me. 'If you're trying to get me to apologize, I'm not going to.'

'Why would I want you to apologize?' she asked. 'I need your help.'

I raised an eyebrow. 'Help? You expect me to help you?'

She shook her head. 'No. I'm asking.'

I frowned. 'Help you with what?'

She bowed her head. 'A new Sleep has overtaken the palace,' she said. I wasn't sure whether to laugh or cry out in horror. 'It's terrible. The victims are plagued with nightmares, and nothing wakes them.'

'Wait a few days,' I said. 'It'll probably blow over. Now leave me alone.' She didn't know it came from me? I tried not to heave a sigh of relief.

'No,' she said. 'We've been waiting. We've tried everything. Cold water, searching her body for poison, Prince Ferdinand tried kissing her. Nothing works.'

'Like I said, wait. And quit bothering me with minutiae.'

'But it's been nearly a week!' she cried.

I froze. 'A week?' I turned to her. 'Wait. *You* didn't get the Sleep?'

She frowned at me. 'Obviously, or I wouldn't be here asking for your help.'

'But I just heard,' I said. 'My sister heard in the market, the princess had caught the Sleep.'

'My sister. It's old news,' Willow said. 'We couldn't keep it contained any longer. It must have slipped out with the baker's order or something. It happened the morning after I met with you. Something awful happened when I used that spell on the thorns.'

'It doesn't work?'

'No, it does work. And I knew it would work, and got cocky. Lavi saw me get too close and got scared, and tried to pull me out of range. Then I botched the spell because she distracted me, and we both got caught by the thorns. We fell. There was this awful crunch, and Lavender hasn't woken up since.'

'Probably just knocked unconscious,' I said.

'No,' she told me. 'Her dog fell asleep too, and then several of the cooks and our head baker. Whatever it is, it's contagious.' She dug her arm out from under her cloak and pulled up her sleeve. The red lines of half healed scratches contrasted her skin. 'When Ferdinand pulled us out of the thorns we were both bloody and scratched. I was pulling thorns and splinters out of my skin for days. But Lavender was already asleep by then. I can only assume that the magic I cast on the thorns made them . . . oh, gods, I don't know. They were part of the curse on my mother, maybe they remembered the other half of the curse, too, and put Lavender to sleep when they pierced her skin.'

I frowned at her. It wasn't bad logic, if you didn't know about my sleep spindle. 'You say there was a dreadful crunch when you fell?' I said. 'Did you happen to see threads caught in the hedge afterwards?'

'No,' she said. Then she hesitated. 'But . . . Lavender was knitting something for the poor. There was an entire hank of yarn tangled round her neck. Why?' She took a step forward. 'Did you hear something? Were we unable to keep this as quiet as we thought?'

I turned and rubbed my forehead. I felt very agitated now. 'And you were pulling splinters from your skin. Both of you.'

'Yes,' she said. 'Well, no, Lavender seemed all right. Except for that stick that punctured her shoulder when I fell on her, but that was my fault.' I closed my eyes. My drop spindle had more than pricked the heiress's finger. It had stabbed deep into her flesh. The princess was still talking. 'I think it only caught Lavender because she's the real heir. Or something. Maybe it only works if it creates a Sleeping *Beauty*, and I'm really not.'

I glanced at her. She really had no clue that I had anything to do with all this. I took a deep breath. I didn't know what this meant. The curse I had spun was in the princess's blood now, would not unwind as time passed by. This was no longer a temporary curse I had created. The Lyndar Princess was indeed cursed to an everlasting nightmare sleep.

I felt torn. I was elated at how well my revenge had come out. But this was now an unknown spell. If it was still a contagious sleep, as I had intended, how would it play out? 'You say it's contagious?' I asked. 'In what way? Do the people have to be near her? Touch her?'

'No,' she said. 'People are falling asleep all over the palace.'

Faerie Light, but that was bad. I hadn't keyed the spell to the palace. I had keyed it to the people. In fact, I had keyed it towards my hatred. 'Who did you say fell asleep first?' I asked. 'The heiress, her little yappy dog, and who . . . ? The baker?'

'Our head baker, two undercooks and a serving maid were the first to succumb. But it seems pretty random.'

Yes, I knew the palace baker – she'd thrown a stone at my sister, once, knocked her out for a day and a half. And if I had to guess, I'd wager that the two cooks and the serving maid who'd fallen prey were the ones who went to the market on Stormsdays, and often recognized me. And I despised yappy dogs, they alerted people to my presence. The spell was perfect. And now it was spreading, likely along the lines of my hatred. I hated everyone in the palace, yes, but I hated many, many more than that. If it was weaving through the palace to unconnected victims, eventually it would work its way out of the palace, to the people outside. It would weave its way to everyone who had ever said a word against the Nameless, it would touch everyone who looked down upon me and my kind. That meant – eventually – everyone.

A quiet, angry part of me grinned in triumph. Good! They all deserved it! Every rock thrown at me, every time they tried to hang me, every angry mob that attacked me, all of this would be avenged. And yet . . . and yet . . . Cursing the kingdom forever hadn't been my intention. I looked back at Will. Why hadn't it all gone as I'd expected it to go? If Will and maybe a few others had fallen asleep for a few days and woken up knowing what it was like to be Nameless, it wouldn't have caused serious damage. This had a very ill potential. Especially considering I had no idea how to undo it.

That thought gave me pause. 'What makes you think I can do anything about it?' I asked. Maybe she *did* know.

'I don't,' she said. 'I need to find Mistress Cait.'

'Faerie Caital? You need to find Faerie Caital?'

'Yes,' Will said. 'She's the faerie who saved mother a hundred and twenty years ago.'

'And caused the interregnum,' I reminded her.

She sighed. 'Yes. But she's the only one who could ever do anything about this kind of curse. The queen has sent a message to the Winnowinn clan, but she's not optimistic that they can help her. They were the ones that granted her Mercy, and Mercy isn't a very difficult gift to grant. Apparently. As far as faeries go, Mother says they aren't very powerful.'

I shook my head. 'No, they aren't,' I muttered. 'Ice magic is all temporary, melts away.'

'But Mistress Cait granted Life out of Death, and that's a very powerful spell. If anyone left in the kingdom can still help us, it'll be her.'

'And why are you talking to me?' I asked.

'Because she lives in the enchanted forest,' Will said.

I frowned. 'And?'

'And so do you. So I thought that you might be able to find her.'

I baulked. 'Me? You expect *me* to find Faerie Caital for you?'

'No one else can,' Will said. 'Mother hasn't been able to get a message to her since my christening.'

'And why do you think I should fare any better?'

'Because you're a magician,' Will said. 'And you live here!' She gestured to the towering trees around us. 'Actually *in* the enchanted forest.'

'This isn't really the enchanted forest,' I said. 'This is just the . . . borderlands.'

'You're still the closest thing to an expert on it in the kingdom,' she said. 'Next to Cait.'

'You know, just because the forest hasn't killed me while I'm hovering on the borders doesn't mean it's going to welcome me with open arms if I go traipsing through it looking for Faerie Caital . . . who, by the way, grew that forest to keep the furious people of the kingdom away from her during the interregnum. Hiedelen's armies would have gleefully killed her, and she knew it, not to mention the occasional angry mob. The forest is a protective labyrinth. I can't just go walking through it.'

She tossed her head in frustration. 'But if you could find a *way*. There *has* to be a way to contact her!'

'If she's even alive,' I pointed out.

'She's alive,' Will said. 'The Winnowinn clan have told us that much. She visits their fastness every year for some faerie harvest or other.'

'The Ceremony of the Light,' I said. I'd never been to a Light Ceremony, not since I was old enough to remember. My mother still went through the motions every spring, but she says it isn't the same in the shadows. 'And it's a renewal, not a harvest.'

'Whatever,' Willow said. 'But apparently it's not for months, and at the rate this Sleep is spreading, that'll be too late.'

I shrugged. 'So sorry, Princess. Not my concern.'

'My *name* is Will!' she snapped.

She really loved rubbing that in, didn't she? 'I don't care,' I snapped back.

'Would you care for another book?'

She had my weakness, didn't she? 'On what?'

She pulled a well bound book out of her cloak. '*The Zarmeroth Cycle.*'

Oh, she didn't! 'Where did you get that?'

'It was buried in a courtier's private library,' she said. 'Misfiled, so it escaped the purge.' She held it out for me. 'If you help me find Mistress Cait, it's yours.'

My eyes narrowed. 'What makes you think I'll help you? I might just take the book and run.'

She turned to show me the spine. 'Vol. 1,' it read. 'Oh.'

'Yes. It comes in three volumes. I'll give the other two to you after I talk with Cait.' She pushed the book into my hands.

I looked down at it. It was another well worn, often read tome. I wanted it, but I was beginning to wonder about her. 'Why are you doing this?' I asked. 'This book has been loved.'

She nodded. 'Yes.'

'By you?'

She nodded again, this time looking down at the snow. 'Yes,' she whispered.

'So why give it to me? From what I understand, these books are your most precious possession. More valuable to you than your crown, your kingdom, your fine jewels. Why do you give me this gem of your collection?'

'Obviously I'm no better at protecting them than anyone else,' she said. 'Besides. If your sister were under a curse, wouldn't you be willing to sacrifice every *thing* you own to get her back?'

'Yes,' I said. 'But my sister and I love each other. Yours burns your books and insults you to your face.'

'And has every virtue I've ever wanted, and isn't about to be sold off in marriage to someone she hasn't a prayer of loving!' Will snapped. 'Yes, I hate her!' She glared at me. 'And that's why I have to do this. I hate her, and it's all my fault she's like this. And if it means I have to sacrifice the gem of my library, or suffer through a thousand hardships or cut out half my heart and feed it to Ferdinand's hawk, I'll do it. I'll even crawl on my hands and knees to a complete stranger, begging for his help.' She fell to one knee in the snow, her head bowed toward me. 'Please,' she said, with surprising dignity. 'Please.'

This was it. This is what I'd wanted, a princess of Lyndaria in the dirt, bowing to me in respect. Why did it make me feel lower than ever? 'Get up,' I said. 'I'll come and tell you when I know how to find her.'

She looked at me. 'You mean you'll find her for me?'

What did I just say? My throat didn't hurt, so I'd obviously meant it. 'I guess,' I said, trying to figure out what I was saying. It was really hell not knowing who I was; I kept saying things I hadn't meant to. I clutched the book to my chest, making it very obvious that I did intend to keep it. 'Now get out of my forest, and don't come here again.'

She stood up and then sank into a respectful curtsey, as if I was a nobleman, or a clan master. 'I thank you,' she whispered. She turned to leave, back towards the road and the palace. She paused when she reached the edge of the clearing. 'Let your sister keep the scarf,' she said. 'It looks very nice on her. I'd have brought an extra cloak, if I'd known she was in rags.'

I said nothing, only stared at her out of the shadows. She turned her back on me and trudged on through the snow.

I stood for a long time watching her go, clutching my precious first volume of *The Zarmeroth Cycle*. The kit's voice cut through my reverie after a moment. 'Your spell didn't work.'

I looked back at her. The scarf was wrapped elegantly around her head, effectively covering her ears and still fashionable enough that it wouldn't draw undue attention. It looked a bit out of place amidst her rags, but a little dirt would quickly hide that. And it was warm. 'My spell worked fine,' I said.

'Your spell was supposed to be temporary,' the kit reminded me.

'You heard?'

She nodded. 'I like her,' the kit said. 'She seems honest.'

'She probably is,' I said. 'If I remember, Honesty was supposed to be one of the virtues her mother received from the faeries. Such gifts tend to inherit down.' I looked down at the book. I'd forgotten about the faerie virtues until Will had mentioned the Winnowinn clan and their gift of Mercy. I had a fleeting thought; I wondered what virtue I would have given the princess, if I hadn't been a child, and I had been invited to the christening of Princess Amaranth. At the moment, the virtue I had granted to all of them had been Suffering. That wasn't much of a step down from my aunt's gift of Death.

'How are you supposed to find Faerie Caital's tower?'

'I don't know,' I said. 'Maybe I won't.'

'You promised!' the kit said.

'No, I didn't,' I said. 'I said I'd come and get her when I knew how to find Faerie Cait. Not that I'd actually work at finding her.'

The kit glared at me. 'They may call us demons, but we're not. If you start telling lies, you may actually become one.'

'I'm not going to become a demon,' I growled.

'You're already acting like one,' the kit said.

'What do you know?' I said. 'You're just some Nameless child.'

'I know that you made her believe you'd help her, and you took that book in payment,' she said. 'You tell too many faerie lies, it's not too much of a step before you start being able to tell real lies. And then what'll you be?'

'A Nameless rake,' I muttered. But she was right. I was already telling lies. They hurt my mouth, but I told them. What did that make me? 'I still never promised her.'

'Then promise me!' the kit said. 'You promise me right now that you'll do everything in your power to find Faerie Cait *soon*! And that you'll keep your tacit promise to Princess Willow once you do it.'

'If there's anyone in the world who can't order me about—' I began.

'Promise!' the kit snapped.

She may have looked about eleven, but the kit was fifty years old, and not about to be sidetracked again. I sighed, trying not to laugh. 'Fine,' I said. 'I'll probably get eaten by a dragon or sucked into a quagmire, but I'll try to find Mistress Cait. Soon.'

'And you'll tell Willow how to find her.'

'I swear,' I said.

'On our lost names.'

'Oh, Faerie Light!'

'Swear!'

'I swear on our lost names. Satisfied?'

She tilted her head and looked at me. 'And you wouldn't lie to *me*, right?'

I kissed her pale forehead, which looked regal under the royal blue scarf. 'Never, my kitling,' I said. 'You're all I have left.'

Chapter 10

Will

'They've grown more than a foot this time,' the captain of the guard said.

Will looked down at the chart of measurements she was keeping. 'That's impossible.' She looked at his knotted cord. He was right. His fingers were held well past the fourth knot. 'That's more than twelve feet in two weeks.'

'And that's just here by the main gate,' the captain said. 'We can't even measure the areas near the East Wing any longer.'

Will sighed. The thorn hedge's growth rate had increased exponentially since Lavender's affliction. Will had pored over every record of the start of the Interregnum, her grandmother's diaries, the guard's reports, even the servants' records and the ordering of supplies for the kitchens and stables. She could only think that the thorns were preparing for another interregnum.

When Amaranth had been struck by the spindle, the Sleep had come upon the rest of the castle within a day. There had barely been time to lay Princess Amaranth on a fine couch and prepare a formal court to announce the fulfilment of the curse. The Sleep had then overtaken the palace so swiftly that the old king and queen had suffered their slumber upon their very thrones. The noblemen who had come to hear that particular court had been very put out to discover, upon their awakening, that their titles and lands had disappeared in the ensuing century. Not to mention the hundreds of sundered marriages, the discovery of grandchildren now older than themselves, the tragic loss of family fortunes which the sleeping had had no way to circumvent.

Once the Sleep had firmly established itself, the first layer of the thorn hedge had grown up in a night. According to the one record of the period (from a nobleman who had arrived late to court and thanked his stars every day for his carriage's cracked axle), there was at least a foot of writhing, bloodsucking briar roses by the time he had arrived the next morning. No one else thought to take detailed records of the growth of the thorns since this nobleman, but there were some peasants' records reporting when the palace road had to be abandoned and when the palace mill had to be closed. The road, which ran about fifteen feet from the palace wall, was finally declared unsafe about twenty years after the start of the Interregnum, and the palace mill, which had been situated on River Friene about a hundred feet from the Eastern Wall, was ultimately abandoned during the interregnum at about year sixty. Which meant that, apart from that first night of sudden growth after Princess Amaranth's curse, the hedge had been growing at slightly less than a foot a year.

Since Lavender's sudden Sleep, the hedge had been growing at several inches a night, despite its being the dead of winter. At first even Will hadn't noticed. By the time five days had passed, no one could miss it. Since Amaranth had woken, due to many interventions, the royal family been clearing and battling the thorns with some success, and it had been down to a hedge a mere ten feet thick around most of the palace. Now it was approaching a forest again, twenty feet thick if it was an inch.

It worried King Ragi. Ragi was the only man who had ever penetrated the thorns when they were more than ten feet thick, all the virtuous woodcutter's sons having entered the palace when the hedge was comparatively thin. He was often caught staring out the window at the rapidly growing hedge. At night one could almost hear it, rustling, stretching, spreading its roots and growing, growing, growing in the darkness.

There wasn't anything Will could do about it, but she kept records. It made her feel a little less useless. 'Thank you, Captain,' she told him.

He nodded stiffly and turned his back. Will sighed. Had the rumours finally gotten to him, too?

Will had first noticed the rumours the very evening of her return from her meeting with Reynard in the forest. At first they'd only appeared to be whispers. 'I'll wager she's *happy* about it!' Hints. Innuendo. No accusations, only a general feeling of unease about her.

Recently the rumours had been growing stronger. Will had even seen not-so-veiled hints in one of the local broadsheets. Her impassioned cry of, 'I'll kill you!' that she had shouted just as Lavender had burned her book was being reprinted again and again. There was even some repetition of the argument Lavender and Will had had in the hedge, when she'd questioned Will's magic. Will wondered who'd repeated that? Narvi, or one of the courtier's children who had been snowballing in the fields? She refused to suspect Ferdinand.

The last few days she had been getting threats. At first it was just accusations pushed under her door. 'I know it was you.' 'You can't hide from the truth.' 'Magic is only practised by the evil.' Then it was actual threats. 'The same will come back to you.' 'Treason is a hanging offence.' 'The hedge will take its own.' She had asked for guards to be posted at the door of her room, but there were not any guards to spare.

As Will entered the great hall she nearly fell over someone's leg. She thought someone had tried to trip her, as people had been doing ever since Lavender's sleep, but when she looked behind her it was clear this was not the case. 'Oh, seven hells!' The guard at the right of the door had fallen asleep. He had slid down the wall and his head was lolling. His battle axe lay forgotten on the floor. He snored gently. 'You! Why didn't you report this?' Will asked of his partner, who stood at the opposite side of the door.

He looked up from where he was nodding on his halberd. 'Sorry?' He blinked at his partner. 'Oh, hells!' He started and took a step toward her only to have his eyes droop again.

'Oh, no.' Will jumped up and caught him as he fell. There had been quite a lot of broken bones and cracked skulls from people who had been alone and standing when the Sleep finally took them. It wasn't an instant process, as Ragi had pointed out. It wasn't a swoon. It was a true, pervasive drowsiness which finally overcame you. It was so subtle you barely noticed it.

Will propped the guard next to his partner and went to find someone to take them to the West Wing. The West Wing was where they put all the victims of the Sleep, including those who had been brought in from the surrounding countryside. It didn't seem to be contagious in the same way an ordinary plague was. People who had never visited the palace were often struck. They hadn't had many victims from outside Lyndaron, though they'd had some stalwart farmers who hadn't set foot in the city since last harvest. It appeared to be completely random where the Sleep would strike next.

Before Will left the entry hall her eyes were caught by the immense portrait of her sister which now graced the receiving wall. It was fourteen feet tall. Inside it her sister stood, twelve feet from hem to head, dressed in her lavender silk, her yappy little fluff of a dog curled in her arm, in a

135

way he would never have permitted had he been his rampant, squirmy, awake self. The portrait painter had been commissioned less than a week after the sleep, and he had worked day and night, with the help of all of his apprentices, to have it completed quickly. It had been hung two days before, the paint still sticky. Amaranth had wanted it completed by Midwinters – Will's wedding day. Five days away.

If there was to be another interregnum, Amaranth wanted any potential rescuer to have no question as to what the princess looked like.

Will heard someone coming down one of the two elegantly curving stairs which framed the receiving hall. 'Excuse me, we need some help here!' she called up, not even looking to see who it was. Anyone would help.

'You are asking help . . . from *me*?' came an unctuous voice from the stairs.

Ah. Anyone would help except him.

King Lesli leaned over the balustrade and peered at her. 'And what would appear to be the trouble, Your Highness?'

'The same as ever, Your Majesty,' Will said with a respectful curtsey. 'More victims of the Sleep.'

He cocked his head at the sleeping guards. 'Guards who fell asleep at their post in *my* country would be whipped, and possibly executed,' he said, then he laughed. 'It is a shame this isn't Heidelen land.'

Will was not going to be baited by him again. 'Sir.'

His eyes shifted to her without any movement of his head. 'Princess Willow. Have you gained some courtesy in the past weeks?'

'As you say, sir,' she said, with a respectful curtsey.

He frowned. 'I think I almost liked you better before this fiasco,' he said. 'You had spirit then. I like horses who have spirit. After they are broken they are a highly superior ride.'

136

'I'm certain you are a fine rider, Your Majesty,' Will said dully.

'*Are* you now. I don't think you are certain of me at all.' He smiled at her in a way she was sure she didn't like. 'And perhaps you shouldn't be.' He looked down at his hand, examining a jewel on his finger. 'This is not my function, but I believe I passed the messenger, who was supposed to fetch you, asleep in the upstairs hall.' He looked back at her. 'Your mother wished to speak with you.'

'When was this?'

'About an hour past. She's in her chambers.'

Will frowned at him. 'What were you doing in my mother's chambers?'

Lesli smiled at her. 'Merely working out some of the details of the union of our households. Some very important issues had to be risen and laid.' His eyes narrowed and flickered up and down her body. 'I suggest you speak with her.'

'Indeed, Your Majesty.' Will curtseyed again, her mouth tasting of bile. She hated that man. She hated him more with every passing day. His unctuous, slippery incivility was enough to try the patience of the Goddess of Forgiveness herself. Amaranth was the only one who could stand to spend any time with him, thanks to the faeries for the gifts of Patience, Nobility and Wisdom. Bravery probably wasn't hurting Amaranth any either.

When Will knocked on the door of her mother's chambers she heard her in heated discussion with someone with a kitchen accent. 'Enter!' Amaranth called as she continued her discussion.

'I tell you, I bain't stayin' here one more night!' said the current head chef. She had once been assistant to the third underchef, but the kitchen staff had been among the first to succumb. No one was sure why.

'You may of course return to the city, if you refuse to work for us, and to forego your annuity once you retire,'

Amaranth said. The chef squeaked indignantly at that, as if the very idea hadn't occurred to her. 'However, you should know that the city itself is under quarantine.'

'Quarantine!' shouted the chef. That she should shout at the queen surprised Will, but she wasn't trained as an upper servant, and everyone was tense and uneasy these days.

The queen was unperturbed. 'Yes. We do not know exactly why or how this Sleep spreads, but it would seem prudent to prevent it from touching as much of the kingdom as possible. The walls of the city have been closed, and no one goes in or out.' This wasn't strictly speaking true. Will knew about the quarantine, and she also knew that those few Sleeping who succumbed from outside the walls were brought in, though their families were usually not permitted to leave again. If it wasn't for the fact that the Sleeping needed no food, (at least the magic of the Sleep seemed to be the same as the old Sleep in that regard) there would have been starving people in Lyndaron this winter.

'So even if I leave this cursed castle, I won't be gettin' away from this Sleep?'

'I'm afraid not, Bethel,' Amaranth said. 'However, if the Sleep *should* take you in the streets of Lyndaron, you may leave a note on your person requesting that you be returned here, to be encouched in the West Wing with the rest of our staff.'

The chef squared her shoulders. 'I'll stay, Ma'am,' she said. 'But I bain't be pretendin' I likes it!'

'As you will, Bethel,' Amaranth said. 'Your feelings are your own.'

As Bethel walked past Will she distinctly heard her mutter, 'If we just cut out the *source* of this thing, we could all sleep in our beds without fear.' She was looking right at Will as she said it. Will knew better than to say anything against the rumour. It would only make her appear more guilty.

Queen Amaranth held her hand to her head in weariness before she looked up at Will. 'I sent for you *four hours* ago. Where have you been?'

'I never received any message,' Will said. 'King Lesli thought he saw the messenger asleep an hour past.'

The queen groaned.

'We just lost both the front entry guards, as well.'

Amaranth threw up her hands. 'Of course!'

Will frowned. 'Mother? Why do we not leave the palace? We could request that my marriage to Narvi be performed in Hiedelen. I'm certain King Lesli doesn't mind *where* I marry.'

'He is under quarantine as well,' Amaranth said wearily. 'He actually suggested it. He said he feared the Sleep would spread through his kingdom, should he leave.'

'But this doesn't seem to be like a plague,' Will said. 'You and I and Father haven't succumbed. Ferdinand has never left Lavender's side, and he's still wide awake.'

'We don't *know* how this spreads,' Amaranth said. 'I'm taking no chances.'

'But Mother . . . the thorns grew a foot last night.'

She looked up at her. 'An entire *foot*.'

'More, actually. The kitchen entrance has entirely closed over.'

'Is the main entrance in any danger?' the queen asked.

'Not so far. But I've ordered the road sown with salt.'

'Is that helping?'

'It seems to be keeping the main entrance clear,' Will said. 'But if we didn't have a crew of twenty on it every day, it would have closed up already.'

'I'll be sure that the clearing crew is assigned priority,' Amaranth said, making a note on her chart. 'We're having trouble keeping up the staff. They fall asleep so fast, and replacements are getting hard to find.'

'Hire more from the town.'

Amaranth shook her head. 'They fear the castle. Which is madness. The Sleep hit the market area the hardest.'

'You haven't had *any* luck contacting Mistress Cait?'

She shook her head. 'No. I spoke again to Junco Winnowinn.' Junco had been by the day after Lavender fell to Sleep, but he hadn't been much help.

'The faerie? He was here? Why didn't you summon me?'

'I did. You did not come. There were quite a few things I needed to discuss with Junco Winnowinn, and it would have been better had you been here at the same time. As it is . . . . Well. Things are getting worse, Willow. The West Wing is full up,' Amaranth said. 'We have to abandon the commoners to tend to their own Sleeping. I've written down tending procedures to take into the town. Find the victim a warm, dry place, kept from possible rats or vermin, things like that. I'll need to get it to a herald.'

'The royal herald fell prey this morning,' Will told her. 'I can take it to his apprentice.'

Amaranth sighed, pulling the sheet of parchment from beneath a pile on her desk. 'Thank you,' she said. 'And I must remember to tell every official to appoint a replacement should they succumb. Remind the apprentice herald to choose a new apprentice and to give him the minimum training immediately.'

'Yes, Mother.'

Will took the sheet, believing that to be all, but Amaranth called her back. 'Willow, there's something else I needed to discuss with you.'

'What?'

'I need to tell you that as of this morning I have reinstated the laws against magic.'

Will didn't understand what she was saying at first. 'You've what?'

'Reinstated the laws restricting magic,' she said. 'There is too much risk associated with such practices, given our circumstances.'

'What do you mean, too much risk?' Will asked, too flabbergasted to even be upset.

'We don't know what has caused this Sleep,' Amaranth said, 'we don't know what is encouraging the thorns, and have no idea how other spells might interact with this ensorcelled affliction. As a result, at King Lesli's suggestion, I have reinstated the Hiedelen ban on practising magic.'

'But Mother . . . how will we solve this problem if not *with* magic?'

'The faeries are, of course, permitted to continue with their practices,' Amaranth said. 'But for their own safety I've a note recommending that all of the Winnowinn clan remain in the north, for now, preferably in their own fastness. This way there will be no confusion.'

'But Mother, this is madness!'

'No,' the Queen said. 'This is politics.' She studied Will's expression. Will felt about ready to burst into flame, and she probably looked it. 'As my daughter, and the current presumptive heir, you will be expected to obey these laws as well.'

'But . . . what does Father say?'

'It doesn't matter. He is not the hereditary ruler of this kingdom. I am. But since you ask, as it happens, he does in fact agree with me.'

Will's world was crumbling. Her only source of nourishment was now illegal? 'Why have you done this?' It came out as a whisper. Will had wanted it to come out a wail.

Amaranth was too harried to be too sympathetic, but her gift of Kindness shone in her face. 'King Lesli pointed out the possible evils of permitting magic in this uncertain climate,' she told Will. 'The people of Lyndaron are already up in arms. They're frightened, and they are frightened of magic.

They're not used to it. It was illegal for a hundred years. It has only been permitted for less than half a generation. As their queen, I need to reflect the will of the people.'

'The people don't know anything about magic,' Will said. 'They've never learned about it. They don't know what it can or can't do, they don't know whether it's dangerous or not!'

'They believe it to be dangerous,' Amaranth said. 'That is all that matters at this stage. If I do not respond to this, they may well retaliate against us in fear.' She took a deep breath. 'You realize if such a retaliation should occur, the one most likely to suffer would be yourself.'

Will blinked. 'Myself.'

'Surely you aren't ignorant of the rumours about you.' She picked up a sheet of paper. 'I have received a report this very morning citing supposed proof of your black arts, the vindictiveness of your spirit, and how you instigated this sleep by feeding your sister the blood of murdered children.'

'*What*?' Amaranth showed Will the paper. It was barely legible, written in charcoal on brown parcel paper, with hardly a full sentence of complete grammar and more spelling errors than Will could count. 'This is nonsense!'

'Of course it is,' Amaranth said. 'But that didn't stop this person from believing it true. If I can assure the people that my daughter has complied with the new regulations against magic, and that she is therefore a lawful and honourable person, it is possible that their distrust of you would thaw.'

'So I have to abandon my magic,' Will said. 'Sell myself into marriage to Narvi. Curb my tongue. All for the sake of you and the people.'

'You can spit in *my* face, Willow, if it makes you feel better,' Amaranth said. 'I will endure your hatred with dignity. But as far as the people are concerned, yes. You must obey.'

Will was half tempted to follow her advice and spit on her, but the idea made her feel childish. 'Your will be done,' she said with a curtsey, 'Your Majesty.'

She turned to go. As she opened the door she heard Amaranth behind her. 'I'm very proud of you, Willow. So very, very proud.'

Will was glad to hear it, but she'd rather have had her own life and none of her mother's pride.

She passed the message off to the apprentice herald, and then headed down toward her chambers, pulling out her keys. She always locked her chamber door, ever since the first threat. She inserted the key into the lock and then backed away in horror.

Upon her door, scrawled in a red liquid she suspected was animal blood, was a new message. 'Die in flayms Deman Wytch'. Will cried out and snatched her keys back. It was all too much. Between the threats and her marriage and this new injunction against magic, her supposedly strong will was crumbling. She screamed again, mostly in anger this time. She turned back her head and howled a scream of rage at the gilded palace ceiling.

'Will! I'm coming!' She turned her head. It was her father, pelting down the corridor with something glittering in his hand. 'What is it?' he panted when he caught up to her. 'What's happened?'

Will almost sobbed, and pointed silently at her door.

'Oh,' he said. He took the keys from her clenched hand. 'Could one of you fetch some water and clean off this door?' he called down the corridor.

Will turned. A half a dozen ladies were proceeding carefully down the hallway with something gauzy and beautiful between them. They looked at each other for a moment and then one of them peeled off, carefully handing her section of the gauzy thing to another. Ragi inserted the key into the door and pushed it open, pulling Will inside. 'It'll be all right, Will,' he told her. 'It means nothing, you know.'

Will was sobbing now, but it was half in laughter. This was all such madness! The fates were conspiring against her, and there was nothing she could do about it. Ragi led her inside and set her on the sofa. 'Let me get you some water,' he said. He filled a glass and pushed it into her hand. 'I take it your mother told you?'

Will nodded.

'Will . . . .'

He didn't know what to say. 'I'm well, Father,' Will said. The handful of ladies came gingerly in after him, carrying the gauzy thing. 'What is that?' she asked, brushing the tears from her cheeks.

'Nothing,' Ragi said. 'We'll see to it later,' he added to the ladies.

'We haven't any more time,' one of them said.

'That's my wedding dress, yes?' Will asked.

They nodded as one.

Will stood up and climbed onto a chair. 'Thy will be done,' she muttered to the fates, and let the ladies hang the gown upon her and fit it to her solid frame. The dress was of white and grey, to reflect the mourning the kingdom was in due to her sister. Her jewels were to be jet and deep burgundy rubies. Her veil was heavy, to cover her face completely. Narvi was to be entirely in black. Will wished they'd dress her in black, but white was required due to her virginal status.

A status which was likely to remain intact for some years yet after the marriage. Her arms ached and she was exhausted by the time the ladies were halfway finished with their final fitting. Ragi had waited, presumably to lend moral support, but Will rather wished he'd leave.

As they were fitting her one of the ladies considerately held up a mirror so that she could admire herself. Will's reflection stared back at her with lifeless eyes. The figure in the mirror was massive and awkward, a giantess in a white dress. The grey trim was the same colour as her eyes, and washed them out of her face, turning them to mere shadows. The faces of the ladies reflected about her waist were tense and frustrated. They kept trying to tighten her thick waist, to match the current fashion of willowy and slender. Princess Willow, the furthest thing in the world from willowy and graceful. *Why couldn't they have named me Cabbage or Pumpkin? Something that is judged by how big and wide it can get.* As she stood there the shock of Amaranth's injunction began to wear off, and she began to feel more like a Thistle or a Nettle. Tighter and tighter they pulled on the stays until she grunted with pain.

She lost her temper with the whole situation. 'Forget it!' she said. She threw her arms down and started wrestling off the dress. 'It fits as well as it fits. You're never going to be able to make me a bride as beautiful as Lavender, so just give up! Dress me in a flour sack and tie a belt around it, I'll look fine!' She pulled the dress over her head, and she heard something tear. She didn't care. She threw the dress at her father. 'Or let me wear Father's clothes!' she shouted. 'Give the dress to Narvi, he'd look prettier in it.'

Ragi gently handed the dress to the nearest seamstress. Will stood on the stool in her shift and glared at the figures in the room. 'I'm marrying the boy, not being put up for sale. If he wants to marry me, he can marry me comfortable, not trussed up like a capon!' She got down off the stool. 'I'm done.'

'I suggest finishing your fittings to the dummy,' Ragi said quietly to the head seamstress.

'But it's not exact,' the seamstress began.

'It will suffice,' Ragi said firmly. 'Fit it loose.'

The seamstress took one more look at Will. Will's face must have daunted any further protests, because the seamstress made a clucking noise to her ladies, rather like a mother hen, and like a hen with her chicks the seamstress and her ladies scuttled out of the room, Will's wedding dress flapping like a hen's wings.

'Will,' Ragi began.

'I know, I *know*!' she hissed.

'Will . . . if you don't want to marry . . . .'

She looked up at him. That was the last thing she'd expected her father to say. 'Are you saying I have a choice?'

Ragi looked grave. 'It is a difficult one . . . but yes. Neither I nor your mother will force you into anything.'

Will's anger cooled, though her despair only surged stronger. Being offered the choice only let her see how firmly she was trapped. 'I know what has to be done, Father,' she said. She gazed at him. 'When Lesli told you you had to brave the thorns . . . was there a choice?'

Ragi blinked. 'Yes,' he said. 'I could brave the thorns and . . . basically let myself die, or I could watch my mother disgraced, our estate gutted, our name sullied. There was also a not very subtle threat about the future of . . . .' He hesitated and then said frankly, 'My sisters would have been enslaved, as well.'

'I didn't know you had sisters.'

'I don't,' Ragi said. 'Not officially. Natiniel . . . my mother's . . . friend . . . was forced to find a wife after I was born. It would have been suspicious, otherwise. I spent my summers at their farm off the mill.'

Ragi had never admitted that he was illegitimate before. Will was stunned. 'So . . . you always knew . . . .'

'That my life did not really belong to me. Yes. There are all kinds of choices. Of course you have a choice.'

Will shook her head. 'You know full well I don't.'

Ragi nodded. 'I suppose you'd rather be alone,' he said. 'I'm very proud of you, my daughter.'

'Stop saying that,' Will said.

'It's true, all the same,' he said. And he left.

He was wrong. Will didn't want half a dozen ladies buzzing around her like stinging hornets trying to force her body into an impossible shape, but she didn't want to be alone, either. Her many years of upcoming married bliss with Narvi at college would leave her ample time to be alone. She caught up her skirts and went to see the only other person in the castle whom she knew felt as bereft as she did.

Prince Ferdinand still sat at Lavender's side, reading aloud from a book of poetry. Lavender was no longer in her chambers, but in the antechamber off the throne room. This was at King Ragi's suggestion. He had spent nearly twenty hours wandering around the palace peering into this room and that before he'd finally found Amaranth in the highest room in the tallest tower. It may have been an excellent place for the evil faerie to hide the last spinning wheel in Lyndaria, but it was an abysmal place for a would-be rescuer to find and wake the princess. The courtroom antechamber was on the ground floor, and obvious. If someone, eventually, had to penetrate the palace and find the princess in order to end the Sleep, he wanted her somewhere easily found.

Will knew Ferdinand would be there. He barely slept. When he did, he slept on a cot by the fireplace, refusing to leave the antechamber where Lavender lay, twitching in her nightmares. When she cried out he would smooth her forehead and murmur to her. When she shivered he would wrap her in blankets. Will rather thought the shivering had more to do with the nightmares than cold, but she didn't want to tell Ferdinand that. He was suffering enough. Let him think he could help even a little.

When Will came into the room he looked up from his book. 'Good evening, Will,' he said.

She looked at the windows. The shadows were lengthening. 'Any change?' she asked, knowing the answer.

'Nothing,' he said. He leaned over and touched Lavender's still rosy cheek. 'My poor darling.'

She was twitching with another nightmare. Will knew it was a mistake, but she couldn't help herself. Something about the nightmares drew her. She had to know what was making Lavender whimper in her sleep. Will reached out and took her hand, tying herself to the dream sharing spell. Again, she was sucked through a tunnel into blackness.

Someone is shouting. I was in hiding, but I know I am revealed. There is someone I have to protect, and I can't get to her. There is a horde of angry men between us. Some carry pitchforks, and mean to kill her. They're shouting at us, 'Demon! Evil! Kill it!' I push between the men and they cry out when they catch sight of me. I'm nearly to her, I have my hand on her to protect her. One of the dirty pitchforks stabs into the back of my leg. The pain is terrible, shooting through me until my stomach heaves, and the blood drains from my face. I stumble and fall, screaming, screaming.

'Will! Will!'

Will opened her eyes to find Ferdinand standing over her, shaking her shoulders. There was another sound distracting her, more than Ferdinand's frantic crying of her name. She realized belatedly that it was her own screams. She closed her mouth. 'Sorry,' she whispered, gasping. The dream had frightened her, but she suspected it was Ferdinand's hands on her shoulders that was really making her tremble. She was very close to his lips.

'What was it?' he asked, and she could smell his breath. He smelled of violet water and wine.

'Her nightmare,' Will said. 'There was pain. Fear.' She shuddered.

Ferdinand's face crumpled and sucked in breath, holding back tears. Will wanted to reach out to him, but kept her hands at her sides. He swallowed. 'Does my reading help her, do you think?'

Will shook her head. 'These nightmares are too powerful for any voice to enter. I don't even know who I am when I'm in them.'

He sighed and he sank to his knees before her. His hands slid down her arms to her elbows, but he didn't let go of her. He looked exhausted. His skin was now nearly as pale as his hair. 'How can you do it?' she asked him. 'How can you sit here, day after day?'

'I must,' he said, his voice hoarse with reading aloud. He looked up at her, willing her to understand. She stared at him. His face was haggard and his ice-blue eyes were cracked by red lines. 'I have nothing now but my vigil.'

Will shook her head. 'This can't be why you left your father's kingdom,' she said. 'This can't have been what your fate held in store. You were granted courage and the gifts you needed to defeat the dragon and win the princess, only to sit staring at her bedside day after day, night after night, until you waste away to a shadow of grief?'

'If the only thing I can offer my beloved is a shadow of grief, I will become it for her,' he said. He stared into Will's eyes. 'You do what you must.'

'But what if you don't want it?' she said. 'What if it's tearing you up inside until you feel like you're going to scream? Until you hate everyone around you so terribly that if they could see it they'd shrivel on the spot?'

'I don't know,' he said. He shook his head. 'You're right. I look about me and I envy the happiness I see in others. I envy your father and mother for the love they share. I envy you.'

'You envy *me*?'

149

'You have lost nothing with this Sleep. You have gained again a kingdom.'

Will batted his arms away. 'You know *nothing*. You believed from the first that I wanted to be queen. It was never anything I wanted. When you came home with Lavender I was so relieved! There was never anything I wanted more than for Lavender to come back.' This was it. She told herself not to do it, not to say it, even as she found herself sliding off the bed, onto the floor before Ferdinand, almost into his arms. 'There is nothing in the world I want more than to bring her back . . . for *you*.'

His breath caught, and his eyes closed.

'I so want you to be happy,' she whispered, telling herself to shut her mouth. 'I love you so.'

He almost sobbed. 'Thank you,' he breathed. He reached for her and caught her up in a fierce, warm embrace.

Will's insides melted. Ferdinand, her beloved Ferdinand, had caught her in his arms, held her against his bosom, and she was part of his sphere. He became a part of her, until she couldn't tell where she ended and he began. She could feel the kiss drawing her to him, like a pull on her lips. His breath tickled her cheek, his hands were so strong around her shoulders. His lips were a mere breath from hers. She closed her eyes . . .

And it broke. He had pulled away from her. He kissed her forehead as a brother. 'I know Lavender knows how much you care for us, and want our happiness.'

He thought when she'd said *you* that she'd meant *both of you*. Part of her was very glad she hadn't just completely muddled everything with her impulsive admission. Another part was heartbroken. Had he felt it, between them? Had there been anything on his side at all?

She could tell by his calm demeanour that there had not. He pulled away without any awkwardness, and sat back in his chair. Returning to his vigil over Lavender. He had embraced his sister, as he would embrace a child or a distant aunt. The magic between them was all in Will's own head. She knew this was the case.

That didn't stop it from hurting.

She had to find her feet. They seemed to have disappeared beneath her dress. It was a fight up a mountain to make herself stand. 'Good evening, Ferdinand,' she whispered.

He nodded cordially, but she didn't wait to hear his farewell. She ran.

Damn him! Damn him for existing in the first place! Damn him for being so handsome and charming that everyone fell in love with him. Damn him for making me care for him so. Damn him for not loving me.

Damn me for loving him.

She fled to her chambers. The bloody message had been cleaned off her door, but she barely cared any more. Her door could have been aflame with the fires of all seven hells, and it wouldn't have daunted her, so long as behind it lay escape. She slammed it behind her and flung open the door to her closet. She couldn't see to find her cloak, and it was only then she realized she was still crying. She scrubbed the tears from her cheeks. Ah, there was the cloak. She pulled it on.

She was going to see Reynard. Injunction against magic or no, there was no one else she could trust in her wretched kingdom. Besides, she should make sure he knew that magic had been banned. From the look of his rumpled rags, he couldn't afford to pay a fine and would likely end up imprisoned if he was caught breaking the law.

Mostly she wanted an excuse to flee the palace.

She pushed her way down the black passage to the secret door. She opened it into the blazing sunset. The sun had turned the snow to fire, and the winter thorns were thick, black smoke.

> *For everything that grows and every leaf*
> *That hangs upon the climbing vine or tree*
> *Blessed with sweet flower, wondrous belief,*
> *That my poor will can overpower thee*
> *For I am nature's strength, her arm and hand*
> *That binds the fruitful bounty of the land.*

As always, the thorns ceased their writhing and stopped reaching for her. Reynard's adaptation had made the spell much more reliable. She strode on through them confidently. But long before she reached the edge of the thorns, she could feel her spell weakening. She frowned and peered ahead through the fiery gloom. She should have left the thorns by now . . .

With an angry creak, some of the thorns reached for her. 'AK! *For I am nature's strength, her arm and hand/ That binds the fruitful bounty of the land!*' She said it so quickly that many of the words slurred, but it worked. She looked around her. The thorns were quivering, only barely held back by her abbreviated magic. She could see the well worn path behind her back to her secret entrance. When she tried to look past the thorns to the clear, she couldn't find it. The thorns stretched on and on ahead of her. There . . . no. There! Her mouth opened. Fifty feet beyond the previous border of the hedge, the forest of briar roses stretched on into the gloom.

She couldn't do it. It didn't matter how powerful the spell was. By the time she got through one section of stilled thorns, she'd have to recite the spell again, and she couldn't maintain it twice. Not reliably enough to get her through. Her second recitation was already crumbling, and any second the thorns would be upon her. Her royal blood was too sweet.

She turned and fled back toward the wall. Her cloak caught on a branch, and she bit her lip to keep from crying out and breaking the ill cast spell. She reached the wall before her botched spell shattered, leaving the thorns grasping for her arms. She slammed the secret entrance shut on them, and she could hear them strike against the stone facade of the door. They realized they could not reach into the passage. With a hiss and a shiver, they settled down again.

Will slid down the wall and stared into the blackness for what felt like hours. She was trapped. The main entrance was guarded not only by her mother's guards, but by King Lesli's as well, with their yellow and green livery and the Hiedelen identity tag around their necks like dogs.

She couldn't escape. Her will about the subject be damned, as of this moment, there was only one road open for her. Her duty.

Chapter 11

* * *

Promises are tricky things. You can't just go ignoring them. The failure to start is like a lie. It aches on you. Like a thorn embedded where you can't reach. Throb, throb, throb. You haven't fulfilled your promise. Throb, throb, throb. Time is ticking forward. Throb, throb.

It doesn't help when your kit sister stares at you every time she sees you and asks, 'Well? Have you found her yet?' If I didn't love her so much, it would be enough to make me hate her.

It wasn't that I wasn't trying to reach Mistress Caital. I'd get up every day and set off through the forest. I tried handling it systematically, but once I got past our little glade on the outskirts the forest changed daily. Sometimes I could hear the winter trees groaning and moving behind me as I walked. Sometimes I just closed my eyes and the forest changed with a blink. All I could do was keep muddling through until the forest spat me back out, usually some miles from where I started. It was hopeless.

I wasn't really giving up, I told myself as I headed for the club. Maybe someone there had a clue. Maybe I needed to interact with another magic user. Maybe what I really needed was just a break. The city walls were closed but, even without wings, faeries can climb easily. I made it over the rough stone without issue.

The club was full, but there was no witchfire in the kitchen hearth as I slipped through the window. The subdued murmur

I heard came from what had once been the parlour. I poked my head around the door.

More than a dozen people were clustered in little groups around the room. I'd never seen so many people in the club at any one time. 'Hey, all,' I said.

So many people glared at me my hand went up to check my hood. All was still concealed. 'Well, old rumple's still with us,' said the whore.

The witch looked me up and down. 'I can't believe it! I thought sure you were in the dungeon with the rest of them!'

'Rest of who?' I asked. 'Why's everyone here?'

'Lots of us have had our homes burnt by our friendly neighbours,' the witch said. 'Nowhere else to go.'

'Burnt? Why? What's happened?'

'This,' she said. She thrust a broadsheet under my nose. Very few people in the club knew I could read, but the witch was one of them.

Magic Banned, the broadsheet read. *It has been the opinion of our good Queen Amaranth that, due to the unsettling nature of certain events in the city of Lyndaron and the Rose Palace, that magic and all practice, discussion and sale of magical goods or services are to be banned until further notice.*

The sheet went on to list certain punishments, ranging from fines to imprisonment, depending on how the injunction had been broken, and then useful ways to spy on your family and friends, and whom to tell if you suspected a magic user in your area.

'When was this?' I asked. The broadsheet had no date.

'Two days ago,' the witch told me. 'You hadn't heard?'

'I've been busy,' I said.

'Old Shine wanted a word with you before he went. He was waiting for you.'

Winnowinn was still in town? 'Why'd he want a word with me?'

'Dunno. I think he's up in the observatory. He was expecting you today, must have a bit of foresight that faerie.'

'Must have,' I muttered. I backed out of the subdued parlour and up the creaking stairs to the observatory. I wondered if Junco knew the Sleep spell was mine.

'I saw you come in,' he said as I slunk into the observatory. 'I told the witch to send you up.'

'I had questions,' I said. 'What's going on? Why suddenly ban magic?'

'I think it has to do with this Sleep that has infected the princess,' Junco said. 'They're taking all precautions.'

I shook my head. 'They can't think this has anything to do with the local hedgewitches.'

Junco shrugged. 'Doesn't matter what they think. This is what they've done. I have to get back to Fortress Frost, but I wanted to talk to you.'

I prepared myself for a fight. 'Of what?'

'Before they got all paranoid about magic again, they summoned me to the palace. Well, they summoned Mistress Isolde, but she sent message to accept me in her stead, lest there was aught she could do. There isn't. This spell is beyond us. It draws shadows 'round your heart, and absorbs any magic which tries to fight it, only making it stronger.'

I swallowed. This was a Nameless spell indeed, cast in shadow, drawing in all because there was a void to fill. I hoped he hadn't noticed that. I made quite sure I was standing in the shade.

'When it became clear I could do nothing the queen grew quite angry. She demanded that I contact Mistress Caital, and they all grew considerably irate when I told her I could not.'

I raised an eyebrow. Was Will talking about me? 'The reason they reinstated this law is because you refused to contact Faerie Caital?'

'I didn't refuse,' Junco said. 'We can't contact her because she doesn't want us to. She was always a little eccentric, and she's gotten worse since the end of the interregnum. Queen Amaranth didn't believe me when I said that only those Cait wants to see are allowed through the enchanted forest. It wasn't until after she accepted we couldn't reach her that this law came down.'

'So you can't get through the forest either?' I asked, hoping I didn't sound obvious in my inquisition.

He shook his head. 'I've asked. Several times. The forest keeps sending me away.'

'Wait, what do you mean, you've asked? If you can't contact her, how can she know to send you away?'

'I've asked the forest. That's both the door and the guard at the door. If the forest doesn't let you through, that's the end of that.'

Ask the forest. That hadn't occurred to me.

'Why do you care about Caital?' he asked. I had been rather blatant.

'I'm living by the edge of the forest,' I said truthfully. 'It's good to know one's environment. Why did you want to talk to me?'

'They're banning faerie magic, now,' he said. 'I've been banished back up to the fastness. If I show my face outside again I'll be arrested with the rest of them.'

'They are truly arresting *all* magic users?'

'Aye. At the moment the Winnowinn clan is to stay in their fastness. If this persists, the queen tells me we may be banished from the kingdom altogether. I thought you should know.'

'What difference would it make to me?'

'I want you to get out of the kingdom.'

I blinked. 'What?'

'You heard me. The climate here is about to get very cold towards people like us.'

'But, as you know, I am not like you,' I told him. 'I doubt I'd notice a difference.'

'You may not,' Junco said. 'But I thought it a kindness to warn you all the same.'

'Yes, *such* a kindness. You know full well there's nowhere else we can go. The other faerie clans have been very clear on that point. The Nameless are not permitted to intrude on their territory.'

Junco tilted his head. If I didn't know better, I'd have said he was a little uncomfortable. 'I suspect that an exception could possibly be made in your case. Your taint is by association, not from any crime you yourself have committed.'

'How do you know?' I said. 'I could be committing crimes left and right. I could be the demon they call me.'

Junco shook his head. 'I suspect you aren't a demon.'

'If you're so concerned about us, invite us to your fastness,' I said. 'We'll share your internment in the north.' The lack of response was all the reply I needed. 'No. I thought not. Thank you for your warning, but I'll take my chances with the same thugs who have always been after me, rather than cross borders and deal with fellow faeries who despise me with the added benefit of power.' I turned to go, and then hesitated at the door. 'How does it feel, Junco? To have everyone hate you for what you are? To have your very existence outlawed?'

Junco gazed back at me. 'Not good.'

'You still enjoy watching my envy?'

He looked down, fluttering his white wings. 'I don't pretend to be an angel.'

Whatever reply I might have made to that was drowned out by a sudden scream from below. Without looking at each other, Junco and I both fled down the rickety stairs. Or rather, I fled, he flew. A terrible banging was coming from the front door. The door was nailed shut, but that didn't seem to disturb whoever was on the other side. The door splintered in on itself, revealing an entire squad of the queen's soldiers. Or I thought they were at first; on second glance, half the livery was of the green and gold of Hiedelen's guards. I felt a stab of anger. Of course; my spell puts half the soldiers to sleep, so what does the royalty do? Just go and get more! People were expendable to royals.

Junco turned and fled from the room, no doubt unwilling to be seen amidst this company when he was supposed to be hightailing it back to Fortress Frost. I muttered a spell to try and make myself invisible, as did half the people in the sitting room. Unfortunately, most of the members of the club weren't very powerful, and shadow spells, illusions, and misdirection of attention weren't effective when two dozen trained soldiers in full armour, wielding clubs and crossbows, came storming into a known hideout at high noon. No doubt they'd known that when they came bursting in.

I could have escaped. I should have escaped, frankly. It wasn't as if anyone at the club had ever treated me with any special friendship. I tried to slip out the sitting room and toward the kitchen, but I heard more soldiers at that end of the house, and a few screams from someone I thought was the alchemist, an old man who mostly brewed potions to make small explosions for stage plays and poison rats. Real heart of the criminal world, him. A loud pop made me think that maybe he had a little more fire power than they'd bargained for when they grabbed at his wizened frame.

I was debating finding a window when I saw the whore grabbed from behind by a scarred soldier, who pushed her up against the wall. She was particularly fetching today, all dark hair and red lips. His intentions, when I saw him grappling with her clothes, were obvious. The whore did the only thing she could think of and let go of her glamour. Suddenly he found himself holding a misshapen, mousy-haired wretch with a cleft palate and a crumpled nose. He looked ill, and took out his frustration with his club on her face. The whore moaned, and a crunch told me the soldier had joined the ranks of men who had broken her nose at one time or another. It was a terrible sound.

I lost my temper. My only coherent thought was that could have been my sister. I rushed forward, snarling with every animal instinct of a fox faerie, and launched myself at the man, biting at his throat. He started, surprised by my assault, and dropped his club. Unfortunately, he gathered his wits fairly quickly and pulled out a blade. At the first cut of my flesh on my hip I twisted in his arms, bringing my knee into his groin. Unfortunately, he had armour there, and I bruised myself, but I also hurt him enough that he let go of my shoulder. I twisted, snarling with the pain, and elbowed him in the throat. He fell to the ground, choking, but probably able to recover. I reached down and pulled the blade from his hand.

I don't know if I meant to kill him with it or not. I had killed men before, always in defence of myself or my family, usually with their own weapons, and always in cases of extreme rage. The Nameless have poor impulse control. But before I'd even half decided, I was distracted by the face of the whore.

She still wore no glamour, blood streamed from her battered nose, and her face held the lines of hardship, but that did not disturb me. It was the look of sheer terror on her face. Her attacker was disabled, so it wasn't due to him. The cold air breathed over the top of my head, and I realized my foe had torn down my hood during the assault. There I was, faerie and Nameless for all to see. So far, only the whore had the opportunity to notice.

I'd seen that look before. A cross between disgust and horror. Then her expression changed to pure confusion, and I could guess what she was thinking. She couldn't decide whether or not to start screaming about me. She had a valid point; as far as popular opinion went, I was a thousand times more terrifying than any soldier, or any witch. If she'd suddenly announced me as a Nameless, all the soldiers would instantly abandon the other members of the club and make a beeline for me. Yet I had also just saved her, and the whore had a naturally generous heart. I could see her deciding whether or not to sacrifice me. Then her eyes opened wide as they focused on something over my head, and the decision was made. 'Behind you!' she squawked, her voice lisping without her glamour. I whirled and spied another soldier, red and white in Lyndarian livery this time, coming behind me with a club.

I ducked and twirled, hooking my leg around my assailant's ankle. He tripped and fell onto his recovering comrade. I grabbed the whore's shoulder, pushing her toward the guarded door. 'Medusa,' I hissed at her.

'What?' The hurt in her eyes would have been comical if I knew she hadn't been as insulted and harassed as I before she'd learned enough magic to conceal her face.

'Glamour,' I clarified. 'Make a glamour, a gorgon, some of them might think it's real.' I didn't have time to explain further, as another half dozen soldiers in assorted livery came streaming into the room from the hallway, some of them smoking from a tiny bomb the alchemist must have secreted about his person.

With sudden understanding the whore's eyes opened wide, and then turned an unpleasant shade of yellow. They grew large in her head, and her mousy hair began to move and writhe in the form of dozens of snakes, and her face . . . I was surprised to note she did not change her face much. She must have had utter hatred for her natural form. I found myself wishing that I could whip up a glamour that my own innate power wouldn't burn off in a few hours. I could have created an illusion on a human, but on myself it wouldn't last. It wouldn't have mattered much; my darkness would still have bled through.

The whore dashed away from me, roaring with false ferocity, and I lifted my hood and made to follow her. As I raised my leg, someone grabbed it. One of the soldiers I'd felled had grabbed hold of my ankle. I was unable to maintain my balance and fell, catching myself with my arms. I rolled, twisting my captor's wrist, and kicked my heel at his face. I missed his nose, which I'd been aiming at, and caught him instead in the forehead. He blinked, stunned, but unless I'd managed to concuss him, he probably wasn't hurt.

I didn't have time to check, however, as the whore had frightened the men at the door, and they were finding convenient excuses for getting out of her way. Some of them braved it out and threatened her with clubs, but she was hissing away some spell, and it seemed to disconcert them. The others had decided I was less of a threat, and determined to come at me instead.

They were on me in a second, before I'd even had a chance to get up. I clawed and bit and kicked with all the skills a lifetime of being hunted had taught me, but six strong men, when I was already forced onto the floor, were a bit much even for me. My arms were brought behind my back. I pulled and strained, but with a final and awful sounding click, a pair of iron manacles were slapped around my wrists.

I was moderately fortunate, there. The more earthen fae aren't as susceptible to iron poisoning as the more airy spirits.

I've been told that iron poisoning isn't as prevalent a problem among the fae as it was in my great-grandparents' time — there has been a lot of interbreeding with humans. Most who do spinning magic can actually use the properties of iron to heighten their work, using the inherent forces inimical to magic to channel and strengthen our spells through the iron spindle. It makes them harder to undo. I'd even been stabbed by iron on a regular basis, and while it does make me nauseated, I haven't died from it yet. But there isn't a single faerie, earthen or otherwise, who actually likes having the stuff bound around them. It did not burn at a touch or instantly make me lose all my magic or stop my heart or do any of the other myriad things that iron poisoning could do to a particularly sensitive faerie. What it did do was make me feel heavy and very tired. I think if I'd been glowing, my light would have dimmed a bit. But I was in shadow, so no one noticed.

Most of the soldiers continued to pursue other members of the club. One of them dragged me by my bonds to the hallway, where the alchemist and the witch were similarly bound. I thanked my stars that my hood hadn't been tossed down in my struggle this time. 'Over there!' the man said, throwing me against the wall. 'And any mumbling or spell chanting and I'll pierce you through.' He loaded his crossbow meaningfully and leaned against the wall.

'Caught you too, eh?' the witch muttered.

'My own fault. I wasted time with the whore.'

'She get out?' the witch asked.

'Think so,' I said. 'Didn't have time to look.'

'I said no talking!' our guard snapped. The witch and I both frowned at him. 'And don't look at me with those evil eyes!'

I rolled my evil eyes and considered the iron that lashed my hands around my back. My magic wasn't strong enough to rid myself of them without a spindle. It was really a curse needing tools, sometimes. I looked at our guard. 'What are you going to do with us?' I asked.

The man shook his head and blinked at me. Was he drunk, or trying to place me? Oh, hell, he wasn't one of the market guards, was he? We really had to leave Lyndaron and find some other city, we were getting too well known here. Was I in shadow? I couldn't tell.

'The boy asked a question,' the witch asked, rattling her chains. 'What are you going to do with us?'

'Prison!' the guard spat. 'What did you think? Foul beasts that you are. If I had my way, I'd see you all executed on the spot.' He fingered his crossbow. 'We are given permission to kill, should there be excessive resistance,' he said pointedly. He glared at me again. 'So don't try anything.'

I glanced over at the alchemist, who seemed about to pass out. I opened my mouth to give words of comfort, as I would have to the kit, but I realized that I had none to give. I sighed and looked back at our homicidal captor. His companions were up the stairs and in the basement and still chasing the few of us that had escaped down the snow crusted streets. This man was watching us alone. And as I stared at the man, he yawned.

I caught my breath. Yes! I *did* know this man. He'd chased me and my sister before in the market place. My Sleep was slowly trickling through the tendrils of my hatred, and was about to touch this man. I wished I had some way to control it, but I had no idea how, and no tools to experiment. If it took long enough for his companions to get back to us, we could get up and sneak out from under his sleeping nose. We'd still be chained, but at least we'd be away from that crossbow.

A violent shudder from the alchemist caused me to look over at him. 'Are you all right?'

'My heart's not good, lad,' he wheezed, more loudly than before.

'I said no talking!' With a crack the crossbow shot its bolt. It is possible that our captor had aimed for the spot between the two of us, and was too addled by the Sleep to get it right. Whatever he meant to do, the bolt pierced my shoulder, effectively pinning me to the wall with a thud. I let out a brief second of an agonized scream, followed by a stream of curses which had both the witch and the alchemist staring at me in bewilderment. Half the curses had been faerie ones. I hissed and tried to pull myself from the wall. The pain shot through me in a thousand lightning bolts, and I gave up that idea. Panting with the pain, I glared at the soldier, who gaped at me, his eyes dull. Then, as if he was the one who had been shot, he sank to his knees and fell into an unwakeable Sleep.

'Serves you right, you currish, hell-witted hedge pig, may you dream of cramps and bone-gnawing starvation, and chew your own murderous arm off in your sleep!' I growled. The witch whistled, impressed. 'Oh, shut up,' I snapped, glaring at her. I listened. The kitchen seemed quiet. I glanced toward the door. 'Get out of here while you still can.'

'But you, lad,' the alchemist said, his voice wavering. I think he'd realized that bolt might just as easily have gone through him.

The look I gave him made him back up a step, his chains clanking.

'He's off for it, Ed,' the witch muttered, hoisting herself to her feet. 'And he knows it, too.'

'I said to shut your mouth,' I growled at her.

The alchemist wasn't hearing that, though. With his old hands, which were in truth younger than mine, he tried to pull the bolt from the wall. It felt like he'd stabbed me with a red hot poker. I think I screamed as my vision went black around the edges, and I definitely let loose with another round of insults.

'Off with you!' someone grunted through my stream of vitriol. 'I'll take care of him.' The sounds of clanking chains indicated that the witch and the alchemist had obeyed.

I blinked to clear my head, and was blinded by white light. 'Get the marrow out of here, Winnowinn! This isn't your fight, remember? You're only banished to your fastness.'

'Oh, shut up,' Junco said, echoing my tone exactly. He blew on my wound and a sudden blessed coolness numbed my entire left arm, including my screaming shoulder. I couldn't hold back a sigh of relief. He pulled the bolt from me with a sudden twist, and I was loose from the wall. I felt nothing but icy numbness from the wound.

I took a deep breath. 'Why didn't you fly out from the Observatory?'

'I did,' he muttered, examining my wound. 'Have you ever heard a Nameless faerie scream before? It isn't a pleasant sound.'

'No, it's not,' I growled. 'And yes, I think I might have heard the sound once or twice.'

'Oh, seven hells, this isn't going to be pretty,' Junco muttered.

'Neither are you,' I taunted, my teeth chattering with the cold.

He glared at me and slapped my arm. I groaned through my teeth. Heat and pain flooded back through my body. 'Sorry,' he said. 'You'll freeze to death if I keep that in place.'

I gritted my teeth. At least the bolt wasn't inside me any more, but it was possible I'd bleed to death before I managed to close the wound. Particularly without a spindle. Oh, *why* did I have to waste my only spindle on revenge? Why hadn't I taken the time to make a new one? 'Why are you helping me? You don't even like me.'

'I may not like you, but if they catch you here, they'll kill you.' This was true.

'Why not let me die?' I snarled.

'Why not let you live?' he retorted. 'Far more heinous a punishment, yes? This is going to hurt.'

'It *already* hurts!' I snapped. I'd been pierced by crossbows before, and it always hurt.

Holding his hand to his lips Junco blew again, this time forming a long icicle which he wielded like a wand. I didn't know much about ice magic, so I had no idea what he was about to do. Good thing, because if I'd known I'd have tried to stop him. With a deft twist, Junco grabbed me around the neck, bending my head to the ground so that I couldn't run from him. And without ceremony, he forced the icicle deep into my wound.

I screamed with the icy pain of it. Junco would have been able to hold on to anybody else, but I was a faerie, and had been Nameless for most of my existence. I twisted out of his grip and whipped him in the face with the chain of my manacles. Junco hissed, backing up. 'Good Light, man, keep that stuff off me!' he shouted. He lowered his hand, revealing a nasty red welt on his cheek. Obviously, Junco was more sensitive to iron than myself.

'Not when arrogant ice faeries are trying to kill me!' I yelled back.

'Trying to save your worthless life! I can't believe you let yourself get caught in the first place. Couldn't you just spin your way out the wall or something?'

'How do you know that?'

'I'm no fool. I can spot someone's gift a mile away. Don't you have a spindle?'

'No.'

'Then you're going to need some help with the shackles, aren't you? Now don't move.'

I pulled away. 'When you nearly slaughtered me the last time? I don't think so!'

'How's your shoulder?'

I blinked. The pain had lessened, though my shoulder felt very cold. I glanced down. The place where the wound had been was filled with ice, that leaked the occasional drop of meltwater to join the bloodstains on my shirt. 'What did you do?' I asked.

'Patch job. I told you it wasn't going to be pretty. It should heal up in a day or so. Keep yourself warm. If you get too cold you'll just freeze solid.'

'Thanks for imbedding ice in me in the winter.'

'Best I could do,' Junco said. 'Better than bleeding to death. Now do you want the manacles off or not?'

I smiled, showing all my teeth. 'Yes, please,' I said, falsely congenial.

Another spell that wasn't pretty; Junco, muttering at the inelegance of the magic, forced ice into the lock until it clicked and broke. The iron bands fell with a clink at my feet. 'There,' Junco said. 'Now get the hells out of here, and don't come back!'

'No fear!' I snapped, jumping to leave. At the door I stopped. I grunted, hating myself before I'd even turned around. I glared at him, my eyes narrowed. 'Junco Winnowinn,' I said, giving him his full name. 'I suppose I am in your debt.'

Junco glared at me in turn. 'Pay it back by trying not to be an ass all the time,' he said. 'You can start by saying thanks.'

'I'll keep that in mind,' I said, and I turned to go again. 'Thanks,' I whispered, without turning around. He didn't reply. I didn't really want him to. I slipped out the club through the kitchen.

Of course, it couldn't be that easy.

'There's one of them!' someone shouted.

Faerie Light, why did there have to be more of them? Six guards, all with crossbows, waited at the end of the alley. The alchemist was held by one of them, but the witch seemed to have slipped past them. I was all out of magic. I held up my hands to surrender, but those crossbows looked serious. I couldn't take another shot, not if I expected to live. One of the bows snapped loose, a loose trigger or a warning shot, and the bolt pierced the snow between my feet. I closed my eyes, knowing that the moment they removed my hood I'd probably be killed anyway.

A burst of white fire flared up between me and my attackers, and a small hand pressed a pad of goat's hair into my palm. I wasted no time staring at the fibre. With a deft twist I spun a crude shield. Four crossbow bolts whizzed past me out of the fire. A fifth, aiming straight for my stomach, hit the goat's hair shield and burst into real orange fire, hissing as the ashes landed in the snow. 'Thanks,' I said to the kit.

'Don't thank me, just run,' the kit said, grabbing me by the sleeve. 'They just set the building on fire.' I looked up. Sure enough, smoke was wafting from the front facade. I hoped everyone had either escaped or been arrested, because the club was so dilapidated it was sure to collapse in on itself. 'Good!' I said. 'Can you make it bigger?'

She frowned. 'I can make it look bigger. Why?'

'Distraction. If they're all busy fighting the fire they started, they won't have time to chase us.'

The kit shrugged and threw her hands at the flames. The flickering orange flames and the black smoke was quickly joined by a series of glowing white fires that took up artfully on the houses surrounding the club. She laughed wickedly as the false flames took.

We ran off together away from the burning club.

'What are you doing here?' I asked when we were sufficiently far away to no longer draw suspicion.

'You may not have any foresight, but our ma does,' the kit said.

'I thought she lost it when Da left.'

'No. She just didn't want to admit that he wasn't ever coming back. She saw you die about an hour ago, told me to go and stop it.'

'Oh,' I said. 'Die? Really die?'

'She seemed to think so.'

'It was just a crossbow bolt through the shoulder. Junco patched me up.'

'Junco Winnowinn?'

'Yeah. I'll be half frozen for the next two days, thanks to him.' And also alive.

'She didn't say you were shot,' the kit said. 'She said you died.'

I ran my tongue over my teeth, considering this. 'I'm alive,' I finally said. There didn't seem to be anything else to say on the subject, but the prediction made me nervous. 'What made you think of the goat's hair?'

'All I could find between our burrow and the club.'

I let the matted piece of hair fall. Goat hair didn't bind as well as wool, but it would work once. 'It did the trick. Thanks. You go tell our ma I'm all right.'

'Where are you going?'

'I have a promise to keep, remember?'

'But you're bleeding.'

'Not any more. I'm fine.' I kissed her forehead and left the road, taking the fastest route to the enchanted forest.

I entered from the south-west, a good two miles from where our burrow was. The snow was thin on the ground beneath the trees, and the stillness was unnerving. Unlike my little corner of the forest, there were no winter birds, and the tree tops were too far above for the wind to sing through them.

I had always felt the trees watching me, listening to me. I could only hope that Junco was right. I walked quickly through the forest. 'Mistress Cait!' I called. 'I'm calling on you!' I kept calling out for more than an hour. Suddenly I laughed. This was useless. My only consolation was that there wasn't anyone else around me to see me act the fool. The forest was just as uninviting as ever. I was hung up on briars, caught in snow drifts, confused by eerie sounds and generally led astray by every possible method. 'Mistress Cait! I'm calling on you on behalf of the princess of Lyndaria!' Nothing. The winter forest didn't even seem to be listening, by now.

'Damn you,' I muttered. 'I risk my life for that thrice-blasted princess, and what am I to get in return? Not even her gratitude, I'll bet. If she hadn't offered me the books, I'd never have done it. Waltzing up to *my* burrow, dreadful as it is, presuming I'd risk myself for her. What's she got to worry about, up in her pristine tower? She's got food and fires. She *knows* who *she* is. Princess Willow Lyndal, second in line to the throne of Lyndaria. Presuming my spell is ever broken and she isn't the heir presumptive. She certainly has all the qualities of a princess. But here I am, I promised to find you for the princess of Lyndaria, and I have no idea why the hell I'm doing this, because I'm the one who caused the damned sleep in the first place. I'm standing on my own in the middle of an empty forest talking to TREES!' I slipped and landed face down in the snow. I growled with frustration. 'Damn you, witch!' I yelled. 'Why couldn't you have a front door to knock on like anyone else!'

You know, said a voice from the trees, *just because we let you pass through the forest doesn't mean you can insult me at will.*

I surged to my feet. 'Mistress Cait?' It hadn't quite sounded like a real voice. It was a clicking whisper of the wind through the barren winter forest. 'Mistress Caital, was that you?'

In a manner of speaking, whispered the trees.

'You must have known I was in your forest,' I said. 'Why haven't you spoken earlier?'

You haven't told us what you wanted until now.

'I'm here on behalf of—'

This is only an echo, said the trees. *Your true message must be relayed in person. I cannot truly hear you.*

I looked about me. The forest all looked alike. 'Where are you? Which direction?'

My tower is in the centre of the forest.

'Where is that?' I asked. I'd gotten completely turned around as the trees shifted about me.

Follow my wolf. She will lead you.

I looked about me. A slim grey wolf stepped out from the shadow of the tree. She shone in the dark forest as if she stood in bright sunlight, like a faerie. One who wasn't Nameless, anyway. I liked her. 'Hello,' I said. I held my hand out for her to smell. She sniffed it for a moment, and then she bit me. I yelped, snatching my hand back. A few drops of blood spilled onto the snow. 'Guess I know better than to pet a wolf,' I said, no longer liking her in the least. 'Lead the way, she said.'

The wolf looked over her bony shoulder and loped off.

I was hard pressed to keep her in sight as I followed, despite her shining. She ran like the wind itself, dashed and wove between the trees. Half the time she left no footprints at all, and even running as fast as a faerie can run, her four legs were faster than my mere two. I'd wanted to try and mark the trees, or at least the direction of the sun, but we seemed to be going in twists and spirals, as if I was being spun into the centre of the forest.

We came upon the tower so suddenly that I almost ran past it. It stood all by itself, with no garden or ruins to mark it. It looked very much like the immense trees we were running past, but I realized it was made of greyish brown stone instead of greyish brown wood, and it had no branches. It towered above me, and I blinked at it. At first I thought there was no door, but the wolf snapped at my ankle, and I sidled away from her against the wall of the tower. The moment I touched the wall it moved beneath my weight, and warm firelight touched my shadowed hand. I poked my head inside, knowing already that in this bright room my darkness would stick out like ink on blotting paper.

The wolf, however, did not share my worries and harried me inside the chamber. Quite deliberately, she leaned on the door after I entered, closing it behind us. The room was filled with plants and vines, some of them dried for winter, but most of them alive and writhing. Even the furniture seemed to be made of living plants. Stunted trees that were shaped like low benches, climbing vines that held lamps and lanterns, a flowering shrub that held a round tabletop. Apart from the plants, everything was in disarray. Dead bouquets lay dustily in the corner, and half-empty teacups still teetered precariously on the edges of shelves or collected mould beneath the benches.

All of this disarray was punctuated by the figure that must have been Mistress Cait herself. The faerie woman was tall, taller than me, but willowy. Her wings were small in comparison, and a deep moss green. Her hair was green and brown, and at the moment there were dead sticks in it. I frowned at those sticks. No, those weren't dead. They were dormant. Cait actually had vines as part of her hair, and they were leafless now, for winter. Her skin was brown and soft, like earth, and her eyes were the bright green of new leaves. They didn't quite focus on me as she said, 'Ah. I was wondering when you'd make your way here. Taken you at least fifty years longer than I would have thought. Care for some tea?'

I blinked. 'Tea?'

'Yes. Tea. It's a hot drink. I make it from dried leaves boiled in water.'

'I know what tea is,' I said angrily.

'Oh, you do?' She looked almost disappointed. 'Well, I have some ready here. Let me get it for you.' She went to a hedge on the wall and tapped it a few times. It moved and writhed, and slowly, from somewhere deep in its depths, pulled out two teacups and a steaming teapot. Then, without any further instruction, it began to lay the tea things out on the table. Within a few minutes the shrubbery table was laid with an elegant tea, complete with tablecloth and tea cakes. Mistress Cait gestured for me to sit down, but the hedge wasn't finished yet. It pulled out crumpets and jam and a set of linen napkins. 'That's enough,' Cait muttered. The hedge dragged a candelabrum from its innards and set it in the middle of the table, and was just reaching for the fire to light it when Cait slapped it. 'You'll set the house on fire again!' she told it, and the tendrils retreated quietly back into the hedge. 'You'll have to forgive her. We haven't had guests in over a decade. She does so love to show off!'

'Her?' I asked.

'My honeysuckle. She makes an excellent serving maid, though she's not as good at clearing as she is at setting.' She perched on what I had thought was a dead stump, which promptly grew roots the moment she sat on it and pulled her deftly up to the table.

I sat gingerly on what I hoped was a non-mobile low-trained tree limb, at just the right height for a bench. 'You were expecting me?' I asked.

'Of course. For years, now. I've always wondered why you hadn't come. When you came to live in my forest I thought, surely *now* he'll come to see his hostess, but no. Not once.'

'I've been looking for you nonstop for the last two weeks,' I said.

'No you haven't,' she said. 'You were wandering through my forest, disturbing my trees, stirring up my leafmould, but you weren't coming to see me.'

'Yes, I was,' I said. 'I'd been sent to get you by—'

She cut me off. 'You were sent?' She glared at the wolf for some reason. 'You didn't come on your own?'

'No,' I said. 'Was I supposed to have?'

Cait sighed and set down her teacup. 'Sad, really. Ah well, can't be helped. So, why did you come again? I forgot.'

'I haven't told you yet.'

'Oh.' She looked down at the wolf. 'So I didn't forget.'

The wolf turned her back on her and slunk up the stairs.

'Poor Ylva,' said Cait. 'She never will forgive me. So, you were saying?'

'I've been hired to find you by Princess Willow Lyndal,' I said.

'Hired? *She* hired *you*?' Mistress Cait laughed until she spilled her tea. 'Oh, this is bound to be interesting! Why did you agree to this?'

'She offered me something valuable in exchange,' I said. 'She needs me to give you a message.'

'And that is?'

'They need you at the palace at once,' I said.

'No they don't. I can't do anything for them.'

I blinked. 'You already know?'

'Know what?'

'You know that you can't help?'

'Can't help with what?'

I sighed. It was like talking to an imbecile. 'Princess Willow sent me because they need you at the palace to break a Sleep spell which has ensnared the princess.'

'Will?'

'No, not her. The other one.'

'Oh, *Lavender*.' Mistress Cait laughed. It sounded like the tinkling of bells. 'Of course she's gotten herself into trouble.' She eyed me curiously. 'But why did *you* come to give me this message?'

'Because the princess thought I could do it.'

'But why did you not refuse?'

'I told you, she offered—'

'Something valuable, so you said,' Mistress Cait said. 'But as valuable as what you'll lose should I do as she asks?'

I was confused. 'What do I lose?'

She tilted her head at me. 'What do you have to lose?'

I scoffed. 'Nothing.'

'Exactly,' she said, with a tone of triumph.

Somehow I thought I was missing at least one element of this conversation. I tried again. 'I was told to give you a message. You're needed at the palace.'

'By who?' she asked.

I felt like I was going to scream. 'By Princess Willow!' I barked.

'Oh, she'd have to ask me that herself,' said Mistress Cait. She turned back to her tea and pulled a crumb cake off the tray. 'Ylva! Come back down! He's your guest as much as mine.'

'Buff,' came a canine voice from the stairs.

'Oh, come now. Don't you feel just a *little* ashamed of yourself?'

With an angry snarl the wolf launched herself back down the stairs and began barking at Mistress Cait. Cait raised an eyebrow once or twice, but otherwise ignored the barrage of angry barks.

'I was trying to help,' Cait said when the barks finally ceased.

A low growl was the reply.

'Please yourself,' Cait said. 'But I'd want to get to know him.'

The wolf walked up to me and sniffed me. I narrowed my eyes at her. She bared her teeth. I growled. So did she.

'So much for that,' Cait said with a somewhat wistful sigh. She stood up. 'You go and get Will and bring her here,' she said. She pushed an empty canvas bag at me. 'Take this to your mother and sister.'

I frowned at her. 'How do you know . . . ?'

'I know all about you.' She smiled. 'You're living on my land. But I knew you even before that. I'm sure the kitling is hungry. Take this to her. And don't go wandering my forest unless you have the princess with you. She's the only one who can do anything, anyway.'

I clutched the bag. 'What in Light are you talking about?'

Mistress Cait sighed. 'This conversation is getting us nowhere,' she said, which I rather thought was my line. 'You go and get the princess and bring her here. Everything should come out all right by then.'

'Why can't you just come with me to the palace?'

Cait laughed her bell-like laugh. 'Oh, that wouldn't do at all! Truly my Nameless little fox faerie, I know it goes against your nature, not to mention your principles, but you really ought to try and do as you're told, at least once.' She took me by the shoulders and pushed me out the door. 'That way,' she said, pointing to my left. I looked to the left, and then turned, ready to demand that she explain herself. But this was her forest, and her tower was already out of sight. I sighed. If I'd still had my spindle, I could have woven a path for myself back to her, but it would have been a strain.

Fine. I guessed the only way to solve this mystery, and fulfil my promise to the kit, was to go and get Princess Willow. Very well. I set off in a direction, trusting to Caital's magics to lead me back to my burrow. My instincts served me well. In far less time than it had taken to get to Mistress Cait's tower, I tripped on a snow-shrouded root and found myself thrown almost violently into the spider glade.

I went back to the burrow, where I found my mother outside in the cold, trying to add to the pitiful stack of deadwood we used for our fire. She looked up at me with profound relief the moment I came into sight. 'Oh, praise the Light! I thought I'd lost you!' She ran forward and hugged me.

I grunted. She'd pressed on my icy wound. I'd almost forgotten the thing, but the pressure reminded me with a vengeance. 'I'm well enough, leave off,' I muttered, pushing her away. 'Didn't the kit tell you I was fine?' Then I realized I was being rude. 'Thanks for sending her. She saved my hide.'

'She told me you were injured.' She pounced on my bloodstained shoulder.

'I said leave off. It was just a crossbow bolt. I've lived through worse.'

'I've barely dragged you through worse,' my ma reminded me.

'Well, Junco Winnowinn's patched it with an icicle, or something of the kind.'

My ma insisted she be told every detail of the raid at the club, and I told her what I wished to. I was a bit ashamed of myself for wasting my chance at escape by saving the whore, so I left that bit out.

'And Winnowinn helped you? Oh, that's a good sign.'

I frowned. 'A good sign of what?'

'Maybe they'll accept us back into society, dear. I'd love to see another Light ceremony before I pass on.'

'Not in a hundred years,' I muttered.

She looked at me frankly. 'We both know I might not have that much time,' she said.

I searched her face. She was looking old. 'Let me make you a spindle,' I pleaded, not for the first time. 'Just a little one.'

'I can't take the risk, dear heart. Someone needs to be here for your sister, and with you putting yourself in harm's way all the time . . .'

'I only do it because you won't!' I snapped. 'What's wrong with you? Why don't you *fight*?'

My ma blinked at me. 'Why do you fight all time?' she asked. She sighed. There were new lines on her face, come since my Sleep had come over the palace.

'I'm sorry, my ma,' I heard myself say, and was surprised that it wasn't a lie.

'Brother!' The kit slid out of the burrow to wrap me in a hug herself. She stepped back almost instantly. 'What's that?'

I glanced down at the empty canvas bag. 'Something Cait pressed on me as I was leaving. Don't know why. It's empty.'

'Mistress Cait? You found her?'

'Aye.'

The kit had taken the bag from my shoulder and opened it. 'By the Light!' she breathed. She pulled out a roast chicken on a wooden plate, surrounded by carrots and buttery turnips, still steaming. 'She gave you a faerie gift!'

I blinked. I'd heard of faerie gifts before, but I myself had never had the leisure time or the excess wool to set about making one. The bottomless horn of spirits, the harps that played music on their own devices for all eternity, or, such as this, a never-empty bag of food. A continual spell on an object like that took a great deal of time and quite a bit of power. 'Let me see that.' I pulled the bag back and examined the seams. Why would Caital have given us something as precious as this? There didn't seem to be a time limit on the spells, which meant it would provide food forever, at least until the bag itself wore out. There was only a limited number of spells twisted into the seams – this magic was close enough to my spinning magic that I could read it fairly easily – no more than twenty or so, and most of them appeared to be vegetable dishes. Not surprising, given Caital's apparent green sorcery. I reached inside and drew out a loaf of crusty white bread and a bowl of steamed shelled peas.

'Oh, thank you Mistress Cait!' the kit cried at the trees.

My ma, however, was not impressed. 'High time she felt some sympathy.' She snatched at the bread and broke it evenly, handing a piece to each of us. 'I'll only eat her food because we've nothing else, but she does not hold my gratitude.'

'Why not?' the kit asked, her mouth full of chicken leg.

'She wasn't much help when they stripped me of my name, now was she?' my ma snapped, and she slipped back into the burrow hurriedly.

I shook my head. 'I don't understand her.'

'She was about to cry,' the kit said. I hadn't noticed. 'She misses other fae.'

I sighed. 'Give me some of that chicken,' I said. I pulled a breast off and folded it into my piece of bread. 'I won't be back until late.'

'Where are you going?' the kit asked.

'I have a promise to fulfil, remember?' I reminded her. 'Now that I've found Caital, I have to take the princess to see her. That's me, the nameless errand boy for the royalty.'

The kit grinned around her bread. 'I'm sure Will doesn't see you like that,' she said, and took a big bite.

It didn't matter much. That's how I was seeing myself, and it made me feel strange.

An hour later I was sitting in a rose-steeped palace, couched in shadow on a beam of the ceiling, staring down in awe at the most beautiful sight I'd ever seen. It was not riches or gold, it was not fine art, it was not arrangements of roses or flowers, and it certainly wasn't some member of the royal house. It was an antique spinning wheel, fashioned out of briskly oiled dark oak, kept impeccably by palace servants. This was my great-aunt's infamous spinning wheel, the one that had cast Princess Amaranth into her century-long sleep. The 'deadly spindle' had been removed, but even from a distance I could see that someone who knew nothing about spinning wheels had supervised this. A second spindle, and even two spools for winding thread, were attached to the base of the wheel, so naturally formed that they appeared part of the design. The wheel had been fashioned with its spare parts inclusive. No doubt this spindle was for either finer or coarser work than the one that had been removed, and the attachments of the spools would allow for easy plying of yarn. If I'd had any wool I could have sat down at that wheel and been spinning in less than a minute.

I was positively drooling with envy. I hadn't seen a spinning wheel in over seventy years. Even the sight of it made me long to feel the wood under my hands, the pull of the living wool, the even click of the pedal under my foot. It was more beautiful and more seductive than any woman. If I could have, I'd have walked off with the thing right there, hang the princess, hang the Sleep, hang Mistress Cait, and hang – until it died in agony – the thrice-cursed law against spinning. But unfortunately, the wheel was locked behind an iron gate – a kind of cage – perched in stationary splendour beneath the royal crowns and the fine jewels of the Lyndal family.

Moreover, two guards stood at attention on either side of this vault. I'd had difficulty enough sneaking past the guards at the front gate. The thorns were angry, and hungrier than I'd ever seen them. They'd even caught at my jacket, no doubt longing for the blood that still stained it. I'd twisted two of the sharp strands together in a primitive spin, causing the thorns to quiver in consternation and release me, but I wouldn't have wanted to be caught in the midst of them without my spindle.

I reminded myself that I wasn't going to be able to drool over the spinning wheel all night. Not if I wanted to fulfil my promise to that wretched princess. And it was at that moment that I heard the sounds of a chase from the hallway, and a woman's voice shouting, 'Kill her!'

The two guards glanced at each other knowingly before resuming their rigid stance. Contempt surged. They were paid good money to guard things. Didn't they ever guard people? Apparently not *this* person, whoever it was. A terrible foreboding gripped me. I slipped over the rafters and out the door, leaving a heartfelt curse in my wake. The two guards suddenly drew their weapons, looked around in fear for my disembodied voice, but I wasn't going to waste time playing with them. Someone down the corridor was screaming.

Chapter 12

Will

Will was a bride. By tomorrow evening, she would be a wife. It felt like an sentence of execution.

That was probably why she was here again, standing at Lavender's bedside. Prince Ferdinand was, mercifully, asleep on his couch. Will was pretty sure the Sleep hadn't overtaken him, because his face was peaceful.

She knew she shouldn't do it, but she couldn't help it. She crept to his side and knelt beside him. His strong, handsome features were softened now, in sleep. His cheeks were pink, and his fine hair was tousled. She wanted to say he looked like a little boy, but he didn't. He looked like a *man*, the kind of man her husband-to-be was not, and – it seemed at the time – never would be. She could have stared at him all night.

He shifted in his sleep and made a small masculine sound that made Will's heart quicken. She wanted to curl up beside him. Instead she contented herself with reaching out her hand to brush a lock of hair from his face. He twitched, and she half feared, half hoped he would open his eyes. For a brief second the whole scene played out in her head. He would open his eyes sleepily, and find her bending over him. In a dream state their lips would meet. He would be unable to control himself. They'd fall in a breathless, clutching tumble to the carpeted floor, right beside her Sleeping sister, who would never, ever awaken.

In reality he shifted himself until his back was towards Will and began snoring gently.

She laughed at herself. Despite all her attempts to quash it, this love for Ferdinand was relentless! *And damned silly*, she thought.

No. She knew she had to marry Narvi on the morrow. And she knew that she would have to endure many long nights before she really had a husband. And, even then, she wouldn't love him.

Deprived of Ferdinand's beautiful sleeping face, she turned back to her sister. Lavender was twitching again in her sleep. What was she dreaming? Every dream was different. Will bit her lip. What if she started screaming again? There was no one here to pull her from the dream. And it was magic. Everyone would know that she had broken the injunction. No. She determined not to try.

Then a little imp whispered in her ear, *why not*? If the Sleep overtook her, if the dreams drove her mad, she wouldn't have to marry Narvi on the morrow, and Hiedelen surely couldn't blame Lyndaria for it.

In the end, she had to know. The horror of the dreams was like dragon wine – too strong to stomach, but she always wanted more. She reached for Lavender's forehead and closed her eyes. She searched for, and found, her dream-sharing spell.

I'm hungry. A terrible gnawing monster is wrestling in my stomach. I'm so hungry I'm chewing on discarded bones, like a dog. They are rancid and have been thrown in the dirt, but I'm desperate. I gnaw on them like an animal, and try to wrestle against myself. There is no such thing as dignity where hunger is concerned. I crack the bone and am thrilled to discover rancid, fatty marrow inside. I cut my tongue trying to lick it out. If I could sell myself into slavery to keep myself from this kind of hunger, I would. But there is no choice. No one would even be willing to keep me a slave.

Will opened her eyes, feeling sick. There was no terror there, no pain, but the hunger and the shame and the self-loathing were worse than those. She could still almost taste the rancid bones she'd been desperately gnawing. Nausea writhed inside her. She poured herself a cup of Ferdinand's violet water and rinsed her mouth. What *were* those dreams? She was always the same person in them, and she wasn't herself, but she didn't know *who* she was, either. The faces were indistinct when she tried to remember them. Most of the faces of her pursuers were generic, interchangeable. There were others in the dreams, those she loved, had to protect, and not being able to keep them safe was part of the horror. But their faces always eluded her. Her own character eluded her.

Will took a deep breath. It was foolish, really, she thought. It was just a series of the most horrible things one's mind could conjure, meant to make the Sleep less a rest than a punishment.

She paused at that thought. A punishment? Who would send a Sleep as a punishment? Well, who would want to punish Lavender?

I would, she realized. *I'd want her punished for stealing all the better virtues, winning the love of the kingdom, being perfect in every way, having Ferdinand. I'd want her punished for burning my book, for not letting me indulge my magic.* Will hadn't cast this Sleep upon Lavender, or upon anyone, nor would she. But if it wasn't an accident, what was it? And who would have cast it?

Will debated touching her again to try and find out, but she couldn't bring herself to endure another session of her nightmares. Not yet, anyway. She knew they'd call her again soon enough. Instead she banked the fire in the grate and left the chamber.

185

The halls were dark and echoed without the myriad footmen and servitors. The palace seemed deserted. Spider webs were beginning to grace the corners, as the regular staff dropped off to Sleep one by one, leaving their half-trained apprentices and completely new hires to perform twice as much work as usual. The smell of roses was tainted with dust. The West Wing, Will knew, smelled of decay as the Sleeping bodies sweated in their nightmares. Will was in a nightmare herself, wandering empty corridors, awaiting a life of loneliness.

She heard something strange coming from the corridor. Some kind of commotion. She figured someone else must have fallen asleep, and hurried on to help.

When she turned the corner she did not see what she had expected – someone prone on the floor. Instead, she saw her bedroom door open, and half a dozen of her things strewn on the floor. A hand mirror, her black cloak, and quite a number of her books – all innocent ones, as her magic books were still hidden behind her closet. Will's chambermaid was sunk to her knees just beyond the pile, in tears. Will rushed over to her. She looked up in horror. 'I'm sorry, mistress! I didn't know what they were about! Randy kept on at me and on at me, and I just let him in to have a look! I didn't know he was going to—'

She was drowned out as someone poked her head out the door and glared at Will. 'There she is!'

Will drew herself up to her considerable height. 'What is all this? I demand an explanation!' She recognized the intruder to her chambers. It was her sister's head lady-in-waiting, a pretty but loud little thing called Ginith. She did not look chagrined. 'I presume you're the vandal who keeps scrawling illiterate insults upon my door? I hope you realize what kind of trouble you have brought for yourself, young woman. Do not think that this will go unpunished.'

Ginith smiled at Will in a way she was sure she didn't like, and Will soon found out why. The lady was quickly flanked by an entire crowd of castle members – youths, mostly. Will recognized two of the stable hands. A collection of three girls with stained aprons Will assumed were scullery maids, and that nasty underchef called Bethel were with them. Two more of Lavender's ladies-in-waiting followed, looking unsure of themselves, followed by the falconer's assistant, a youth who had lost his eye last year showing off to a lady by keeping the lethal creature on his shoulder. Ginith smiled at the falconer's assistant. 'Get her,' she said, her voice deadly quiet. The crowd made a move, almost as one.

Will was no fool. She ran, pelting down the corridor, her skirts flying behind her. She could hear them chasing her, their voices echoing round the empty hallways. She called out but there was no one awake to hear her. At least no one inclined to help.

Compared to Lavender, Will was fast, strong and vigorous. Compared to the palace stable hands and the iron-armed scullery maids, she was pampered and soft. They called things out to each other as they followed close behind. 'Head her off!' 'To the left! The left!' Ginith, trailing behind the more sturdy members of her mob, calling, 'What are you waiting for? Grab her!' and the falconer muttering, 'We'll get you, witch!' Will couldn't run fast enough. Her shoes were slick palace slippers, and she would have traded her left arm for a pair of boots. She tried to turn a corner, skidded, and lost momentum. Within a few more steps she felt a beefy hand clutch at her arm, and she was jerked to a halt. Strong bodies pushed her against a wall, and she was surrounded on three sides by the mob.

They held her there for long moments. None of them seemed to have any sense of what to do with her now that they'd caught her. They were angry and scared, not at all assured that what they were doing was right. Ginith was apparently the leader of this rabble, and she and the other ladies were trailing behind the main group. One of the scullery maids seemed ashamed of herself. 'It'll be all right, miss,' she said. 'We just want to talk to yas.'

'Aye, and then we'll cut her throat,' muttered the falconer. 'That'll end the spell.'

Someone elbowed him in the ribs. 'Don't anger the witch!'

'She'll give you the evil eye,' the scullery maid said.

'You don't know what you're talking about,' Will said, trying to muster some nobility. 'Are you under the impression that I have something to do with this Sleep that is infecting the palace?'

'Aye,' snapped a different scullery maid. 'And we'll see you do something to stop it!'

'If only I could,' Will tried to explain.

'Don't let her talk!' Ginith shouted behind them. 'She'll bewitch you with her spells!'

Will rolled her eyes, 'Oh, please. Magic doesn't work like that—' But she didn't get the chance to explain how it did work. The falconer's assistant grabbed her by the back of her hair and yanked. Will's coif collapsed with a ripping sound, and she didn't pretend it didn't hurt. He had twisted her as he grabbed her hair, so she went with the turn, catching him with her body and throwing him against the wall. He lost his hold on her, and Will, still twisted half to the ground, butted him in the stomach. Or tried to. She missed, and he made a very painful sound as her head connected with a different part of his body.

'Kill her!' Ginith screamed, still some ways down the corridor. Someone reached for Will, and she stomped on his foot. Still crouched, she tried to push through the mob, but the stable hands grabbed her arms, none too gently. Seeing the falconer curled in agony on the floor, she intentionally kneed one of them in the groin, and tried to elbow the other one away.

Will might have been half a head taller than the tallest of them, and she certainly made them pay for capturing her. But in the end, she was simply outnumbered. Then Bethel pulled a carving knife from her apron and brandished it toward Will's face. She stopped struggling. That blade was wickedly sharp, and she had no weapons.

Wait. That wasn't true. She had one weapon at her disposal – fear. She narrowed her eyes and bared her teeth, groaning like a beast. Then she started reciting gibberish. 'Mole sweat and toads' tongues, bats' blood and aprons!' The hands that held Will's wrists loosened, and she tore her arms away, raising her fingers like claws. The underchef was frightened white. Her hand holding the carving knife trembled, and she took a step back as Will advanced on her.

'She's bluffing!' Ginith said, finally catching up, and she launched herself at Will, prepared to scratch her eyes out with her long nails. Apparently tricks wouldn't work on Ginith. Will raised her fist and bloodied her nose. The other lady's maids squealed hysterically in horror, worried that the poor lady would be disfigured for life! (Somehow, Will losing an eye wasn't as worrisome to them.)

She glanced at the underchef, the biggest threat with her knife. But she was frozen in panic with their leader bloodied. Will pushed past the whimpering ladies and ran again.

Then she heard it, from behind her. Ginith, her voice slurred from her broken nose, shouting out, 'Any one of you catches her, I'll see you get an hour alone with Princess Lavender!'

That disgusting whore, selling out the princess's virtue! Will would have to tell Ferdinand – she was pretty sure he was always with her, but they'd have to be sure. The offer revitalized the men in the mob, and Will heard boots clomping after her. Will's stamina was gone. She was grabbed, thrown to ground, and a boot planted firmly on her back. Someone twisted her arms behind her and bound her hands. There was only one thing left to do, and that was scream. Will opened her mouth with a scream that would make a dragon cover its ears. As they hauled her onto her back she screamed even louder. Puffing with the exertion, Bethel the underchef joined her captors and pulled a truly gruesome kitchen rag from her apron pocket. With deft hands, she gagged Will with it. It tasted of rancid bacon and stale breadcrumbs. Will screamed around it, but the sound was terribly muffled.

Ginith came up behind them, then. Will was trussed up like a pig on a spit, and Ginith was terrifying. She held the underchef's blade in one hand, and her eyes held a strange light above the bloodied wreck of her face. 'You are going to bleed, witch!' Ginith mumbled.

Will could see it in her eyes. Ginith was really going to kill her. A burbling spring inside Will sank to her stomach, and she felt ill. All her strength was gone, all her wit was bound, all her fascinating, pretty, useless spells, none of them could save her life. She closed her eyes, awaiting the blow.

Then she heard a scream. A collective scream, as every one of her attackers cried out in alarm. She opened her eyes to a sudden inferno of orange-white fire, so bright it nearly blinded her.

Fire engulfed the hallway, and Will's captives scattered in panic through the flames. Many backed away, one fell to her knees, crying and trying to smother the flames which surrounded her body. Out of the blinding fire a hand grabbed the back of Will's dress and hauled her backwards. She shrieked and lashed out, trying to escape this new captor. He cursed and cuffed her lightly, grabbing her roughly by her bound hands. 'Come on!'

It was only then that she recognized the voice. Reynard? She would have called the name out, but she was gagged. Was it Reynard? What was he doing here? Will let him take her, then, though she was barely able to walk.

Reynard dragged her down a corridor and into an alcove three turns from her pursuers. It was the kind of alcove where courtiers had sinister intrigues and secret assignations, so there was a convenient bench which Reynard threw her ungently into. 'There,' Reynard said. He knelt down and bit at the binds which held her wrists shut. To Will's surprise, they parted under his teeth. 'You undamaged?'

Will pulled the foul-tasting gag from her mouth the moment her hands were free. She spat and scraped her tongue against her teeth. 'Yes,' she said, her mouth pulled in distaste. 'Well enough, anyway.'

'Can you walk? That won't keep them forever, and they're probably already looking for you.'

Will poked her head out of the alcove, but he had made too many turns, and she saw only darkness up the corridor. A tiny tongue of orange fire was flickering from her hand. 'The fire doesn't hurt,' she said, examining it. 'You did this?'

'No, I suspect it arriving exactly at the same time as I called it down was a complete coincidence.' He looked at her flickering hand. 'Just shake it off. It sticks to magic.' He ran his hand down hers and the cold flame died.

Will felt a little shaky. Between nearly being killed and then suddenly being engulfed in an inferno, she supposed that wasn't overly surprising. 'H–how did you do that?'

'It's only foxfire,' Reynard said. Will suppressed a smile. Of course Reynard knew foxfire. She'd seen a spell for it in one of her books, but she hadn't been able to make it work. 'It's harmless. My sister does it better than I can – mine always die quickly, and stay small. I didn't want to deal with repercussions if I actually hurt them.'

'No, that's *great*,' Will said. 'For all of me you could have killed them!'

He blinked at her. 'I could go back,' he offered. Will wasn't sure he meant that or not.

'No,' she said. 'I'd rather stay with you.' He scoffed at that. 'I'm just glad to get away from them,' she clarified.

'Did they really mean to do what I thought they meant?'

'To kill me?' He nodded, and Will laughed shakily. 'I think some of them did. I think some of the others just meant to teach me a lesson. But if it had continued, I'm pretty sure it would have gotten out of control.'

'And you didn't have a single spell that could help?' The scorn in his voice was clear.

There was nothing to say to that, so Will just raised a hand in defeat.

He frowned. 'Why were they after you?'

She sighed. 'It's a long story.'

'You think I don't have time?'

'I think you'll probably agree with them.'

Reynard scoffed. 'If I agree with the majority of anyone who lives in this palace, I want you to hunt me down and hang my skin on the wall.' He glared at her. 'Honestly, Princess, how bad can it be?'

Will swallowed. 'They think I cursed my sister with the Sleep.'

Reynard raised his red eyebrows almost into his hood. 'Oh,' he said. He paused for a long moment. 'Seems a bit unfair. It would seem I was right to stop them, I suppose.'

Will laughed giddily. 'Aye,' she said. The burbling spring which had sunk to her stomach came burbling up again, causing strange fish to come swimming through her chest. She caught her breath and tried to laugh again, but no laugh came out. Just a hoarse, shaky wheeze, and her vision seemed grey.

Will only realized she had sagged because Reynard suddenly had to hold her upright. 'Oh, hells,' he said. He propped her up and made her rest her weight on him. 'Is there anywhere you feel safe?'

'My chambers, I think,' she said. 'I was on my way there, when . . . when . . . .'

Reynard interrupted, impatient. 'Aye, and where is it?'

'This way.' She pointed.

Reynard draped Will's arm around his shoulders and barked at her, 'You will *walk!*'

Will didn't know if the words carried some kind of spell or if it was just his irritation, but she found herself walking – shakily. 'Wh-where are you taking me?' Her voice shuddered along with her body.

'Somewhere safe where you can sit down. You'll need some water and food, if you can get some, and somewhere quiet for at least twenty minutes.'

She felt very ill. Her cheeks were hot and her breath came hard. Her heart was still beating wildly in her chest, and everything had taken on a sharp edge. She could see farther down the corridors, and she could hear everything. A mouse scuttling along the passage made her head jerk toward the sound. 'I think I'm sick.'

'You're not. Not really.'

'How do you know? What's going on?'

He frowned. 'My sister calls it going Chase Crazy. It's a type of panic you feel only after you've gotten to safety. Haven't you ever been in mortal danger before?'

'No.'

'Figures.' He turned the corner she had indicated and looked down the corridor. 'Which door is yours?' he asked. Then he stopped. 'Oh. I'd wager that one.' He began leading her toward her door.

It didn't take much to see what had tipped him off. Some of Will's things were still strewn in the corridor, and her door hung open. Moreover, it had the word 'Murderer!' scrawled on it in an unsteady hand. 'You gamble well,' Will said.

'One of my many gifts,' he said with a black humour. He shook his head. 'Don't you have better security than this?'

'Not enough guards,' Will panted. 'They keep falling asleep. And they don't want to help *me*.' She looked around. There was no sign of her chambermaid, though most of Will's more valuable things had been heaped in a pile by the foot of her bed. How very considerate of her.

Reynard grunted and pushed Will through the door, then closed it behind them. He still had her arm around his shoulder. It was very strange having her arm around someone who was tall as she was. Particularly as she always thought of Reynard as small, since he hunched so. As valiant as it seemed, he shrugged her off onto the couch without ceremony, as if he wanted her off him as quickly as possible. That seemed doubly certain as he then began brushing off the arm which had held her, as if she had lice.

Fortunately, the maid had lit the fire, so the room was at least warm. The warmth was bringing the rose scent out of carpets, and Will saw Reynard sniff, rubbing at his nose. He looked very irate and uncomfortable, like he wished he was someplace else. 'What are you doing here?' she asked.

'What do you think?' he said irritably. 'I told you I'd come get you when I knew how to find Mistress Cait. I'm here.'

'Just in time, by the way. Thank you.'

He paused. 'For what?'

Will swallowed. 'I'm pretty sure you just saved my life.'

He rubbed his face. 'Oh, the irony,' he said with a groan. 'Aye, I suppose I did. Too bad that doesn't change a thing.'

'It does for me.'

'Not for me.' He seemed very angry at her for some reason. He didn't seem like the man who she had met at the monument. He was more like what he'd been around his sister. She wondered if he'd been putting on an act when she saw him at the monument. She opened her mouth to ask him what she had done to make him hate her so, but he cut her off before she could speak. 'As soon as you stop shaking we can go.'

'Go?'

He scowled. 'To Faerie Caital's. That is why I'm here, after all.'

'You really found Mistress Cait?'

'You think I'd have risked my life to come and see you if I hadn't, Highness? No thank you, I'm not so fond of your company as all that.'

Will blinked at that. 'How *did* you get here?'

He lifted up a rip on his rumpled russet tunic. 'With some difficulty,' he said. Will supposed that meant this rip was new. She suddenly noticed stains on his russet jacket. They were almost the same colour as the dye, so she couldn't be sure, but she thought they were blood. Damned thorns. Before she could mutter sympathy, he went on, 'And I'm counting on your little stilling spell to get you out.'

'But you found Mistress Cait. Why can't she just come here?'

'She *won't*,' Reynard barked. 'She said to bring you to her. I said I would, because I'm a blasted fool, and I've a promise to keep. So let's go.'

Will shook her head. 'I can't.'

'What do you mean? I see no chains binding you to the walls.'

'But there are bars made of blood-sucking briars.'

'So? I made it past them. It isn't all that difficult.'

Will shook her head. 'They have a taste for royal flesh. It takes a troop of men armed with swords just to get any of us through the main gates now.'

'So, get your troop of armed men and let's go.'

'I can't.'

He took a deep breath and spoke slowly and patiently. 'You see, I'm not sure I follow you, Princess. I spend weeks trudging through a forest, risking my life, I nearly get murdered by your mother's guards, and when I finally find your precious Mistress Cait you say you won't go.'

'I didn't say won't. I can't. They've outlawed magic. Even Mistress Cait is almost a criminal now.'

He brushed off his hands. 'So, you won't break the law.' He started walking backwards with contempt on his face. 'But here you are sitting with a criminal, which must be a great trial to you, so I think I'll get that worry off your hands.' He put his hand on the door.

'I think the law is senseless,' Will said.

He scoffed. 'You'd be right.'

'But I can't ask my mother to give me the troops to get me out the main gate. Even Mistress Cait is under house arrest.'

'What? Whatever for?'

'Because she hasn't come to help. They're calling it a mild form of treason. If they see her, they'll bring her in in chains.'

He nodded. 'Oh, aye. That'll surely get her wanting to help you.'

Will threw up her hands, exasperated. 'I told you I thought it was foolish. I don't even think this was Mother's idea. King Lesli has been poking her left and right.'

'Lesli?' He froze and then took a few steps toward her. 'Lesli, Hiedelen Lesli?'

Will nodded.

'What's he to do with this?'

'He's been here since before the Sleep. He wouldn't leave. At first he said he wasn't afraid, and then the quarantine went into effect, so he's still here.'

'He didn't argue the quarantine?'

'None of his men have succumbed,' Will told him. 'I think he thinks he's immune. He's not of the Lyndar line, and he's royal. Royalty could walk through the Sleep.'

'The old Sleep,' Reynard said with a sly anger. 'This is a new one.'

'I know,' Will said. 'But he's here. Amaranth is . . . I don't know what she's thinking, actually. There were treaties involved with Lavender marrying his son Dani, and now he's almost up in arms. This injunction on magic was his old law—'

'I know.'

'—and now he's managed to bring it back. Which means that Caital won't be permitted to help, which means the Sleep will keep getting worse.'

Reynard frowned. 'Why would he do that?'

'I think . . . .' Will sighed, and then voiced her suspicions. 'I'm pretty damned sure he's hoping for another interregnum.'

'Why?'

'He could be regent again. Lyndaria would be his.'

'Hiedelen's laws.' The words were a growl. Will wondered what annoyed him so much. He didn't look much older than Lavender, so the Hiedelen laws couldn't have affected him. Maybe they'd imprisoned a family member.

'Well, it's Lesli's guards at the gate now. Most of ours are asleep.'

He looked at her. 'Couldn't you give them some excuse? Some reason you *have* to leave?'

Will shook her head. 'Not tonight. It's no secret I'm not thrilled about the ceremony tomorrow. They'll think I'm trying to run away.'

He dismissed that. 'We could use magic,' he said.

She shook her head again. 'It's illegal.'

His eyes narrowed and he stared down at her. 'Does that really matter?'

'No,' she said, realizing as she said it that she meant it. 'But I don't know any spells that'll help me sneak past the guards and the thorns at the same time. I know a shadow spell, but the gate is always flooded with torches, there are no shadows to hide in. And the moment the thorns smelled my blood they'd be on me like a pack of ravenous hounds.'

'Doesn't your stilling spell work?'

'Not very well. My secret exit is grown over, and now there's a veritable forest of briars. By the time I'm halfway through the spell is fading, even with the extra power you put on it, and there I am surrounded by man-eating briars. I can't get all the way through.'

He seemed thoughtful. 'But you do *have* a secret exit?'

'Well, yes,' she said. 'It used to work wonderfully. Took a bit of running before you augmented the spell.'

A wicked grin suddenly brightened his features. Will was taken aback. He was both frightening and very seductive in that moment. He squared his shoulders. 'I can get you through the hedge,' he said slyly.

'You can?' Will looked him up and down, with his rumpled clothes and his angry freckled face. 'How?'

He gave a bit of an uncomfortable sigh. 'Not honestly,' he admitted. 'I can't do it alone, I'll need help.'

'I'll give you any help I can.'

'Not from you,' he said, annoyed. 'Not directly, anyway. I need a tool.'

Will shrugged. 'All right. What?'

He hesitated. 'How serious are you about the breaking senseless laws concept?'

Will thought about this. 'So long as no one, and I mean *no one*, is getting hurt . . . pretty serious.'

'You won't like it.'

'I need to see Mistress Cait.'

'I need to steal something.'

Will raised an eyebrow. She'd always known he was a thief, but for some reason this surprised her. At the same time, she didn't hesitate. She stood up. 'What are we going to steal?'

He looked her up and down. 'You'll need your shadow spell.'

She didn't hesitate. She breathed all eight lines of the shadow spell and felt the darkness close around her instantly.

He grinned at her. 'Well done. Come with me.'

Chapter 13

* * *

It shouldn't have surprised me that the princess knew the shadow spell. It wasn't all *that* difficult a spell, and she did have a veritable library of magic books. She did not protest as I led her down the corridors, until we came to the vaults. Only then, as we gazed upon the barred cell that contained the royal jewels, did she baulk. 'I'm not stealing the crown.'

I glared at her. 'I don't want your fool crown.' I turned, pointing to the darkly glowing spinning wheel that waited patiently to be loved. 'I want *that*.'

'That?' The shadow of the princess cuddled up beside me. 'You want the spinning wheel?'

I nodded. Reverently, I realized.

She looked at the wheel, and then at me, thoughtful. 'Why?'

'No concern of yours!'

'If I'm about to steal it, then yes, it is.'

'I need it, all right?'

'You know that's a national treasure.'

'It's wood and pins.'

'With a history.'

I sighed. 'As much as I'd like to, I'm not going to take it with me.' I grunted, annoyed. 'Someone should, though. It's not right to let it go to waste.' It always made me wonder what the wretched law did to the economy of the country.

'Does it really not trouble the country having to import all your textiles?'

'We don't import all our textiles.'

I laughed, looking down at her. 'Yes, you do.'

'No,' she said, as if speaking to a child. 'We export the flax and fleeces to Hiedelen, and they send us back thread.'

I blinked. 'Is that really efficient? Who makes money on this? Hiedelen's carters?'

She frowned. 'I guess . . .'

'Is there a tariff on the importation of the fibre?'

'Well . . .' She stopped, then looked quietly angry. 'Actually, I think there is. And you're right. That goes directly to the Hiedelen crown.'

She wasn't half stupid, this one. 'Have none of you realized how outdated this ban on spinning wheels is? I guess I could see it when Amaranth's father was worried about the curse, but Amaranth was already pricked by the time she was sixteen. Why keep the law in force after the fox got into the coop?'

Will was still frowning. 'Habit, I think. Now that you mention it, I don't think my grandfather intended the law to still be in force after Mother was asleep. But then, he was asleep, too, very shortly afterwards.' She shook her head. 'Actually, I can't think why the law was never rescinded during the interregnum. According to the histories there was lawlessness for about seven years after the interregnum started, until Prince Alexi sacrificed himself.'

'No, there wasn't,' I said. 'There was rampant law*fulness*. All the governmental officials had the right to do as they pleased, without superiors to report their atrocities to. People were tortured to death for littering in the streets.'

She glared at me. 'That can't be true.'

'It is.'

'Where did you read this?'

I blinked. I was letting my age show. 'Never mind. Are you going to help me with this, or do I get to go home?'

The princess frowned, then squared her shoulders. 'What exactly did you have in mind?'

'If you can get them to open the door of the vault, I can sneak inside and use the spinning wheel to get us, and it, out.'

She looked at me, annoyed. 'I wish you'd told me that in my chambers,' she said, and she ran off on me, leaving me staring after her in bemusement. I finally shrugged. Either she'd be back or she wouldn't, and either way it wasn't my problem.

A while later she came back, her hair fixed and a cloak over her arm, sans shadow spell. Something glittered in her hand. As she walked past me she whispered, 'You coming?' but she didn't look at me. I twisted my own shadow spell into my hair and followed along behind. She approached the vault without fear. 'Open up, please. The jewels selected for tomorrow are unacceptable.'

The guards bowed. 'We weren't informed by your mother, Highness.'

'You think with all this she has time to do this personally?' She held up a glittering diamond necklace that reminded me of Winnowinn's glacier. 'This is far too ornate for a time of mourning. I've come to exchange it for my grand-mother's sapphire.' She held up a large brass key. 'I have the second key.'

'Ah,' said the guard. 'I suppose that's all right, then.'

Then he actually turned and inserted a key into one of two locks in the vault. Apparently it took both the guard and a member of the royal family to open the vault. Willow opened the other lock, and she held the barred door open wide for a moment before she entered. A moment in which a dark shadow slipped into the vault before her.

For the first time I touched the spinning wheel. I felt a hum as I touched it, a cold, calculating efficiency. There was no hatred, no desperate vengeance in my aunt's spinning wheel, such as had created my own Sleep. Just sheer willfulness and relentless determination.

While Will made a big show of exchanging the ornate diamond necklace for a more plain and older-fashioned one of diamond and sapphire, I pulled a ragged thread from my hood and threaded it through the mother-of-all, creating a leader line. I had thought, when I first saw the wheel, that it was maintained by the palace staff, but I knew at a touch that the longevity of this wheel was entirely my aunt's doing. The machine fairly dripped with magic, as if it had been immersed in oil. Magic to keep the dust off, to keep the joints oiled, to keep the leather drive solid and in place on the flyer and the fly wheel. I snatched a spindle from the lower rack and screwed it into place, keeping one ear on the guards.

Being surrounded by iron did sap my strength a little, but I had more than enough to twist the wheel widdershins and tighten the leader line, using that twist to tighten the blood vessels in their throats. As the blood was cut off from their brains their heads began to weave dizzily. With a silent nod, they both lost consciousness and fell to the ground.

Will caught one of them as he fell, but the other collapsed against the cage, making the whole thing rattle and slamming the iron shut around us. I felt sick. 'There!' I said, still holding the thread. 'Get me out of here.'

Will lowered the guard carefully and opened the door of the cell. 'What did you do to them?'

'If you want them to die, by all means, keep me here chatting,' I said. 'We don't have much time.'

She stepped quickly over the guard, and I released the leader thread, letting their blood flow freely once again.

Their colour returned instantly. Their consciousness wasn't far behind, I knew. I hoisted the wheel against my chest, like carrying a chair, and like carrying a chair, it was awkward and hindering. I came through the cell door backwards, and Will ran ahead of me . . . in the wrong direction. 'Where are you going?' I hissed. 'The exit is that way!'

'No it isn't,' Will said, and she pressed a wooden panel on the wall. With silent hinges, the wall twisted on itself, leaving a gap two abreast, into which she disappeared. With a blink of surprise I followed after her, hoping there was enough space within the wall for the spinning wheel.

There was, but only barely. As the guards groaned with their revival Will closed the panel behind us, leaving us in comparative darkness. 'What did you do?' Will whispered to me.

'Nothing,' I said. 'Just put them out.'

'How?'

Explaining that I could have done the same thing by squeezing their throats didn't seem like the best thing to say at that point. 'It doesn't matter. They'll wake up any second.'

'Unless the Sleep takes them while they're out.'

Shrug. 'Not my concern. Is this your secret exit?'

'Down there, turn left, second right, third right, then—'

'Inside the walls?' I asked.

She nodded her head. 'Let me go first,' she said, and then tried to get past me. The spinning wheel made that difficult in the cramped passage. She twisted then turned, but she was not a narrow figure, and the magic on the wheel resisted any attempt to climb over it.

'Oh, for Light's sake!' I reached over the wheel and hoisted her off her feet, sliding her backwards over the wheel, which spun in protest. She gasped. I don't think she'd been picked up since she was a child. Anyone less strong than a faerie would have had a tough time of it. For a stunned moment she stood in the dark, my hands still holding her ribs beneath her large, warm arms. I could feel her breathing. I deliberately released her. 'Your exit?' I said pointedly.

It took her a moment to find her voice. 'Right. This way.' She turned and headed down the passage, leaving me to drag the spinning wheel behind me.

It wasn't pitch dark. Occasional stars of light shone through the walls as breathing or spying holes let air and sound into the passage. It smelled musty, and I could see spider webs in the corners, but it was evident that someone tended here, or it would have been filthy. 'What is this place?'

'Shh,' she said. 'Whisper. These are the escape routes,' Will said. 'They're to enable us to escape a siege or a coup. Only the royal family knows about them.' She walked on a short ways before looking back at me. 'You realize I'm trusting you with a pretty big secret, here, right?'

I frowned. 'You're trusting me?'

'Yea.'

Well, that showed poor judgement. There probably wasn't anyone in the country who hated her and her family more. 'Why?'

She shrugged. 'I don't know. Probably because I need your help.' She looked back toward me in the gloom, but I doubted her human eyes could see me. 'And you do keep helping me.'

I tried not to choke. I did keep helping her, almost entirely against my will. It was bizarre. 'Don't count on it,' I said, brusquely. 'I expect payment.'

'You'll get it,' she said. 'All three volumes of *The Zarmeroth Cycle*, I promise you.'

I sniffed. 'I'd better.'

We travelled the rest of the way in silence. Eventually she twisted round a corner and stopped so abruptly that I bumped into her. I sniffed as the smell of roses in her hair caressed my nose. 'This is it. You'd better stand back, the thorns are pretty querulous just now.'

I dutifully stood back and let her open the door. I should have put her behind me and opened it myself. The moment the door opened there was a creak and a shriek, and four tendrils of thorns lashed out at the princess. She stepped back with a gasp and tried to close the door, but two of the canes were already through, and, as if the hands of a vengeful army, they started prying the door back open. 'Sorry!' Will panted, wrestling with the door and the thorns that were reaching for her wrist. 'I told you they've gotten more aggressive!'

'Maybe you should recite the stilling spell *before* you open the door?' I asked, keeping the spinning wheel well behind me. I couldn't risk it getting grabbed by the thorns, or we'd never get out of here.

Will took a deep breath and muttered the spell. With a quiet sigh the thorns wiggled and then settled, as if tucking themselves into bed. 'Good,' I said. I pulled open the door to a solid wall of thorns. 'Now. Sit down, and don't get in my way.'

She slid sideways past me, enveloping me in another cloud of rose scent. She did not dart past me as quickly as I would have wished – likely her size made it difficult in the narrow passageway, and her skirts were tangled in the thorns that had attacked her. She hesitated against me as she extricated herself from the briars, and for another heated moment I felt her practically in my arms. Something about it reminded me of Lynelle, and rage surged inside me. 'Get off me!' I growled, and I heard her murmur an apology as she twisted away down the corridor.

Trembling with rage from that burst of memory, I grabbed for a handful of the quiescent briars. I twisted the selection of thorns into the leader thread. Ignoring the prickles on my fingers I tested the tension, positioned my foot on the treadle, and threw the wheel forward. With a leap of a living thing the thorns pulled from my fingers as if they were nothing more solid than threads of flax, the magic inherent in my spinning, and in my aunt's faerie spinning wheel, pulling the stiff wooden briar canes into a soft and pliable fibre before it spun them into thread, which in turn was pulled around the spool.

Will watched me for three pulls, her eyes growing wide. 'What are you—'

'Quiet.'

It was strange spinning the thorns. I had spun grasses and even pine needles into ropes and thread and — once — into gold, but the thorns welcomed the spinning in a way I had not expected. Whatever they were turning into — and I hadn't decided, I'd simply spun the briars and let them decide what they wished to be — was heavy and very smooth, almost more like silk than flax. But whatever they wanted to be, it certainly drew the power from me. If I hadn't been sheathed in darkness I could tell I'd be glowing brightly from the amount of magic that surged through me. I couldn't spare much attention from the spinning itself, because within a few moments the thorns awoke from their enforced sleep and started thrashing at Will again. She muttered the stilling spell again without being asked, and I spared a glance of thanks in her direction. While I could have muttered the spell myself while I spun, it was tricky holding two spells at once, particularly handling this much power.

Spinning a path through the thorns took about an hour, while the moon rose quietly in a cloud-studded sky. Rather than carefully ply the threads I made — I was only trying to get us through, after all — I pulled them whole off the spool whenever it grew full, leaving the threads in tangled little nests behind us as we progressed through the forest of briars.

Then, with a final cracking of canes, with one last pull of the wheel, we were through. I hoisted the spinning wheel out of easy reach of the thorns and stepped back. My shoulder ached icily, and my neck had a crick in it. I hadn't spun so much in a long time. The wheel was a joy to touch, but that much spinning was no mean feat when you were performing magic along with it.

Will had followed silently along as I'd inched my way through the forest of thorns, and she followed me now. She held a little nest of thread in her hand. Like everything else, it was silver and blue in the moonlight. 'What did you turn this into?' she mused.

'Doesn't matter,' I said. I wasn't sure myself, I had only let the thorns take on the form they wanted. 'Flax probably. Or something like it.'

'It's heavy,' she said.

'Forget it,' I said, snatching it from her. I jammed the thread into my pocket and hoisted up the spinning wheel. I positioned the wheel under a tree which would keep the snow off it. It was just too big to take with us. 'Make sure you fetch this when you get back,' I said. 'Or rest assured, I will.'

'Let's go,' she said, and strode on ahead of me, her feet squeaking in the snow.

I caught up to her fairly quickly. 'You don't know where you're going.'

'The enchanted forest, I presume,' Will said.

'Yes, but where?'

'That's where you come in.'

'Right,' I said.

We lapsed into silence for a long time. She had a long stride. It felt very odd to me. I rarely walked anywhere with anyone. I kept myself hunched to hide my height, but I hardly needed to with Will so tall. Her legs were almost as long as mine.

I could feel her looking at me, long sidelong glances before turning back to herself. Then she'd look again. I was waiting for her to speak long before she finally opened her mouth. 'What did you do back there?'

'Got you through the hedge,' I said. 'That's what you wanted, isn't it?'

'But what kind of magic was it? I've never even read anything about it.'

'I suspect all the books on spinning magic were the first to be burnt.'

She shrugged. 'Probably.' She stared at me, her brow furrowed. 'So how did you learn it?'

I turned to look at her. 'I promised to bring you to Mistress Cait, Princess,' I said, 'not to give you a treatise on my personal history.'

She looked away. 'Sorry,' she said, but I could tell she didn't mean it. I strode on ahead. 'Ahm,' she said, utterly unable to keep quiet. 'Re—'

I whirled on her. '*What?*'

She swallowed. 'I only wanted to thank you again for coming tonight,' she said. 'They really were going to kill me.'

This was getting on my nerves. '*Stop* – thanking me for that!' I said, my words clipped with anger.

She swallowed. 'You regret it,' she said.

Her wide grey eyes caught me as she said that. I glared. 'Saving the life of a Lyndarian princess was not on my list of aspirations, no.' I strode on ahead.

Her next words came quietly, calmly, with neither pleading nor anger. With mere curiosity she asked, 'Why do you hate me?'

Damn. 'Who says I hate you?'

'You do,' she said. 'Every time you glare at me and snap at me like some fox puppy. You turn disgusted whenever you get close to me.'

I closed my eyes. 'It's just my nature.'

'You've a very strange nature,' she said. 'Are all magicians misfits?'

I looked at her sidelong. 'What do you mean?'

'Well, you're obviously not your average run-of-the-mill Lyndaroner. And I . . .' She looked down at her ill fitting dress with distaste, 'I don't fit anywhere.'

I scoffed. 'You know where you fit. You're a princess. You *know* who you are.'

She frowned. 'I guess,' she said. 'That doesn't mean I find it comfortable.'

I strode on ahead, at faerie speed. 'Do you intend to talk all night, or would you like to get to Caital's tower before daybreak?'

Will ran a few steps, and then fell into step beside me. We continued on to the enchanted forest in silence.

I didn't take her anywhere near our burrow this time. I took a more direct route and we approached the forest from the north-west. Here the smaller, younger trees had been cleared for the road, so there was no buffer of normalcy between the blank white canvas of the winter fields and the sudden city of enchanted trees. The enormous trees were shrouded in cloaks of snow, and sparkled prettily in the moonlight. I strode into the shadows beneath the trees without a blink, but Will hesitated. I glanced back at her. 'Are you coming?' I asked.

She stared up and up at these trees, wide around as towers and taller than her palace. 'Yes,' she said finally. 'Yes, I am.' The snow squeaked under her feet as she took the final few steps into the forest. Then the sound faded as the magic of the forest turned the snow into a thin white carpet.

'I'm coming to see Mistress Cait,' I announced to the trees.

'What are you—'

'Shh! I bring the Princess Willow Lyndal with me.'

The trees moved with the wind a bit, shedding quiet handfuls of snow. '*Proceed*,' they whispered.

'What, no wolf this time?' The trees didn't answer me. I shrugged. 'Guess that's all we get. Come on.'

'Who were you talking to?' Will asked.

'The trees,' I said. 'Didn't you hear them?'

'The wind?'

I looked at her. She truly hadn't heard the whisper. 'Caital won't let us through unless we ask,' I said. 'They told us to proceed.'

'Oh.' She gestured me ahead. 'I guess we go on, then.'

'Stay behind me,' I said. 'I don't trust this place. I'm not sure Cait's all there, really.'

It took a long time to get through the forest. The night was growing colder, and the wind had picked up. Even before it started to snow I had noticed Will growing perceptibly slower. 'Can you hurry up?' I asked her.

She squared her shoulders and picked up her pace, but I knew she was putting up a front. It was very cold. *I* found it cold, and Will wasn't a faerie. The frozen numb pain in my shoulder had spread down my arm, and I kept flexing my fingers to keep it at bay. Will kept huddling down into her cloak. When she started to shiver, I wanted to lose my temper. Instead, I found myself becoming worried. 'Are you all right?' I asked.

'Yes,' she said, but her teeth were clenched to keep them from chattering.

When the snow began to fall, at first I was glad. Usually that meant the temperature would climb a bit. No such luck. The wind caught the snowflakes and blew them against the skin like shards of glass. It began as just an annoyance. I pulled my hood low over my brow and lifted the mantle over my face. Soon the whirling snow was a positive torment. Will was wrapped so deeply in her fine cloak that I could barely see her eyes. That cloak. It may have been warm, but it wasn't made for heavy work. It wasn't meant to withstand a blizzard. Which was what this snowstorm was rapidly becoming. I growled at the trees. 'You aren't making this very easy, you know!' I shouted at them.

If there was an answer, it was lost in the roar of the wind. 'This journey wasn't so long the last time I took it!' I shouted again. I took Will's arm and pulled her along beside me. She was stumbling. 'You're going to kill her!' I expected Cait's tower to appear as I turned around another tree, but it did not. 'Oh, for the love of Light, I can't lead her through this! Is there nothing you can do?'

We walked onward. It surprised me at first that Will didn't ask what I was yelling for, but when I looked at her it became clear she was nearly past all speech. It was all she could do to keep on her feet. I growled, snarling at the very forest. Will tripped in the snow, losing her footing. I lost my grip on her, and for one minute of obscene panic, I lost her in the whirling snow. 'Princess!' I called out. '*Princess!*'

I heard a very thin cry waver through the wind. 'H-here!'

I followed the sound, falling to my knees. Will had fallen into a black hole in the snow. With a chattered whisper I heard her mutter a spell. I couldn't quite catch it, but a tiny glimmer of light no brighter than a candle flame appeared cradled in her shaking hand. I scoffed at the trees. 'This is the best you could do?' I asked them.

They did not deign to reply.

I crept in beside Will. We were in a burrow, much like my own, although this appeared a natural hollow created by roots and water and erosion, perhaps helped along by some animal. It was very small, and the ground was frozen. I sighed. 'I guess this gets us out of the wind.'

'Y-yes,' she whispered. Her little witchlight wavered and went out. 'S-sorry,' she said. 'I c-couldn't ho-old it.'

'That's all right,' I said. 'I can see.' But that faded light worried me. Being mortal, it was her own renewable life force that powered her magics, and if she couldn't maintain so simple a spell as a light, that force was fading. Her cloak was covered in snow. I took it off her and shook it in the entrance. She was so cold her face was blue. I sighed. I'd suffered enough winters in burrows that I knew what had to be done. I knew the ground was frozen, and my own coat was covered in snow as well. I took it off, shook it in the entrance, then lay it on the ground for her to curl up on. Then I curled beside her and pulled the cloak over both of us. 'Sorry,' I said. 'I don't like it any more than you do, but we'll freeze.'

'It's a-all right,' she said. 'I r-really d-don't mind.'

I wasn't as prone as a human to shivering, but I was pretty cold myself. My ice-patched wound ached with a dull, cold throb, pulsing the cold through my body. Oh, hells, Junco had warned me not to get too cold! I wished I had my spindle. Damn me for an imbecile, giving it up for a pointless revenge. Serve me right if I died of the cold, huddled in a hole with my worst enemy.

No, it didn't! I didn't want to die, enemy or not. I'd already saved her life once today, she could jolly well return the favour. 'Come here,' I said roughly, and pulled her shivering body to mine.

'Hoh!' she breathed. 'Oh, you're so warm!'

Compared to her, I was. I was tempted to push her away again, but something stopped me. She huddled up against me so trustingly, much like the kit did. Instead of pushing her frozen form away, my hand found its way down her arm until it rested on her stomach. There it stayed, feeling the convulsive shudders that passed through her again and again.

Her body felt too large and sturdy to be so cold. I wasn't sure she'd be able to warm herself, and I knew there wasn't enough of me to warm her. There was just so much of her to warm back up. I pulled her a little closer and reached for her hair. 'Don't move,' I said. I had no spindle, and I was out of wool, but she had an abundance of fine brown hair. I took a tendril and began twisting it around my finger.

'What are you—?'

'Shh.' I continued to spin the lock of her hair until I could spin heat in with it. Then I bent the twisted tendril back onto itself, so that it plied together into a small hank of string. The moment it came together the heat spell took effect, and I could hear the same groan of relief that my sister gave when I warmed her. It sounded very different coming from Will's throat. I sighed with relief myself. She was so much more pleasant to hold when she wasn't a shuddering rock of frozen flesh. She seemed to melt back into a human against my chest. 'There,' I said. I dug a stick out of the detritus beneath us and split it with my teeth until I had a rough hair pin. I pinned the hank of spell together at her scalp. 'Don't undo it,' I said. 'You'll break the spell.'

One hand reached up and gently touched my lock of a spell. 'What did you just do?' she asked, sounding languid.

'Spun some warmth with your hair,' I said. I slowly placed my hand back on her stomach. 'It's not the best spell I've ever cast. I don't have a spindle.'

She made a small sound. 'It's strange that you can do magic with spindles,' she said. 'How did you learn it, when spinning is illegal?'

'My mother taught me,' I said, 'when I was small. Before she grew too frightened and abandoned the skill.'

'She stopped, but you still spin? How? Don't you need a wheel?'

'I make drop spindles out of wood. I can work those by hand, but it's not as even a thread.'

'Isn't it risky?'

'It's a damned fool law,' I said frankly. 'That's where my greatest gift lay. I wasn't about to let some archaic policy dictate my life.'

Will sighed. 'Yes. I suppose that is pretty silly,' she whispered. She settled in more comfortably, her now warm body moulding against mine. 'I wish I knew why you were helping me.'

'It's not that much of a help,' I said. 'I think I've nearly killed you.' I frowned. 'Either I or Mistress Cait.' I looked down at her. She looked rosy and sleepy. The scent of roses was overpowering. 'What makes you so sure she's going to help?'

'She helped my mother last time,' she said.

'Did she really? From what I can see she saved one life and caused the deaths of countless others. Which faerie is the truly evil one?'

She seemed to lose her patience. 'Then would you rather Hiedelen became regent again?' she asked.

'No,' I finally admitted. I hadn't thought, when I considered my revenge on the Lyndarian line, whether the alternatives would be better or worse.

'Mistress Cait is the only person who can possibly help. If Cait won't, and the Winnowinn can't, than the kingdom is done for.'

'They're only sleeping,' I muttered.

'They're being tortured.'

I was silent for a long time. 'I know,' I said quietly.

'I didn't think you cared.'

'I don't,' I said, my voice hardening.

'Then why are you helping me?'

Because I'm enjoying watching my revenge work through you, I thought, but the thought made me feel ill. I didn't think it was true any longer. I was acutely aware of the scent of roses. It permeated her clothes, her hair, her very skin. There was another scent I caught as my nose touched her temple, buried under the roses. The scent of her hair, heady and sweet and very human. I took a deep breath, drinking her in. It had been a long time since I'd held a woman. 'I don't know,' I finally said. My lips brushed her skin as I whispered.

I think my confusion showed in my voice. Will shifted to face me until my hand lay on her waist. 'Are you . . . ?' She paused. 'You sound tired,' she finally said.

My wound was aching, and I was exhausted from the events of the day. I'd poured a great deal of power through me clearing a path through the thorns. I was drained from pain and exhaustion and cold. And the princess's grey eyes were deep as the sky. I closed my eyes to escape them. She shifted, and then, light as a moth's wing, I felt her chill fingertips on my cheek. 'Where did you come from?' she breathed at me. Her fingers lightly touched my lips.

'From the shadows,' I whispered. I said it without thinking, and I wished I hadn't. I was about to pull away, to turn my back on her, to stop the line of questioning which would lead, ultimately, to nowhere and nothingness. But before I had a chance, to my surprise, she kissed me. *She* kissed *me*, her lips soft and confident. I pulled back half an inch, taken aback, but she only waited for me. I could feel her nearness, and it was as if a thread was pulling me to her. Our lips met again, only for a moment, then again, and again. I kept trying to pull away, and I couldn't make myself do it. I could feel her solid weight beside me and that wasn't close enough. I'd thought back at the monument that I was trying to seduce her. Suddenly *I* was the one who wanted *her*, no connivance, no agenda. I just wanted her.

It had been years since I'd let myself get close to a human. Not since my disastrous affair with Lynelle had I dared risk such an intimate connection. I guess I was hungrier than I'd thought. I kissed her as a starving man given good food.

With an unintentional gasp I pushed forward until she lay half beneath me, her arms sneaking over my shoulders. I could feel her body beneath mine, welcoming my weight, and our breath mingled as we kissed again and again. Her heart beat faster, and mine, which was less subject to mortal whims, wasn't exactly steady, either. She held me passionately, her hands caressing my shoulders, my face, reaching under my hood to touch my hair.

My hood! I pulled back as if I'd been burned. I knew what would happen if she pulled it back. The realization. The horror. The retaliation. I wanted none of it. I didn't love her, couldn't love her, but for some reason I didn't want her to hate me. I opened my mouth to apologize, to make up some excuse . . .

'I'm sorry,' she breathed.

I blinked. 'What?'

'I'm sorry. I shouldn't have done that,' she whispered. She looked nearly in tears. 'I was using you. It was inexcusable.'

The princess I had used to curse her own family was using *me*? All right, *this* I had to hear. I lay back down, slowly, and wrapped my arm around her shoulders again. 'And *how*, exactly, were you supposedly using me?'

'I'm sure you've heard,' she said. 'I'm engaged to be married.'

'So I understand. You have quite a wait, though.'

'No. I'm to be married at midwinters. Tomorrow.'

'Tomorrow?' She'd said something about a ceremony before, and I'd dismissed it without even hearing it. A gush of something I could only define as rage rushed through me. I wasn't even sure who I was angry at. It didn't make sense, so I dismissed it, too. 'To whom?'

'Narvi Hiedelen.'

I growled under my breath. Hiedelen again. I hated that family as deeply as I hated Will's. Possibly even more.

'We've been betrothed since the day he was born,' she went on. 'I have to marry him. It's even more important now that Lavender's asleep. I always knew I'd have to marry him someday. But I thought I'd have time. Time to . . .' She sighed. 'I don't know. I guess I'm just dreaming. I'm not the style of lady who is embraced by the ideal of courtly love. The attention without intention, the kind of court that was paid to Lavender since she turned fifteen. But I thought maybe . . .' She looked up at me. 'I only wanted a taste. Just to know what it felt like. To fool myself that someone . . . could love me. The half-chaste kisses in the corridors, the poetry left beneath my door. But no. All I get is death threats. They're making me marry Narvi *now* because of the Sleep. And Ferdinand,' she added in a whisper. 'And now I won't know what it is to be loved. Even in play.'

I scoffed. 'Your husband will pay ample attention to you.'

She shook her head. 'I'm to be married to a nine-year-old boy. He's not terrible, this isn't a curse, and yet it feels like it. It'll be seven years at least before our marriage can be . . . really real. In most opinions, that would qualify me as an old maid, or at least someone who married very late. I just wanted to know what it would be like to really . . . You're the only person I know,' she finished. She sighed. 'I know I'm royalty, so you don't want to anger me. But I also know I'm not handsome, and I know I'm big and I'm awkward and just a lot of trouble for you. So . . . I'm sorry. I didn't mean to . . . upset you. I was being selfish.'

I touched her cheek. She felt soft as feathers. 'You're not unhandsome, Will,' I said. I didn't realize until after I'd said it that I had just used her name. The first time I'd admitted to it. I shuddered. It hurt to think of it. I took a deep breath to steady myself, and only found myself drowning in the scent of roses. I swallowed. 'And you can't use me. Not if I'm already using you.'

'How are you using me?' she whispered.

I grinned, a mischievous black humour trickling into my voice. 'That would be telling.'

A responsive shiver went through her. I could feel it all through my body. It did unwelcome and delightful things to me. I knew better than this. I knew the kind of hell that I'd be thrown into again if I let this continue. I told myself to control myself.

A real faerie who knew his own name might have had more strength of will in the matter. They can take control of themselves, force themselves to act the way their reason tells them. The Nameless are more subject to whim. It's one of the reasons why we're so hated, so, possibly rightly, feared. I wanted to kiss her again, so I did. It was reckless, it was dangerous, it was ill advised, but my lips met hers as if they were sleep after a hard day. I was able to keep enough hold on myself to be careful, kissing her gently, keeping my arms around hers so she couldn't reach for my hood again. She relaxed into my kiss. I could feel her opening like a flower beneath me, welcoming me. She made a small, heart quick-ening sound and wrapped her leg around mine.

Oh, yes. Oh, no, oh, hell. I pulled back, slowly, looking into her face. Her eyes were languid and hungry, glittering as she looked up at me. I knew it was too dark for her to see my features much, but I couldn't help seeing everything about her. At this range I could see much of her mother in her.

The largeness of her eyes, that was Amaranth the Beautiful. The shape of her nose, likewise. Her hair was brown like winter leaves, but the fineness and the curl, that was Queen Amaranth. She may say she did not inherit the gift of Beauty, but she was beautiful, in a strong, severe way. The strong chin and the plain cheekbones and the coarseness of her face were not so much unhandsome as unexpected. The determined set to her mouth was softened now as she looked back up at me. She was only considered plain in comparison to her delicate porcelain sister, whose transient beauty was likely to fade as she aged.

What was I doing? She would give herself to me. She would. I could feel it in her body, see it in her face. She would let herself fall in love with me. Since that had been my goal in the beginning, I didn't know why I was feeling so confused now. Wasn't this what I wanted? But it wasn't. Not any more. What I wanted was to love her, and I couldn't. I knew I couldn't. And I couldn't let her give herself up, not to me, who only wanted to harm her. I took a deep breath and kissed her once more, softly, half-chaste. The sweetness of it made her catch her breath. 'You should rest, Princess,' I whispered. 'We still have a long walk once this storm lifts.'

She blinked once or twice, then sniffed. 'Right,' she whispered. I rolled aside and tucked her beneath my arm, gathering the cloak carefully around us. Her head rested against my chest, warming my heart beneath that icy wound. I reached up to stroke her hair. I think she fell asleep, but I stayed staring out at the swarms of swirling snowflakes.

I didn't know what I was doing. I hadn't abandoned my purpose, the complete collapse of the Lyndal line. Nor was I taking this useful avenue towards that design, which confused me. If I were to claim this princess now, I could announce her disloyalty to the Hiedelen prince. Undoubtably, that would cause a war. Possibly even Will's execution. The repercussions would spiral through her family. Lavender was already unmarriageable. Amaranth would be without an heir. It would be perfect.

So why wasn't I doing it? I knew I could change my mind. It wouldn't take much effort on my part to foster my will onto Will. It would be her will, really. She wanted more than what I had just given her. I was a faerie, naturally seductive, and she felt herself beholden to me for many reasons. She was more than curious, but too inexperienced to press the issue.

I also knew I wasn't going to do it. I wanted to — every hungry, lonely corner of my body wanted her — but there was too much more to it than that. I told myself it was simply too dangerous to risk it, but that was a lie. I didn't care about danger any more. How much worse could things get? Everyone already wanted me dead. My heart had been broken so many times that it knew the procedure. I was basically safe. But she wasn't. The truth was that I knew I couldn't live with myself if I did it. I couldn't break another woman's heart. Not after Lynelle.

I also felt as if I'd been half coerced into this. That Mistress Cait and her enchanted forest had compelled us into this tiny, inadequate shelter, forcing us into each other's arms. What function could it serve, anyway? Nothing good.

No. Best leave it as it was. I would lead her to Cait, and things would unfold from there.

I wished I knew my own name, if only to curse myself by it.

Chapter 14

Will

Will opened her eyes to stillness. The roaring winds outside had faded, and the moon shed dim, silvery light into their hollow. The only sound she could hear was her own breathing. She felt Reynard's chest beneath her cheek, rising and falling slowly. She felt a gentle tug on her hair, and she realized he was idly running his fingers through it. Despite the cold, it felt good to be lying beside Reynard, to feel his body against hers. She was confused. As much as she enjoyed it, it wasn't Ferdinand beside her, and that knowledge galled her. She was curled beside a lover – or as near to a lover she was ever likely to get – but it wasn't the one she'd wanted. Reynard was handsome enough, but there were things about him she actively hated.

She didn't like the way he skulked and slunk about. He had a rather obvious contempt for her, and that annoyed her. He was selfish and almost cowardly, stealing the gift she'd given to his sister. And his greed was beyond limit. He might have counted as a friend, but he was a friend she had to buy. That wasn't real friendship.

Except . . . except. He was hard to pin down, this one. He had saved her life. Without asking for reward. He'd risked imprisonment to get her out of the palace. He had shown her the secret of his spinning magic. As much as she trusted him, he was trusting her, whether he knew it or not.

In the end, none of that even mattered. The biggest thing about Reynard was that he was not, nor could he be, a friend to Princess Willow Lyndal. He was poor and rough and roguish, and the princess couldn't risk herself or her country to such an association.

But Will was two people. She was the public princess who was going to marry Prince Narvi tomorrow, the noble Willow Lyndal whose life was devoted to her country and her people. But she was also Will, an overly big, outspoken critic of royalty in general, who wanted only to study her magic and never go to another ball again. Will was her father's daughter, a rough, lowborn child more of a miller than a queen. Princess Willow's life was her country's, not her own. And Will's life was shackled to Princess Willow.

Reynard could be Will's lover. He could never, ever be Princess Willow's. Besides, Princess Willow was in love with the world's most wonderful prince . . . who technically belonged to her sister Lavender. Will and Princess Willow hated one another. The princess hated being big and plain and longing for things that a princess could never have, like freedom and magic. Will hated having to force herself into being a princess, like shoving her big body into a dress that didn't fit, leaving her uncomfortable and constricted.

There wasn't enough of her to fill both roles, but there was too much that didn't fit into either one. Each part of her spilled out into the other, and left her scattered and out of place.

Leaving her here. She had abandoned everything it was to be a princess so that she could fulfil the role and become the princess she had to be. What on earth was she doing to Reynard? It was inexcusable to kiss him like that! But she hadn't been able to help it. He'd been so close, and it felt so good to be warm again after the cold. And he had seemed so . . . lost. She thought he was telling the truth; he didn't know why he was helping her. Her gratitude had bubbled through her, and Will's little voice had sounded inside, saying, *This is it. Your chance to be your own person for once. You'll never get another opportunity.* So she took it.

He had tasted of wood smoke . . .

Will hadn't moved at all, so it surprised her when Reynard said, 'We should go.'

She looked up at him. 'How did you know I was awake?'

He looked at her with a slight smile. His teeth flashed white in the dark. He had the most wicked smile she'd ever seen, toothy and impish. It was strange seeing him smile. Usually he did nothing but scowl. His red-brown eyes looked very large in the dim light. They disengaged from each other and Reynard wrapped her cloak more properly around her. She swallowed. 'About . . . what happened . . . .' She stopped. She wanted to talk about it, but she didn't know what she wanted to say.

'Best to forget it,' Reynard said.

Will nodded, but she wasn't sure if she was agreeing or just acknowledging.

They climbed through the snow and back out into the night. The wind was still rattling the winter trees, but it had also blown the clouds away. Bright patches of moonlight punctuated the snowy forest. 'I'm turned around,' Will said. 'Which way?'

Reynard shrugged, pulling on his coat. 'It doesn't matter. Mistress Cait decides direction and distance here, to some extent.'

A low growl made the cold creep up Will's spine with icy fingers. 'What was that?'

Reynard turned and glared with a combined look of relief and frustration. 'About time you showed up!'

Will followed his gaze. In a tiny ray of moonlight a silvery wolf was standing, hackles raised. Her eyes glowed green, and Will took a step backward. The wolf frightened her.

Reynard, on the other hand, seemed merely exasperated. 'And where were you two hours ago when the storm hit?' he asked. 'You could have saved us quite a walk.'

The wolf barked, then growled, and Reynard tossed his head in scorn.

'You can understand what it's saying?' Will asked.

'No,' he said. 'But a growl is pretty universal.'

The wolf stalked forward, and Will took another step back. The moonlight seemed to follow it, and it still shone even in the shadows. It growled at Will. 'Follow her,' Reynard said, but she frightened Will terribly. She reached out and took Reynard's hand. It stayed stiff for a moment before curling around hers, and they followed after the wolf together.

The sun was already rising by the time they found Mistress Cait's. Will was surprised by the brown tower that looked so like a tree, but Reynard had been expecting it. He knocked on the wall, and a door appeared under his hand. It opened into a bright room, and Reynard hesitated. 'You should go ahead,' he said.

Will looked back at him, lurking in the shadows outside the streaming light from the doorway. 'You're not coming in?'

He shook his head. 'I'd better not.'

Betrayal stabbed at her. 'You're abandoning me here?' she demanded, angry. 'How am I meant to get home?'

'I'm not abandoning you,' he said.

'What would you call it?'

He snorted in annoyance. 'I only agreed to get you here, not play nursemaid.'

Will glared at him. 'You coward,' she snapped.

He scowled. 'What did you call me?'

'You heard me. Is it Caital who scares you, or are you suddenly afraid of me?'

His face went blank with incredulous rage, and Will nearly laughed. It was so easy to get him angry.

'It's himself he's afraid of, dear,' said a voice from behind her. 'Don't worry about him. He doesn't know what he's going to do from one minute to the next. But that's his own problem, not yours. Turn around, let me look at you!'

The faerie woman who stood behind her looked like the head gardener at the palace, that greenness to the edges of her eyes, though the gardener's eyes were actually brown. Will had known, from what Lavender told her of her christening, that Mistress Cait seemed to be part plant, but Lavender's childhood memories hadn't done it justice.

'You took your sweet time!' the faerie said, taking Will by the shoulder. She opened Will's cloak and seemed to survey her dress. 'I was expecting you all hours ago!'

'Your wolf, and your forest, decided to play us a trick,' Reynard said from outside. 'She left us lost in the frost. You should teach her some manners.'

'I've been trying for over a hundred years,' said the voice. 'Ylva's never been easy to tame.' She looked out into the darkness. 'Though in this instance . . . Well. Come in, you're letting in a draught!'

Reynard hesitated, then sighed and came in, hovering as close to Will's back as he could. He really *did* seem afraid of something, though it didn't quite seem to be Cait.

'Just ignore him,' Cait said, pulling Will towards the fire. 'Let me look at you!' She took Will's snow-laden cloak off and shook it into the fire, which hissed as the lumps of snow fell into it. She cocked her head on the side and regarded her as if she were a tea table, and she was wondering if she had forgotten the cream pitcher. 'I must say, I'm proud.'

Will was a little embarrassed. 'Ahm . . . thank you.'

'You *should* thank me,' Cait said. 'I've done my best by you.' She examined Will's hand and lifted her palm to measure her height. 'Yes, I think I've done quite well. It all failed with Lavender, of course, but the eldest are always hard to refine.'

The wolf barked and growled. Will started, but Cait only laughed.

'Oh, don't mind Ylva. I think she's learned her lesson where royal families are concerned.' She looked over at Reynard. 'Unlike some people.'

Will glanced at Reynard, but he was across the room, lurking in the shadow cast by the stairs, like some petulant schoolboy (which at his age was pushing it). 'I'm afraid I don't know what you're talking about,' Will said.

'I'm talking about you,' Cait said. 'I think you've turned out *very* well.' She smoothed her hands down Will's ill-fitting travelling dress. 'Now this is my idea of a princess!'

'Ex-cuse me, if you're trying to make a joke, I don't have time for games.'

'A joke?' She looked at Will curiously. 'You think this a joke?'

'Well . . . yes. I'm probably the least princesslike princess in the history of Lyndaria.'

'Exactly!'

Will was a bit lost for words. 'I don't follow,' she said.

'That was my goal, you know,' Cait said. 'I was hoping someone like you would be the result. I did my best to keep out those blasted arrogant princes. I thought, now, if poor Amaranth wakes up to some inbred monstrosity, nothing is ever going to go right for her. She's too wise, too sensitive. Those pompous, overbearing, lordly little creatures would crush her! She'd wither under their black thumbs. No, she needed someone to counter all her perfections. I was hoping for a gardener, but a miller's well enough. I must say, I was impressed with the selection of your father.'

'She didn't select my father,' Will said. 'She had to marry him because he rescued her.'

'I didn't say she selected him,' Cait said. 'My thorns did. And they did very well by the look of things.' She looked Will up and down. 'I haven't seen you since you were a baby, of course, but I've heard about you. Smart as a whip, a sense of humour and purpose, a disdain for frivolity, and above all a gift for magic! *You'll* shake things up, and about time, too. You're a great success, Willow.'

'Wait a minute,' Will said. '*Your* thorns?'

Cait frowned at her. 'But of course my thorns. Whose did you think they were?'

Reynard stepped up at this point. 'It is widely believed they were a product of the interregnum.'

Cait frowned at him as if trying to remember who he was. 'Oh. Well, yes, but no. I planted them to protect poor Amaranth when the Sleep claimed her. Poor dear.'

The wolf barked again.

'Oh, can't you *ever* let that go?' Cait asked her. 'It was over a century ago!'

'What is she saying?' Reynard asked.

'She's just being stubborn,' Cait said. She turned back to Will. 'Now. Princess Willow.'

Will was standing dumb. She searched for her voice. 'The thorns are *yours*?' she hissed.

Cait wrinkled her forehead. 'Did I not just say as much?'

Will was appalled. 'Have you *any* idea how much chaos you have caused?' she snapped. 'How many dozens, even hundreds of innocents have died in their clutches!' Will's entire world view cracked. She was suddenly frightened. She had thought Cait was meant to be the good faerie, the saviour, the one who abhorred death and preserved her mother. Now it seemed she was a heartless, thoughtless maniac who believed it best to murder innocent people and animals all for some misguided belief about who the princess should marry.

Cait was not offended. Indeed, she hardly seemed to notice Will's outburst. 'Of course the thorns are mine,' she said. 'That is where my strongest gifts lay, in my plants. You just walked through my sentient forest, isn't it impressive?'

'The forest is sentient?' Reynard asked.

'If a little scattered,' Cait admitted.

Reynard chuckled. 'Considering its progenitor,' he muttered.

Cait did seem to notice that. 'Have more respect for your elders, young man.'

Will shook her head at her. 'That's just his way,' she said. 'I was talking to you. If the thorns are yours, I demand, by right of inheritance, that you remove them. Immediately.'

Cait raised an eyebrow. 'Ah. Well, I thought one of you might ask that one day.' She turned and poured a cup of tea from a table she had set by the fire.

Will took a step toward her. 'And?'

'Tea?' she asked.

'Tea?' Will was appalled. 'Tea? Someone could be bleeding to death in the thorns this moment, and you're offering me tea?'

'Why shouldn't I? I can't do anything about them. I'm afraid they're there to stay.'

Will was not going to be denied. 'If you put them there, you can take them away again.'

Cait leaned away from Will, who looked like a firecracker about to go off. 'I can't. Any more than your mother can make you keep your mouth shut. My children have power over themselves, after a while.'

Will's breath caught in defeat. 'You can do nothing about them?' she asked. 'Nothing?'

'I'm afraid not. Their life is their own, and no longer mine.' She smiled, looking out the window at the towering trees. 'I sometimes wonder what this forest will do once I'm dead and gone. It is very fond of me.'

Will scoffed. If it took on the kind of life her so-called protective thorns had, it would go marching through the countryside slaughtering entire villages. Cait regarded her with concern. 'You seem very distraught, my dear.'

'My palace has been besieged by your thorns,' Will said. 'They grow a thousand times faster than weeds, a veritable forest of bloodthirsty, flesh-tearing death.'

'Don't exaggerate,' Cait said, 'it detracts from your veracity.'

'I'm not lying,' she said. 'They've been growing a foot a night since Lavender took ill.'

'They're growing that much?' Cait asked.

'Yes!'

Her brow furrowed. 'That *is* curious. They must be very worried about you.'

Will blinked. '*Worried* about me?'

'All of you,' Cait said. 'They are semi-sentient, you know. I did create them to protect you.'

'Then why do they try to kill me?' Will asked.

'Well . . . protect Amaranth, I should say,' Cait amended. 'If you threw *her* into the centre of the briars, no doubt they'd twine around her like lovers.'

'Until she was bled white,' Will muttered.

'Oh, no. Well, they might not ever let her *go*, so she probably would die in the end. But they'd never pierce her skin.'

'They seem to like mine.'

'Well, that's because you aren't her, dear,' Cait said.

Will sighed. 'But Lavender is,' she said. She wanted to melt to the floor. Will's perfect sister. True to form, she hadn't a scratch on her when they carried her from the thorns. They had picked her up, shredded her clothing, but Cait was right. They hadn't tried to hurt her. Once again, Princess Lavender exceeded all expectations of perfection, the distillation of all that was blessed about Queen Amaranth, with some delightful specialness all her own. And Will was the dross left over. And the thorns knew that as surely as everyone else did.

'Now, you didn't come to berate me over my children,' Cait said. 'This young man here told me he was hired by you to find me.'

'Yes,' Will said. 'A new Sleep has overcome my sister, and is slowly engulfing the castle, and the surrounding area. It's a terrible thing. The afflicted are plagued by nightmares of . . . dreadful potency.' She swallowed, remembering the fear and the horror and the hunger.

'Why come to me?' Cait asked.

Wasn't that obvious? 'I need you to tell me how to break the Sleep.'

'Oh, I can't do that,' Cait said.

Several things went through Will's mind at that moment, but the only one that really seemed to matter was, 'Why not?'

'It isn't my spell.'

'The last Sleep wasn't your spell, either!' Will shouted. She was losing it. 'The curse upon Mother wasn't your spell, but you managed to counteract that!'

'Not very efficiently,' Cait said. 'I couldn't remove the curse entirely, I could only soften it. Ylva's still furious at me over it.'

'The wolf?' Will was losing her patience over this wolf. 'What has the wolf got to do with anything?'

'You don't know?' Cait tilted her head to the side. Will suddenly realized that she wasn't entirely sane.

'Know what? Why would I know anything about your wolf?'

'Ylva's the faerie who cursed your mother,' Cait said. 'As I said, she's very touchy.'

Reynard surged to his feet. 'Her? You?' There was a terrible moment of silence that burned the very air. Will took a step away from him. He looked very frightening just then. He pointed at the wolf. '*You!*' So quickly that Will could barely follow his movement he launched himself forward and grabbed her by the scruff. The wolf yelped and growled, and Reynard held her down by her throat. 'Do you know what I've been through because of you? *Do you?*'

The wolf continued to growl and tried to snap at his face.

'Go ahead and try it!' he snarled.

Will took several more steps back. She knew better than to get between two dogs fighting. If the wolf and the fox were about to go at it, Will wanted to be as far away from the two of them as possible.

Cait, however, did not seem at all perturbed. 'Stop this,' she said calmly. A honeysuckle on the wall began to move, much like the thorns when they were reaching for blood, and fixed themselves around Reynard and Ylva's legs, pulling them physically apart. Ylva barked angrily, but Will's eyes were fixed on Reynard. As he was dragged against the wall he smouldered with a fury Will *never* wanted to see directed towards herself. His brownish eyes were glowing red, and he seemed to writhe in darkness. He was positively terrifying.

Cait addressed the wolf. 'Ylva, you know perfectly well he's quite right. You weren't thinking very clearly, and the whole Stiltskin clan suffered for it.'

Reynard's head snapped to Cait. 'What did you say? What was that name?'

Cait glanced absently at him. 'Stiltskin. Don't obsess over it, you'll forget it again within the hour. I can't make it stick to you.'

Reynard sagged, defeated, but he snarled between clenched teeth, 'Then let me kill her!'

'I won't do that,' Cait said. 'She's my sister.'

Reynard blinked. 'You mean you're my great-aunt?' he asked

'Only a little,' Cait said. 'Ylva and I had different mothers. She was very offended when I was invited to the palace for Amaranth's christening, and she wasn't. She was the eldest and I was the youngest, and she thought I had little business there.' She turned to Will. Will was busy staring at Reynard in confusion. Reynard had faerie blood? 'Your grandparents had invited a representative of every clan, you see, and since I represented both Caital through my mother and Stiltskin through my father, they thought they had both clans covered. Oh, unlike your people, faerie names follow the female line. But Ylva didn't see it that way. She thought I was too spoiled as it was.'

Frankly, Will couldn't give a bent copper for historical family feuds. 'You're a faerie,' she whispered.

Reynard looked at her, his dark face completely unreadable. He strained against the vines, but they did not slacken their grip. Will couldn't say she was upset about that. He took a deep breath. 'Yes,' he admitted.

Will took a hesitant step toward him. 'You don't shine,' she whispered. 'You . . .' She searched his face. Everything she had ever heard about the Nameless flashed through her head. Uncontrollable. Fickle. Violent. Unknowable. She searched his face, and saw nothing to dispel her suspicion. He was no longer skulking in the shadows, but the bright firelight cast no brightness over his face. Nameless. Shadowed. That explained it. It explained all of it – his quicksilver mood swings, his smouldering hatred, his skulking and his lying. And he had never told her his name. 'A demon.'

He flinched angrily at the word. 'Gah! I *am not*. I am Nameless, yes, but if I was a demon I'd have done something dreadful *long* before now.'

Will took one more step toward him. She knew the answer already. Amaranth's gift of Wisdom damned her in that moment. She had been happier not knowing. 'But you have. God of Death!' She breathed. 'God of Death, Doom and Destruction, the wool!' She backed away from him, horrified. 'The wool!' Lavender had been tangled in wool when she fell to her Sleep. And Reynard was a spinner. Will still had one of his spells twisted into her hair. With a sudden shudder she clawed at it, ripping the elflock from her scalp. She cried out as she did it, as she'd torn the whole lock of hair out by the roots. She could feel a thin line of blood trickling down her temple. 'It was *you*. This Sleep is *yours*.' Her voice trembled and roared, seeming to come from some other place, where her horror echoed.

He didn't deny it. She wished he'd deny it. She wouldn't have believed him, but she wished he'd deny it. Even a doubt would have made her feel better.

Cait frowned. 'I thought you knew that, too,' she said

Will whirled on her. 'You thought I knew? You thought that I was callous and bloodthirsty as you and your blasted doom-laden briars?' She pointed at Reynard. 'You thought I'd spend a minute around some Nameless cursed demon if I *knew* what he was? What are you, as evil as he is?' Will took a step back, all of her mother's admonitions and Lavender's fears echoing through her head. 'No. No, it's the magic, that's what it is. It's driven you all mad! Arg!' It pained her to admit it, but Amaranth was right. Hiedelen was right. She held her head in her hands. 'What have I done?' She turned to Reynard. 'You used me. You even admitted to it. And I, ah! I didn't listen! You used me to get to Lavender. You just wanted her, the real princess, and I didn't even see it!'

He lost his temper. 'Actually,' he snapped, 'I didn't care if the Sleep cursed you, her, your wretched parents, or anyone else in that blasted palace! Every last one of you, living rich and warm and well fed, the entire kingdom bears your filthy *name*.' He struggled against the honeysuckle. 'I wanted you to *suffer*.'

Will choked. 'Well,' she said, her voice quivering. 'You got your wish. I'm suffering. We're all suffering. The kingdom will be taken by Hiedelen, and everyone will suffer for it. I hope you're content enough.' She took a step toward him. Her voice low and dangerous, she growled at him, as if it were a curse. 'I'll see you suffer, too,' she rumbled.

'Too late,' he whispered.

Will searched his face, his wretched, shadowed, lovely face. And she had kissed those lying lips. 'Tell me.'

He raised an eyebrow sarcastically. 'Tell you what, exactly?'

'How do I undo it?' she demanded. 'How do I break the Sleep?'

He growled in his throat. 'I wouldn't tell you if I knew, *Princess*.'

The use of her title was what did it. She had been trying to get him to call her Will, again and again. She had taken him into her confidence, she had made herself vulnerable, and he'd thrown it in her face again and again. And now, he had to do it again. He knew what she was. She had told him . . . everything. And he had used her.

She hit him. An open-handed blow across the cheek. He didn't pretend it didn't hurt. She drew herself up to her full height. 'By the authority vested in me by right of inheritance,

I hereby sentence you to arrest. You will be brought before the queen to await judgement for your crimes!'

Cait laughed, a surprisingly merry sound in the charged air. 'You don't think I'd let you arrest my great-nephew, do you?'

Will rounded on her. 'You too are under arrest,' Will said. 'For the wilful murder of four Hiedelen princes, and untold others.'

Cait tossed her head. 'Oh, honestly. Listen to yourself, Willow. You have no power here!'

With a swallow Will looked around her. Suddenly, she realized what a precarious position she was in. For the first time, fear clutched at her. Everything had changed. She had gone with a friend to find an ally, and instead discovered she'd followed an enemy to a callous, disinterested criminal.

She backed a step towards the door. 'What do you plan to do with me?' she asked. She was suddenly glad of her gift of Bravery. She was terrified, but she stood against it easily. Her voice did not tremble in her fear.

Cait shook her head. 'Well, this is madness. I'm sending you home, clearly this is a waste of all of our time.' She sighed at her and glanced at Reynard. 'Shame, really. Off you go!' And she thrust a dry winter rose into Will's hand.

The rose twisted and wrapped itself tightly around Will's arm. The thorns pierced her flesh, and it stung worse than nettles. 'Ah!' Will scrabbled at the thorns, and a few drops of blood from her wrist fell to the ground before everything went dark around her.

Chapter 15

* * *

'Well,' Cait said. 'That's got rid of her.'

I was more worried than I wanted to be. 'What did you do to her?'

'Just what I said, I sent her home. She'll open her eyes in the front hall of her palace, probably a little dizzy, but perfectly fine. It's so touching that you care.' I couldn't tell if she was being sarcastic or not, and I frankly didn't care. 'Too bad, really, I had such high hopes. If you promise to stop trying to kill your aunt, I can let you out of that honeysuckle.'

The wolf growled.

'No, Ylva, you got yourself into this,' Cait said. 'Until he's gone, you can just stay there.'

I narrowed my eyes at the wolf, the glowing, named wolf. I considered this promise. I knew Cait could probably tell if I spat out a lie. Stop *trying* to kill my aunt. If I succeeded, it wouldn't be a try. She also didn't make me promise not to hurt her. 'I promise,' I said.

'Hm,' Cait said, but the honeysuckle slowly released its hold on my arms and legs. I pulled myself from it and took a deep breath. I hated being bound. I stared at my lupine aunt. Things were more clear in my mind. The story made much more sense when it was explained as a family fight with a strong overtone of sibling rivalry. When faeries fight amongst ourselves, it can turn very bloody. We feel any emotion much more strongly than most humans, and rarely let it be tempered. Our emotions run very pure. Any anger would not be easily tempered by familial love, but would be easily strengthened by years of familiarity and a forest of resentment. Like the resentment I felt right now.

'Do sit down,' Cait said. 'It's clear you know nothing.'

'I know much,' I growled.

'I mean, you know nothing about us,' she said. 'Your history, our people. I'm appalled, frankly.'

I glared at her. 'How could I know anything?' I said. 'I've been Nameless since I was an infant. Shunned by faeries, hated by humans, who would have told me a thing?'

'Well, I'd have thought my niece would have taken it upon herself to educate you.'

'There are many things,' I said through my teeth, 'that my mother will not let herself talk about. Things that hurt her.' I sat stiffly on the bench I'd tried before. 'I don't understand.' My voice was still clipped with barely controlled rage. 'That wolf over there is clearly Named.'

'Well, it's not her original name,' Cait said. 'That's lost forever. Even I don't remember it. I sometimes even forget Father's clan name, but it always comes back. Father was never rendered Nameless, after all.' She handed me the cup of tea she had poured for Will, and I pushed it back, causing it to slop over her green dress. She set the cup down without resentment. 'I named Ylva,' she added.

I shook my head. 'How could you do that?'

'Well, first, you clearly know nothing about us, or you'd know all of this. We faeries aren't even strictly faeries any longer, though we're as close as we can be. Do you know how we came to this world?'

'Through the Light,' I said. 'The Festival of Light celebrates a journey from a place we left so long ago that there is no memory, nor even true record of it.'

'Yes, and since those first faeries came through the Light from . . . wherever they came from, we've been interbreeding with mortals. The first faeries were immortal, unless they were killed, and they created their own Names at birth. These names were immutable, and could never be stripped. However, there have been too many years, too much dilution of the blood. While we are long lived, we are no longer immortal. And our Names no longer grow from our blood. We are given them by our parents, while we are infants, and still pure.'

'I remember,' I said. 'Mother tried to name the kit. I remember her trying, but I can't remember the name.'

'Well, the name we are given weaves into our blood. As we are still mostly faeries, we need a Name, a proper Name, to understand ourselves, to take hold of our more . . . impulsive tendencies. I suspect if you were named you wouldn't have cursed poor Lavender.'

'I don't think she's so poor,' I snapped, but Cait only laughed.

'Be that as it may,' she said. 'Our name is what binds us to the Light, and keeps us connected to what we once were, when our ancestors first passed through to this world. When the Stiltskin name was stripped from Ylva, and through her the entire Stiltskin clan, you were cut from that Light. Names can no longer bind to the darkness in your blood. You can't recall what your name was. You can't find a name that becomes you. For all intents and purposes, you are no longer truly a faerie.'

'I am,' I said.

'Yes,' said Cait. 'And that is where the problems arise. You are a faerie without the Light, and without any control. This makes you very dangerous, and all the humans know it.'

A vision of the kit formed in my mind. The kit, white and beautiful, glowing like a true faerie. She'd be an angel. I took a deep breath, and then voiced the most important question in my life. 'How do I find the Light?' I asked. 'That bitch over in the honeysuckle has found hers. How can my family earn back its name?'

'Well, there is where we run into a conundrum,' Cait said. 'I'm not sure that you can.'

I felt as though someone had just struck me. I'd had hope dropped before me, and I was seeing it crushed before my eyes. 'How did *she*?' I said, and it came out very softly. Tears stabbed my eyes.

Cait's tone turned gentle. 'I gave a name to her. I took pity on her. Fifty years into the interregnum I found her wandering my forest, still angry, still vengeful, and half dead. When I found her, she tried to kill me, and failed. Then she begged me to kill her. She didn't want to live Nameless any longer. I made her a deal. If she would serve me for a hundred years, in a magicless form, I would grant her a name. She agreed. It took me five years to find it, and I was only able to do it so quickly because I'd known her all my life.'

'So *quickly*?'

'The only person who can give you a name is someone who knows your heart. Every corner of your heart. Predict every nuance of your thought. I know my sister. We may hate each other, but we have always been family. It took me five years to understand the changes that had taken place in her during her fifty years wandering Nameless, but she hadn't changed all that much. She was still my sister. So I named her for the wolf, and in another twenty years or so she will be a faerie again, just like me.'

'I know *my* sister,' I said. 'You mean I could name her? Any time?'

240

Cait shook her head. 'Such a thing isn't within your power. Until you know yourself, you can't begin to know another properly.'

I looked at her. My great-aunt, mad as a march hare, with daisies for a mind. I knew the answer before I voiced the question. 'Could you name us?'

'That is why I'd expected you earlier. I thought it would be common knowledge that I had taken Ylva in. I expected your mother to join her, but she didn't. I suspect it was that fox father of yours. Red Jack was always sure he could name your mother. He never could manage it. He never truly had a grasp of her heart. Or yours, apparently. Too distrustful.'

'Don't blame this on Da,' I said, but it was without heat. I felt drained. She was right. He'd left after the kit was born. He must have realized he'd never know her, either.

'I don't,' Cait said. 'He was fully a fox faerie; always a wanderer. It was in his nature. I was impressed that he stayed with you and my niece as long as he did. He couldn't name her, so he finally left. I cannot name you either. In the end, I don't know you. I don't know your sister, I don't know my niece. It was possible, back when you were younger, that I could have grown to know you. But as of now, you've been Nameless so long, I doubt anyone could. When you came to my forest I asked my trees to look you over. Not a one of you is knowable. Your mother is broken, so there is too little of her spirit to find. *You* are so buried in resentment and distrust that whatever is beneath is beyond retrieval, even, I suspect, by yourself. Your sister is an enigma. She jerks from optimism to hollow emptiness with no prediction of when, with never a hint of a self in her entire life. You may understand her, but I certainly couldn't begin to.' She pushed another cup of tea at me. 'I'm sorry,' she said.

I bit my tongue to keep from crying. I didn't know why I felt like this. I'd never expected to be anything but Nameless.

I hadn't lost any long-cherished hope. And yet I felt like I did when Da left, and everything seemed empty and dying. Without even thinking about it I took the tea, and this time I swallowed some. It was warm, but I couldn't taste it. 'We will always be Nameless,' I whispered, and my hands trembled around the teacup.

'Yes,' Cait said.

I couldn't even remember the clan name she had said. Something starting with an S. Or was it a C? Cirrus? Seren? It was lost — to me at least. I took a deep breath. 'I suppose that's it, then.' I set the teacup down with a clink. I stood and turned my gaze to the wolf. She was watching me distrustfully. Quite rightly. My next act was not an impulse — I had intended to do it from the moment I was released from the vines. I strode the few steps toward her, and with a furious kick I broke her lupine jawbone. She yelped and whined. 'I very much hope your little prank with Princess Amaranth was worth it, Great-aunt,' I said. 'Pray you never meet me again. I can't quite bring myself to kill a bound enemy, but take this as a token of my appreciation.' I lunged forward and bit her ear, tearing half of it off. I spat the corner of furred flesh to the ground and listened to her whimper. I wanted it to leave me satisfied, but I felt hollow.

Cait shook her head. 'Impulsive Nameless nephews,' she muttered. 'You're very like her, you know.'

I whirled on her. 'Say that again and I'll bite you too!' I snarled.

She was holding something out to me. 'Here.'

I took a step back. 'What's this?'

'It's for you.' It was another sack, the same as the seemingly bottomless one she'd sent me home with before.

'What, the other one about to run out?' I asked.

'Oh, no,' Cait said. She reached inside and pulled out a chiffon cake with sliced cherries atop it. 'But this one does desserts.'

I wanted to push the cake in her face and dump the bag over her head, but the thought of the kit with an éclair the size of her head stopped me. We hadn't had anything sweet since I broke into the bakery fifteen years ago. The kit was still a child. I took the bag and stalked out into the snow, alone.

Against my will, I briefly wondered if Will had gotten home all right, but I banished the thought. She thought me a demon. She was no longer any of my concern.

Chapter 16

Will

Despite Cait's assurances that she was sending her home, Will half expected her new bracelet of thorns to slit her veins and leave her bleeding out her last. Instead, she suffered only one small scratch. The pain of the scratch seemed to turn her inside out until she was nothing but this mild stinging pain. Cait's tower chamber, her shrubs and vines and teacups, all swirled into a tiny point, which then exploded again, unfolding like a flower. When it did, Will was no longer in Cait's tower. She had arrived, with a crack as loud as a firework, in the centre of the receiving hall.

Will staggered and clawed at her wrist. If this was a briar like the ones surrounding the palace, it would just twist tighter and tighter until Will's blood splashed onto the floor. But it was dead and lifeless, and fell from her without a struggle. Will wanted to pick it up and examine it, but she didn't have a chance, as the sound of boots and the mutters of frightened soldiers quickly surrounded her. She looked up to find a selection of guards holding swords and crossbows forming a ragged, breathless circle around her. 'She's come back!' one of them shouted over her head.

'Of course I've come back!' Will snapped. She was too tired and angry and frustrated to really focus. 'Let me pass. I need to speak with the queen immediately.'

'You just stay right there, Highness,' said a deadly voice. Will turned to look, and frowned. It was Captain Warren.

'What's going on, Captain?' she asked. 'I insist that you let me pass.'

'Stay still, Highness,' he said firmly. He raised his crossbow a little, and his brow furrowed. He looked very much as if he didn't want to have to pull the trigger, but several of the others didn't look quite so averse. Will suddenly realized it was no accident that the guards had surrounded her. She felt an unpleasant sensation up her spine as her back realized it had four ninety-pound-draw crossbows pointed at it, bolts set and ready. Crossbows had been known to misfire on occasion. Will wanted to turn inside out.

She cleared her throat, and two of the crossbows shook a little at the unexpected sound. 'I have no intention of disagreeing with you fine gentlemen. I surrender myself into your capable hands. If you would be so kind as to lead me to my mother or father, I'm sure we can clear up this little misunderstanding.'

'Just stand there, Your Highness,' Captain Warren said. 'Don't move, I beg you. The king's already been called for. He expressed orders to be fetched should you dare to return.'

'Yes,' Will said, a little relieved. 'I'm sure my father can sort things out to everyone's satisfaction.'

Captain Warren shook his head. 'Not your father, Highness.'

Will frowned. 'Who . . .' she began, but she already knew who he meant. She swallowed. 'What's happened?' she asked in a lower voice. 'While I was gone. Has something happened to Mother?'

'The which you well know,' said a loud, accented voice from behind her. The creeping sensation up her spine clutched at her, and she flinched. Very, very slowly, she turned around.

King Lesli was standing by the stairs, surrounded by quite a little knot of frightened looking courtiers including . . .

ah, of course. Ginith. She would be in the thick of things, wouldn't she.

'Your Majesty,' Will said, curtsying in her travelling clothes. 'I apologize for my appearance, but you have an unfortunate habit of failing to catch me at my best. These kind gentlemen inform me that they are following orders issued by none other than your illustrious self. May I ask what has occurred that you find yourself in a position to issue orders in Lyndal's house?'

'The overthrow of my nephew's household by his conniving witch daughter,' Lesli said. He nodded at two of the surrounding guards. 'Bind her. No knowing what tricks she can pull if her hands are free.'

'Bind her mouth, too, Your Majesty,' Ginith said. 'She could still mutter spells at any of us.'

Will stopped herself from rolling her eyes. Someone might take it for the beginning of a spell, and then ten inches of pointed ashwood would embed themselves rapidly into her torso.

Lesli narrowed his eyes. 'A fine notion. You, see to it.'

He had pointed at Captain Warren. As hands grabbed Will's wrists and none too gently trapped them into manacles, such as were used for common convicts, Captain Warren took a hesitant step forward. He reached into his pocket for a clean handkerchief. 'Forgive me, Highness,' he muttered as he wrapped it loosely around her head. It was a much less intrusive and unpleasant gag than the one Ginith and her cronies had forced into her mouth earlier, but it was no less degrading for that. Particularly before half the court guards.

Will's mouth closed on the clean linen, and she sunk her teeth into it. Her eyes bored into King Lesli until he actually looked away.

'What shall we do with her, sire?' Captain Warren asked when he was finished.

Ginith stepped forward brazenly. 'The dungeon!'

Lesli looked amused for a moment.

Warren stood before Will. 'You can't do that, sire. She is the royal heir of Lyndaria.'

'Of course we can't,' Lesli said. He was too disciplined to let the disappointment Will saw in his eyes colour his voice. 'I had no intention. I've already called for a trial, which shall be held within the hour. In the meantime, I suggest we set her, guarded, in the antechamber with the fruits of her crimes.'

'Are you sure that's wise, sire?' Ginith asked. 'No telling what she might do to them!'

Lesli turned his gaze on Ginith, and she took a step back, realizing her error. 'Of course, you would know the best, sire,' she said hastily.

'Indeed.' He pointed at Warren. 'You. Choose four of your men and stand guard on her at all times.'

Someone tried to take hold of Will's shoulders but she whipped her gaze back at him and he shied off. With her head held high, with as much dignity as her rank could possibly lend her, she marched steadily and serenely through the throne room to the antechamber, where her sister was laid in state.

She suspected the truth before she was brought in. Lavender was no longer alone in the room. Another bed had been brought in and set up opposite Lavender's lovely dais. This bed was larger and even more ornate. Will recognized it immediately as the antique bed from her grandmother's chambers. As she expected, the figure laid out in antique silk – her coronation dress, if Will remembered correctly – with her fine, slivering hair spread delicately over the pillow, was Queen Amaranth. She was frowning unhappily in her dreams. Beside her, looking as much like a farmhand as he ever had despite the velvet suit they had somehow gotten him into, her husband Ragi was curled on his side, wrestling furiously with a nightmare.

Will tried not to react, but she swallowed. Reynard had done this. Wretched, wicked Nameless. She made a small sound of frustration. It sounded odd and muffled, and it drew movement from a shadow beside Lavender's bed. 'What's this?'

Prince Ferdinand rose to his feet as gracefully as a wave of the sea. He turned his attention to Captain Warren. 'What is this? What are you doing to a member of the royal house?'

Captain Warren opened his mouth and frowned. It seemed to take him a moment to find words. 'Pardon me, sir. I'd forgotten you were like to be here, or I'd have insisted on another place. We'll just find another chamber, if you please, sir.' He bowed and began walking backward.

'Nonsense!' Ferdinand rushed forward and pulled the gag gently from Will's face. 'You'll not drag this young woman around her palace in chains! Whoever ordered such a thing?' He glared at Captain Warren. 'I can guess. You tell your new master that he is not the only one with a claim to the Lyndarian crown. Until this young woman has been convicted, she is currently in a position of regent until her mother's or sister's awakening. Go.'

Captain Warren shook his head. 'I'm to guard her, sir.'

Ferdinand strode behind her and began fearlessly taking bolts from the crossbows. 'If two of your men with swords at the ready can't guard a young woman in a closed room, than your entire regiment needs restructuring and retraining, and quite possibly new leadership. A point I will be sure to bring up with Queen Amaranth upon her awakening, which, I might point out, may well be any minute of any hour of any day.' He pushed the bouquet of bolts into Warren's hand. 'The key, if you please, sir!'

Warren hesitated. 'I have orders . . . Highness.'

Ferdinand laughed. 'Indeed. Have you finally remembered that I, too, am visiting royalty, betrothed to the heiress, with as much claim as your wretched Hiedelen king? You do not treat a royal prisoner as you would one of your common stales.' He held out his hand. 'You may inform His Hiedelen Majesty that it was my royal command.'

Warren thought for a brief moment and then pulled the key from his waist. 'Here you are, sir. But we must remain here as guards.'

'As your conscience dictates, gentlemen,' Ferdinand said, closing his hand around the key. He turned back to Will and unlocked the manacles. 'Are you all right, Highness?' he asked her in a quieter voice once the bands of iron had fallen to the carpet.

'Yes,' she lied.

Ferdinand wrapped his arm around her shoulder and led her quietly to a couch.

'Sir,' called Captain Warren. 'I'll need to stand near to hear what the two of you are plannin'.'

Ferdinand turned his ice-blue eyes into a frozen glare that stopped Warren in his tracks. When it became clear that Warren wasn't about to press the issue, Ferdinand softened a bit. 'Your ordinary charges are not royalty, Captain Warren, nor is guarding political prisoners originally your assigned responsibility, so I shall let this misinterpretation of your role pass. For now. In the meantime, you will maintain a respectful distance between yourself and our royal personages. And as you had outrageously presumed to gag the princess, I find it unlikely that you had direct orders to listen in on her conversations. Am I correct?'

Captain Warren decided to cover his confusion in efficiency. 'Men, at attention,' he said. 'Swords at the ready.' He stood with the others by the doors.

Ferdinand's hand on Will's shoulder smoothed the uncomfortable clutching feeling she'd suffered since she'd noticed the crossbows. 'I thank you,' she whispered.

'No need,' Ferdinand said in a low voice. 'The palace has been in a state of chaos since you vanished.'

'I tried to make it back in time for the wedding,' she said.

Ferdinand laughed. 'That should be interesting,' he said. 'You can see what's occurred since your departure. Do you know they've already arranged a trial?'

Will nodded. She already knew what she had been arrested for. The rumours had gone from whispers to accusations. With the king and queen out of the picture, Heidelen had taken those accusations and turned them to charges. Will was to be put on trial for bewitching her own family. She wasn't very worried. They'd never be able to prove she had any part in this, and once she had told them all of Reynard and Cait's betrayal, they'd turn their search to finding him. 'When did the Sleep take them?'

'It took your mother yesterday morning,' Ferdinand told her.

'*Yesterday?*'

'Aye. Your father had hidden it, trying to find a way to keep it from Hiedelen's men. After the attack on the royal vault there was a general outcry, and then no one could find you. Lesli was furious. He personally oversaw a search of your rooms, and he said it looked as if you had packed in a hurry.'

Will scoffed. 'My rooms were raided by a bloodthirsty mob! Ask my chambermaid.'

'I'm afraid she's asleep. There was a sudden surge in cases in the last eighteen hours. First Narvi fell prey, which threw Lesli into an uproar.'

'I thought the Hiedelen were immune.'

'So did we all, but first Narvi, and then half of Hiedelen's guard. It all seemed to happen in one fell swoop shortly after midnight. One minute, all the men from Hiedelen seem immune, and the next, yawning and nodding and snoring all around. Hiedelen grew very quiet then, drew all his men into his chambers and didn't come out for three hours. Everyone was terrified. We thought he was plotting some kind of revenge. When he finally did come out, all he did was demand that Ragi let him see Queen Amaranth. No more of his men have succumbed, though, which is making things difficult, as the rest of the palace seems to be falling like rose petals in autumn. We're down to mostly Lesli's men as guards, now, as you may have noticed.' He nodded at the men behind them which, apart from Warren, were all Lesli's. 'Also, there doesn't seem to be anyone left any more who doesn't believe you're some evil witch.'

Will grunted in frustration. *Damn* Reynard to the darkest hell! 'When did it take Father?'

'About an hour ago, I suspect. That's when the dreams started, in any case. But he's been unconscious since last night. After they couldn't find you, they did a careful count of all the royal jewels, assuming you had taken some to finance your escape.'

'I never touched them!' Will cried.

'Shh!' Ferdinand hissed, looking over her head toward Captain Warren and his men. 'They discovered that immediately, but what was taken was bad enough.'

'The spinning wheel,' Will said. 'But it isn't really missing. If you go around the back of the palace, it should still be there.'

'I know,' Ferdinand said. 'Sitting in the middle of a large cleared swathe through the thorns.'

'Right,' Will said. 'You've found it then?'

'Yes,' Ferdinand said, seeming a little uncomfortable. 'My hound found it, actually.'

Will grinned. 'Good Edelweiss,' she said praising the white fleethound, but Ferdinand looked so grim that her smile died on her face. 'Ferdinand, what do you need to tell me?'

He took a deep breath. 'Lesli was adamant about seeing your mother, particularly after he found out about the raid on the vault. He said he couldn't risk marrying his grandson to a witch, and she had to know it. Your father said that Narvi being asleep made the entire issue moot, and they would discuss it and sign a treaty when the crisis was over. They argued. Lesli pushed past him to get to your mother's chambers. You know we don't have enough guards, and your father was doing the best he could on his own. Lesli discovered Amaranth, and found that Ragi was trying to hide her condition. They fought. It was quite heated, apparently.'

'How do you know?'

'Your mother's chambermaid was trying as hard as she could not to be noticed in a shadow by the clothes press. According to Helene, Lesli accused your father of being nothing more than the son of the chairman of the miller's guild in the Duchy of Ethelbark, and your father grew enraged. He said Natiniel was an honourable man, and a far better choice than Lesli's weak-brained younger brother. At that point the argument came to blows. Your father had Lesli down, and Lesli surrendered, and then attacked your father with a jug from behind. Ragi went down. Hiedelen said he succumbed to the sleep, but I'm inclined to believe Helene. Your father was in and out of consciousness until a little bit ago, but he stopped waking to my hand, and the dreams started. I think the Sleep did finally catch up to him.'

Will sighed. 'You're *sure*?'

Ferdinand smiled ruefully. 'I've been sitting by Lavender's side for weeks. I think I know what the Sleep looks like. He didn't have it before, but he's suffering it now.'

Will rubbed her forehead and glanced over at her father. She wished he was only suffering a blow to the head, and would sit up, bleary eyed but awake, stride forward and make everything better. But there was little chance of that. 'I'll check and see,' she said. 'There's only one way to know if his nightmares come from the Sleep or his own troubled mind.'

'Later,' Ferdinand said. 'You need to hear the rest. Lesli announced that both the king and queen had succumbed to the Sleep, and he was taking over again as regent. But the only way he could do that was by revoking your right of inheritance, and he could only do that by accusing you of treason. So, as of now, you're officially accused of causing the Sleep.'

'I didn't, you know,' she said. 'But I do know—'

Will didn't have the chance to say that she knew who did cause it, because Ferdinand went on, 'And he has proof.'

'Proof? What proof?'

'You're a magic user and a thief. He has proof of the one and witness to the other.'

'I'm not a thief.'

'You stole the spinning wheel,' he said. 'And the guards were there to see it. Sort of. And apparently you attacked a handful of innocent servants who were wandering the halls. Ginith bears witness to this.'

'That bitch tried to kill me,' Will snarled, just like Reynard.

Ferdinand grimaced. 'I believe it. Why do you think I stay by Lavender's side all the time? She's been trying to lure me away so that her gentleman friends can have their vile way with her.'

'I know,' Will said. 'She mentioned it.'

'She says you cast spells on them and set them on fire.'

'I do use magics,' Will admitted. 'Small magics mostly, charms really, but that was never against the law until Lesli came along and made it so.'

'It's against the law now, and he has a hundred witnesses to prove you've done it. And I wouldn't call spinning deadly thorns into skeins of purest gold a small magic.'

'Gold?' Will blinked. 'Into *gold*?'

'Yes. I can see why you didn't want to reveal this little trick, given the renunciation of spinning in this country, but don't you think you could have given your parents a hint? They say Lyndaria has been in desperate need of finances due to all of Hiedelen's exploitation over a hundred years, and according to your sister, the thorns have been a serious threat.'

'But I *didn't*,' Will said.

'Don't be so modest,' Ferdinand told her seriously. 'I suspect it's the only thing keeping you alive right now.'

Will blinked. 'What?'

'You heard me,' Ferdinand said. 'They didn't discover the skeins of gold until after sunrise. Before that, Hiedelen had ordered all his guards to kill you on sight, before you could do more witchcraft. Only after he discovered *that*, did he arrange for the trial, should you dare to reappear.' He sighed and gently touched Will's cheek, causing little frightened birds to beat their wings in her chest. 'I'd half hoped you had run for good, Will. Gone out to seek your fortune, as I had.' He smiled. 'I could see you going far. If you'd asked me, I'd have given you my horse and hawk and hound to set you on your way.'

Will shook her head. He didn't understand her at all, did he? 'And leave Lyndaria in this mess?'

He shook his head back at her. 'Lyndaria is already lost, I fear.'

Will pulled away from him. He gave up too easily. 'So why haven't you left?' she asked.

He smiled. 'Without Lavender, I am lost too. If my fate be to sleep beside her for a thousand years, I will take it and gladly, rather than be without her.'

She stared at him. He was mad. Love had driven him mad. He was still beautiful, still kind and courageous and noble, but Will never wanted him or anyone else to be so bound to her that they'd rather be dead than without her. What a useless, senseless way to structure your life! She still loved him, but if she had to choose between wasting away beside his lifeless, or rather sleeping, body, or living, she'd have chosen life. She would have honoured her love with her life, not with her death. Her death would be nothing more than a waste. And if he had asked her, she'd have said she wanted no more and no less from him.

It suddenly occurred to Will that Lavender was mad, too. She was willing to sacrifice, her sister, yes, but her country most of all, to marry this man. She was more willing to start a war, to condemn thousands of people on both sides to death, rather than live her life without this man. What a selfish, small-minded, vicious way to behave!

What did that mean? That Will did not truly love him? She did not think that was true. Her love felt as real as any other emotion, as real (though different) as her love for her mother and father. But she had Amaranth's gift of Wisdom, and perhaps that light helped her to see through the fog of love.

She suddenly understood the comparison between poets, lovers and madmen. All of them were blinded and made foolish by some passion or another.

Reynard had been blinded, she realized. He was blinded not by love, but by hate. *Wait*, he had said. When she'd first come to him for his help when the Sleep had taken Lavender, he had told her to wait. That the spell would go away in a few days. Had something gone wrong, then? Had his revenge taken a more sinister turn than he'd intended? He was wildly powerful, so long as he had a spindle in his hands. Will had gathered that. He'd been keeping his magic hidden, as he kept his height and his ears and his shadows hidden. He was Nameless, and the common wisdom was that they were dangerous simply because they were faerie powerful, without the cool faerie reserve. But he had saved her life, more than once last night, and had never threatened her in any way. If he had wanted her dead, he could have killed her easily. If he had wanted her disgraced, he'd had that opportunity too.

Will did not trust him, but suddenly she couldn't bring herself to hate him.

She frowned at Ferdinand. 'I could never leave Lyndaria,' she said. 'Not like this.'

Ferdinand smiled at her sadly. 'You're braver than I,' he said. 'I'm . . . I'm sorry.'

A groan from her parents' bed made her start.

'Just a dream,' Ferdinand said. 'Just another dream.'

Will stood up. 'I have to know if it's the Sleep,' she said.

The guards shifted uneasily as she moved to her father's side, but at a sharp look from Ferdinand they did not try to interfere. She sat on the side of the bed, and took her father's hand in hers. 'Father,' she hissed. 'Father, please.'

His face was like so many faces she had seen these last weeks, twisted in terror, moulded into grief. She knew Ferdinand was right even before she reached out to place her fingertips on his brow. But, for more than one reason, she had to see the truth.

I'm sick. I can barely breathe and my body is burning. I can't get up. I'm being tended, but I'm in a dungeon. Or I might as well be. A hollow under the earth. It is cold – so cold. Terrible, biting winter cold, and the hollow is dank and damp and I'm too ill to fix it. I need to protect someone, but I'm too sick to take care of her. I want a bed. I want broth. I want peace. All I have is rags and damp and a hand to hold mine. I almost wish the hand wasn't there. If it wasn't, I could give up. I could let go and let the illness take me. But I am loved, and my life does not belong to me alone. I cannot steal it from them.

Will pulled her hand away, shivering as if the illness were still with her. She held herself tightly. How could Reynard have done this, to her sister, her mother, her father? Will turned to Amaranth. The queen's breath was coming in shallow gasps and her hands were clenched. Sweat dewed her forehead. Will gently took her hand. 'I'm here, Mother,' she whispered, but she knew she couldn't hear her. 'Mother, I don't know how to help you.' Will smoothed her brow with the damp cloth, but she knew it wouldn't help. Not against . . . She quietly instigated the spell.

I'm hiding. They know I'm here. There are many of them, with gleaming weapons. More of those terrible pitchforks, and heavy shovels, all of them as deadly as soldiers with swords and arrows. I'm hiding in a space so small I can scarcely breathe. I can't see them, but I can hear them, coming for me, looking for me. My heart is beating so loudly I'm sure it'll give me away. I have an impulse to simply burst out, and tell them I'm there, just to end the suspense, the constant terror that they are about to find me.

When Will opened her eyes she was curled in a ball on the bed, trying to hide. She pulled herself back to a sitting position. Ferdinand was no longer watching her. He was back at Lavender's side, tending the princess in her nightmares. What was this? The nightmares were too specific for just a punishment. There was something more. Will reached out one more time.

I'm lonely. There is a terrible blackness of emptiness. There's no one I can trust, no one to run to. I am hated by all. I hate them back. I hate myself more than any of them. So, so alone.

Will gasped. 'Reynard!'

She finally understood. These weren't merely a punishment, not a simple series of horrors. These dreams, these terrible nightmares, were flashes of Reynard's life. The life of a wandering criminal, a prisoner shackled by his flesh. 'God of Wonders,' she muttered. And she had cursed him to his face, called him a demon, threatened to arrest him. He had done wrong, cast a cruel spell upon innocents. But thinking of his sister, his small, pearly white sister with the sharp, mischievous teeth, Will swallowed. Protect them. Protect her. In the dreams he needed to protect her. He wanted to die, but couldn't let himself, for her. Reynard *had* committed a crime in creating this Sleep, there was no doubt of that. But he had suffered his punishment before the act.

Will reached out for Ragi's brow again, but did not search out the dreams.

They left her alone for a long time. She actually slept for a few hours beside her father on the bed. It was well after noon when a guard in Hiedelen livery was sent to fetch her. 'Why is she unbound?' he asked, angrily.

'There is no cause to bind an unconvicted princess in her own palace,' Ferdinand said angrily.

'And who gave you authority here, Illarian?' the guard snapped, and Will recognized him as Lesli's personal bodyguard. His name was Levi. He was actually a relative, some illegitimate son of one of Lesli's cousins. He clearly felt no deference toward Ferdinand's status.

'Queen Amaranth,' Ferdinand said. 'When she betrothed me to her daughter.'

Levi laughed. 'Oh, aye, that's sure to take you far.' He gestured to Warren. 'Tie her up.'

'You truly intend to parade her at trial trussed up like a suckling pig?'

As Warren reattached the manacles the guard pulled a gag tightly around Will's mouth. 'Not going to trial. Already convicted,' he said.

'What?' Will said, but it came out a muffled shriek through the gag.

Ferdinand tried to stop him. 'Then I demand to know where you are taking her!'

Levi half drew his sword, using the hilt to bash in Ferdinand's fine nose. 'Get your paws off me. I follow orders from King Lesli himself!'

'He is no king here!' Ferdinand cried out.

'More than *you* are, Illarian. Hold him back!' Levi snapped at Warren's soldiers. Will stood up to her full height and looked down at Ferdinand, shaking her head to tell him it was all right. She looked from him to Lavender, hoping he'd catch her meaning; she needed him here to watch over her family.

He nodded, and a line of blood trickled from his nose. He wiped it with his black gloves and returned to his vigil at Lavender's side.

Which meant Will stood alone. Keeping her face stony, she allowed Levi and his men to lead her back through her palace. She kept her eyes straight, but couldn't help but hear the murmurs as the servants and remaining courtiers caught sight of her being led through the corridors. Finally, her cheeks burning with shame, she was led to her mother's study. The door was guarded by no less than six of Hiedelen's remaining attendants. Without ceremony, Levi pushed her through the door, still bound and gagged.

Lesli sat at Queen Amaranth's desk, dressed in more formal attire than he had been before. 'I've just come from your trial,' he said, his tone unctuous and unpleasant. 'I'm ashamed to call you my kin, Highness.'

Will had a dozen things she wanted to say to that, her gifts of Honesty and Wit raking at her tongue, but the gag forced her to remain polite.

'No doubt you've guessed at the outcome. I stood up valiantly in your defence, but in the end the prosecution was simply too formidable, the evidence against you too apparent.'

Will's eyes narrowed, the only act of defiance she was capable of, bar butting him in the nose and kneeing him in the crotch, two options she considered. But the guards were right outside, and she would likely be tortured for such an attack.

Lesli leaned back in Amaranth's chair. 'You know,' he said, 'when I was a boy, I always wondered what the interior of this palace looked like. There were tales of gold-draped walls and gem-encrusted furnishings. Every tapestry a king's ransom, every rug a baron's fortune. I was highly disappointed when your father brought this place to life. Ageing wood and drafty corners, every article a hundred years out of date, and failing to maintain its splendour. Truly heartbreaking when your childhood dreams are spoiled by the reality.' He leaned forward. 'Do you want to die?'

Will stared at him. He knew the answer. She wasn't going to give him the satisfaction of begging silently for her life with a gag in her mouth. He lifted a little nest that was sitting on the desk. 'I'm sure you know what this is, my dear,' he said. Will blinked at it. In the light of day, the little tangled skein of thread was clearly gold. She didn't even have to touch it to know. The heavy way it sat in his hand was enough. And Will knew how heavy it was; she'd held one not so long ago. 'I must say, I was impressed. You do realize that the art of spinning straw into gold was lost more than a hundred years ago.' He pulled out a strand of the thin, silky wire. 'But this is even more impressive. Those thorns have become a true nuisance. There was a time, after your father proved less than loyal to me, that I considered invading this country. But I realized it was pointless. Kingdoms that still dabble in magic cannot be held without taking the royal seat. The thorns made taking this palace impossible, and sieges take so much time. Time an old man like me doesn't have.' He smiled at her in a way she was sure she didn't like. 'Or maybe not so old as all that.'

He idly began wrapping the thread of gold around his index finger. 'You have been sentenced to death. However, if you would care to place your fate at the hands of the gods, I can arrange for you to undergo a trial.' He twisted the gold between his fingers. 'Yes, a trial, such as we have in my kingdom for witchcraft. If you fail the trial, you will die. If you succeed at the trial . . . I will think of some other fate for you.'

Will glared at him over the gag. He thought much of himself if he thought she would follow his false thread of hope for a moment.

'The East Wing has been overrun with thorns, has it not?' he asked. 'None ever uses that portion of the palace for fear of being throttled and bled to death. There are many rooms which hold now nothing but solid canes of these deadly briars. Am I correct?'

Will guessed where this was going, and it wasn't going to be pleasant. If he was proposing what she suspected, she was already dead. Her body just hadn't realized it yet.

'Your trial is this. I am going to shut you into one of those East Wing rooms, those rooms entirely overgrown with briars. You will have one night, and your spinning wheel. If, in the morning, you have not spun every last briar cane into gold, you will be hung publicly upon the gallows, your body burned, and your ashes scattered in an undisclosed location. You will be branded as a traitor to your country, and people will use your name as an insult.' He smiled. 'Ah. And if you are found bled dry in the morning, I will exonerate you.

Announce you were falsely accused and your remains will be buried in state.'

She stared at the nest of gold thread in his hand and gestured to it with her manacled fist. And if I succeed?

He frowned, then his face cleared when he understood what she was asking. 'Ah, you want to know what happens if you succeed.' He smiled again. 'If every single briar has been spun into gold, and you stand, hale and whole in the midst of the glittering. What a fine picture that would make. Should you succeed in this way, you shan't be killed in the morning. That is all you need know.'

Will sighed.

'I already know where I shall put you. Guards, take this woman to the East Receiving Room. There you may unbind her. Treat her respectfully,' he added. 'She is of the royal line. The spinning wheel is all ready for you, my dear.'

If hatred alone could kill a man, Will would have been a murderess and glad of it at that moment.

Chapter 17

* * *

As always, it was much easier to find my way back to the burrow than it had been to find the way to Cait's tower. The kit jumped up from under a snowbank as I approached, surprising me. She was rosy cheeked and well fed, thanks to Cait's eternal bag of food. Even though her weight had not begun to fill out, it was strange seeing her without that look of hunger in her eyes. I stared at her in wonder for a few minutes, imagining what that silver-white hair would look like illuminated with the Light of a true faerie. It hurt my heart. 'Gottcha!' she cried, and hurled a loosely packed snowball into my face.

I sputtered and she dashed behind a tree, awaiting my returning volley. I wished I was in the mood to play with her. She rarely had the energy and freedom to play. Neither of us had had much of a childhood. I brushed the snow from my face and reached into the bag. I pulled out what appeared to be a cinnamon bun and hurled at her instead, still steaming with ensorcelled heat. She caught it deftly and looked at me awed. 'Cait gave you another bag,' she said.

'This one does desserts,' I said, but I couldn't sound pleased about it. 'Where's our ma?'

'Collecting firewood,' the kit said.

I heaved a sigh. 'Good.' That meant the burrow was empty. I crawled in and curled up. I hadn't slept last night.

It took me a long time to get to sleep. At first I kept thinking of Cait and Ylva, and how we would never be anything but Nameless. Unknowable. I think I growled under my breath as I tried to pursue the elusive slumber. Then I thought of Ylva's crimes, and how that had resulted in so much hardship. Thinking of Ylva's crime made me think of Will, and her anger at Cait's wall of thorns which had caused so much death. And then I was thinking of Will.

Damn.

The scent of roses. The scent of *her*, thick and very human. Her body had been so soft and so strong beneath mine. Stop that, I told myself. Stop it, she hates you, you're Nameless. She called you a demon. The last thing you need, the absolute last thing you need is to get obsessed over some other human, risk another Lynelle. Damn Lynelle to the depths of the darkest hell, and damn Will along with her!

It wasn't working. The scent of roses was still hidden in my clothes where I had held her. Finally I gave in and just thought of her, how she had reached forward to kiss me, how she'd simply waited for me to come back. She thought herself unhandsome? What madness! She was probably comparing herself to that pale, washed-out twig of a sister. The scent of her hair was enough to lead a man to hell. I turned my head and breathed in the scent that still lingered on my shirt sleeves. Finally, curled around a warm human body which was not there, relishing a scent which was rapidly fading, I lulled myself into sleep.

My dreams were unpleasant. I was chasing a wisp of light, through a snow-covered forest. A light no more real or substantial than the kit's baby attempts at foxfire. Sometimes I could see by it, but mostly it was just a hovering twinkle darting behind black trees. I needed to catch it, and I kept getting closer and closer, until I had it cornered, or so I thought, near a hollow under a tree, like our burrow. I darted in after it, but inside it was a large ballroom, and there was Will, gleaming like a flame in the darkness, spinning at the spinning wheel. She had caught the light and was spinning it into a gleaming thread that I knew I was not permitted to touch. I was furious that she had stolen the light from me, and I launched myself at her. She turned into Ylva as a glowing wolf, and savaged my arm with teeth made of ice.

I yelped and sat up too quickly, knocking my head on the curved wall of the burrow. My arm was all pins and needles, the icy patch on my wound half melted. I was healing, but it almost hurt worse for that, the pain kept less at bay by Winnowinn's icy bandage. On an impulse I sniffed at my sleeve again. My father might have been able to read the trace of Will's scent still on it, but my nose wasn't so strong.

I poked my nose out of the burrow and saw my ma sitting by our pile of firewood. She was ostensibly piling more wood neatly atop it, but I could see she'd stopped in her labours. Her hand was running idly over Mistress Cait's new gift. A small layer cake was sitting on the snow before her feet. I grunted a greeting and she looked up at me. 'You're awake,' she said.

'Aye.'

My ma looked very sad, and a little afraid. 'You should eat that,' she said. 'You'll be needing it.'

I frowned. 'What's the matter?' I asked. I glanced around. 'Where's the kit?'

'She's gone to town to check up on your princess,' she said. 'You'll be going off again in a bit.'

'Don't presume to foresee me,' I snapped. 'I'm never going to see that bigoted clod again, and even that will be too soon.'

'You'll go,' my ma said. 'And you'll die,' she added in a voice bleak as the winter. 'Either you'll die, or she will.' She stared straight at me. 'I told you you were being reckless.'

There was nothing to say to that. I picked up the cake, which was made with fruit and nuts and held some wholesome weight beneath the sweetness. After a few bites I looked over at her. She looked immensely sad. 'Did it never occur to you,' I asked, 'to go and see Faerie Caital after . . . what happened?'

My ma looked up at me. 'Don't listen to what she says. She's mad. She's always been mad.'

'She says it might have been possible, once, to find a name for us.'

'There was never any hope of that,' my ma said. 'She never knew us. I saw her barely twice in my lifetime.' She closed her eyes. 'She couldn't possibly. That much I could see.'

I shook my head. 'Since when have you been so willing to foresee anything?'

'I never stopped seeing,' my ma said. 'I only stopped saying.'

I finished the nut cake in silence as the sun sank quietly in the sky. I heard the kit returning before I saw her. When I saw her I lurched to my feet, preparing to do battle. Her face was twisted in pain and rage, and she held a crumpled piece of paper clenched in one fist. 'What is it?' I asked.

The kit launched herself at me. 'You've killed her!' she shouted. 'You evil, nameless demon brother, you've killed her!'

I caught the kit by the arms and held her away from me. Dark tears were streaming down her face, steaming slightly in the cold air. She was the one who looked demonic, the fires of hell smoking down her cheeks. 'Who have I killed?'

'Willow! Princess Willow!' She wiped her face with the royal blue scarf the princess had given her, her faerie tears bleaching spots of it a yellowish white. 'They've condemned her to death for spinning the thorns to gold and putting the royal family to sleep, and it's all your fault!'

'Condemned her to death?' I asked. 'What are you talking about? She's getting married this morning.' The thought caused a stab of rage through me, towards her and towards Hiedelen's entire country.

'No, she's not,' the kit explained, pushing the crumpled broadsheet under my nose. 'Narvi's fallen asleep, Willow's been accused of treason, and now they're going to kill her unless she can spin the thorns, and I know she can't do it, because *you* must have done it, and now she's going to die because of *you!*' The kit hit me on my wounded shoulder and I grunted with the pain.

'Stop it!' I said. I grabbed her around the neck and held her under my uninjured arm, bent double so she couldn't hit me again. She flailed, but I knew how to hold someone who was trying to hurt me. As she struggled, I glanced over the broadsheet that the kit had brought. Damn. The kit was right. Somehow last night, between my power and the inherent magic of my aunt's old spinning wheel, the deadly thorns had chosen to spin themselves into gold – it was probably that flash of annoyance I'd gotten when Will had reminded me of Lynelle that did it. Gold and death and Lynelle always tangled together in my mind anyway. It wasn't just a little trouble the princess was in, either. It really was a sentence of death, and it really was my fault. 'If I promise to go and help her, will you stop hitting my wounded arm?'

The kit ceased her struggles and nodded beneath my grip. I let her go and she tilted her head, stretching her neck. She sniffed and wiped her face again, further bleach-staining the scarf. 'You're really going to help her?' she whispered.

I stared at her. 'You care so much,' I said. 'Don't you find it exhausting?'

She shrugged with a little smile on her face. I thought of Will lying against me last night, warm and welcoming. I thought of her stiff and cold, her head severed by an executioner, or bled by my mad aunt's eccentric thorns. I couldn't let it happen. 'Yes,' I said. 'So help me, I'm really going to rescue the wretched princess.'

'No!' my ma called out. 'Don't you see? It's happening.'

'See what?' I asked. 'Truly, my mother, what do you see? What do you see that can be worse than *this*?' I gestured to the barren wood and the frozen ground and the tiny, filthy burrow.

'I see thorns and gold and blood. I hear screaming. I see death.'

'Whose death?'

'Just death, like a golden shroud, a white hand that touches where it will, a claw of thorns.'

I lost my temper, something I never had a strong rein on at the best of times. 'You see nothing!' I snapped. 'You thought I would die yesterday, and here I stand before you!'

'My foresight has never failed me before,' my ma said. 'As I would spin the threads I could see the threads of time, follow them to their ends, and if they are not changed they will always go where I see them lead.'

'You haven't spun a thread in a generation,' I snapped. 'And if you know so much, why have you not prevented it? Why didn't you warn us when we were about to be ambushed, or when the winter was going to be hard enough that we half starved and our fingers turned numb from the cold? Why did you not see the hell you were bringing us into, even before you'd let the council strip our names from us?'

'You blame me?' our ma asked.

'I blame you for nothing,' I shouted. 'But I have no faith in your visions. Why did you not foresee the spell I would cast, foresee this sentence of death on an innocent girl? And while I'm asking, why did you not foresee Lynelle's fate?'

'I did,' my ma said quietly. 'You would not have believed me then, either.'

I thought of Lynelle, wiry and coarse, but fragile as a climbing vine, pulled up by the roots. And I thought of Will, sturdy as a country heifer, tempered by refinement as pure as gold. I thought of her slaughtered on a butcher's block like a heifer. 'I can't let it happen again,' I said. 'You know I can't.'

'Yes,' my ma said. 'I know.'

The spinning wheel was gone, but the swathe I had cleared through the thorns the previous evening was unguarded. I thought this curious, so I was cautious until I approached the wall and realized the reason. The door through which Will and I had come was so camouflaged that even I couldn't see it, and I knew it was there. It took more than a quarter of an hour of hunting to realize where the hidden catch was and slide the passage open.

The secret passages of Will's were difficult to traverse without her help. There were more turns and dead-ends than I had anticipated, leading to convenient spy-holes and secret weapons caches. Finally I found a panel that led to a corridor, and I left the dark, unmarked passageway behind.

The broadsheet had said that Will was being kept in a room full of thorns, and that probably meant the East Wing. I took a deep breath and headed east until I came to a door that had only recently been unlocked. Dust covered the walls of the corridors, and most of the valuable objects and statues had been removed, making the entire place feel abandoned. This must have been what the palace had been like when King Ragi had picked his way through the sleeping people and finally found his princess in the uppermost tower. The corridors were relatively clear, only the occasional shrub sneaking under some of the doors, testifying to rooms that were past occupancy. The few windows were boarded up, and clawlike hands of briars grasped through them.

It also didn't take much scouting to figure out where Will was being kept, and I found her fairly quickly. The frustrated scream might have had something to do with it.

The door of the room she was in was locked, but I could hear someone cursing when I put my head to the wood. The door was iron-bound oak, and I wasn't going to be able to break through in a hurry. But a window stood nearby at the corner. I muttered Will's stilling spell and pried the boards off the cracked glass. I crept into the briars themselves, climbing amongst them like a squirrel. A few twists and I was able to angle towards a window high up in the wall of the room in which Will was being held.

It was not hard to get inside. The briars had broken this window, and no one had bothered boarding it up. I had to move the briars aside, and got a little scratched. I climbed up onto a beam and watched for a moment, mostly trying to figure out how to approach.

It was Will, of course. She was not sitting weeping in the corner like any normal princess would have, faced with execution. No; Will was wrestling with the thorns. She was pulling up canes with her bare hands and cursing them with inventiveness. It was dark, and the torchlight flickered, so I couldn't understand what she was doing at first. She continued to wrestle with the thorns, and as I watched she became helplessly tangled. She tripped, fell, but got hung up on the sharp canes, and hung suspended a few inches from the ground. She forced her way back to her feet, but was so hopelessly tangled that I couldn't see how she'd get herself out. She stood in the middle of her thorny prison and yelled at the moon. A fiercer and more mournful bay I've never heard from a wolf. I couldn't bear to watch it any more. I jumped from the beam to the centre of the room.

I probably seemed to have appeared from out of thin air, and Will gasped. I didn't ask if I could help, I simply began separating the stilled thorns. 'Have you grown to love them so much?' I asked once I'd cleared a slight path.

Will tore her way out of the thorn hedge, ripping gashes in her clothing and her flesh. Bits of broken briars clung to her hair and were embedded in her sleeve, and one was still piercing her neck. I reached forward very gently and pulled the briar from her flesh. She hissed with pain. Analogies failed me. She looked exactly as if she'd been wrestling with thorns half the night. Her clothes were mere threads, more hole than cloth, and the only reason they still afforded modesty was due to the fortunate layers, and a few strategic knots she had tied to keep them together. Her flesh was riddled with lines of red, and blood stained her skin. A scratch arched across her face, and her eyes were haggard.

'I . . .' She blinked at me a few times. 'What are you doing here?'

'I was about to ask you the same question.' I reached out and pulled a bramble from her hair. She cringed, but did not back away from me.

'Awaiting execution,' Will snapped. 'What does it look like?'

'They decided to execute you with thorns?'

'It was Lesli's idea. If the thorns kill me, I'm not guilty of using the spinning wheel, and I'm therefore innocent of cursing my sister. If I'm able to spin them into submission, I am guilty. It's a double-edged sword.'

I frowned. The spinning wheel stood in the only clear spot in the room, in a patch of torchlight. 'So why are you wrestling with the thorns?'

'Because if I'm guilty, Lesli has promised me the punishment is not death.' She threw up her scratched hands. 'Given the choices, I'm choosing life.'

'You think *you're* going to be able to spin the thorns?'

'No,' she said. 'But I was willing to try.'

A drop of her blood was running down her cheek like a tear. I caught it gently with the back of my finger. 'At the risk of your life?'

'They'll kill me whether I try or no. And I still have the stillness spell.' With a striking hiss the thorns answered her, as if in defiance. 'Blast! *For I am nature's strength, her arm and hand/ That binds the fruitful bounty of the land.*' The briars writhed and quivered and then fell again into submission at her spell. She panted. 'They're adapting to the spell, though. They stay still for a shorter and shorter amount of time.'

I could see the spell had cost her. She was no faerie, connected to the magic as a fish to water. Her magic drained her of her own life force. Rest and time would replenish it, mortal as she was, but it wasn't a bottomless well. It wasn't that the thorns were adapting. She was losing power, weakening herself. What with her exertions last night and the magic she was expending here, she was likely in a terrible state. I looked at the ground with a sigh, horrified by what I was watching. I shook my head and turned back to her. 'And when it stops working?'

She stared straight at me without pleading or expectation in her eyes. Fear there was in abundance, but it was a defiant fear. 'I'll die, won't I.' She sat down at the stool by the spinning wheel. 'They'll come to check in the morning. If I'm not dead by then, and the briars aren't spun away, they'll hang me publicly in the courtyard. If they don't decide to just tie me up here and leave me to the thorns.' She looked up at me. 'Why are you here again?'

I searched for a thousand different lies I could tell her, and finally stumbled on the truth. 'I heard you were in trouble.'

She kept her face very still as she said, 'I don't flatter myself you've come to help me.'

I glared. 'Why would I help the daughter of my enemy?'

She twitched her eyebrow in acknowledgment. 'Right. Come to gloat?'

I stared at her evenly. 'I didn't expect you to think well of me. But am I gloating?'

She smiled with a black humour. 'Not very efficiently,' she said. She ran her finger along one of the angry scratches on her wrist. 'So why are you here?' Her voice was so quiet I could only hear it because I was a faerie. I was silent for a long time and she stole a glance at me. She looked away when she saw I was still staring at her, but in that one flicker of her eyes I could read the pleading there.

I desperately wanted to hate her. 'I like watching you suffer, remember?' I said, but the words hurt. I flexed my jaw, remembering where she had hit me. 'I suppose you think this predicament is my fault.' I *knew* it was my fault, but I couldn't say it.

Will shook her head. 'I went to you willingly,' she said. 'You may have a wicked streak, but I'm a damned fool.'

I looked around at the thorns. 'Why are you playing this silly game? Why don't you run?' I asked.

She sighed. 'I thought about it. I even tried, but . . .'

'But?'

'For one thing, I'm not a faerie. I'm heavy and clumsy and human. I find it a lot harder to climb these thorns than you seem to.'

She was big, tall and square, but she was anything but clumsy. Perhaps she was only comparing herself to her willowy older sister. 'You could do it,' I said, though it was a guess. I wasn't sure whether a human *could* scale the thorns as I had, stilling spell or no.

'I probably could get out of this room, yes, and end up impaled on a crossbow bolt.'

I winced as she said it, and rubbed my shoulder.

'Besides. Where would I go? Leave here, wander the earth, take Ferdinand's horse and hawk and hound and go off to seek my fortune?'

'Why not?' I asked.

'Because everything's still falling apart here. Hiedelen has everyone marching to his tune, everyone's falling asleep, and I can't just let the kingdom go.'

'Why not?' I asked again.

She looked at me seriously. 'You feel you have to look out for your sister, don't you?'

I didn't answer.

'I have an entire kingdom to protect. I can't run away, I can't turn my back, and I can't even let myself die.'

Something about that statement made me feel ill. 'Is that what you want?'

'No,' she said. She swallowed what must have been tears. 'No, I don't want to die,' she whispered.

'And I don't want—' I began, but I didn't know how to end the statement. I didn't know what I wanted or didn't want. 'What will you give me if I were to help you?' I said instead.

'Help me escape?'

'You just said you didn't want that. He's given you an impossible task. Very well, it's not impossible for me. But what do I get out of helping you?'

She opened her mouth in surprise. 'Well, anything,' she said. 'Gold. Jewels.' She held up the necklace around her throat. 'Do you want this?'

I lost my temper. 'What would I do with that?' I spat. 'You know I can't sell it. None would buy it off me. I certainly can't wear it. It would be stolen from me in a day. I can't eat it, it wouldn't keep me warm. What good would it do me?' I bore down on her. 'I am Nameless, do you remember? Hated by all! Hated by you! A nameless, evil demon.' She winced as I used her words against her. I turned away. 'I don't know why I came here. You have nothing for me.' I started climbing the thorns back to the windowsill.

'Wait,' she called after me.

I hesitated, then looked back. She stood, straight and defiant by the spinning wheel. She touched the wheel and stared at me, her winter eyes cold. 'I'll give you my library.'

My emotions warred again. I was touched, but I wanted to be cruel. 'You mean that?' I asked. 'Every book?'

'Every. Single. Book,' she said.

My eyes narrowed. I didn't want to believe in her. 'How do I know you'll keep your word?'

'The books are in a secret chamber behind the closet in my bedroom. I'm sure you can find them. Go and get them after this, if you want.' She turned from me and touched the wheel again, gently rocking the wheel back and forth with her fingertips. All defiance left her voice then. 'Take them even if you won't help me. What good are they to me dead?' She shook her head. 'I'd rather they were taken by someone who wouldn't burn them.'

The despondency in her words angered me. It was so unlike Will. 'Move!' I shouted. She started and took a step back. I seized one of the thorn canes she had already broken off and fed it into the wheel. 'And keep your mouth shut.'

It was more difficult spinning the thorns than it had been the night before. They argued with me, as if they knew what had happened to their brethren outside, and were resisting. After the first spool was wound I was panting. I stood up to fetch more thorn canes only to find that Will had been collecting them as I worked. 'Does this help?' she asked.

'I didn't tell you to help me,' I growled.

'I know.' She didn't smile, but there was a hidden lightness to her face. I swallowed, but I allowed her to bring me all the briars she could, until her strength failed, and her spell faded, leaving the thorns wild for her blood. It was twice as hard to spin them into submission after that. I made her sit by the door while I carried the spinning wheel from one corner of the room to the other, chasing the writhing briars. My own fingers were pricked and the sweat stood out on my brow. My already rumpled and ragged clothing gained more rips and tears as the winter thorns warred against my magic.

But what else could I do? I couldn't just leave her to die. Any more than I could have cut off my own arm.

I couldn't.

The sky was already paling when I finished. There were no more briars fighting in the room. Small piles of glittering thread were scattered like bird's nests on the ground. Will was half asleep, her bloodied head resting on her scratched arm. The continued stillness of the spinning wheel seemed to rouse her and she opened her eyes. 'You did it,' she whispered.

'Of course I did it,' I snapped. I was trembling with exhaustion, and I was still hurt by her earlier snub. 'And I expect payment.'

'Go and collect it,' she said quietly. 'You're welcome to it. And anything else you want from my rooms. I think there's a white cloak that would look lovely on your sister.'

Well, *that* made me feel awful. I couldn't decide what I was doing. Wasn't I the evil Nameless demon who wanted everyone to feel pain? 'You'll be all right now?' I asked. For some reason I didn't want to leave her. 'Is there anything else . . . ' I trailed off.

She shook her head tiredly. 'No. There's nothing else you can do for me. But thank you for asking.'

Stone crushed my heart again. 'People like you have no business offering thanks to demons like me,' I said, scornful.

'I suppose not.' She sat up fully and leaned against the wall. 'I'm sorry I said that,' she said. 'Whatever else you are, you're not a demon.'

'It would be easier if I was,' I admitted.

Only one torch had lasted this long, and its yellow light made her look as golden as the threads I had spun. Her tattered rags revealed rather more of her flesh than modesty dictated. She looked like some exotic statue of a fertility goddess. I couldn't keep my gaze from trailing down her form. 'Can I ask you something?'

'Can I prevent you?' I asked, dragging my eyes back to her face.

'You can fail to answer.'

I waited, expecting her to either ask or let it go.

She asked. 'Is it . . . very hard . . . being Nameless?'

I hadn't expected that. Something twisted in me. 'What makes you ask?'

'To do something so awful . . .' she whispered. 'To hurt so many people so casually . . . something has to hurt terribly inside you.'

'I didn't ask for your pity, Highness!' I snapped.

'No. You simply cursed a kingdom to a never-ending Sleep.'

I looked to the wall.

'Why did you do it? What had we ever done to you?'

I didn't have an answer.

'We hadn't hurt you,' Will went on. 'We didn't even know you existed.'

'Exactly,' I spat. 'You didn't know and you didn't care.'

'How would you know? You never petitioned us, never asked for sanctuary or leniency. Amaranth held a public court once a month for any who wanted to appeal to her judgement.

We would receive dozens of letters appealing situations far less sympathetic than yours. Why would you only punish us, instead of ask for our help?'

I didn't have an answer for that, either.

'How does cursing my sister gain you anything?'

'It doesn't,' I whispered, the words falling like feathers.

'Then take it off,' she said. 'End the Sleep now, and I'll see you're acquitted of it. If everyone wakes up, Lesli will have no claim. Everything will be over.'

I finally looked at her. I didn't want to look at her, the red and gold of blood and torchlight shining on her face. But she wouldn't believe me if she couldn't see my eyes. 'I can't. The spell was only meant to tangle into your fingers as you unwound it. It would have faded when the thread was removed. It might have danced about a bit, as coarse wool will, but it wouldn't have done this. Instead it wove itself into Lavender's blood, like the spell that cursed your mother. It wasn't supposed to do that. I don't know how to unravel it.'

Will's head sank onto her hand. 'I wish you'd just told me,' she said. 'In the forest, when I went to find you.' She stared through the empty space before her. 'I feel such a fool.' She turned her gaze back to me, and her eyes shone. 'I want to hate you.'

'I thought you did,' I said. 'Nameless demon. Remember?'

'And a liar, as well,' she pointed out. 'I thought faeries couldn't lie.'

'The Nameless have to learn,' I muttered.

'Part of me does hate you,' Willow said to me then. 'It isn't so much what you are. It isn't even what you've done – mistake or no. But you lied to me.'

'I can't lie very well,' I said honestly.

'But you never told me the whole truth, either,' she said. 'That bothered me.' She looked down at her fine rags. 'Particularly after . . . , that. Under the tree.'

'I only wanted you to trust me,' I said. 'It meant nothing.' The lie hurt, but I said it anyway.

'I know that,' she said, closing her eyes. 'That's why it hurt.'

I couldn't help but ask. 'Did it mean something to you?'

'I already told you I was using you,' she said. She stared into my eyes. 'We're the same, you and I. Both of us discontent with our lot. Both of us starving for one thing or another. That's what it meant.' She looked away again, down at the knots of gilded thread. 'And that was the lie.'

I couldn't stay any longer. This was going to eat me alive. 'You live your life, Princess,' I said. 'Live it well.' I climbed up on the windowsill to leave.

'Live well, my Nameless friend,' she called after me.

I nearly turned around. That she should still call me her friend, after everything, was almost more than I could bear. But I left without another word.

Chapter 18

Will

'Well, well, well,' King Lesli said, surveying the scene. About the room the nests of gold glittered in the morning sun. 'I expected to hear of your death or your failure, but it seems here that you've succeeded in your task.'

'Yes,' Will snapped. Her scratches stung and her muscles ached from sitting on the cold stone, and she felt half frozen. 'Have I established my innocence, yet?'

'We shall see,' Lesli said. He smiled at her in a way she seriously didn't like. 'I suppose we must tend to our princess. Guards, take her somewhere where she can be bathed, and give her something . . . decent to wear.'

Will looked down at herself and blushed. Her garments were tattered beyond recognition, showing a brazen amount of flesh. She grabbed at her chest to cover herself. King Lesli laughed.

As he had men collect the fruits of the night's labours Will was led, without ceremony, to a guest bath chamber. She was not even permitted a robe or cloak to cover her indecency. The bath was filled by more guards, and she was not to be permitted privacy.

She wrestled with her position for a moment, and finally decided she didn't care enough. Without asking permission she rigged up a screen using the edge of a mirror, a vanity stool, and a bath sheet. She stripped off what was left of her clothing behind that and sank into the tub.

It was bliss. The hot water stung at her scratches for a moment, and then smoothed the worst of the aches away, while her muscles unknotted slowly. Had Reynard *ever* been permitted the luxury of a hot bath? she wondered. How would he tend to his scratches? The heat slowly eased its way from the bath to her face, and hot water slowly leaked from her eyes. Why had he helped her? She couldn't understand what his motives were. She wished her hatred of him was clear as the water, but it was murky, tinged with gratitude and blood. She shook her head to banish the tears.

When she got out of her bath she found a fine velvet dress laid out for her. The guards still hovered over her like a flock of vultures, but she threw the dress over her head and dressed beneath it as though it were a tent. She was relieved that they didn't try to touch her, or even leer at her awkwardly undressed state, but they clearly had their orders. She supposed some of them might have even remembered she was the princess.

She did not ask them what their orders were, and they did not volunteer the information. She decided to pretend they weren't there, so she did what she wished. She crawled onto the guest bed and curled up to try and catch some true sleep. Sleep was slow in coming. Every movement and hiccup of the guards caused her to jolt back awake, wary of attack. Finally the two sat down and began to play at cards, and she relaxed. She wished they had brought her to her own rooms, or any of her mother's, as there were secret panels that led to the royal passages, but Lesli probably knew such things existed and was keeping her far from any room with such an escape route.

It was past midday when the door opened. Will had been sleeping lightly, and woke instantly. 'Leave us,' said the voice of King Lesli. She sat up in bed, her heart beating wildly.

'So,' he said. He sat down on the bed beside her, far too close for comfort.

'Get away from me, sir,' she said.

'You're in no position to give orders, Highness,' he said, and he snatched the comforter down. He seemed disappointed that she was dressed in velvet and not in a silk nightgown.

Will rolled off the bed and picked up a metal figurine on the bedside table. 'Don't come near me,' she growled.

'Guards!' Lesli called. The door opened and two men with crossbows at the ready entered silently. Lesli looked at her pointedly. She set the figurine down. 'Much better. You can leave us,' he said to the men, and they nodded, closing the door behind them. 'Don't try that again,' he said. 'It really would be a pity to have to kill you. You're far too valuable to me.'

'I don't belong to you,' Will snapped.

'Oh, I think you do,' Lesli said. 'This kingdom belongs to me, this palace belongs to me, and you, my dear, are my own personal property.'

'I am not.'

Lesli sighed. 'I forgot how troublesome the young can be. Do you expect me to announce, "are too!" in a fractious voice? You should know better than that.'

'I've played your little game, passed your little test. I'm innocent. Set me free now.'

'I told you that you would only be proclaimed "innocent" if you were to die.'

Horror clutched her chest, but she ignored it. 'Well, I haven't died, and I've done all you asked. What do you want of me?'

Lesli smiled an oily little smile. 'You're far too bright for your own good, little Princess. You see, you were right when you commented on my policies. Hiedelen's economy has been steadily declining for the last fifty years.'

'Oh. Ever since you got your hands on the kingdom?'

Lesli's eyes narrowed. 'I'll thank you to keep your mouth shut.'

'Don't bet on it.'

Lesli squared his shoulders. 'I'll teach you the kind of manners we expect in Hiedelen.'

'Is that where you're sending me next? There're no thorns there, Lesli. No gold for your coffers.'

'On the contrary, Princess, I intend to keep you right here, spinning thorns. For me.'

'It'll never work. You'll never be allowed to keep the only Lyndaran heir a prisoner in her own castle, your lackey. The people would never accept it.'

'You're right. They wouldn't. I couldn't possibly keep you as my prisoner indefinitely. I have another proposition in mind.'

Something in his tone unnerved her, and the word worried her still more. 'What kind of proposition?'

'An alliance, my dear lady.'

'With your country? I'm well past trusting any treaty with you, and I think Narvi's a little beyond acquiescing to a marriage.'

'For the moment, yes. Possibly even forever. A shame I'll have to keep the new bride under lock and key, to prevent her from doing some other terrible thing. But the people will understand the need to control you.'

'You've no more sons left to marry,' Will growled. 'Unless you know how to wake Narvi or bring Dani back from the dead.'

'I wouldn't risk my grandson on a witch like you. Far too delicate, even if he was not indisposed. No. I intend to marry you myself.'

Will was appalled. He couldn't be serious. 'I think not.'

'You don't seem to understand. I'm not leaving you with a choice.' He turned around. 'Bring him in!'

The door opened and in walked two guards carrying a figure in chains. Will thought at first he was threatening her, saying this is what I'll do to you. She wasn't intimidated. Then she saw that the threat was not toward her own person. 'I'm sure you recognize this.'

She did. It was Prince Ferdinand.

His fine black clothes were stained with grey dirt, and many places were darker with his blood. His fair hair was tangled and matted with substances Will didn't want to identify, and an ugly purple bruise marred his handsome face. He cradled one arm in his other hand as if it was broken. Will scrambled to her feet. 'What have you done to him?' She ran to him and fell to her knees, trying to see if she could help him. He lifted his head weakly to look at her, and then let it fall again. Whatever they had been doing to him, there was more damage than Will could see.

'Only letting you know what the consequences of your stubbornness would be. This entire palace is filled with help-less victims. This one was not helpless. He was caught trying to sneak you out of your imprisonment last night. He had his horse, hound and hawk ready to spirit you away. Falcon makes a surprisingly rare casserole, if you ask me, and my dogs love horsemeat.'

Will glared at him. 'You *killed* them?'

'Better them than the prince,' Lesli replied. 'You have one more chance. Tonight I'm going to set you in the East Ballroom.'

Will stared at him in shock. 'That's a solid wall of thorns!' Not to mention it was also four times as large as the room she had been bound in the night before.

'It is,' Lesli said. 'If you can't handle it, just say so.'

'I can't handle it.'

'Very well. Guards? Shoot him.'

'What?' Will stepped in front of him. 'No!'

284

'Are you willing to spend the night in the ballroom?'

'You *know* I can't spin that much in one night!' she cried, desperate. She didn't even know if Reynard would come back, and it was all he could do to spin as much as he had.

'I suggest you try.' Lesli leaned toward her and stared into her eyes. 'Now, this is what is going to happen, Princess. Tonight you are going into the East Ballroom. You are going to spin me enough gold to finance my armies for the next year. Once you have done that, I will announce to the people that you are indeed innocent of your family's blood. You and I will marry, and this kingdom, and all of its assets and treasures, will be mine, including you and your surprising little talent. You will be treated as the queen you are. I'll even let you keep this broken jack as an amusement.' He smiled unpleasantly. 'Do you think I haven't seen how your eyes follow him? He's yours. All you have to do is spin for me, for at least a few hours every day.'

'And what about the Sleep?' she asked. 'It isn't going to break. It could take you next, or me, or half the kingdom.'

Lesli shrugged. 'I'm not worried. If it becomes too much trouble we shall simply execute all who are infected. As for myself . . . I know I can withstand it. I can even keep you safe, I'm sure. Safe enough to keep you by my side, spinning as a good wife should.' He reached out and touched her face. 'I could even come to be fond of you. Perhaps I'd have to crush that overactive throat of yours first, if you never learn to keep your mouth shut. I'd much rather you simply learned to behave yourself.'

Will yanked her head away and spat at him. Lesli's eyes burned for a moment before he composed himself. He calmly wiped his face. 'On the other hand, I can leave you tied up among the thorns until every drop of your blood has been drained away. I can have this pet of yours torn limb from limb before your eyes, and then start hacking pieces off your mother and your father and your beautiful sister. I'm sure we could find some other uses for her, as well. An entire parade of the king's guard, performing a little show for your benefit. I might even make a first appearance.'

'You dare!'

'You accept, then?'

Will hesitated. This was giving him legitimacy over the kingdom. This was selling her life. It was fruitless anyway, because once the king found out she could not spin the thorns into gold he would have her head. But then King Lesli made a gesture with his finger and Ferdinand groaned behind her. His broken arm had just been wrenched. 'All right!' she cried. 'I accept, I accept!'

Lesli smiled. 'Well chosen, Princess. I'll let you get back to your rest. I'm sure you'll need it for this night's work.'

Chapter 19

* * *

The previous night's work lingered. My icy shoulder pulsed with pain, coursing through me, bleeding over into my scratches. Every muscle ached with fatigue and residues of spent magic. I was so exhausted I couldn't fathom journeying back to my burrow. Instead I slept in Will's royal passages, curled up behind the baking oven by the kitchens, in a narrow dark corner which was both warmer and more spacious than my burrow, if less cushioned. I woke to the sounds of a row in the kitchen as a half dozen cooks cried out in protest.

'It's nothing to do with me!' someone with the vocal range of a herald shouted over the din. 'Those are the king's orders, and you get to decide how to go about it.'

I tried to ignore their outcry and go back to sleep, but phrases kept drifting to me through the walls. 'But the best of the joint was used two days ago for that fiasco of a wedding!'

'I'm not making another subtlety.'

'How are we expected to whip up another wedding feast when the head chef fell asleep yesterday?'

'It needn't be so fancy as we'd been plannin'. After all, we's in mournin'.'

'But this be the king himself! We can't be foisting him off with some dog chuck and call it a weddin' feast!'

'He b'ain't our king.'

'He is at that, ye young jade!'

'Calm down, everyone!' someone announced in a commanding tone. The noises subsided as someone started issuing individual orders. 'We have until tomorrow,' she continued, 'we can have something reasonable prepared by then.'

'Presumin' as that witch don't get herself killed!'

'I don't see why he has to marry her. Ain't she just as evil even if she *can* be makin' gold?'

'Ain't *his* gold if he don't.'

My brow twitched. I'd thought Narvi was asleep. So be it. Willow had passed her test and was innocent. The wedding was back on. She could have her kingdom, and my hands were clean.

In fact, she owed me, didn't she? I thought I remembered the general direction of Will's chambers, so I traversed the royal tunnels for an hour, stretching the residue of too-potent magics out of my system. I knew I had found it when I turned a corner and stumbled, not upon a weapon's cache, but upon two shelves of worn books. I tested the door I found just beyond them and found it opened into a closet full of Will's things. I closed the door again and perused the shelves.

Will's secret library was astounding. The shelves went on for quite a little ways, far more books than she had lead me to believe. I realized quickly why. Though she had some seventy odd grimoires, spell books, and books on magic theory, not all the books were actually on magic. The rest were old stories that told of magicians or sorcerers, children's stories, faerie tales. These had never been banned, but for a princess they were probably shameful. I ran my fingers down them very lightly, feeling for how much power they had, and how much they had been loved. These were beloved books, cherished, taken out one at a time and devoured again and again.

What was it about her? Sometimes it seemed as if this life of a princess would suffocate her. At other times it seemed to be all she wanted in the world. Why hadn't she run when I offered to help her? Why not abandon this place of greed and sleep and blood, go and find a life for herself? I had to admit I liked that idea. Will, off on a journey with her questing beasts, her tenacity and strength of will sending anyone who opposed her into cartwheels of confusion. She certainly confused the hell out of me.

But I also knew she wouldn't leave. And she wouldn't leave because I had cursed her palace and her kingdom and left her the only caretaker Lyndaria had. I'd taken her family from her. That was the one thing I had never lost. We lost our names, our property, our place in the world, but we had always had the family. My ma and the kit, and even Da before he went wandering. In my envy for all the things I had not, I had taken from Will the only good thing I'd ever had.

Will's question of the night before ate at me. Why had I done it? So what if I hadn't intended it to be so terrible a curse. Why had I done it at all?

I wanted to be evil. Things would have been so much easier if I really was evil, after all. This act had clinched it. I should take her books and leave the kingdom to its fate. But I couldn't. I couldn't bear the thought of taking her books from her. I had done too much harm to her already. Instead of taking the books I actually pulled the two books she had already given me out of my shirt and replaced them in the glaringly obvious empty spaces on her shelves.

Still, it was time to get back to my own family.

I turned back the way I came, creeping down the passages in the dark. My faerie eyes could see well enough, but there were no distinguishing marks in these royal routes. I had just turned a corner and found myself faced with another staircase that led up, when I needed to stay on the ground floor. I backtracked until I came to the turn off and turned the opposite way. Suddenly I heard a groan come through the walls. 'Not so grand are you now, eh?' said a voice, followed by much laughter. 'Teach you to go about trying to set witches on decent, honest folks!' I heard a scuff, and then a grunt, and someone cried out in serious pain.

I was already boiling inside. There was nothing more I could do for Will, and my own situation was just as dire as it had ever been, but someone was being ganged up on – someone who approved of 'witches' – and I hated that with a passion. Perhaps *this* I could do something about. I felt around the wall, one wood, one stone, until I found a catch and opened a panel into a grand chamber filled with equally grand sleeping people. On the floor there was one not so grand, dressed in sober black, curled up in a protective ball as three men in Hiedelen livery kicked him into submission.

I had no spindle, little strength, and even less imagination. I realized as I stood there that I had no idea what I planned to do to stop them. The three stared at me as I came out the wall as if I was a ghost. 'Demons!' one of them shouted. 'Run!' And to my utter surprise, they left off attacking their victim and fled for the door.

I frowned and reached for my hood. I'd forgotten it. There I was, pointed ears, large slanted eyes, dark as a shadow in a bright room. Moreover, I was stained with blood and sticky with dusty cobwebs from the royal passages. 'Well, that was easy,' I said. I made sure I was hooded for the benefit of the victim, who was still curled in a tight ball, protecting his face and vital organs. I lunged for the door and locked it behind the fleeing guards.

The pitiful figure on the ground looked up hesitantly. In a surprisingly regal voice he said, 'And whom do you presume to be, sir?'

I nearly laughed in his face. 'I'm a friend of the Princess Willow,' I said. 'You're in no position to sound as if I've just interrupted court.' I bent down and examined his chains. 'What are you bound for?' I asked.

He glared at me. 'I don't know you.'

'I don't know you. Tell me what you're bound for, or you can stay this way.'

'Did you say you're a friend of Will's?' he said. He shook his head. 'This is some trick to get me to confess to some wrongdoing. I trust you not.'

I rolled my eyes. 'Your arrogance tells me you're royalty,' I said. His arms were free, but one of them was clearly broken. The chains encircled his ankles, and then were bound quite firmly to an iron ring in the wall, ostensibly a torch holder, but firmly embedded in the stone wall for all of that. 'Damn. They're iron. I'm not very good with iron; hold on a minute.' I looked around the room to see if there was anything I could use. My strength was frail and I'd no spindle. The room was abundant in brocade and silver, but very limited on spinning accoutrements. 'I'm guessing you're Narvi,' I said absently. 'Older than I was led to believe.'

'No,' the prince said. 'I am Prince Ferdinand of Illaria, betrothed to the Princess Lavender.'

'Oh, him,' I said, even more absently.

'And your name, sir.'

I did laugh, then. A high, giddy giggle bordering on hysteria. 'And it *always* comes back to that,' I said. I turned back to him and examined his arm. 'You might have to stay here for now. I can't find anything to free you with.' I pointed at his arm. 'I can do something about that at least.'

'Don't bother,' Ferdinand said as I pulled one of the shawls off the bed to turn into a makeshift sling. 'The guards will be back in a moment, with reinforcements, and likely Lesli himself. Don't worry about me. Find the princess. Free her, help her to leave this place.'

'Tried that,' I said, working on his arm. 'She won't leave. Don't move, I need to make sure the bone is in place.'

To his credit, Ferdinand bore the pain stoically, without even a grimace. 'You found her? Spoke to her? When?'

'Last night,' I said. 'Here, hold this.' I put a corner of the makeshift sling in his mouth. 'This has to be still if I'm to do anything for it.'

'You tried to free her?' Ferdinand said out of the corner of his mouth.

'Yes. Stubborn as an ox, that one.'

Ferdinand sagged. 'I knew they didn't need to torture me. Ow.' The sound was more confusion than pain. 'What are you doing?'

'Trying to knit this together, at least a little,' I said. 'Light, I'd kill for a spindle. I need your help; try to think about the arm that doesn't hurt.' I performed a rather ineffective repeat of the spell I'd worked with Will at the monument. I twisted the power together in my mind, but I was weak. The break was not healed, but at least the broken bones had a tenuous connection to each other. I sighed. 'Best I can do without equipment. Should be a little better.'

'I thank you,' Ferdinand said. 'I take it you have something to do with magic? Are you Will's tutor?'

'Something like that,' I said. 'Now will you tell me why you're trussed up like this?'

'I was caught last night trying to open the door to the East Wing. I had my beasts ready for her, and . . .' this was the only time any emotion touched his voice, 'they slew them before my eyes.'

'Their power was spent, anyway,' I said gently.

'They still saved my life a dozen times,' Ferdinand said. 'And now Hiedelen and his lackeys have robbed me of them.'

'If you cared so much about them, why were you giving them to Will?'

At that moment a groan from the bed caused Ferdinand to start. He crept over to his betrothed's side and took her hand gently in his uninjured one. 'I owe Willow,' he said. 'I've performed her a terrible disservice, and I had to rectify it.'

'What disservice was this?' I asked.

'I refused to marry her.' He shook his head. 'Her father suggested it, just before Amaranth fell victim to the sleep. If I had, Will would have been safe from Hiedelen's intrigues.'

'What makes you think she would have agreed?' I said, and my voice sounded very small.

'Oh, there was no question there,' Ferdinand said. 'She's too honest, in her face and her looks as well as her words. The secret is not very well kept. She's in love with me.'

I swear my very heart stopped for a moment at those words. I didn't move or blink or even breathe. I stared at Ferdinand's bent head and heard nothing through the sudden silence that had engulfed me. It took me a few moments to realize that Ferdinand was still speaking.

'I should have treated her with less friendship. I did not know how lonely she had been in this palace, how neglected she was, how shadowed by her sister's charm and beauty. I was trying to become her brother. I did not realize her passion, her isolation, her hunger.' He shook his head. 'It was cruel of me. And worse. I know I should have rescued her. I know Lavi would have asked it of me, with her kindness and her nobility. And but for her, I could. If Lavender were dead or wed or gone from me, I could do what I must. I could take Will away from here, wed her to protect her station, win again Will's kingdom in Lavender's name. I've always known she loved me. I've known it since before Lavender Slept. Poor Will. She and I are alike in many ways. I could love her if I did not know there was a perfection such as this.' He brushed the lily-white brow of the princess in the bed. 'But while there is a chance of Lavender needing me, I must stay by her side. Not such a hero, am I?'

There were a thousand things I could have been saying to this, but none of them surfaced over the sudden rush of realization I was suddenly drowned in. Will was in love with Ferdinand. It made terrible sense. That night in the forest. The way she had whispered his name, as if it hurt her heart to even mention him. She said she was using me, wanted someone to hold her, to make love to her. She had been speaking in generalizations, but it was Ferdinand who held her heart. It was he whom she wished was courting her. It was because of him that she hungered for someone's touch. It was because of Ferdinand that she had kissed me.

I stared at the prince. He was wounded and haggard, but I could see the masculine beauty in his face. He held his shoulders square, stood like a man, not like my habitual slink. He was almost as tall as Will. Tall and strong and regal, a hero in his own right. And what was I? A nameless, homeless demon faerie, embittered by years of hardship, filled with rage and utterly hopeless.

What did it matter? It's not as if it made any difference, the comparison between us. Because I didn't want Will. I hated her. I hated her very existence. 'It doesn't matter,' I said bitterly. 'She'll be married to Narvi on the morrow, and you'll be safe with your sleeping stupidity.'

He either didn't catch my last words, or let them pass, because all he said was, 'Narvi? No, the sleep took him the night Willow spun out the thorns. Lesli's marrying her himself.'

'Hiedelen? Lesli? That ancient, boorish tyrant who can't abide magic?'

'Apparently he can abide it just fine when it's spinning gold out of dross,' Ferdinand said ruefully.

Rage surged through my veins. That greedy, exploitative slime eel! That puffed-up, arrogant tyrant! That darkness cursed, overbearing goose-catcher with delusions of godhood! Will, marry *him*? Horrifying images flooded my brain, of Will in a white dress standing by his side, of her feeding him the traditional honey cake at the feast, of her huddling in bed waiting for his massive bulk to come and crush her, bearing his horrid children, turning to him, bowing to him, saying, 'Yes, my husband,' the sparks in her winter eyes shrouded by misery, her strong form reduced to fat through domestic captivity, image after image of my Will deteriorating in the clutches of that beast.

My Will? *My* Will? I had to stop thinking of her like that. She wasn't mine. I didn't even want her!

Didn't I?

I hated her. I detested the Lyndal line, blamed them for my misery, and Will was a part of that, a strand in the rope of hatred that had been slowly strangling me my whole life. I despised her.

I had to hate her. Because if I didn't hate her then the intensity of what I felt for her had to be something . . . else.

If I had known my name, I would have realized how I felt before that moment. It wouldn't have taken a litany of mental tortures to tell me that I . . . loved . . . her . . . .

Damn! Damn damn, damn damn, damn damn, damn and damn! I was in love with her. Hopelessly, desperately in love with the blasted princess of Lyndaria. Of all the stupid, atrocious things to go and do! I was tempted to go up to Ferdinand and tell him to slap me, right hard. How had I fallen in love with her? True, she was witty and lovely and honourable and brave and, oh, love of Light, how was I supposed to endure this?

I had to kill this. I had to slaughter this right now, before it grew so deep I was wounded forever. I knew how this kind of thing had to end. But it didn't matter, because it was already too late. Married. Married to the king of Hiedelen. Married! There had to be some way of stopping this. 'We have to get her out of here.'

'You said she wouldn't go,' Ferdinand said. 'I know she won't. They tortured me as a lesson to her. If she runs, I die. She'll never let that happen.'

My guts clenched, and I nearly hit him. 'You can't let her go through with this,' I said. 'You care for her, don't you?'

Say no, a part of me begged.

'Of course I do,' Ferdinand said without emotion. He caressed the princess's cheek. 'But Lavender . . .'

'How could you choose that nothing over Will?' I demanded.

He dropped to his knees, his chains clanking. 'I don't expect you to understand,' he said. He looked up at me. 'We're in love.' He turned back to her. 'So long as there's still a chance . . . the slightest chance . . . .'

Clearly Ferdinand was going to be no help. I jammed my hands into my pockets, and what I found there made my fists clench in bitter hope. An idea had come to me. It was elegant in its simplicity, and another step on my path to utter damnation. 'I'll kill Hiedelen,' I said.

Ferdinand's eyes snapped to me. 'Kill Lesli?' he asked. 'How? He's protected at all times. Guards stand around him with crossbows at the ready.'

'I have a way,' I said.

'What way?'

'I'm a magician, remember? Where is he?'

Ferdinand cocked his head. 'Likely on his way here,' Ferdinand said. 'Do you hear them? Coming to investigate his guards' call of "demon". Was that an illusion? I didn't see it.'

'They'll only bring more guards. I need Lesli.'

'He'll come,' Ferdinand said with confidence. 'Anything to do with magic and Lesli expects to be contacted personally. He killed my hound himself.'

'Then expect the world to be rid of one more dictator,' I said, and opened the panel of the royal passage. 'Keep him talking as long as you can. I'll need time to pull this together.'

It wasn't long, and Ferdinand was right. I'd barely had time to prepare before the door was burst open by a dozen heavily armed guards, whose eyes darted back and forth across the room, crossbows at the ready. Following these, his face serene, was Lesli Hiedel himself, twisting a narrow piece of wood, probably a pen, idly between his fingers. 'Why, Ferdinand. I expected you to be eaten up by demons. A few of my men here had quite a shock for a moment.'

'What they saw was a manifestation of their own guilt, binding and beating an innocent man,' Ferdinand said, his head held high in defiance. 'Come to finish the job, King Lindwyrm?'

'Calm yourself, Prince Ferdinand,' said King Lesli, with an oily smile. 'I'm here to release your bonds.'

'You need a jester's cap and staff to make a proper joke, Your Majesty. I am not amused.'

Two more guards came in flanking the king, and he nodded towards the prince. 'Release him. It's been enough.'

One unlocked the chains and the other disconnected them from Ferdinand's form. Lurking behind the panel, peering through a strategic peep hole, I twisted the strand of gold I had slid into my pocket on my first night's work. I had never before used my magic to kill a man. It was one of the ways of truly becoming a demon. To use your own magic to snuff out another's life could twist your mind, twist your magic, turn everything you did to evil, turn you into a warped and dangerous version of yourself. If I had done such a thing as a pure faerie, undimmed by Namelessness, I would have had my name stripped from me for what I was about to do. But what more could they do to me? So my sister was right, and I truly was heading toward evil; able to lie, able to kill, unable to do any good with my powers. If I killed Lesli, every spell I ever performed from this time on would cause harm somewhere. So be it. Will's life was worth it.

'Is this some cruel trick?' Prince Ferdinand said from across the wall, 'Or are you finally going to execute me?'

'On the contrary, my dear Prince. I need you very much alive.'

Ferdinand gently protected his wounded arm with his uninjured one. 'Whatever for? To play your fool, or to fight some beast? Win your wars for you? You've slaughtered my horse and slain my hawk and hound. I don't see what good you think I can do for you.'

'Quite a great deal. You're here with your beloved slumberer, not in the dungeon. I've let you relax and recover. I've even supplied you with food and drink. Now that I've displayed you to the princess, you can be of great value to me. I need you to keep my dear wife in line. Presuming she survives this second test I've set her.'

'Another test? What is she to do this time? Turn dirt into diamonds? Starlight into silver? I'm sure she'll bleed her own blood into rubies just to please Your Majesty.'

Hiedelen laughed. 'I thought you might not have been aware of much when I brought you to the princess. Pain has a way of blocking out all else. All I ask of her is the same as before. I'm not so particular as to require more than one wonder from my wife. Please don't mistake me, Prince Ferdinand. I have no delusions about my young bride-to-be. She is not in the least fond of me.'

Ferdinand was buying me time, I knew. The spell was difficult to cast. I'd no spindle, and I was not accustomed to killing people. The spell I'd used to subdue the guards at the royal vault was the closest I'd ever gotten, and I'd had a spindle then. The spell would be easiest to cast if I could somehow get the thread about his person, but crossbows would kill me as surely as any other, so I couldn't attack openly. I couldn't cast a true invisibility without a spindle, either, and the room was too bright to sneak up on him using a shadow spell.

The king continued. 'Until I can wring a child or two out of her, I'll need you as leverage to keep her in line.'

'You don't know her,' Ferdinand said. 'You don't need me. She'd care about anyone.'

'Possibly true,' Hiedelen said. 'But if that is indeed the case, I can kill you now.'

One of the guards raised his crossbow.

Prince Ferdinand stood straight and tall. 'Do your worst.' I was impressed. He wasn't all show, this Ferdinand. I could see why Will loved him.

Hiedelen laughed and moved his chin. The line of the crossbow changed, pointing instead at the sleeping maiden on the bed.

'Ah, no!' Ferdinand flung himself upon the bed, shielding her with his body.

'Ah, so there is someone you care about as well,' Hiedelen said unctuously. 'What a weakness this affection is.' My heart twisted. I agreed with Hiedelen. Wretched fondness. I'd heard a saying somewhere; a cat may look at a king, and a knave may love the princess, but only the cat will be satisfied. Something along those lines. It was true enough, in the end. I was wasting my time and my powers on someone who would never throw herself in the path of a crossbow for my sake. No, but she would for Ferdinand. He was straight and tall and honourable as a prince should be – a fitting match for her. I was darkness incarnate.

'So,' Hiedelen said. 'Willow will behave because I have you. You will behave, because of *her*.' He pointed to the sleeping princess. He looked Ferdinand up and down. 'I don't know what tricks my betrothed has been teaching you, but no more demons. I don't permit magic from just *anyone*, you know. You might find it more difficult conjuring illusions without any hands.'

As Hiedelen turned to leave I pulled the knot tight in the golden thread. It should have worked. His throat should have closed as if I had him locked in a noose. Hiedelen thirsted for the gold I created; I should have been able to spin a spell around him without any trouble. Instead the thread snapped in my hand, and I was thrust against the opposite side of the passage by a failed spell.

Failed spells are a bit like being kicked by a horse. They tend to leave you winded and shaky for quite a while, and sometimes things are broken inside you. Not bones, but it takes a while for one's magic to settle back into something one can utilize. I gasped and slid down the wall to the ground, my heart beating fiercely. By the Light, what had happened? Hiedelen was protected in some way. Magic slid off his oily personality as water off a duck. Some shadowy power pulsed from him, as if he had a real demon protecting him.

No wonder he didn't worry about the Sleep. He knew he was immune.

After a little time the light brightened, and Ferdinand snuck in beside me. 'Are you well, my friend?' he asked. 'Have you cast your spell? Will we be hearing the death knell of King Lesli at last?'

I searched for a little while until I found my breath. 'No,' I said. 'He's protected in some way.' I grunted. 'I need . . . rest. Failed spells are the worst.'

'I'll fetch you a pillow,' Ferdinand said. He was actually very thoughtful, and he fetched a pillow and wine and cheese for me. I found myself hating how gallant he was. He was exactly the kind of creature Will deserved. If the kit were older, I wouldn't have even opposed her considering someone like him as a marriage partner. Finally he left me alone, safely concealed behind the wall, and returned to his beloved slumberer.

I lay in the darkness for a long time, trying to put myself back together inside. My magic ached, still humming as a metal gate hums when struck by a hammer. It galled me how Ferdinand tended that wretched princess. I could hear him murmuring endearments and comforts when she cried out with nightmare flashes of my life. She couldn't hear him. Why wasn't he upstairs, tending Will's scratches, guarding her virtue as she slept with her exhaustion? I wished I could be. I wished she wanted me there.

I lay thinking for hours, meditating on Will, on Ferdinand, on Lavender. In the end, I dreamed up a plan. It was not a good plan. Like executing a man with my magic, it was an act that would finally ensure my road to hell, but it didn't matter. Condemned to Namelessness since I was an infant, in the end there was no way I could have grown to be anything but a demon.

When I finally closed my eyes it was to a smile. Lynelle had been right all along.

I took my leave of Ferdinand without making my exit known. I was afraid he'd ask what I meant to do, and it was not something he'd ever permit. As the sun set it took me a little time to find where they had put Will. I knew it would be somewhere in the East Wing. I searched for a while before I realized, if this was to be her final test, it would be the most difficult one.

Sure enough, she was in the East Ballroom, a room the size of our clan's grand house before our names were stripped from us. She was sitting on her own in the deepest centre of the thorns. She was dressed this time in hunter's leather, a wise decision. There were much fewer fresh scratches on and about her, as she wasn't even trying to wrestle the thorns into submission. As I watched her, she muttered her stilling spell again, but she wasn't putting her full power behind it. The thorns trembled and shook. 'Will!' I hissed.

She gasped when she looked up at me, and I thought I caught tears in her eyes. 'You came.' The words came in a whisper that tore as fiercely as the thorns. She hadn't thought I would.

I was stung by her disbelief. 'Of course I did. Think I'd spend this much effort on you and then leave you to die?'

'Maybe you should,' she whispered.

'Pardon?'

'I don't have anything else to pay you with.'

I blinked. I'd forgotten she didn't trust me. I'd forgotten that I was supposed to hate her. 'I'll think of something,' I said.

'Why?' she asked.

Her innocent question annoyed me. Now that I knew the truth, saying anything else was a lie, and lying was painful. Wretched beautiful thing. 'I like having you in my debt,' I said, as that was true enough.

To my surprise she began to cry. 'Why not you, too?' she muttered. 'I have nothing to give you. There is nothing left of me.'

'Oh, Will, that's not true,' I said, very quietly.

I think she heard the tenderness in my tone, because her tears slowed. She sniffed. 'Have you truly come to help me again?'

'That's what I said, isn't it?'

'But why? Why do you keep helping me? What's in it for you?'

Your happiness, I thought. 'I know what I want,' I said. 'And you can give it to me.'

She swallowed. 'What?'

I want you to be free. I want you to have the happiness I can never have. I want you to have light and life and love, and I can give you none of that. Except like this. 'I want . . .' The lie burned at my throat, but I forced it out. 'I want the first born of Lyndaria.'

'What?'

'I want the heir. The first born.'

'You want my unborn child?'

'What would I do with a baby?' I glared at her. 'No. I want your entire kingdom. I want your sister, the heir to the throne.'

Will went white. 'What did you say to me?'

'You heard me.'

'But she's asleep.'

'It's my spell,' I retorted. 'I can deal with it.' That wasn't true; I had no idea how to reverse it, and still didn't really want to.

'Then why don't you?'

'Because I want your kingdom,' I said again. The lies were burning my mouth by now, and I wasn't sure how much longer I could keep it up.

'I can't agree to this,' Will said. 'I'm not the queen.'

'Upon your mother and father's incapacitation, you are the only capable member of the royal house of Lyndaria. This makes you regent, if not queen.'

'But King Lesli—'

'Burn Lesli!' I shouted the words, and they rattled the thorns. 'Do you want to live or don't you!'

Will gulped and looked about her, and at that moment the thorns shook off her stilling spell and writhed towards her. I grabbed one of the tendrils and twisted it into a knot.

Droplets of my blood trickled down the cane as the thorns stiffened and retreated with my spell as dejected as a slapped puppy. My resolve had increased my powers.

She stared at me, her eyes wide with something like fear, or awe. I wondered what I looked like. Probably something demonic. 'I-I do want to live,' she whispered.

'Done, then!' I cried, and darted past her, diving for the spinning wheel.

The lovely old wheel felt familiar in my hands by now, and I almost sighed with relief at the touch of it. I felt more complete with a spinning wheel at my fingertips. It was as if everything came together.

The spinning of those thorns was the hardest thing I ever did in my life. Before I was halfway through, my strength was failing. Each successive skein took longer and longer to spin. I was red faced and sweating long before I was finished. Finally I took off my hood and jacket. Golden lines of thread were burned onto my vision when I closed my eyes.

I couldn't have done it at all but for Will. Long after her stilling spell failed she continued to wrestle the thorns, bringing fresh canes to me again and again. Her leather clothes were sufficient armour against the least insistent of the briars. Once or twice I had to leave my spinning and go to rescue her when a briar had her by the ankle or she was surrounded by writhing thorn canes. She never cried out for my help, always insisting that she could do it herself.

The birds were beginning to sound in the pre-light of dawn, and I still had at least four more skeins of thread to spin. 'Hurry!' Will whispered. Lines of blood caked her face and hands, and her hair was a nest of broken thorns. 'If they see you here, they'll kill me all the same.'

'You think I don't know that?' I snapped. I twisted the last line of thread and tore off the skein. 'Give me another briar.'

She helped me feed more briars into the spinning wheel as the sky turned purple, then red. Only little shreds of light peeked through the briars which were plastered against the vast windows of the ballroom, but it was enough to see that we were running out of time. I could tell that Will wanted to ask me something, but I didn't have breath or energy left for talk.

There was still one pernicious bush in the corner where two windows met, probably the mother bush that had spawned all the rest of the briars in the ballroom. 'I can't break it!' she cried out as it grabbed for her.

'I'll bring the wheel over,' I said, and tried to get to my feet. I swayed as I stood, my exhaustion gripping me. It was all I could do to stay upright as I grabbed the spinning wheel and dragged it behind me.

I could see the line of the briar snaking up over her head, but I hadn't the strength to cry out to her. I dropped the wheel and tried to point, but she was exhausted too, and didn't understand. Earlier in the night this would never have been a danger. Will was too alert, and I was fast on my feet. But with the sand running out of the hourglass, I had poured almost every ounce of my strength into these blasted skeins of worthless gold, and Will was pale faced and wide eyed with fatigue. The branch wrapped itself around her throat with a satisfied creak.

Will screamed for all of a second before her air was cut off. Terror gripped me, and that gave me strength. I clutched the spinning wheel and took off across the ballroom running. Will was dangling like a rag doll. The branches creaked and swayed with their prize, and Will had been pulled off her feet, nearly to the ceiling. 'You will not!' I shouted at the thorns. Of course they had no reaction, other than to start inching tendrils toward me.

I kicked at them, feeling no fear. 'Just hold on!' I called to the dangling princess. Will thrashed and pulled at the briars, breaking off narrow canes, but the thick branch which held her was past her strength to break. Not past my magic though, I hoped.

I began pulling canes through the spinning wheel, starting with the central branch, almost a trunk. I was surprised I could get a grip on it, but with a strand of gold to start it, it spun as well as all the others. I tugged. With a shriek of splintering wood the plant cracked. It let Will go, and she tumbled through the air, only to fall on another branch, which promptly wrapped itself around her. At least she could breathe again. I could hear her coughing as I readied myself to pull another cane. 'The thorns!' Will choked.

'I know!' I said, but I spared a glance at her anyway. She wasn't just informing me of her predicament. She was pointing at me. Two tendrils of briar had worked their way around the front of the spinning wheel. I abandoned the branch and pulled these furtive tendrils into the thread.

'Ah!' Will cried out then, and I grabbed for the previous branch. I looked up at her, and saw what had caused her cry. A particularly nasty thorn, as long as my hand, had pierced Will's chest, near her heart. She was gasping around it, and her face was twisted in agony. With a fierce pull I grabbed the base and yanked the entire branch through the wheel. It pulled from her chest with a sucking sound and *whirred* through the wheel, scratching my cheek as it came past me. Another branch, and another. Only a few more to go.

Will was dangling over me now, her eyes wide with fear, and her blood fell on my hands. It was bright red, not the deep red blood of a wound, but the true heart's blood of a slaughterhouse. It slowed my work, but I wasn't about to let it stop me. The briars trembled and shook, as if they knew their time was up. One sneaked around my arm, but I couldn't let go of the branch which held Will. It had her by the throat again, and she was losing too much blood. I pulled the branch through the wheel and Will was thrown against the wall as it surged. She slid down and landed awkwardly on her hip.

The last branch was firmly embedded in my flesh, and I wrenched it out with a cry of pain as I forced it through my wheel, through my magic, and onto my spindle. I let the wheel stop and I sagged as I let my magic die. Where had I found the strength at the end? I panted and pulled my eyes to Will, who lay crumpled on the floor, blood streaming from her chest.

I knew where I had gotten the strength, because the sight of her brought more. I crawled my way to her side and pulled her to me. She was only semi-conscious. Her mortal blood stained my hands. The wound in her chest was too deep, she was losing too much blood. That blood was so bright — I'd never seen blood so bright from any creature that had lived. I had to close the wound somehow. But I couldn't. I couldn't reach the magic, I had no strength at all. No! It wasn't fair! I sobbed with the injustice of it all, and tried to find a reserve of strength within me.

There wasn't one.

No. I refused to accept that. I'd survived brutal winters and furious mobs and starvation and illness and I wasn't about to give up when it came to this terrible, wonderful, misfit princess. We hadn't come this far to have it end now, at her moment of victory. I reached behind me and yanked at the spinning wheel. It toppled over, but the spindle turned, and a line of golden thread rolled towards me. This thread had a rose tint, alloyed with her heart's blood, and the blood from my bleeding hands. I grabbed it and yanked it from the spindle. I went through the motions of twisting it into a spell, but despite the blood-charged thread, there was no power in my knots. It was futile.

Will shuddered under my hands, and her heart stopped. Everything stopped. Her eyes gazed unseeing at the ceiling. In that moment, she was dead. She was still warm, but she'd lost too much. It was over. All that would come now was the death rattle.

Will was dead, and suddenly it didn't matter any more that I couldn't do anything for her. She'd been doing it all along – exhausting herself, draining her own reserves with her magic. I couldn't reach the innate power I'd always had access to, but nothing could separate me from myself. I reached inside me and fuelled the spell with my own life force. I probably speeded up my ageing process by a fifth with that spell, shortened my life span by near a hundred years, and I didn't care. The twisted thread reached out from my hands, flowing into the wound, binding it closed as if with needle and thread.

It hurt. If I had peeled my own skin off to save her, it wouldn't have hurt as much. It hurt too much to even scream, but I held it. Where my golden spell bound her, she healed instantly, the power of my own life restoring hers. Her heart stuttered, and then beat steadily. Will gasped and coughed blood, and her eyes flickered, life returning to her. The spell was finished. I collapsed.

For long moments I let myself lie half on top of her, feeling her breathing beneath my cheek, listening to her still beating heart. It was such a wonderful sound. The smell of roses was swallowed by dust and leather, sweat and blood, but the feeling of her life beneath me was the most wonderful thing in the world. After a little time she shifted, and I let my weight drag myself from her. I curled on the floor, and Will's hand reached up and touched my cheek. My eyes flickered open and I stared at her. She was covered in blood, her throat bruised, her eyes shadowed. But she was wonderfully, beautifully alive. 'I'm so sorry,' she whispered.

And at that moment, the door opened.

Chapter 20

Will

With a sudden reflex of panic Will cast her shadow spell. She was not even sure how she figured out, in that second, how to cast it on another, or how to cast it without using all the words, but she did it. In the time it took the men to unlock the door and enter in force she had cast the spell on Reynard and forced herself up using the wall. She had to get away from him, or someone would notice the disconnected shadow lying beside her. She inched her way along the wall.

The door had been opened by a guard, who came in and stared in wonder at the skeins of gleaming gold in the otherwise empty ballroom. Two more guards pushed past him, and another figure knocked him aside without apology. It was Prince Ferdinand. He looked far better than Will had seen him last. His broken arm was in a sling, and he was washed and rested, despite his deep bruises. He strode across the room and caught her with one arm just as her strength failed. 'For the love of all the gods, forget that dross and fetch a healer!' Ferdinand shouted.

'Just . . . get me . . . out of here,' Will whispered to him.

Two of the guards ran off, but the third began collecting the skeins of gold into a small trunk which he had brought with him. Will wanted to laugh at the absurdity of it. Of all the things in the world to be doing! Reynard was behind her, and she wanted to take care of him, and she couldn't. He'd just risked his life for her, that she knew. But she couldn't even stand without help, and she felt weak as a day-old kitten.

Ferdinand led her away, and lay her tenderly down on a couch. She didn't care where she was or what she was doing. She needed water and food and sleep. She managed to get some weak wine into her before she lost all strength and plunged into an exhausted slumber.

She dreamed of fighting thorns, and forced herself awake with a cry the moment she noticed she was dreaming. Even in her sleep, Will remembered enough to be afraid she might never wake. Ferdinand was there when she sat up. Of course, Ferdinand had brought her back to the antechamber, where he could keep an eye on Lavender. 'Will!' he breathed with relief.

'Are you all right?' she asked him.

He laughed, but it almost sounded like a sob. 'Yes. I'm well enough.' He buried his head in his good hand. He pulled away and looked back at her after a moment. 'You looked half dead.'

'Bled white, I know,' Will said, forcing herself to her feet. She was shaky and dizzy and ravenous. There was no food, but a decanter of that delicious weak wine was waiting on a tray. She seized it and drank straight from it, not caring for decorum. In the state she was in, it was the drink of the gods.

Ferdinand grimaced as he watched her, and turned his face to Lavender. Will stopped guzzling the wine and looked at him. His eyes were shadowed. 'I should have stopped them,' he said. 'I should have come to get you. I'm sorry I didn't.'

'They almost killed you the last time.'

Ferdinand shook his head. 'I could . . . I *should* take you now. I'm sorry I didn't marry you when your father suggested it, when Lesli was working on your mother.'

Will blinked. 'My father suggested you marry *me*?'

Ferdinand nodded. 'It would anger Lesli, but it would have gotten him to leave the palace. Only to prepare for war, but a fair war was better than what was happening to Amaranth, he said. She wasn't herself. It was dangerous. And your marriage would protect you.' He lightly touched Lavender's autumn hair. 'I knew he was right, and I would have done it with a content heart . . . but I couldn't bring myself to forsake her. Not to protect you. Not even to save your kingdom.' He looked up at her. 'I'm only a hero when it comes to Lavender.'

Will buried her head in her hands. It was so ridiculous!

'I could have spared you all of this,' Ferdinand went on.

Will shook her head. 'We can never know what could have happened,' she said. 'Even if you'd agreed, Mother would still have succumbed, the Sleep would still be spreading.'

'But you wouldn't be drenched in blood.'

'It's only a few scratches,' she said, looking down at herself, but even as she said it she remembered she was wrong. Just at the end there had been that terrible thorn, more a stake, really. Sure enough, there was a ragged, blood-stained hole pierced in her leather bodice. She turned away from Ferdinand to look beneath for damage. She was still covered in scratches, some of them deep enough to scar, and her throat was bruised, and she felt dizzy and thirsty and weak – didn't some of her books on healing magic say those were symptoms of severe blood loss? But beneath that ragged hole her skin was unbroken. Except when she moved into the light a twisted line of gold was etched into her flesh just above her left breast, like a strand of golden yarn. It branched at the edge, and little flecks of gold bled from it until it looked like a few branches from a briar. She knew enough to know that mark was above her heart. So that final attack had truly happened. So why was she still alive?

Reynard.

'Move,' Will said, whirling to Ferdinand.

'What?'

'Move!' she told him again. 'I have to find out something.'

'What?' He looked confused and grief stricken, but he moved out of her way.

Will took his place on the edge of Lavender's bed. There was no spell for what she was doing, but *The Zarmeroth Cycle* had a whole chapter on the magical power of mere words. She tried to pour her magic into her plea. 'Lavender?' she whispered to her. 'I know you can't hear me, but you've been asleep the longest. I think you've seen everything, witnessed everything. I need to see the worst of it. I need to see the worst moment of his life. I need to know what he was like before he turned so angry and bitter. I need you to find that dream, find that memory, and bring it to the surface. Find it for me, Lavender!'

Will had no idea if this makeshift spell would work, but it was the only thing she could try. 'Whatever happens,' she said to Ferdinand, 'don't pull me out of it.'

He nodded, his eyes wide.

She closed her eyes and sank into the deepest trance she had ever gone into. The blood loss made it easy. Then she reached into Lavender's dream.

Her name is Lynelle.

I am the equivalent of the age when most human men begin to think about a wife. I think I have found one. Lynelle is a woodsman's daughter. Her mother was the village herb-woman, and knew a few charms, so she doesn't look down on magic.

Lynelle is fun. Dangerous. Wild. She runs through the forest in bare feet, and has very inventive curses when they find thorns or sharp stones. Her dark hair is always tangled with sticks and leaves, her fingers stained purple with berry juice or green with lichen from climbing trees. She laughs easily. She even laughs at me, and my gloominess. We meet in the forest, in the shadowy places.

We have a game we play. When she first asked for my name, I said, 'I am mine own self.' She laughed.

'Hello, Mineownself,' she said the next day. 'Unless that isn't really your name.'

'It isn't,' I said. 'I'm One-you've-greeted.'

'Hello, Oneivegreeted.'

Every day she asks for my name, and every day I have another coy reply. Until I say, 'I'm a dancing man,' and I catch her in my arms and twirl to the sound of the wind in the trees.

The false names grow less and less coy. I'm your friend. I'm your dear friend. I'm someone who loves you. Now that I have met her I've become so many things besides Nameless that I almost don't mind. For the first time in my life, I'm not hollow inside. Then the day comes and she confesses she loves me too. From then on when she asks, I am always, 'Your-beloved.' I don't even need to be myself, so long as I am beloved of Lynelle.

I spin her a golden ring out of the yellow wheat. When she asks me who I am, I catch her hand in mine and I sink to my knees. 'I am your husband, if you'll have me.'

A broad smile spreads over her face. 'Really? You'd really marry me?'

I stand up and take her chin in my hand. Of course, she has no dowry, but I care nothing for that. 'There is no other maiden in the land who had the power to catch my heart. But you've done it. And I want to spend every moment of your life with you. I will lay my spells at your feet, and all my magic will belong to you, because you *are* all my magic.'

She is blushing bright pink by now, and her face is

314

scrunched up in delighted embarrassment. 'I'd love to marry you. Anywhere, any time. Yes! Yes!' She throws her arms around me and I feel as though I have wings. We kiss, and the world flies away, and all the shadows leave my heart.

But they cannot leave my face.

Lynelle says she has to go and tell her parents, that they'll be so happy. And then once again she asks who I am. 'I'm your betrothed,' I say, as happy as I've ever been.

'No, really,' she says. 'It is a fun game, but I can't very well tell my mother I'm marrying Mineownself, now, can I?'

'Tell them you are marrying your true love,' I say quietly. I refuse to listen to the warning bells in my heart. 'That is more than enough.'

Only then does she realize I'm not playing a game with her. Her smile turns serious. A little frown touches her brow, though she still looks at me with love. 'You . . . truly refuse to tell me your name? Ever?'

'I can refuse you nothing. You know that.'

'Then why won't you tell me?' She takes a step toward me and touches my chest with just the barest tip of her fingers. 'Is there something I need to know?'

I take a deep breath. 'Can't we stay as we are? We're happy like this, aren't we?' I reach up to touch her dark hair, but she steps away from me.

'B-Beloved? Please tell me what this means.' She sounds truly frightened.

'Don't be frightened,' I say. 'There's nothing to fear from me, I swear it on all I hold dear.' I smile at her. 'I swear it on my love for you.'

'How can you love me if you're truly keeping secrets from me?' She takes another step back. 'What are you hiding? Are you a-already married, or, or, wanted for a crime, or . . . .' She chokes on a sob. 'Tell me. Please, tell me.'

'I've done nothing wrong,' I say. 'But you won't understand. Lynelle, if you'll only trust me, trust in my love for you—'

'No!' Her voice is panicked now. She looks around her and realizes we are alone in the clearing. This fact has never frightened her before. 'You're frightening me, please. I love you, you know I'll always love you, what could be so terrible that you must hide from me?'

I want to hold her, to kiss the fear from her face. 'Lynelle. Lynelle, beloved, please. It is nothing terrible, and you have nothing to fear, from me, from anything. Believe me. I'll keep you safe, always.'

'How can I believe you when you lie to me? How can I trust you if you're keeping secrets? How can I marry you if I don't know who you are?'

I cough an exasperated sigh. 'I could never lie to you. If I would lie to you, I'd tell you I was named Ren and was the son of a woodsman and that my mother was murdered by bandits. I could tell you my name was Grumblebone and I was the seventh son of a seventh son of a grand house fallen into ruin by my uncle's drinking and gambling. I could tell you any one of a thousand lies, each of them more plausible than the fact that I *cannot* tell you my name!'

Her face is more questioning now than fearful. 'Why can't you?' She takes a blessed step toward me. 'Are you under a geas? Are you—'

'No,' I cut her off. 'Can you not just let me love you, and have an end on it?'

She blinks at me a few times, and then nods. I heave a sigh of relief and wrap her in my arms. 'Thank you.' I kiss her then, and she lets me. As my lips travel down her jaw and to her throat her hands wrap around my shoulders. Then with a jerk she pulls back my hood.

I am exposed. Exposed before I could tell her – as I meant to do on our wedding day. Before I can pull the hood back, distracted as I was, she has already seen. Her scream echoes over the valley. 'Stop! Lynelle!' I cry out, trying to calm her.

But now she is backing away from me as if from a poisonous snake. 'Demon,' she whispers, her voice raw with terror. 'Demon, Nameless!'

'Yes, yes, I'm a Nameless faerie. But I am not yet corrupted. I've done nothing wrong!'

She screams again and runs from me, looking over her shoulder as if afraid to turn her back on me. It is pointless, though. I am a faerie. I am faster than her. 'Lynelle!' I catch her up and hold her firmly. 'Lynelle, stop this, I'm still the same man! I am still your dear friend, still your beloved! Nothing has changed between then and now. You did not fear me then, why fear me now?'

'Demon!' she spits the word in my face and begins to sob in horror. I release her, staggering backward as if from a blow. The moment her arms are free she begins wrestling at her hand, as if afraid the ring I had given her is fused to her flesh, is as an iron manacle, binding her forever to me. Of course it comes off. It is only meaningless gold.

I fall to my knees, desperate. What can I say to her? How can I make her understand? But her lovely bare foot comes up and meets my jaw, and I am thrown backward, and dazed. She pulls her gathering knife which she uses to collect mistletoe and tansy and stabs me. I could pull away. I could cast a spell on her. I don't want to. The knife comes down.

The well used blade plunges deep inside me, grating against bone. It glances off my ribs, and I still breathe. My heart beats. It doesn't matter. Though my life continues, she has already stabbed me through the heart. I stare at the sky as she runs away from me, my blood pulsing onto the ground. No longer her beloved. No longer anything but shadow.

My sister finds me, tends me, forces me back to some semblance of life. When I recover I hear Lynelle was found at the bottom of the ravine, her neck broken from the fall. My sister tells me it isn't my fault. I know that it is.

Will knew this dream. In a briefer, less detailed form, it was the first dream she had visited, as Lavender lay wasting on her bed. Stabbed, wounded, but it was the grief and the shame that cut to the soul. Will tried to reach further, desperate to find any hope in that terrible moment, but she didn't have the chance.

Hands grabbed her and pulled her away from her dream, out of her trance. Tears her wasted body could ill afford to lose were streaming down her face. She thought at first that Ferdinand had broken his promise, but he was standing by the bed in horror. The hands that held her belonged to Hiedelen's guards. 'Sorry, my lady,' said Captain Warren, stepping before her. 'We're under strict orders not to let you get away with any more magic. You're to be bathed and made ready before the evening bell.'

'Made ready?'

'For the ceremony,' he said without expression. The door opened behind him. A gaggle of women came in carrying the wedding dress she had been meant to wear for her marriage to Narvi. And leading them up was – of course – Ginith.

I lay exhausted, expecting to be seized and arrested at any moment, but the sounds of Hiedelen's lackeys collecting the fruits of my toil continued around and about me. They weren't seeing me. I struggled my eyes open and all I saw was in shadow. I blinked. A tangled skein of blood alloy thread was within a few inches of my hand. I reached for it, and it disappeared into shadow. It took me a moment to realize I was shrouded in Will's shadow spell. She'd altered it on the fly. *Well done, Will*, I thought. I surreptitiously pulled the skein into my shirt and pulled my exhausted body deeper into the shadow near the corner.

Unfortunately, the movement made more noise than it should have. The nearest guard looked in my direction. 'Eh?' he said. 'Who's there?'

'What is it, Levi?' one of his friends asked.

'Dunno, I just . . .' He frowned at the shadow in which I was crouched. He nervously touched the Hiedelen soldier's tag around his neck and then approached my shadow.

I wasn't up for it. If it came to a fight, I was already dead. He reached out into the shadows and made contact with my right arm.

It was pure reflex that saved me. He touched me, I started back, and my arm caught on his tag. He pulled back, startled, and the cord holding the tag snapped, leaving it twisted around my wrist. 'Here!' the guard shouted. 'Here, it's . . . it's . . . .' His words were drowned in a yawn. I felt a surge of hatred, and even before the yawn was finished he listed sideways, and sank to the floor, a victim of the Sleep.

His mates came forward to collect him. 'So much for Lesli's protection,' one of them said. 'I told you it wouldn't work.'

'Do you want to be the one to tell him that?' his friend said.

'No!' said the other with feeling.

They frowned at their sleeping comrade. 'Let's leave him here. Let someone else tell the old windbag his charm's not working.'

'Better them than us. Let's finish quick.' He laughed. 'Without Levi counting every strand, what do you say you and I each . . . ?'

'Just one or two, eh?' They hurriedly stuffed a few skeins of gold into their pockets, and finished the rest so quickly that it never occurred to them to even glance at the shadow that Levi had been trying to warn them about.

I was left staring at a Sleeping guard, holding the soldier's tag on a roughly spun woollen cord, whose spinning I recognized all too well.

My dark spell was still twisted into the wool, but there was something else there, too. Something which made me uneasy. It was as if my spell was overlaid with another, an oily, greasy magic, manipulative and so subtle as to almost be unrecognizable. A very specific type of manipulative magic, that could use another's spell, or another's will, and turn it to his own devices. This spell was no longer wholly my own.

Of course! Someone had used the spell itself as a shield for select members of the guard. If someone knew enough to turn my hatred against itself, using that hate to keep the Sleep at bay, then mightn't they know enough to turn the Sleep itself to their own devices?

I lay back and tried to think of how the spell had spread. First to Lavender, pierced by the spindle. Then to her wretched dog, in close proximity. After that, it travelled through the lines of my hatred, touching those who had harmed me personally first. From what I had gathered, my hatred for Hiedelen and his men hadn't struck me fully until I realized that Will was marrying Narvi – and out of all of the men from Hiedelen, hadn't it struck Narvi first? But I desperately hated Lesli, and it wasn't touching him, so he must be guarded. Somehow, just after the surge of my hatred had taken out Narvi, he had gotten hold of my spool of wool and was using it as a shield for him and his men. But when I had attacked him and failed, that hadn't been the Sleep; that was an attempt at cold-blooded murder. This Sleep spell wouldn't have protected against that.

But my spindle would. The broken spindle: the drop spindle I had been using for more than a dozen years, the spindle that held the memories of warming spells for my sister and spells to help us escape from our foes and even that wretched gold ring for Lynelle; that spindle had been the channel for my power for long enough that it was as powerful as any more traditional faerie's magic wand. Anyone with even a moderate gift for magic, particularly the oily, manipulative kind I could feel on this woollen cord, could turn that spindle into a fierce protection, with every pulse of love and hatred I had felt in the last decade. And Lynelle had been no more than seven years ago. Oh, Light, the strength of the emotion in that spindle! What had I been *thinking?* Of course, I hadn't been thinking. I'd only been feeling – hatred, revenge, self-loathing for having met Princess Willow and not hating her on sight. I'd liked her. That was what made it so terrible for me. Everything that happened, right from the very beginning, had been because, in one charged, irritated, amused conversation, I had grown fond of the Princess Willow Lyndal.

Cursed, Nameless fae, I wasn't good for anything.

I hadn't the strength to do anything about it just then. I could barely see straight. I needed to rest. The hollow in the marble floor left by that blasted thorn bush was a good size to curl up in. It reminded me of my burrow, actually. With the sounds of Levi's nightmares for company, I tucked myself into a ball and tried to regain some energy.

I'm not sure you could call it sleep, but the day passed in my little hollow.

It was the wedding bells that pulled me from my stupor. I didn't recognize what they were at first, only that a musical crashing echoed around the palace and rang from the hills. By the Light, I'd stayed too long! I jumped to my feet—

And realized I should have gotten up slowly. I reeled and fell back to the floor.

I spent a few moments on my back, watching the room spin above my head. Then I crawled onto my hands and knees and used the wall to get to my feet. Oh, black dark, how was I supposed to stop this wedding?

Get there first, I decided. Figure out what you're going to do when you get there.

Will

The wedding was not a grand affair of pride, pomp, and circumstance. There weren't enough people awake in the castle to fill the palace chapel, so Lesli had elected to hold the wedding in the throne room, where the guests wouldn't rattle around so much. There were barely forty guests, and at least a quarter of them were upper servants, hastily stuffed into holiday garb. The resident members of the court were in attendance – those that weren't asleep. Otherwise, the only other guests were Heidelen's guards. They ringed the throne room, and the bishop seemed uneasy. Will was deposited at the newly erected altar by Captain Warren. Ferdinand entered and watched from the doorway of the antechamber, his face pale as if he were feverish. Will shook her head at him gently. There was nothing he could do.

Apparently, Lesli had spent the last three days having as much of the spun gold as he could embroidered onto one of his royal blue velvet coats. He positively glittered standing by the bishop; as gaudy as a gypsy, only three times as wide. The design was fairly simple, a twisting vine, more the tendrils of a grape than of the climbing roses, but it covered the coat from chin to hem. The sight of him swathed in the spoils of all Reynard's hard work made Will feel positively ill.

She gritted her teeth as the bishop began the liturgy. She'd been prepared for this. She'd been prepared to marry someone she didn't love for her country. She'd just thought it would be a harmless little boy, not the epitome of evil himself. As the ceremony continued something melted in Will. As the bishop droned on and on about the sanctimony of the marriage state and how the gods would smile upon the couple, she started to cry. She did not sob, or even bow her head. The tears trickled one by one down her face, but she stood straight and tall and stony faced as the bishop ate up the words until she had to agree. *I do*, she had to say. *I do*. And she could. For her country, for her sister, for everyone, she could do this. Bravery. She had that virtue, after all. She could face anything. Even this.

And then someone behind her screamed. She thought it was Ginith.

The entire congregation shifted, turning to look at the figure that was trudging slowly up the isle behind them. More screams followed Ginith's, and Will almost didn't blame them. Reynard looked terrible. He was hunched and scraggly. His ragged russet clothes were crusty with dried blood, and the shadows swirled around him like mist. The tattered remains of Will's shadow spell weren't entirely gone from him, so he seemed wreathed in darkness. He had forgotten his hood. With his eyes blazing red with exhaustion and his face white as driven snow, he looked the personification of evil.

'Guards!' Lesli called out behind her. 'Fetch the guards! Kill that demon.'

Reynard glanced about him as if he'd only just realized what was going on. The guards at the sides of the room moved as one, fitting bolts to crossbows. 'No!' Will cried. She wrenched her arm from Lesli's grip and flung herself to Reynard, shielding him with her body. His hand gently squeezed her shoulder. 'No, you can't kill him!'

'Move away, Princess. This is no concern of yours.'

'I won't let you kill him!'

'He's just vermin!' Lesli barked. 'Guards, shoot him!'

Captain Warren shook his head. 'Not with the princess in the way. If you'll pardon me, sir.'

'Then seize her!'

Reynard grabbed her then, hard. 'I want my payment, Princess,' he announced. 'You made a promise.'

The words sounded hoarse in Will's ears. Of all the times to collect! There had to be something else going on.

'You *know* this demon?' Lesli snapped.

Will glared at him. 'He's not a demon!'

'Foul witch! Associating with demons. Criminal activity in such a noble rank. Guards! Guards!'

Ferdinand surprised Will by coming to her side. 'Quite right,' he said evenly to Lesli. 'If she is such a criminal, it would be unwise to wed her. Why not leave her to her own kingdom's justice and return home?'

'Leaving who in charge?' Lesli asked. 'You?'

'Why not? I was to be heir to the kingdom upon my marriage to Princess Lavender.'

'But you aren't married yet, Prince Ferdinand! And that witch beside you has broken the law of this realm and used foul magic—'

'You're one to talk,' Reynard called from behind Will. 'You're a magician yourself.'

There were several gasps around the room.

'What did you just say?'

Reynard poked his head between Will and Ferdinand's shoulders. 'You've your own gift for magic, and you use it, too. You're shrouded in a magical protection, of a very specific kind. Many of your men, are too.' He pulled a woollen cord from his pocket and held it out towards the king. 'I wonder what the noblemen of this realm would think if they discovered that you had a shield against the Sleep . . . and weren't sharing it with them?'

Will gazed at Reynard, and she knew he was telling the truth. She glared at King Lesli, with his blue velvet coat and his fine fashionable powdered wig and his expensive gold rings. 'You were using magic to manipulate Mother,' she realized. 'That's why Mother was listening to you, when she's been doing everything all her life to get the kingdom out from underneath your oppression. You've been using magic all your life, haven't you? Why else did Father willingly come to sacrifice himself on the thorns?'

Reynard piped up, 'And why else would your own brother take your place to die on them fifty years ago?'

'Why else banish magic,' Ferdinand added, 'unless because you don't want anyone to know what you're doing?'

'Lies!' Lesli cried. 'Conjecture! You can prove nothing.'

'Yes I can,' Reynard said. 'Check his person. He and all of his men have a spell cord just such as this. How long have you had it, Lesli? You could have protected others with that spell, shielded them from the Sleep, like the king and queen, but you didn't want to.'

'I only discovered the spell cords in the Princess Willow's chambers. *She's* the witch!'

'We've only your word for that,' Will said, leaping on the lie. She knew, now, that that rough wool was Reynard's sleep spell, and she thought it likely that Lesli had only discovered it when he searched her chambers the night she went to see Mistress Cait. Still, he had used it for his own devices, and as such had been caught red handed. 'Why didn't you offer this protection to my father? Or Ferdinand? Or Captain Warren?'

Captain Warren cleared his throat. 'Failure to disclose vital information to the crown in a time of crisis is a hanging offence, sire.'

King Lesli gave him a withering look. 'Only if I am a citizen of Lyndaria.'

'If you're proclaiming yourself as regent,' Will said, 'then you are.'

Lesli's eyes narrowed. 'This is a farce. They're all corrupted by the demon, and you can't prove I've ever touched a rag of a spell.'

'Oh?' said a crisp, clear voice from behind the crowd. 'I can fix that.'

White fire engulfed the room. Most of the people screamed, and Ginith was the loudest of all. As quickly as the cool inferno had risen, it faded, leaving only a few tendrils of flame here and there, in particular around Reynard and Will. Up beside them strode Reynard's little sister, still burning with foxfire. 'Hey there, Princess,' she said, and Will smiled at her.

'What are you doing here?' Reynard asked.

'Our ma's been out looking for you. We were worried. You've been gone almost two days. I told her I'd go get you.' She turned back to the people. 'People of Lyndaria! My foxfire clings to magic. Everyone look around you. If anyone's still glowing, you know they're a magician.'

The fire burned steadily around Will's hands, with a burning flame near her heart. Reynard positively flared with it, the brightest thing in the room with a shadow at its core. To Will's surprise, a handful of the guests glittered here and there, and the bishop held a steady glow in his hands.

And King Lesli glowed from top to toe like a torch. Will suspected much of the reason was his gold-studded coat, but some clearly surrounded his mouth. Unless he had been eating the gold, Lesli had been speaking spells of his own.

'Lies still!' King Lesli cried out. 'This . . . urchin is obviously working with them. Another criminal.'

'Still,' said Captain Warren. 'I'm beginning to wonder about some of my own actions over the last few days, Your Majesty. It might be best to investigate this further before we proceed with any permanent arrangements.'

Lesli's eyes narrowed then, and he glared at Captain Warren. 'I do not intend to allow a handful of spurious rumours to deprive me of what is rightfully mine.'

'Yet you'd do the same to me,' Will snapped. 'What proof does anyone have that I did anything to my sister? That I'd ensorcel my own kingdom? Magic was never against the law until Lesli came among us and made it so.' The guards seemed ready to listen to her, so she stepped away from Reynard to take a better stance. 'From the moment of my birth I have been devoted to this kingdom. I have obeyed every law, respected every tradition. I am my mother's daughter, and a rightful heir to the Lyndal bloodline.' She pointed at Lesli. 'This man is a usurper who has done nothing but sap this country of its finance and strength from the beginning of his reign! Beside whom do you stand?'

There was a murmur from the crowd.

'She stands beside a Nameless demon!' Lesli shouted. 'And that is the *only* thing that is keeping you alive, you witch.' Lesli lunged and grabbed Reynard by the arm, dragging him from the protection of his sister and Ferdinand. Reynard was still too weak from his last night's labours to struggle much. Lesli turned him around and held a sharp pointed piece of wood to his throat. Will blinked. She knew that piece of broken wood. It was that wooden wheel that she had taken from her cloak. The wheel that had still had a strand of wool around it. Ah, hell, she realized, this was Reynard's drop spindle! The one he had used to cast the cursed Sleep. And it was sharp

327

and deadly as a poniard, and if her studies served her, likely to pierce Reynard with his own magic if it should be used against him. No shield can protect you from yourself. 'If I kill your demon, you'll have no power against me.'

'He is *not* a demon!' Will said heatedly.

'No one move!' Lesli shouted.

Will was exhausted, Ferdinand was broken, and Reynard had a sharp, deadly stake held to his throat. She glanced wildly at Reynard's sister. 'Can you do anything?'

'Illusions,' she said, panicked. 'Intuition. My brother's the one with the power.'

Reynard's hands had moved into his pocket, and Will could see him twisting something with his fingers. *Oh, please let him spin himself out of this!* 'Warren,' Lesli shouted, 'I command you to clap that woman in irons!'

'Don't you do it, Warren!' Ferdinand shouted.

Warren was used to following commands. He was never one to make decisions on his own. Ginith, however, had no such internal war. She leaped for Will and grabbed her wrists. 'I've had enough of *you*,' Will snapped, and kneed her in the stomach. Ginith fell to the ground, her fine skirts billowing around her beautifully.

'Don't do it!' Reynard's sister cried, and Will turned from Ginith to see Lesli twisting Reynard's fine fingers backwards, as if he would break them. The spindle dug into Reynard's flesh, and the tip of the broken shard was stained with blood.

'What's this?' Lesli said. He pulled a tangle of red gold thread from Reynard's hand, breaking the spell he was trying to spin. Lesli chuckled. 'Why thank you. Every ounce of gold helps.' He squeezed the snarl of spun gold tightly in his hand.

Will screamed. It felt as though Lesli had his hand around her heart, and was crushing it. She fell to her knees, and Ferdinand went with her. 'Will!' he cried, catching her with his good arm. Her hand went to her heart, and she looked down. All she saw was the still glowing tongue of foxfire that showed magic had been used there recently.

Reynard watched her fall, his eyes wide with panic, and then his lips curled viciously. With a fierce snarl, he twisted his neck and bit the hand the held the spindle, hard. He barely seemed to notice the new line of red that grazed his collarbone. Lesli cried out in horror and shook his hand, tearing the flesh, but effectively disengaging the biting fox. The broken spindle fell with a clatter to the ground. Lesli also ceased squeezing the little skein of thread, and the pain around Will's heart faded. Reynard fell and scuttled to her, taking her by the arm that wasn't already occupied by Ferdinand. 'I'm sorry,' he breathed, Lesli's blood upon his lips. He lightly touched her glowing chest. 'I'm so sorry.'

Will looked from Reynard to Lesli, who still held the skein of gold. Of course! Reynard did magic by spinning threads. The gold briar on Will's chest was the same red gold as that tangle of thread. In tending her wound, she realized, Reynard would have used the nearest thread to hand, and that would have been the same spool she had been dangling over, where her blood had poured. That gold was alloyed with her blood, and was holding her together. Whatever Lesli did to it happened to her, too. That was why Reynard was apologizing.

Maybe she could use it against Lesli. Sympathetic magic, as in the one unburnt chapter of *The Ages of Arcana*. She'd never had access to the kind of power that magic needed, but the thread was her own life's blood mingled with Reynard's faerie magic. It should be wildly potent. But what could she have the thread do that wouldn't mean her own death?

The thread was once a briar. Briar fed and strengthened by blood. Royal blood. The more it got, the more it wanted.

But the piece of the thread that Will held was connected to her heart. How much more blood could it possibly have?

And then she knew. *The Zarmeroth Cycle* had taught her how to guide her will. If she used that skill as well as the sympathetic magic in her royal blood, it might just work. But she needed help.

There were two choices. Ferdinand knelt straight and tall at her left hand, noble and severe in his mourning black. He was beautiful, handsome and brave and honourable, a true prince charming, perfect in every aspect. And Will didn't even look at him.

'Kiss me,' she said to Reynard.

The skulking Nameless stared at her, his face pale and bloodstained beneath his shadows. 'What?'

'Just kiss me!' she said, and she took hold of his face and pressed her lips against his.

As before, he stiffened for a moment, hesitating, and then the hunger Will knew burned inside him surged to the fore. His arms wrapped around her and he groaned. He tasted of blood and harvest and autumn fires. His teeth were sharp, but caressed her lip gently. He gripped her very tightly, drawing her to him, making her a part of him. As if it were the last time for either of them – which it might have been. Her heart, as she had known it would, beat wildly against her chest. The blood surged in her ears, and there was nothing but Reynard's dark kiss. Will felt ferociously alive.

Some part of her knew something was going on apart from the two of them, but it was very hard to concentrate on that. Particularly since letting herself get caught up in the moment was essential to her plan. Her heart had to beat, and she had to feel every pulse.

Finally someone's scream broke their kiss, and a hand grabbed Will's arm. A large hand. A desperate hand.

King Lesli stood beside them, threads of red gold creeping over his face and hands, growing from the snarl of golden thread in his grip. As her heart had raced, the thread had been charged. Golden briars, alloyed by Will's own blood, and Reynard's magic. They pricked and pierced him, growing stronger with each drop of his blood they consumed. Royal blood, oh, so sweet. Whenever the red gold thread touched the golden threads on his coat, the embroidered vines twisted too, constricting about him, as hungry for his blood as the briars they had been spun from. 'You . . . *witch*!' he spat at Will, but the briars crept into his open mouth, and blood dripped from his lips. He screamed, more of a gurgle, really, and his hand let go of her. Will and Reynard scrambled backwards, as far from the reaching branches as they could get.

Most of the spectators had fled. The room was mostly empty. Only Captain Warren, Ferdinand, Reynard and his sister remained. And Ginith was screaming herself into hysterics in the corner.

Will glanced at Reynard's sister, the most hale of her little band of followers. 'Can you do something about her?' she asked her.

The girl gave a smile easily as wicked as her brother's, and sidled up to the woman. She slapped her hand across Ginith's mouth and pulled it away. The waiting woman's mouth was gone, sealed into a solid line. She was screaming through her nose now, which was at least quieter than her previous hysterics. Will hoped it was a temporary spell, but she wasn't going to say anything just then.

King Lesli was almost gone, now. What pieces of his skin they could see had sprouted golden briars, and he was barely swaying. His screams had ceased, and the gold briars were slowing their growth. Will put her hand to her heart and took a deep sigh of relief.

Captain Warren looked down on her. 'I'm afraid this does not look good for you, Princess,' he said. 'I'm beginning to be inclined to believe that Lesli has been undermining this country, but there's still no proof that you are innocent of this Sleep, or that Lesli has actually done any wrong whatsoever.' He looked Reynard up and down. 'Consorting with the Nameless is still an offence.'

Will glared at him. 'Why? What's he done? You don't know. Why condemn them based solely on what they are?'

'They've already been convicted of something.'

'Yes, but you don't know what it was, or what the circumstances were. If they *have* done something bad, who's to say they mean to do so again?' she asked. 'It's like the laws on magic. Wait until he commits a crime before you condemn him. Or me.'

Reynard touched her hand. 'But you know I have,' he whispered, too low for anyone else to hear.

'Yes, but he doesn't,' Will hissed back.

The golden bush in the centre of the room shivered once and then went still. Forever. Captain Warren looked at it. 'I'm not sure that was legal either, Your Highness.'

Will shook her head. 'There's no one left to order you to arrest me,' she said. 'Go and watch the populous. Perhaps we should prepare to evacuate Lyndaron, before the Sleep takes absolutely everyone. Mother wouldn't hear of it, but she was under Lesli's influence. Prepare a council of my mother's advisers: yourself, the highest ranking nobles, the guild leaders, the elected members of the town council, and anyone else you think should have a say. We'll hold a meeting. All of us can decide what would be best to do. If that includes arresting or executing me, I'll abide by the council's decision.'

'And in the meantime?' Captain Warren asked.

'You have no orders in the meantime,' Will said. 'So leave us.'

Captain Warren regarded her for a moment, and then nodded. 'As you wish, Your Highness.' He collected Ginith from the floor, where she had collapsed in muffled sobs. 'What about her?' he asked.

'She'll be better by midnight,' Reynard's sister called out. 'Unless you want to take a knife and cut her open.'

Captain Warren looked at the red-faced lady. 'I think I'll trust you until then, miss,' he said. He led Ginith tenderly from the throne room.

This left only Will, Reynard, his sister, and Prince Ferdinand, gathered by the golden briar which was once King Lesli of Hiedelen. Reynard looked at Will. 'Leaving won't work,' he said. 'The spell is spread by hatred, not by distance.'

Will looked him over. 'Meaning you'd have to stop hating?'

He looked down. He didn't say it, but he was sorry. 'It wasn't meant to pierce her flesh,' he murmured.

'Just give me nightmares,' Will said. 'I know.'

He didn't apologize. Instead he turned to his sister. 'You should go,' he told her.

'Not without you,' she said. 'Our ma's going to kill herself with worry.'

'I'll be along soon,' he said. He turned to Will. 'There's something Will promised me.'

Will frowned. Something very strange was going on here. Why in all the green earth would Reynard have any interest in her sister? She had to work this out, but he was right. She had promised him. Maybe she *would* offer herself up for arrest, after all.

Before they left, Reynard paused and spoke a word to Ferdinand. Will couldn't hear what he said, but Ferdinand nodded gravely and said, 'You have my word.'

Both Reynard and Will were exhausted. At least Will had had a chance to clean up – Reynard looked something like a walking corpse. He followed her into the antechamber and Will took one last look at Ferdinand. His ice-blue eyes watched her as she closed the door.

The room seemed dark, despite the bright windows and the winter sun shining in. A beam of golden light pierced the gloom and bathed the sleeping princess in its glow. Reynard stood very far away from Will.

'Here she is,' Will said. She gestured to her beautiful sister, her flower-petal skin and her autumn hair and her full, full red lips. 'She is beautiful. And I did promise.' Reynard stared at her, his face as dark and unreadable as ever. 'So this is what you wanted all along,' Will said.

Reynard did not answer at first. Finally he croaked, 'Yes.'

Something he'd once said nagged at Will. *I don't lie very well*, he'd said. Faeries were supposed to be honest; this was why they were able to impart that gift to others, such as Queen Amaranth. Lying made Will feel ill. She wondered if it did the same to him. She pressed for another lie. 'It must make you happy, achieving your goal.'

He swallowed. 'Yes.'

She frowned. 'What were you saying to Ferdinand? Were you telling him he should give up on Lavender, because she'd been promised to you?'

'Yes,' he croaked. He glared at her. 'Can I take my prize and go?'

'I think you're lying,' she said. 'I think you asked him to look out for me.' He blushed, and Will knew she was right. Damn it, she knew what he was doing. It was sheer madness, but she knew. She smiled in wonder. 'If it was Lavender you wanted, why go through me? If it was only the princess you cared for, why was it only when I was hurt that you could break away from Lesli?' Will took a step towards him. 'Why keep coming to save me? Why agree to look for Mistress Cait, if you were the one who cast the Sleep all along? Why risk your life to save mine?' She took another step. 'No answer?'

'Too many questions,' he whispered. His eyes were closed, and he refused to look at her.

'I'm no fool,' Will said gently. 'I was born with the gifts of Bravery, Honesty, Wit, Wisdom and Mercy. I can see clearer than most.' She stepped toward him again. 'You don't want Lavender at all. You've never even met her.' Tears of sympathy were brewing somewhere behind her eyes. 'You're doing this for *me*. Somewhere along the line you started to *care*. You're only offering to take her because you think that's what I want. You think if you take her then I can have Ferdinand and live happily ever after.'

He refused to look at her. He reached back and pulled up his hood, shrouding his face in deeper shadows. 'I never said any of that.'

'No. You didn't have to.' Will reached out into the shadows to touch his cheek. 'I don't want Ferdinand,' she told him. 'She can keep him and his mad love.' He looked up at her, and his eyes were painfully deep. Something strange had happened to Will. She felt a deep warmth inside, a fondness. Not the rushing, heart-quickening distraction of perfection that Prince Ferdinand caused. Not the burning delicious ache that had hurt her every second of every day. This feeling was . . . unfathomable. It almost felt like amusement. The feeling glowed inside her, warm and precious. It didn't hurt at all.

'You hate yourself so much,' she told him. 'So much more than you think you hate anyone else. You're so full of hatred for yourself that it spills out into everything. And it grates against you, pulling you in ways you'd never have gone, in any other life.' She shook her head. 'You poor Nameless faerie. You aren't anywhere near as bad as you want to be, are you?' She wrapped her arms around his skinny shoulders. 'Reynard.

My rumpled Stiltskin.' And with all the tenderness of that warm, inner glow, she kissed his shadowed cheek.

Reynard

How to describe the indescribable? How to encompass the miracle, as the name bound to me, engulfed me, became me? I cried out in pain, as if she'd stabbed me. But it wasn't pain. It was wonderful and terrible and powerful, drowning me in something I didn't know how to contain. It was such a sudden and enveloping cessation of a pain I hadn't even known was there that I reeled with it. I pulled away from her and sank to my knees, unable to hold this wonderful Light that seeped through me, from the deepest corner of my soul to the tips of my very fingers. I was warm and cool and burning and soothed and powerful and vulnerable and a thousand other feelings and sensations and beings that I had never even considered.

Will stepped back from me with a gasp. 'Reynard?' she asked, and I flinched with delicious pain at the wonderful sound of it. 'Reynard, what—'

I cried out as she said it again, and gasped, panting with the feeling of it. My heart was broken in that moment, broken more thoroughly than any slight or any attack had ever managed. In comparison, Lynelle had barely bruised me. I was pierced through by the Light, and all the pain and darkness flowed out of me until they pooled in a circle around me. My hands clenched into fists and I ground my knuckles into the floor. My hatred was raw now, unmuffled by shadows, and it was for myself more than for anyone else. Will had been so right. She knew me, knew me better than I knew myself.

That unveiled hatred was countered at the same time by a love I couldn't begin to fathom, a love I could only hear the echo of before. Now the shroud had been lifted, and the love was a powerful surge, a waterfall that threatened to pull me away. Love for Will, for the kit, even for my poor, broken mother. Love for life, and magic, and the world itself, and all the people in it I'd thought I hated. The people I kept trying to save, against my will and my better judgement.

It was as if I'd been deafened all my life, with wool stopping my ears, and Will had pulled that wool away and the sounds I heard were so beautiful and powerful and clear that they hurt. The Light spilled from me, glowing steady and strong, and the shadows faded away.

And as the shadows faded from me, another miracle happened.

The sleeping princess gasped, opened her eyes, and sat up. 'Willow?' Crown Princess Lavender Lyndal tossed her head, looking about herself in confusion. 'Who's that?' she asked, pointing at me.

The Nameless spell I had cast, the shadow spell of hatred and horror, had fled from the new Light that engulfed me. Lavender was the first to stir, but soon there were shouts from all around the palace. As my hatred for everyone died, my spell of hatred died too.

Queen Amaranth sat up and gasped at finding her husband asleep beside her, but soon King Ragi was stirring too, and a horrid little yappy dog that had been sleeping beside Lavender began barking up a storm. The door burst open, and in came Prince Ferdinand, his eyes alight with hope. 'Lavi!' he shouted, and fell to his knees at her feet. Lavender slid off the bed and into his arms, and Queen Amaranth leapt up and embraced Will, rightly suspecting (she was Wise, after all) that Will had found out how to break the spell.

Will started laughing and turned to each of them in turn, trying to explain everything at once. She wasn't getting very far, as everyone kept interrupting. Her winter-thunderstorm eyes sparked with joyous lightning, and her complexion, flawed and sallow, shone rosy in her happiness. She was tall and strong and brilliant as the sun, the single most beautiful, amazing and wondrous creature in the whole of creation. My Will.

I wanted to go to Will. I wanted to thank her. I frankly wanted to fall at her feet and offer her my heart to break, but instead I shrank out of view and slunk out the door. Everything seemed brighter and more beautiful, and I wanted to weep at the wonder of it. There was nothing – not the evening sun shining through the palace windows, not the winter scent of roses that permeated the tapestries, not the glitter of snow on the lawns – that did not hold a new and tangible joy. I yearned to go back to Will. I longed to show her what she had done. But she could never know. I could never tell her. I couldn't stay. One shadow still remained from all the ones my beloved Will had just cast from my soul. I was still a criminal.

I didn't deserve her.

Will

And he was never heard from again.

Chapter 21

Will and Reynard

Or that's what would have happened, if Princess Will wasn't stubborn as an ox.

It took her seven long months to find him. She went at first to his burrow, but it was deserted. She thought that, maybe, he might come back, so she waited. She had not been gifted with Patience, so it was difficult for her. She waited while the roses bloomed into a riot of colour, and Lavender arranged her marriage to Ferdinand – a state affair, with rose petals cast underfoot. It was a beautiful ceremony, and the seamstresses even contrived to make Will look presentable, despite her being forced into a lavender dress that washed out her eyes and felt as if it had been made to fit a seven-year-old.

Will thought Mistress Cait might come to the wedding, but all she did was send a message – a fortune, really – for Lavender. It came on a plain card pinned to a pillow in a baby's cradle made from what looked like a massive living lavender, woven together. The message promised the princess a daughter before the year was out.

Will looked at the note, and looked at her husband-to-be. With Lesli out of the way, and Will's still-dubious reputation, her betrothal to Narvi had been postponed until a more politically advantageous time. She looked back at the note. A daughter, the heir's firstborn, a mere ten years younger than Narvi. Will smiled. A wife at eighteen and a husband at twenty-eight was considerably less strained a union than the alternative. She directed her mother's attention to the note, tousled Narvi's hair with a solemn and formal farewell, and retreated to her chambers alone.

A few minutes later, sans the lavender bridesmaid's dress, she snuck out her secret door dressed for hard traveling. She marched right from there into Mistress Caital's enchanted forest. It spat her out a few times, but she kept plunging back in until Cait's wolf came and led her to the tower. Will was not polite as she demanded assistance in finding Reynard.

She and Cait had a long conversation, at the end of which, Faerie Caital finally presented Will with three walnut shells. Faerie gifts. 'Open them when you need them,' she said.

Will realized she was in her own story. Her happy ending, should she have one, was going to take work.

She supposed they all did, in the end.

She opened the first walnut shell, and out jumped a smallish red fox. Her very own questing beast. He led her over moors and fields and ditches. She walked for long days, sleeping at inns and in barns and even, once or twice, under the stars. It was a summer journey, and she could travel lightly. When she came to the river, the next shell revealed a little cherry wood boat that took her steadily downstream, and finally to the other bank, and then politely folded itself back into the walnut shell for easy transporting. Following her fox she came, after many months, to a tiny village in a distant country.

Roux, whom she had become quite fond of, really, turned around three times in the middle of the road, yawned at her, then promptly jumped onto her knapsack and fell asleep, covering his nose with his tail. Clearly he believed his job was done, but there was no Reynard in sight. Will tried to open the next walnut, but it wouldn't crack. She asked a little girl playing in the street whether she could direct her to the nearest witch or fortune teller, who could tell her what she was doing wrong. She said, 'I dunno about those, but the new faerie just set up shop by the creek side.'

Will asked specific directions and tipped her a copper for her help.

The cottage Will approached was bright with whitewash, and morning glories twined over the door. The garden was a riot of colour – but there were no roses. Autumn was coming, and pumpkins and squash were piled on the door-step. A round, motherly faerie with bright yellow wings sat knitting on a swinging bench just outside. She shone with a buttery light. 'Hello, miss!' she said with a bright smile. Will was dressed in peasant travelling clothes for the sake of anonymity. 'I'm Mistress Stiltskin, is there aught I can do for you?'

'Yes,' Will said, unable to keep the smile from her face. 'I am looking for your son.'

'He's not working today, but my daughter and I could help you. Between the two of us, there's little we can't do. We only need him for the heavy stuff – that unpullable stump, that dying child. You don't want him anyway, he's surly. Too much power for his own good, my son. But anything else, you'd do better to come to us. Charms, illusions, good fortune; tell us your wishes, and we'll see what we can do for you. Modest prices, and we'll take a good trade any day.'

'I need to see Reynard,' Will said evenly.

Mistress Stiltskin looked confused for a minute, but then an enthusiastic voice cried out from the attic window. 'Willow!' A blazing white figure poured from the window, down the trellis, and nearly knocked her over with a hug. 'I knew you'd come! He didn't believe me, but I told him you would! No gift at fortune telling at all, Reynard.'

Will grinned down at her. Reynard's sister was an angel of beauty, her shining face and her flowing hair. A white flame amidst the autumn colours. 'It's you!' she said.

'Kitsune, thank you,' she said proudly. 'Kitsune Stiltskin. But you can call me Kit. Reynard's down by the creek. I won't tell him you're here. It'll ruin the surprise.' She pointed at Will. 'Ma, this is *Willow*!'

Mistress Stiltskin stood slowly and curtseyed deeply, averting her gaze. Will blushed. 'It's all right, Ma'am,' Will said. 'Don't do that. I'm not a princess here.'

'You could be the lowliest scullery maid,' Mistress Stiltskin said. 'I'd bow to you all the same.'

Will didn't know what to say. Kit grabbed her arm and pulled her around the house. 'Go on,' she said, 'he's down by the creek,' and she darted away. Will suspected she was probably going to be watching from somewhere, but she supposed it didn't matter, so long as she didn't interrupt.

As soon as she left, Will pulled out her little red fox, waking him gently. 'Find him, Roux,' she told him, and he twitched his tufted tail and took off down the bank towards a bend in the creek.

Reynard was sitting high on a fallen tree by the creek, spinning something with a new drop spindle. He saw the fox before he saw Will. He folded up his spinning and smiled. 'Hello, there,' he said, stooping down as the little beast pawed at his feet. 'What are you after?'

'Good boy, Roux,' Will called, and the fox dropped to all fours and scampered back to her. She fed him a tidbit of dried meat and he settled down to gnaw it. When she looked back Reynard was standing straight as a rod, staring at her with a look of horror.

It was everything he'd dreamed of, and the last thing he wanted. Will looked lovely, tanned from her summer journey, her hair free from the aristocratic coifs, framing her face in a lovely cloud. She'd grown thinner over her journey, and stronger. She was still sturdy and tall, not at all the fashionable courtly waif people expected her to be. She looked exactly like the hero she already was to him. He wanted to cry out, or weep, or fall to her feet, or flee as he had done before. But he didn't need to. Because he was Reynard, and he could control himself. All he did was stare, faerie tall and perfectly, faerie still.

Will licked suddenly dry lips. God of Love, but he was stunning. Ferdinand would look a pale, washed-out trout next to this red flame. Gone was the skulking stance. Gone were the furtive glances. Gone was the concealing hood. Most of all, gone were the shadows. He shone with a brilliant light, as though his soul was part of the sun itself. But it was still Reynard. She could see the impression of those shadows behind the light in his eyes. He stared at her as if she were a ghost, or possibly a demon come from hell to torment him. 'Will,' he breathed.

'Reynard,' she said with a slight smile.

He cringed at the name. It still hurt to hear it sometimes, a joy too raw, too tender to embrace fully. Kitsune had taken to it with a child's adaptability, and his mother had fallen easily back into the role of Mistress Stiltskin, leader of her small faerie clan. But Reynard was too tainted by the years of darkness to fully be comfortable in the light. And to hear the name from Will . . . Will's clear, rich voice, as it sounded in his dreams, in his errant thoughts, over and over and over, pounding in his head until he had to flee into his spinning or go mad . . . 'How did you find me?'

She took a step toward him. 'Mistress Cait. She gave me him.' She gestured to the little fox, Roux, who seemed to have caught the scent of a squirrel and was spinning in circles, his nose to the ground. 'You kept me walking a long time.'

He turned his back to her, his eyes back to the creek. He couldn't look at her. 'I didn't want to be found.'

She came up beside him and watched his profile. 'Afraid to be arrested?' she asked.

He hesitated. He wanted to lie, and say yes. It would have been such an easy answer, a perfect excuse that had nothing to do with *her*. But lies were even harder to tell in the light, and he didn't like lying to her. Not to her. Will could see the shadows move in his smouldering eyes as he forced himself to admit to something he didn't want to admit to. 'No,' he said. He swallowed. 'It was what I deserved, really. I even considered giving myself up, but . . .' He glanced at her. 'Is that why you've come? To arrest me?'

Will smiled at him sadly. 'I hope you know me better than that,' she whispered.

Why did this have to hurt so much? Reynard closed his eyes, but he could still feel her gaze, burning him.

Will was frustrated. This whole thing was more awkward than she'd thought it would be. It wasn't like the faerie tales; she hadn't found him and taken his hand and walked off happy-ever-after. There was still one more task, one more mountain to climb, and she was afraid she wasn't going to surmount it. If she didn't do this right, she knew he would flee again. She knew how deeply his self-hatred ran, and he didn't believe in happiness – particularly not for himself. And even looking at him was distracting. Oh, but he was handsome. He glowed like a stained-glass window, and his red hair caught the breeze and shone like a flame. 'Your family is . . . looking well,' she said, seizing on a lighter topic. 'I'm glad to see it.'

'I knew Kit well enough to name her,' Reynard said, reminding her it wasn't such a light topic after all. 'There was nothing I could do for my mother, but fortunately Kitsune understood her better than I did.'

'Good,' Will said. 'I did wonder about that. It didn't seem quite fair. I was hoping, but I heard nothing about you and your family. The Stiltskin clan didn't suddenly appear amongst the faeries. You all just . . . vanished.'

'We thought it best to leave Lyndar lands,' Reynard said. 'Once we were no longer Nameless, the other clans had no reason to deny us passage through their territories.' He swallowed. He had to ask, though the answer frightened him. 'Your family? Is everyone . . . ?'

'No ill effects. They're fine.'

'Your sister?'

'Married Ferdinand in the spring.'

His eyes closed. 'I'm sorry.'

'I'm not. They're happy. She wore a gown embroidered with your gold. After that they intended to cut it up and give pieces to all the households that lost working family members in the Sleep, as compensation for the loss of labour. There was even enough gold left over to appease Hiedelen.'

He looked up sharply. 'Hiedelen?'

'Lesli's eldest son,' Will clarified. 'There was a trial after you left. After much deliberation they came to the conclusion that the Sleep was caused by Lesli.' She laughed. 'I didn't disillusion them. There was one final tribute, but now that Lesli's gone, much of Hiedelen's structure seems to be crumbling. Apparently, he was using his magic to influence a lot of opinions. Now they've too much dissension on their plate to argue over our supposed debt. Lyndaria is free.'

Lyndaria was free. Reynard was glad to hear it, after all he'd put them through. But Will . . . 'And your marriage?' he asked.

Will smiled. 'Lavender's firstborn has been promised to Narvi. I read it on a broadsheet at an inn I stayed at. Cait has promised it's to be a daughter.'

That was not what Reynard wanted to hear. 'But you . . . ?'

'Still the witch princess,' she said. 'People are frightened of me. After what happened to Lesli, I can't exactly blame them. Mother and Father probably couldn't sell me into marriage even if they wanted to. Besides, I wouldn't let them. Not any more.'

He looked away as she said that, afraid she'd see the hope in his eyes. He didn't deserve her, there was no reason to hope. Even if she was free, she could never be his.

All she could see was his shining red hair, and the tips of his pointed ears. It was strange seeing them, he'd kept them so hidden. She had a sudden desire to reach out and touch one, let her finger travel down his long, brightly lit faerie throat . . . damn it, he was distracting!

'Oh, ahm . . . .' He realized he was being woefully impolite. 'Please, sit down.' He gestured to the fallen tree he had been sitting on when Roux came up and announced her. She sat, cautiously. He sat down beside her and his eyes darted back and forth from her to the water, unable to look at her, unable to look away. There was something he needed to say. What he kept saying over and over again in his dreams, in the countless conversations he'd had with her while he was sure she was a thousand miles away, content with her life at her now-peaceful palace. While she was, apparently, walking over hill and dale, following her questing beast, to find him. 'I never . . . .' He stopped, and she waited for him to go on. 'I meant to thank you,' he said finally. 'I never got a chance.'

'You never gave yourself a chance.'

'That's true.' He took a deep breath. 'In truth, there are no words to say it.'

'Don't think on it,' she said. She pulled down the collar of her dress and revealed the little golden briar that crossed her heart. 'A life for a life is equal, isn't it?'

Her skin was smooth and unscarred, but the golden line of his spell cord was unmistakable. He'd known it was there – it had as much as killed Lesli, after all – but he hadn't realized she'd ever see it. It was beautiful, in its way. But it was a symbol of something foul, a dark and dangerous experience that she would do better to forget. 'I'm sorry,' he said, touching the golden briar, the smooth, warm, human skin above her heart. 'I didn't realize it would mark you.'

His fingers left a line of heat on her skin that stayed long after his touch was gone. She hadn't realized how closely he'd sat by her. 'You save my life, rid Lyndaria of a tyrant, lift a pernicious ban from our economy, and you're sorry?' She touched the mark gently, tracing the patterns his fingers had left on her skin. 'Besides. I think it's rather pretty.'

'Any effects? Lesli . . .'

'Firmly planted in the middle of the throne room,' she told him 'When they tried to dig him out, I nearly fainted. We think if he's truly killed, I'd die. They decided to let him stay. He's quite decorative, actually. He's growing, but not wild like the thorns, just normally – if you could call a golden briar with the vague shape of a king normal. He bloomed golden rosebuds in the spring. Mother plucked them and gifted them to visiting royalty at Lavender's wedding.'

'Did that hurt?'

'No.' She laughed. 'Apparently, we can prune him without any ill effects.'

He did not smile with her. 'You're all right, then?'

'I'm fine,' she said, serious. 'And you?'

Reynard shook his head. 'I'm all right.'

'You look . . . .' she began, but she couldn't go on. There were no words for how he looked. 'Different,' she said finally.

'I'm not,' he said.

'Aren't you?'

He shook his head. 'Not really.'

'Is it better?'

'It's . . . easier. In ways I can't begin to describe.'

There was a short silence, and she tried again. 'I wish you'd try,' she said.

He heard the double meaning, and his eyes closed. He'd had this conversation a thousand times since he'd left her. Why was it so much harder now than it ever was in his thoughts? But he could deny her nothing. He tried. 'I'm . . . I'm not who I thought I was,' he said, swallowing. 'I didn't . . . I couldn't see myself through the shadows. I'm still learning what it is to be . . . me.' He didn't say the name. He'd only said it twice since he'd received it, once to his sister and once to his mother, so they both could truly know him. 'I haven't changed, really, but . . . it's different. The exact same path feels different in the dark, from in the daylight. I can see where I'm going . . . and where I've been. I can see where I am. I've never been able to do that before. I didn't know myself.' He shook his head. 'I still can't imagine how you could have begun to know . . .'

'The Sleep,' she said. 'No one else can remember the nightmares you gave them. Not one. Not even Lavender. But I do.'

He stared at her, confused. 'But you never Slept.'

'I had a dream-sharing spell, and I . . . I visited one, then another, then another. I couldn't keep away. They were intense and terrible, and—'

'I know what they were.' Reynard's voice was flat.

'And I wanted to see them,' she finished, unwilling to let him cut her off. 'I wanted to be there. I wanted to know.'

His red-brown eyes stared into hers. 'Why?'

Will wasn't sure she could explain. 'Right from the beginning . . . it seemed like they were trying to tell me something.' *And I think I was already half in love with you from the moment you insulted me at Madam Paline's*, she thought. But she didn't say that.

He took another deep breath. He'd just remembered he had to say more than thank you. 'I'm sorry about the Sleep.'

She shook her head. 'I know why you did it.'

'No,' he said. 'You couldn't. Or maybe you could. Maybe *you*. But even I didn't know why, not until I thought about it. It wasn't revenge or pain, not what was in the dreams. Or not really. That was my excuse. I was trying . . . to prove to myself how evil I was. I'd been trying so hard for so long to hold on to what was good in me that everything ached. I was so . . . *tired* of it all. Then I met you, and you were . . . you smelled of roses,' he said quietly. 'You amused me. No one had done that in . . . .' He trailed off. 'And you were the princess. It didn't match what I thought of as me,' he continued. 'And I knew . . . that if you knew who I was, you'd hate me. I thought if I just gave up and became evil − became what everyone thought I was − it might be easier.'

He gave a rueful half laugh. 'I didn't know how much it would hurt knowing myself. I'm not what I thought I was.' He wanted to hold her so badly in that moment that he felt like Will must have felt in the briars − as if a hole had been punched in his heart. He realized if he was still Nameless he would have already reached out for her − or fled. He kept having that impulse, too. But he wasn't impulsive any longer. Very deliberately he turned to face her. He reached out and touched a tendril of her hair, twisting it idly in his fingers, as if he would twist it into a spell. But there was no spell, not really. He was simply learning her. She shivered under his touch, and he didn't want to believe that it meant what his heart longed for. 'It took you to see,' he whispered. He let her go and bent his head to the creek.

351

She took a deep breath, and swallowed, banishing the shiver he had sent through her. 'Mistress Cait explained it to me,' she said. 'About your name. She said if I'd given you the name when I first thought of it — which was the moment I met you, actually — that it wouldn't have stuck to you. Even I probably would have forgotten it, such was the curse. But once I knew you, really knew you, I could, sort of . . . remind you who you were. I learned a lot about you from the nightmares . . . and the rest from what you did. Not how you acted, you always acted like a snarling puppy. But from what you were willing to do.' She touched her heart. After they'd tried to uproot Lesli, and her heart had stopped, she had done a bit of research. She'd known how tired Reynard had been as they finished the thorns in the ballroom, and she knew, better than she wanted to, how deep the wound in her heart had gone. When she asked Mistress Cait about it, she had confirmed her suspicions. 'You poured half your life into my heart, didn't you?'

His eyebrow twitched, and he refused to look at her. 'Only about a fifth,' he said.

His modesty touched her. She reached forward and touched his hand — his bright, long-fingered hand. He'd always kept his fists closed before, she realized. His hands were lovely. Spinner's hands. 'Thank you.'

'Don't thank me,' he said. 'It was what I had to do.'

'I know,' she said. 'And that was how I knew.'

Reynard closed his eyes, ashamed of himself. He knew so much about himself now, and so much of it was unsavoury. Yes, he had saved her — he saved everyone, if he could. But he was shadowed and still angry, and he always would be. To think she'd known it all before he did . . . and still she didn't hate him. Or did she? In the end, she knew him to the core, but he had no idea what went on in her odd, Witty, Wise, Merciful head. 'Why have you come?' he said at last.

'I came to ask you to come back with me,' Will said. 'The ban on spinning has been revoked, and the ban on magic was only Lesli's. We want you at the palace.'

He looked at her then. 'We?'

'I want you,' she said, and then realized how strange that sounded. 'I'd like to learn more magic. I asked if you could come, and Mother agreed. There's still the thorns, and they're still dangerous. And I think you owe me that, at least.'

His expression changed to incredulity. 'You want gold?'

'Spin the wretched things into straw for all I care, just something less deadly.' She smiled. 'Seven-year contract as you help us rid the palace of Cait's briars. After that there'll be land and a title. Huge flock of sheep. Fields of flax.'

He smiled then, a real smile, as he looked down at his knees. She knew what he'd always wanted. She knew everything. But he licked his lips and looked out over the water. Seven years beside her, and unable to hold her. It would be torture. 'I'm sorry, Will. I can't.'

'Would it make any difference if I told you I loved you too?'

He froze in shock. It was as astonishing, in its way, as the moment she said his name. He knew she had known – she knew everything – but that she might feel the same about the vengeful, angry puppy who had nearly destroyed her kingdom, tortured her family, and almost gotten her killed? He hated himself. How could she possibly love him? He turned to her, too amazed to even reach for her, and she smiled. 'I know you,' she whispered.

'You do,' he breathed. He reached out then, and touched her cheek, letting his hand trace down her throat to rest at the little briar above her heart. It beat strong and steady in her mortal chest, a lifetime of strength and Bravery, cleverness and Wit, Wisdom and knowledge, Honesty and passion,

Mercy, and love. All her gifts, and herself besides. 'Will,' he said. Not Willow, not the false name of her parents' title, but herself. Her own powerful strength of Will.

'Reynard,' she whispered, and the name didn't hurt so badly. He would never forget his lifetime of shadow, never feel fully at ease in his own light. But if she could know and accept him . . . maybe he could accept himself, too.

He kissed her then, as he'd dreamed a hundred times, as he did in his mind every night before he could sleep, and never thought he would again. She was drowning in autumn sunshine, wicked laughter, soft spun fleece. As she melted into his arms the final walnut fell from her pocket to the ground, where it cracked open. It was some time before they knew that it held a beautiful red wood spinning wheel, exquisite in its craftsmanship, and like her cherry wood boat, able to sneak back into the shell and be carried anywhere. Roux abandoned his squirrels and curled up beneath it, waiting for them.

And that was really all. Will would have liked to say they lived happily ever after, if she wasn't cursed with both Wit and Honesty. But there was no such thing as happily ever after, no matter how much she loved her faerie tales. But they lived. And they were often happy. And it was always possible for each of them to banish the shadows from each other's lives. And that really is all anyone can hope for.